TAINTED

BY

RICHARD CRANE

This book is dedicated to my father, John, who is the inspiration behind the character Brad Crawford. His intelligence, resourcefulness and determination to put 110% into everything taught me to never give up. I love and miss you.

1933-2010

PREFACE

"They say that you can hear everything when you are in this condition, you know what I mean. It makes me seriously wonder what he's thinking right now...."

Dreams-they can lift you up when you're feeling blue.

Dreams-they can create feeling that you have never felt before.

Dreams-they can almost kill you. They almost killed me. Dead, real dead.

My name is Brad Crawford, a now retired professor out of Tandem Institute of Technology in Springfield, Illinois. I hold a Master's degree in Mechanical engineering and have been dedicated to the field for over thirty-seven years. My gainful occupation gave me one of the most beautiful and lovely dreams I could have ever created. I pushed that dream towards reality and up to the point of perfection, which without warning, turned to lash every breath out of me, every drop of blood from my veins. My lesson was learned, painfully.

The dream, and the objects which occupy it, I can just barely remember, or at least I think I do. Small blurred visions of people and places bounce throughout my mind, ungoverned. Understanding them seems like a lifelong task, but one thing stands clear in my mentality is that dream. It was a crazy idea to begin with and it developed within my last year at the university. I just wanted to do something out of the ordinary for the place before I left. I don't know why I brought Dean Mitchell into it.

Dean Mitchell, now there's a face that remains clear within my mind. It was Dean who led me to this state that I am in, well, not him, but that dream. It sounds confusing because it is confusing. So many debatable visions accompany this dream, and I hope that soon I will be able to sort them once again, if ever, but for now all I can see is that dream. That damn persistent dream.......

PART ONE

DIARY: A daily record of personal experiences and events kept by a person or persons.

THURSDAY

Damn, am I ever tired, seriously tired. This is Dean and I never knew that this project could drain so much energy. Last night, as I reported in my last entry, Brad brought over the EC-380. It took us forever to drag the sucker downstairs and into the basement, but it's finally resting in the pool room. How Brad took it from Mckinley Hall without anyone helping him, I'll never know, but he did. With all that extra weight, I bet his SUV bottomed out a few times on the way over here.

Oh, by the way, I've got another word to add to Brad's verbal dictionary. This one is a gut buster. We had the unit half way down the steps when he mentioned that he has never snaffled anyone before. Snaffled; what a word. It caught an odd look from me, but I still don't know what it means. I'll have to look it up later. Since he was born at least forty years before me, I should expect a generation in there.

Well, anyway, the unit wasn't as complicated as I thought it would be, in fact, to set it up was nothing. It's as easy as plugging in a toaster. The power drained down most of the lights in the house so everything that wasn't needed was turned off. God, I could just imagine the power bill for this month. Brad said he could get the University to pay for it since it is a project for them.

I'm so glad that he got me involved in this project. When he showed me the matrix on the robot, at first, I was skeptical but after all the progress we have made over the last three weeks, I'm as excited as he is. After we got the 380 into place and grounded, we hooked up DD. When we were certain that everything was on backup, I wired myself into the transfer line.

Oh, yeah, I forgot to explain how the 380 works. It consists of a brain wave transfer unit and a thought pattern analyzer. I'm plugged up with six recorder suction tubes, and then the 380 transfers the pattern into DD's memory board. This unit is normally used to transfer computer readouts and programs to a main collector, but we integrated a brain scan machine into the buffer. I was first really scared about doing this but with all the safety precautions Brad took, he said that failure was impossible. It still gave me the heebie-jeebies, (a Brad word). So, in conclusion, all that the 380 does is take my brain wave patterns and my personality and transfers it into DD. Hell, he already has my great looks, might as well give him my great personality as well, if you know what I mean.

When Brad turned it on, everything I saw was doubled. I told Brad about it, and he said it was natural because it's working with the robot's imagery. He also mentioned that I would pass out, and I did.

When I woke up seven hours later, Brad wasn't in the room. My head was fuzzy and my mouth was really dry. I saw Brad's glass of milk on the work table and took a swig of it. That's how I found out it had been seven hours. Needless to say, I'm going to have to clean the area after I'm done with this entry because I spit it out all over the desk.

After that, I pulled off the suction cups from my forehead, and that's when I noticed the great smell of bacon drifting from upstairs. I groggily walked up the steps to find Brad in the kitchen fixing breakfast for me. The clock on the wall said it was half past ten, and Brad informed me that Curt had called wondering why I wasn't in the lab. Brad covered for me and told him that we were working on his SUV.

Speaking of Curt, I wonder if it's time to tell him about what we have been doing. It's been seriously hard to keep him out of the project for he is my best friend, and I'm running out of excuses. Brad and I didn't want him to know because we are going to test our invention on him and Lynette, in fact, Lynette is my first target. If we could fool her, we could fool him. But if we were to run into any problem with completing DD, Curt could help us. In fact, we probably would have finished a lot faster. He didn't receive a full grant from the college for his dashing good looks and the way he is with the women, he happens to be the highest ranked IQ in college history. Of course, his mouth and his attitude don't reflect the IQ. He'll say out loud what others only think because it drives him nuts to be around people who don't use their common sense and he's very arrogant because he knows that people will always need his intelligence. In fact, he's created such a stir with campus police and the board of trustees that I'm surprised that he hasn't been expelled yet. He's crude obnoxious, gross, vulgar and a pervert but I wouldn't trade his friendship for anything. He's always been there for me.

Anyway, back to our progress. I'm sitting in my recliner upstairs writing this and enjoying a cold glass of orange juice. Brad told me he had fallen asleep in the chair next to the 380 downstairs and woke up about thirty minutes before I did. He said that his stomach was growling and came upstairs to fix something to eat. When he heard me rustling downstairs, he cooked more bacon and eggs.

Man, I'm tired. My body feels like it has no energy, but my mind is wide awake. I hate that. While I'm writing this (and eating), I've been watching an old black and white movie on TV. So far three people and one horse has been shot. I'm giving this entry an end.

close: 4:56am

Day 23, Thursday May 4th, 2000, 5:57 a.m.

Brad here with a few words. Dean didn't make the rest of the movie; he fell asleep on the couch. The transfer really wiped him out and hopefully he'll regain his strength before he goes back on it again. I'm calculating that he should only have to be on it two more times for it to complete all transfers. By then we should be able to do a dry run and have DD walk around the house by himself. He should be able to speak as well and voice Dean's vocal patterns. I don't know if Dean had already said this in the Diary or not, but the hardest part is over. Making the body skin and the animatronics was the hardest part. Programming the robot will be easy. Once the patterns are transferred, we should see major results. This whole project is getting really nifty and fun. I can't wait to present it at the Seattle conference next Saturday. Hopefully the project will go well this week, and my report will have significant data to impress them all. Well, now would be a good time for me to get forty winks while Dean is doing the same. I'll retire to his guest room and later we can start round two.

close: 6:11 a.m.

Day 23, Thursday May 4th, 2000, 8:37 a.m.

Oooo is my head pounding. I woke up to find the TV off and Brad gone. My mouth was so dry I went to the kitchen to get a drink of water. It was a task to even walk. You know those headaches that pound every time you take a step? Exactly, that's what I have. Going to the bathroom was even a bigger pain. I was going to go upstairs to my comfy waterbed, but no energy to do so. After I put this pen down, I'm going to pass out once again in this recliner.

close: 8:52 a.m.

Day 23, Thursday May 4th, 2000, 12:42 p.m.

I'm alive and ready to go! Boy, do I feel great. The headache is gone; Brad and I just filled our stomachs with pasta and I had a long visit with the bathroom. We are getting ready to go back downstairs to do round two. I hope I don't have another one of those headaches again, you know what I mean?

close: 12:59 p.m.

Day 23, Thursday May 4th, 2000, 1: 32 p.m.

Brad here with a few lines. It didn't take long to plug up Dean into the chair; he was very excited to continue. The way we made the 380 resulted in a real handy dandy hook up. The robot sits in one chair while Dean sits in the other one. The 380 is between them, and the hook up is just a few electron suction cups that I fasten to Dean's forehead. DD just plugs into his servo, which by the way, connects between his butt cheeks. We had to find an area where nobody would notice it and could get easy access. Of course, pulling his pants down is odd but it would only happen here. Besides, he doesn't have a tally Wacker, so it's not like we are being weird.

While Dean is out, I think it would be best to detail everything about him I can. After all, if this report is going to be the ground foundation of this project, it has to have all the information in it to compare how the robot operates and what it actually receives in the transfer.

Dean Mitchell is an honor student at Tandam institute of Technology. He is in his sixth year and studying mechanical electronics. He is six feet tall, with dark brown hair, hazel eyes, and medium build. He rarely curses, and he always is the nice guy to be around. He always loves to give to others and never asks for things for himself. In fact, he would rather put himself on the spot rather than point out that someone else has a problem. He loves a good movie and enjoys eating out a lot. In fact, he is a hot sauce junkie and loves to take challenges when it comes to hot food. I couldn't last a second on some of the stuff I have seen him eat. I would end up with a wiz bang of stomach problem even if I smelled some of those concoctions. Just the other day at the Pizza Pub, he must have put on at least 20 jalapenos on his pizza. An old geezer like me would have had a cardiac arrest, not to mention the pain that would come from my derriere the next day.

Dean was very well set when his parents died in a car fire about ten years ago during a really nasty snow storm on I-72 heading toward Springfield. It was blizzard conditions, and they just finished a seminar in Decatur when the storm hit. A six-car pileup resulted in two cars burning and the loss of four lives. Due to the white out conditions, rescue teams couldn't see and by the time they were reached, it was too late. I didn't know Dean then, but I do remember reading about it in the paper. They were very wealthy because Dean's father owned a pump company and designed all the pumps himself. His mother handled the office operations, and they had several clients including the United States Navy. Dean wasn't interested in the pump aspect of the business but spent his time understanding the equipment and the technical aspects of the machinery. His cravings for information lead him into mechanical engineering and beyond that. When his parents died, he inherited everything they owned which included the house, cars and the business. He sold the business to his father's silent partner and he immediately went into schooling. This year will be his sixth and final year at Tandem.

He has a lovely relationship with a lady named Lynette Ashbury, and they have been engaged for over six months now. No date is set yet: they are waiting for Dean's graduation, but yours truly gets to give away the bride. Her father died several years ago, and she has no other male figures in her family. Since I have no ankle-biters of my own, it would be an honor to play the part. She is a manager at the Book Nook, and I can tell you she can cast an eyeball. Not only is she very attractive, but she walks very daintily and presents herself as a classy gal. She loves dresses, and I rarely have seen her in jeans. When she walks, her posture is very upright, as if she was taught to walk with books on her head. Even when she sits down, she doesn't slouch. Her speech is very articulate and precise which is refreshing to hear in this world we now live in. One thing is for sure, Dean and she are both hooked on each other pretty good. She is our main target with DD. If we can go the whole week fooling her, then it's made in the shade.

The other target is Dean's best friend Curt Johnson. This dude is a person for the history books. He has the highest IQ that Tandam has ever encountered and is very aware of his surroundings. Getting past him is going to be a real pickle, but if we could pull it off, it would be the bee's knees. The main problem with Curt is that he is very outspoken. He's very arrogant, and he knows it. He has been in a lot of trouble with the university and I personally had to pull some strings to keep him from getting kicked out. One of the saves he had was to design a security system for the entire university. It ended up being so good the government looked into hiring him but found out his character was too much of a problem. The university paid him a lot of bread for it, and eventually he designed several more systems for local businesses. He's got a great cash flow which gives him a lot of free time. I wanted to have him help us with this project, but Dean insisted on using Curt as one of the test subjects. I hope he doesn't blow a gasket when he finds out.

One thing is for sure, not only is he unpredictable but he has the good looks to go with it. He can pick up women faster than a bent eight on a quarter mile strip. His favorite hangout is a strip club called Marvin's, and he probably has nailed every dancer in the club; twice. Being cocky, intelligent and, overbearing can make a person into one loaded cocktail. He has been in trouble with the authorities because he doesn't back down from a fight. He has been trained in Taekwondo, by a private instructor, and is always a comfort when trouble surfaces. He has been running his own school for about five years now. One time I had two boys cut me off on the campus one night, to try to rob me. Curt, just so happened, to be sitting on a bench a few leaps away from us. By the time campus security arrived, one boy was unconscious and the other one was in real bad shape. I'll never forget that night.

Anyway, I thought it might be a good idea to get some information in this dairy about the parties involved so if certain instances occur, we can cross reference the spots. I haven't really read most of Dean's entries and hopefully we are not repeating each other, but soon we are going to have to get another book for this one is filling up. It is now later in the afternoon and I need to run to my office to get something, but I hate leaving Dean plugged into that thing with no observer. Sitting in this recliner across from him is starting to stiffen up my back and I may have to get up and walk around at least.

Well, I'm going to stretch my legs by going to the kitchen and get something to drink. I'll probably not go to the office. I just don't feel comfortable leaving.

close: 4:42 p.m.

Day 23, Thursday May 4th, 2000, 5:21 p.m.

A loud shout from downstairs had me taking two steps at a time, and I almost broke my foot at the bottom. When I got to Dean, it seems that he was having a nightmare. I checked all the stats on the 380, and the brain activity as well, and everything checked out. The transfer is still working. I'm going back upstairs to get my stew before it burns and change my pants.

12

close: 5:37 p.m.

Day 23, Thursday May 4th, 2000, 8: 11 p.m.

My God! What seemed like only 20 minutes was a little over 8 hours! Fascinating! I have no headache, and Brad even said that I had more color in my face. The odd thing was how I woke up. It was quick and sudden like someone just slapped me in the face. I shook my head a couple of times to clear things and that's when I noticed DD and called Brad downstairs.

Surprisingly, DD had stood up and walked a couple of feet away from his chair. It was just enough to break the connection from the 380 and wake me up. COOL! I must have been dreaming in my sleep about walking in order for him to do that. Brad might be right after all. We might only need one more down load and he will be finished. After working on this project for almost a month now, my confidence has doubled.   Doubled, funny joke, huh? I finish the download then all we would have to do is work the voice stabilizer and test him around the house. I don't want to take him out too early and have him break down on us at school or even worse around Lynette. She'd freak out.

By the way, that reminds me that we have a date Saturday night to go to a late dinner and a movie. She said that she would be over about 7:30 after she gets off of work. She really needs a break from that place. One thing about being salaried, a company will work you to death. I can't wait to see her though; I haven't spent much time with her recently. Outside of her working full time at the bookstore and me doing this, we've only had phone conversations. Not to mention that her x-boyfriend is back in town, and she has been on edge ever since. That guy has to be one of the biggest jerks I know. He had a very beautiful, sophisticated lady and treated her like crap. Some guys just don't get it. At times I'd love to punch him in the face, but unfortunately my strongest muscles are in my brains, so I normally wimp out and walk away when I have to deal with the bully. Man, it's been almost three years since she dumped him, you'd think by now he'd move on with his life. I still remember all the things she had to do to make her life more

13

comfortable. She had to move, make her address and phone number unlisted, and even move her lazy butt sister in for security reasons. Don't even start me up about her sister, Kimberly.

Anyway, back to the project at hand. Brad was sitting in the recliner reading a book when this all happened with DD, so he didn't witness it. Brad had twisted his ankle earlier and had it propped up with an ice bag on it. One thing about Brad, he always has his nose in a book. Once he got all the suction cups off my forehead, we backed DD up into his chair. He moved a lot easier and didn't feel as stiff anymore. It still freaks me out how real his skin feels. Not only does the feel freak me out, but if you get up close to his face, it really creeps me out. I seriously think I'm looking at a mirror. I can still remember all that wet plaster Brad put all over my head to make the mold for his face. Boy did that stuff stink. Well, after we secured DD, we ran a test pattern on the 380 and found out that almost 75% of my brain patterns have been transferred into him. Ha, look at me; it's so close that I'm actually calling DD "Him". So, according to Brad one more download ought to finish it, but we have to be careful. There is no telling what DD will do once fully loaded, so for safety reasons, we placed him inside one of my empty metal lockers and padlocked the door. He shouldn't overheat in it and I feel more relaxed knowing that he is secure. Ha, "He". So, to top off this evening with a short celebration, Brad and I are going out to the Pizza Pub, have some pie and a couple of beers.
close: 8:57 p.m.

Day 23, Thursday May 4th, 2000, 11: 41 p.m.
Brad here with a couple of lines. After watching Dean have four beers and almost a whole Buffalo chicken pizza by himself, I thought it might be a good idea that we rest tonight and do the final download tomorrow. I'll sleep here again tonight, but tomorrow I have to get to the office and start getting things together for next weekend. I'm about to bust a gut on this, and it's beginning to become a total blast!
close: 11:57 p.m.

FRIDAY

Day 24, Friday May 5th, 2000, 10:22 a.m.

Brad here, and meanwhile, back at the ranch, that had to be one of the best sleeps I've had in a long time. Dean's guest bedroom has a water bed just like his room does, only smaller. I had one of those puppies years ago and when I got married, we had to switch to a firm mattress because of my wife's back operation. It brings back a lot of memories. Well, rolling along, after a good breakfast, we burned rubber downstairs and got DD out of the locker. It didn't take us long to move him into the chair and plug everything up. Dean also didn't take long for he started to plug himself in and I intervened. I didn't want him to hastily mess it up. I told him from the get go that I wanted all I's dotted and all T's crossed correctly. He calmed himself down and apologized. I told him there wasn't a need to apologize, for I'm just as excited as he is, just too old to flaunt it. Well as of now, he is out, and I'm getting back to my book.

close: 11:05 a.m.

Day 24, Friday May 5th, 2000, 12:43 p.m.

Well, the cat's out of the bag. Brad here, with some bad news. Curt is now into our plan. While I was deep into my book, chapter 11 to be exact, Curt used his key and entered the house upstairs. I tossed my book down and met him at the top of the steps getting ready to come down. He had his usual potty mouth comments, but I managed to get him back upstairs in the living room. My cover story that I've been using about my broken-down SUV wasn't going to hold water anymore. Curt looked at the SUV before he came inside and clearly noted that no work had been done on it. I'm not a good liar so I spilled the beans and told Curt what we had been doing.

At first, he thought I was pulling his leg, well, that wasn't his exact words but I won't repeat them. I told him everything from day one and even showed him this diary, but he still told me that I, well, full of stuff. So, the only alternative was to take him downstairs and show him.

When I first got him into the main pool room, he was shocked at all the equipment we had down there. He also mentioned about how much of a pig sty (once again, not those exact words), the room was. Dean is a clean freak and NEVER has a filthy place. Then he noticed Dean sitting in the chair. Then he noticed the other Dean. I asked him to try to guess which one was the real one and of course he pointed out the directional output of the system was current from left to right, so the real Dean was on the left. Like I said, he would be hard to bluff. Anyway, he approached the robot and was instantly floored. He started jabbering out loud about all the specks and mechanics that was used on the project. Not necessarily talking to me, but he always spoke out loud when he was working. Of course, once again, his vocabulary was laced with his favorite word, which I'll refrain from using here. We did stump him on the texture of the skin, though. After he was satisfied with the first initial meeting, and then did a few vulgar things in front of Dean's face, he pulled me upstairs to fill in all the details. After an hour of this, he said he would go get some lunch for us from the Burger Barn and watch over Dean, so I can get a chance to go to the office for what I need. Good thing because I need to get a jump on things if my presentation is going to stand up.
close: 1:35 p.m.

Day 24, Friday May 5th, 2000, 3:23 p.m.

Holy shit fucks! This is fucking awesome! Just for the record, my name is Curt Johnson and I am God. After I picked up some shit to eat, I let Brad go. He says he's got some shit to do for some big stuffed dick conference next weekend. Better him than me, those assholes. So, I'm babysitting little Einstein downstairs. I've also been reading over this diary for the last half hour and I've never been more fascinated than when I fucked that chick with the double D titties! This robot has to be one of the most advanced computers of our time. How they came up with the skin texture

16

still stumps my fucking ass, and it's listed nowhere in this log. THIS IS FUCKING BITCH'N! The one thing I did notice about this diary is that it's filled with more bullshit about life, feelings, and shit chat than what they really need in this book. I'll fix that.

I was very surprised at all the shit they had in the pool room though. Not only did they have the 380, but the fucking CRT 10, a data processer, a collector unit and even the stabilizer backup assembly. How the fuck did they get all this shit over here? Not to mention the large turd that the board of directors would spray out if they knew it was here. There is also so much shit all over the place that I couldn't believe that this was Dean's house. I've never seen it in such a cluster fuck!

Brad said that this should be the last download on the robot, or DD, as they call it. DD sounds stupid, it sounds like some whore's name down on second street, with double D's! Brad did tell me it was short for "Dean's Double", but I think Donkey Dick would be more exciting.

It's really fucking me up sitting in this chair and looking at both of them. I even noticed that when Dean twitched his hand in his sleep, so did the robot. I wonder if Dean picked his ass, would the robot try doing the same?

I can't believe that they put the 380 hook up in between the robot's ass cheeks. I even noticed that they didn't' even give him a dick. Poor, fella, he wouldn't be able to even enjoy a good masturbation. With a small hydraulic system, I, could build him one. Dean has a small dick anyway, so it would be just right.

Anyway, I see that so far in this book is the nice descriptions of people involved. It was the bomb to read about the comments on me and they're fucking right, I'm arrogant, unpredictable and love to fuck women. But what about the true shit on everyone else? I'll clear the air with a fart and tell it all.

First there is Dean. Clean, proper and nice, Dean makes me want to fucking puke at times. He's fantastic with electronics, of course not as good as me, but can slap the shit together faster than anyone else I know. We met each other when we were very young at the science competitions at the fair. He lived in Decatur and I lived in the Chicago area. We always took first and second place, most of the time it was me at first, but he did beat my ass a couple of times. We really connected when we were put together in a room for the International Contest in Las Vegas. What a fucking great time! At least I was out of the grasp of my deranged fuck of a Dad, but I took first, of course. That's when I found out that Dean had a little demon inside him when we rigged an electric shock panel under a large punch bowl, it was fucking hilarious. Every time a person would grab the ladle, they got shocked. Punch would go everywhere. I laughed my ass off so much; my sides were sore for hours. It was great when we enrolled at Tandem together. It's been a great fucking ride.

He is very shy when it comes to standing up for himself, which is why I always blow smoke up people's ass when he doesn't. The big thing that drives me ape shit about him is that he doesn't have a set of balls to get in people's faces when he knows that he is right, like his truck, for instance. They have been dick'n him around for weeks about the transmission slipping and they haven't fixed the problem. I would have shoved the axel up their asses and without lubricant. He's just Mr. wonderful, kind, and proper and a puke fuck. Best friend I ever had.

Then there is Lynette. Hot damn! The classiest lady I've ever known. She works at the Book Nook as a manager and really knows her shit. She was dating a big asshole named Andy Sorenson when Dean met her in the Book Nook. After a couple of dates, Dean was her new toy. Not a toy as you'd think, though. You see, Lynette is still a virgin. That was the main reason she left Andy Fuck head because he forced himself on her, and white knight Dean came to her rescue. He let her bend his ears and cry on his shoulder. They have been engaged for almost six months now, and I don't think he's even seen her tits. It's pretty impressive for her to be 26 years old and still not taken any dick. That's what I call strong fucking will power. Me, I'd eat the corn out of her poop. She's got these long legs and walks with a strut that makes your dick get hard. I've never seen her run or even walk fast; she has this stride about her that just says, "Fuck me." She has long permed brownish blond hair, and when she talks, the corners of her mouth stay shut. It's like she only talks through her middle of her lips. Really gets me horny just watching her talk. Out of all the women that I've bagged, and it's a lot, I've never had Lynette. And out of respect and honor to Dean, I never will.

Then there is Brad. A father figure if I ever had one. You see, my mother died when I was two and then my Dad proceeded to beat the shit out of me until I was twelve. After all the karate lessons I had been taking from a friend, at twelve is when I beat the shit out of my dad. I moved into a friend's house after that and never saw that Son of a bitch Dad of mine again.

Anyway, Brad was there for me before I came to Tandam. He saw what I had to offer at one of the fair shows and took me under his wing. I was 17 at the time, and he gave me inside tours of the campus. First, I thought he was going to be one of these old sex fucks who took little boys for pleasure, but he wasn't. I don't want this to sound like Brad is a molester, but after everything that has happened in my life, you tend to trust nothing and no one. He did gain my respect as the first adult I really trusted.

Brad wears glasses and has this fucked up habit of picking his nose and then rolling the boogers between his fingers. At least he doesn't eat the shit, he just flings it. He also has a love for classical music. I love that style when they use it for a great kick your ass movie, but listening to it on a regular basis? Fuck that shit. Of course, Brad being 67 years old has a lot of gray hair and does have trouble hearing once in a while; that's when he doesn't have his hearing aids in. He does know his shit well, though, and has been through hell to get where he is now. He always loves to talk about how fucking hard it was to grow up in his time. "Things were harder when I was young." he'd say. "You had to work for everything, and nothing was handed to you like this generation expects!" Eat shit, pal I worked for EVERYTHING! He knows that, which, by the way, is why he respects me as well.

The fun part is he has this language that he uses, the fifties I think, and still can't break the habit. Dean and I still laugh at some of the shit he says. Like earlier in this log, Dean says something about snaffled. What the fuck is snaffled? And we love to tease him about it, but one thing is for sure, I've NEVER heard him swear, which is one reason I do. Hey, someone has to cover for his loss, right? Fuck'n eh.

I did notice Dean didn't want to say anything about Lynette's sister, Kimberly. I'd be glad to be the one to roast that bitch. She has been living with Lynette in her apartment for almost two years now and just sucks all the shit out of her. She "supposedly" has a mental illness and gets government assistance. That bitch bought everything off of her government assistance, or US tax payers. She has a brand-new car, computer and eats out all the time. She blows all the assistance money so fast that she ends up having to borrow money from Lynette all the time. She has no job and just leeches off of everyone, the lazy ass piece of shit. She's fat, ugly, annoying and NO I have not fucked her. I wouldn't touch her with Dean's dick. Someone needs to seriously slap the shit out of this bitch. One time, when Dean and I stopped by to pick up Lynette, Kim called Lynette on her cell phone, from her bedroom, to bring her a coke. I obliged. I took the coke, shook it up, opened her door, and gave it to her. All over her fucking face, her ass, her bed sheets, shit, I think I even got it on the ceiling. I bet she never asked for another fucking coke again. And what's even worse is if she goes with you to, like say, a party or one of their family reunions, she'll bring everyone down at the event. She's always trying to get everyone feeling sorry for her and to become the center of attention. You want attention, bitch? I say tie her whale body up against the wall, and we can all play the game pin the tail on the dumb ass. I guess they say every family has a member that just makes people piss. Kimberly is Lynette's piss.

Well, I hear Brad's SUV pulling up outside, so I'll close for now.

Piss on your neighbor

close: 6:15 p.m.

Day 24, Friday May 5th, 2000, 8:53 p.m.

Brad here, well, so much for our nice clean reading log book. Our vulgar friend has now been added to the butter. I just finished gathering all the things I needed from my office and brought them over here to piece together. In a way I'm very glad Curt is with us because tomorrow we will be testing DD's operation, including the voice stabilizer. If any problems arise, Curt would be the one to solve them. Curt has been in the bathroom for the last twenty minutes and told me that he has a lot of questions when he gets out. I might as well get us both a beer from the ice box because this is going to be a long night.
close: 9:19 p.m.

Day 24, Friday May 5th, 2000, 10:45 p.m.

Good morning, hello, aloha and all that other stuff. I feel great, like I had a massage of all the senses. My eyes are wide open, my ears attuned, my nose is clear breathing and even my mouth feels crisp. It's like the day after you get refreshed from a long fight with the flu. I see that the diary is rapidly growing not only in length but in language as well. I knew that we wouldn't be able to keep Curt out of this. Of course, he cursed me up and down about not letting him in on it in the first place, but after explaining our plans, he seemed to accept it. I guess Brad had explained everything to him from start to now and even next week's plans. Curt suggested that we let him drive as well, but I thought we shouldn't. What if something was to happen and he caused an accident? Seriously? Or worse yet, hit someone walking? I just didn't want to take that chance, and Brad agreed with me. So, Curt will drive him to the university every day.

Well, it's getting late and the other two want to get to bed. We all have a very long day tomorrow, but my problem is that I'm not tired. They are planning to get up at the crack of dawn and start working on the voice stabilizer and his movement. I'll probably sit here and watch some late-night TV. There is always something fun and weird on at this time of night. Hope it's not only infomercials.
close: 10:59 p.m.

Saturday

Day 25, Saturday May 6th, 2000, 6:45 a.m.

We all started the day with breakfast at The Golden Egg restaurant. After Brad had several cups of coffee and Curt exploding on an old lady for writing a check in line, we finally got back home. I'm making this entry quick so that we can start.
close: 6:47 a.m.

Day 25, Saturday May 6th, 2000, 8:35 a.m.

Hi, Brad here. After going over our agenda for the day, I put the two brainiacs to work downstairs, while I start getting my presentation together. If this goes well, I could get one big bowl of chili for the university. In fact, with all the donations maybe they would build a place and name it after me. The Crawford Center has a nice ring to it.

So, the list for the two downstairs is as follows. Dean has to record his voice into the 380 first. He must pronounce each letter in the alphabet and identify it to the unit. The 380 will then arrange the letter according to the dictionary that is downloaded into the CRT 10. They will then test several sentences and words on the 380 first, then if it's successful, transfer it to DD. It should take them a couple of hours to fully verbalize the unit, but they'll get it.

Next, they have to input the following "No" commands into the unit. We all came up with items that needed to be done. Of course, Curt had his usual raunchy things to add.

I still can't believe how frosted he got on that poor old woman. He wanted to get out of the place and get back here to start and she was ahead of us at the register. When she first pulled out her check book, to start writing a check, he razzed her about not getting it ready in the first place. Then when she handed in the check, the waitress asked for her driver's license in which the old woman started digging through her much unorganized hand bag. Curt went ape on her again telling her that everyone asks for ID when you write a check, and she should have had that ready too. Needless to say, the poor woman walked out with her head down and everyone else in the restaurant was eyeballing us. I felt really low being in that party. In a way, he is right. Why don't people think when they do things? But on the other hand, jeepers! I tried to get him to cool it but knew that it was a waste of time. I just wanted to cut out.

Anyway, back to the list. The following commands were placed into the memory of DD;

No eating or drinking, including cravings for food or drink. (Any liquids or food particles would completely shut down his system).

No urges to urinate or defecate. (It would really be a slap in the face to DD if he was to even try it.)

No sneezing, coughing, blowing the nose or flatulence.

No sexual intercourse. (Dean put that one in).

No masturbation (Curt's idea)

No lip kissing. (This is going to be hard to pass unless we figure out a way to make the lips feel wet).

No biting the finger nails. (Dean's bad habit)

No smoking of cigarettes or cigars.

No swimming, showers or baths.

No chewing gum.

No brushing teeth.

Well, got to cut this short and start working on this next week's presentation.

close: 8:52 a.m.

Day 25, Saturday May 6th, 2000, 11:42 p.m.

Brad here again. The boys just ran upstairs and told me that they had to go out shopping for parts. Curt seems frustrated. The word from the bird is that he's having trouble with the voice analyzer, and it needs to be rewired. He said something about a backup microphone and breakers, so he and Dean are going to the local hardware store to get the needed supplies. I, by the way, gotten as far as getting my notes separated. I'm really cranked up about this, but I've got to floor it if I'm going to get this done. I'll pass the diary to one of the boys to fill in when they get back.

23

Day 25, Saturday May 6th, 2000, 1:44 p.m.

Boy, I'm glad the store is right down the street, or this whole day would have been shot already. We had to return to get some measurements that Curt forgot and then head back to the store. Brad threw the diary at me and told me pretty much to let him be alone the rest of the day.

It all started when Curt tried to get DD to say something, and all we got was screeches. First, he thought it was a reverb between him and the 380, but when he tried to move DD around, it never improved. Curt, of course, was cursing up a storm and going over options out loud. When Curt works on a problem, he talks out loud; I guess that makes him concentrate better. Most people think he's flipped out and is just plain weird. So what else is new?

Anyway, while at the Hardware store, several new Curtisim's occurred. Just to clarify, I created the word Curtisim to explain his way of talking. A Curtisim is something that you would say out loud to someone that most people would keep to themselves. The comment is usually rude, obnoxious, or just down right filthy. That is a Curtisim.

So, to start with, when Curt is irritated at a project that he can't figure out, his patience is very short. The voice analyzer and the ocular units have him REALLY on edge. So, look out world, here he comes.

It all started when we first stepped into the entrance. Curt is always moving in a fast pace because he knows what he wants; he goes in to get it, and gets out without hesitation. He doesn't like to "Window Shop", to him it's a waste of time.

Sometimes I think it's a man thing. For instance, when I go to the grocery store for, say, like some bread, I go straight to the bread area, get a loaf, head to the checkout and leave. When I drop off Lynette for a loaf of bread, it takes her close to twenty minutes because she had to see this sale or look at what was new. I would be sitting in the car wondering what was taking so long. At times, if I went in with her, I would be walking next to her talking, and the

24

next thing I know, I've been carrying on a conversation with myself because she stopped two aisles back to look at something.

Anyway, back to Curt. His stride makes him look like he's very knowledgeable of the store. We were only a couple of yards in when some old man asked him if he worked there. The funny thing was that Curt was wearing a blue shirt like the rest of the employees do, so he kind of fit the place. His response was not as bad as I thought it would be, but when the man asked if he knew where the light bulbs were at, Curt responded with "Do you see that corner where all the bleeping light fixtures are at? Does that give you any bleeping clue?" Needless to say, the man scuttled off as we headed toward the electronic area. Curt started mumbling out loud to himself again as he grabbed about 10 items that he needed and told me he had other items in his trailer that he would pick up later. Then we headed for the checkout. That's when it got fun.

First there was a family of four blocking the aisle and Curt yelled at them to move their fat you-know-what's out of the way. When we got to the checkout lanes, he took the 12 items and under lane. There, in front of us, was a woman who clearly had at least thirty items. Curt went off. Between the cursing, all I got was inconsiderate, dyslexic, idiot and get out of here. The lady backed out of the line. The cashier, a young girl, gave him a casual smile and told him she always wanted to do that. By the time we left her lane, Curt had her name, age and phone number. Why couldn't I ever do that? I mean, seriously how does he do it?

As we were heading toward the exit doors, people walked in through them and a guy turned to his wife and asked where all the shopping carts were at? Curt replied, "At the entrance, you bleep," Then as we walked out, the lady in front of us, with a full cart, dead stopped in between the doors and we couldn't get around her. Boy, did she get it.

When we got back to the house, Brad was really into his speech, and we just headed straight downstairs. We have a lot to do.

<u>close: 2:13 p.m.</u>

Day 25, Saturday May 6th, 2000, 3:20 p.m.

This fucking thing is driving me ape shit. The damn voice stabilizer will not interact with the fucking robot! We have loaded Dean's voice into the 380 and still it won't work! Shit! Piss! Fuck! His ocular units are working just fine because what the robot sees is clearly visible on the 380's TV screen and the audio metric unit is the balls, but without the voice output, this thing will just be a piece of shit.

WAIT, I got it! I fucking got it!

Fuck a duck!

close: 3:23 p.m.

Day 25, Saturday May 6th, 2000, 4:10 p.m.

Well, he got it, all right. It dawned on Curt that the voice and ocular units work together to understand sound. The frequency from the 380 was working fine, but the receiving level of volume in his ears was too low. Once Curt turned them up, DD started to speak. It was awesome! I heard my own voice coming out of him! But it was really freaky. Anyway, we did an eye test with him with a poster that I had hanging on the wall, and he read it with no problem, but we did notice that he was turning his head a little too slowly. Curt waved his hand on the side of DD's peripheral vision, and the reaction was also slow. He suggested that we do one more download from me, and it would be complete. We discussed this with Brad and he agreed. Hopefully this will be it.

close: 4:23 p.m.

Day 25, Saturday May 6th, 2000, 5:40 p.m.

It didn't take long for Dean to get knocked out under the 380's power, which by the way sounds like a fucking video game when it's transferring. All the beeping and flashing lights looks like the stage at Marvin's, and I'm waiting for some naked chick to dance her tits over to me and sit on my face. That reminds me, I haven't been there for a couple of days now, starting to get withdrawals. Don't want my dick to go asleep on me. I've always got to keep that boy in shape.

I did have a problem plugging in the robot, though. He was fighting me on why I needed to look at his bare ass. I guess it's really starting to operate to Dean's intuition. After this download I'm going to have to come up with a solution to that problem.

I wonder how it feels to be put under by that fucking machine. I read that Dean had a couple of headaches but other than that, he really didn't explain any effects. Shit, I don't know if I could stand knowing that there was something else that acted just like me. It would be like competing against yourself for everything. In fact, having two Curts would probably rip the world apart.

During his outage, I left to get some parts at my place and came up with a fucking great back up plan. I'm going to build a microphone, into the 380 in case we have further problems with the voice analyzer. Dean could speak straight into the microphone and it would carry out of the robot.

If this download is the last and the robot is fully functional, we plan to put him in Dean's place first thing Monday morning. First, we are going to do some test runs with him around town tomorrow, though. I'll drive him and watch his reaction, while Dean and Brad stay at Dean's with the equipment. I'm half tempted to take it to Marvin's and watch his reaction to naked women waving their snatch at him. If he reacts like Dean, he'll get up and leave, in fact, he probably won't even go in. Dean doesn't like women being exploited that way.

Got to run, Eat shit!

close: 5:51 p.m.

Day 25, Saturday May 6th, 2000, 6:47 p.m.

Just woke up out of the download about ten minutes ago and feel great. This one was very short. Maybe the 380 recorded everything it could and just snapped me out of it.

Anyway, I immediately went over to DD and tested his reflexes. His eyes blinked rapidly when I blew air at them, his head turned fast when I waved my hand and when I said hello to him, he answered back with a perfect sounding hello as well. This is getting weird.

I found the Diary on the pool table and read Curt's last entry, and that's when I noticed the new microphone on the 380. Curt really out did himself this time. I went over and sat in the chair and clicked on the button. I heard a click from DD like turning on a speaker. Then I leaned forward and said "Hello" into the microphone. Within a millisecond, DD repeated it. Of course, after that, I did all kinds of other goofy noises including moans, clicks, and I even pressed my lips to make a farting sound which DD copied perfectly. I was giggling with excitement.

Then, I went upstairs and opened the door into the kitchen. I walked into the living room to find Curt and Brad eating freshly delivered pizza and watching a science fiction movie on TV. It was a good classic black and white, which I've seen thousands of times, and of course Brad and Curt were tearing apart every techno thing in the movie. I pretty much sat down and stuffed my face with a few pieces of pie and stayed out of their conflict. Things were getting pretty mellow until one of them stated the clear difference between reality and fantasy.

The topic was hand laser guns, and Brad said that they could never be able to harness the energy. Curt totally disagreed. Now every time they would get into one of these arguments, they would get really into it. Books would be dragged out; theories would be quoted and even people would be called on the phone to verify conclusions.

Knowing that this would be a long discussion, I went back downstairs and played with DD. Wait, that didn't sound right. I worked on him. Then I got an idea.
close: 6:52 p.m.

Day 25, Saturday May 6th, 2000, 8:55 p.m.
I have now experienced villainy, sneakiness, anxiousness, catastrophe, a heart attack and glorification all with in this last hour.

It all started after my last entry. I got DD up and took off my clothes and put them on him. I told him to go upstairs and see what the others were doing. He walked up the steps with no problem and opened the door. I sat at the 380, in my underwear, and watched the whole thing develop through the screen on the 380. The speakers we had installed gave out great stereo effect and were well balanced like a theater. As I watched the screen, I could see that he had walked into the front room and not to my surprise, Curt and Brad had at least six of my mechanical books spread out all over the coffee table. Their argument was still going on, which was great because they wouldn't even notice me in the room or him for that matter.

DD sat down on the couch where I had just left only moments ago and was glancing back and forth between Brad and Curt. I was practically in hysterics watching this. The tones in their voices told me that they were really getting at each other. Curt was waving his arms around explaining something about laser particle transformation, and Brad was contradicting that nothing could be strong enough to harness that much heat. That's when Curt turned toward DD and asked me for my opinion.

When DD opened his mouth, a loud high-pitched whine emitted from the stabilizer, and it scared the hell out of both of them. I started laughing downstairs for the expressions on both of their faces were hysterical. I have no other way of describing it. Curt flipped DD off, and he had no problem returning the gesture which made all three of us laugh even harder. Curt jumped up in excitement and ran over to DD, called him a name, and then smacked him in the back of the head. That's when I lost visual on the 380 and DD's right eye fell out and rolled across the floor. Cries of anguish, and one loud curse word, could have been probably heard a block from the house. The eye continued to roll across the floor and under my 60-inch television console, but that wasn't that bad part. My heart attack occurred when Brad and Curt were lifting the console to move it, and Lynette walked in the front door.

Now first of all, I had no idea what was going on upstairs because I couldn't see anything. I didn't know about the eye until the other two filled me in with this information later. Of course, I could hear everything that was going on and was very helpless. The other two, on the other hand, had to tap dance their way out of it.

She first asked how I was doing because for my lie this week was that I had the flu. I answered quickly into the microphone that I was feeling a lot better. Then she asked why I was holding my hand over my right eye and that's when Brad answered that Curt and I was sword fighting with cue sticks downstairs and Curt hit me in the eye.

First of all, it was pretty cool that DD covered his eye like he was injured, but come to think of it, I would have too. I heard her high heeled shoes walk across the hard wood floor, and she asked if she could see it. I spoke quickly that the light hurts my eyes, and I already took aspirin for it. I also said that it wasn't that bad, but I would probably have a black eye for a couple of days.

According to the other two, she put her hand on DD's forehead and felt for a temperature. She said that I still felt a little hot and she would get me some stronger medicine. She also told me to take it easy the rest of the night. I grabbed the microphone again and said "But what about our night out tonight?" She informed me that she had her assistant call off and that she was going to have to open the store tomorrow morning, so there would be no movie tonight. I asked if I could just come over to her place for the night and heal there, and she welcomed it.

Curt had told me that she then bent over and kissed DD on the head and told him that she would see me shortly. Just before she left, though, Brad told me she got a weird look on her face at the mess that the boys had all over the room. I heard her say that they need to get a life, and with that comment I heard her shoes walking toward the exit and out the door.

After her car drove off, you could hear screaming all through the house. I ran up the steps to find Brad and Curt jumping up and down with excitement. DD got a puzzled look on his face and asked what all the excitement was about which made us laugh and scream even louder.

Well, an unscheduled test just passed and I'm fully awake with enthusiasm. I'm taking a shower while the other two try to fix our eye problem. I told them that I would help, but they both insisted that I go to Lynette's. They said if they needed anything from me, they would just ask the robot.

close: 9:22 p.m.

Day 25, Saturday May 6th, 2000, 10:02 p.m.

Hello, Brad here with an update. Just after Dean got out of the shower and said he was going to Lynette's, Curt cold cocked him in the eye. At first Dean was pretty rattled but Curt pointed out that Lynette would be even angrier if he showed up with a perfectly good-looking eye. She would have taken the whole thing as a lie and we all know that's a bad idea. I still remember the last time Dean tried to lie out of something. He was really cruisin' for a bruisin then.

It was the weekend of her family reunion and also the grand prix races upstate. All year the two boys planned on the race, and bought expensive tickets in advance, and when Dean heard that the reunion was on the same day, he had to find a way out of it. She was already in Lincoln the night before, so Dean called her that morning and told her that his truck broke down. Later she found out that a friend of hers ran into Dean and Curt at the race. I thought she was going to beat the tar out of him. A couple of days later, she forgave him and things went back to normal.

It's good to know that we got away with that big scene with Lynette a couple of hours ago because if she would have caught on, the rest of the week would have been a real pooper. Just seeing the robot work, in the state that he was in at that time, makes me even more confident that he will fool everyone at the University as well. The big tickle would be fooling the board of directors. But first we had to fix the problem.

We first got him downstairs and into his chair. Curt immediately went to work on disinfecting the eye, which by the

31

way we did find in a pile of dust bunnies under the console. While it was soaking in the solution, I suggested that it might be a good idea to install a power off switch on the robot himself. Since he is a perfect copy of Dean, we wouldn't want it to go off on its own and create a real kettle of fish. Curt mentioned that if we wanted him off, we could just shut off the 380 and that's when I told him that if the 380 was shut off, the collected work of Dean's inputs would be completely erased. This project has been a gas, but I really don't want to start from ground one again. I pointed out to him the large battery backup we had on it in case of a power outage. So, he decided to build the cutoff switch right next to his input feed. Yes, we have to reach between his butt cheeks to turn him on and off.

An interesting point was brought up from Curt, though. He questioned whether or not the robot knew what he was. Did it think it was really Dean or did the programming make it an independent unit? I had never thought of it that way. It really would throw the fat into the fire if it didn't know the difference. To even program a firewall into to it about it being a computer program might endanger the experiment this week. I guess I could always input into its programming that it is an operating unit to resemble a human being.

He also said that he had a devil of a time trying to hook up DD to the 380 when the boys did their last download. The robot was wondering why Curt wanted to get to his butt cheeks. I was afraid this would happen. The robot is so close to Dean that it's going to start wondering why we are doing things that we wouldn't necessarily do to Dean. So, Curt came up with the idea of planting into its matrix a command that would shut off the Robot, without shutting off the 380. Then we would only have to flip on the switch. After several ideas, we decided to make the command word my wife's name. It is not often used, and in a way makes her a part of this operation. I agreed.

So, we split up the duties. I am going to work on the programming and the ocular units while Curt is going to install the cutoff switch and fix the voice analyzer. So, we fixed ourselves a large pot of coffee in the pool room's kitchen and dug in. I parked myself at the 380 and started enhancing some of its command schematics and Curt started on the power switch. I had about busted a gut when I saw the expression on the robot's face when Curt told it to bend over so he could get to his input connection. So, I first inputted the cut off command into the programming. Once done, I spoke Brad's wife's name and DD shut down. Curt bent DD's body over the pool table and started working.

One thing is for sure, I'm glad that Dean's at Lynette's because he needs the rest, and the up and about will do him good. The one thing he's not looking forward to is sitting at the 380 all week during the tests. He will have to monitor the entire procedure from here, while Curt and I chaperone the robot. At least if there is anything he can say to derail a situation, Curt has that microphone installed. I tell you, that boy is the icing on the cake.

Without further ado, it's time to get down and dirty.
close: 10:22 p.m.

Day 25, Saturday May 6th, 2000, 11:42 p.m.
What a fucking mess, but me, being God, fixed it all. After Brad inputted information into the 380 that the robot was an operating unit to portray a human being, I was able to get access to his ass a little easier. I still feel fucking weird sticking my hands into Dean's ass but it didn't take me long to put in a chicken switch.

Moving on to our ocular unit clusterfuck, I replaced the bearing and hookups in the eye socket, and now it's really in there. Let's see if anyone can knock that fucker out now! In fact, I even adjusted the ratio specks on the cameras and was able to get even a sharper image on the 380's screen. I am the shit, and the world is my grass.

So, for the last hour I've been dicking around with the problem of the voice analyzer and the speech. I had everything spread out all over the pool table and was scratching my head when the robot walked up to me. His forehead was buckled like he was in deep thought and was looking at the shit I had laid out. His bottom jaw was one of the pieces on the table and he looked really fucked up standing there. Then he reached out with his right hand and

33

pointed at the left side of the speaker and flipped his hand back and forth. I couldn't understand what he was trying to do. Then get this shit! He grabbed a pen and piece of paper and started writing something down. Fuck me, what a trip! When he was done, he handed me the paper and holy shit, it looked just like Dean's hand writing. It was fucking awesome! The paper said that if I would cross connect the ocular unit and switched the positive to a negative, and vice versa, it would work. How fucking absurd, I thought, what's he trying to do, blow his fucking head off? I asked him if he was nuts, and he shook his head "No". Then he started drawing on the piece of paper the medical output of the human eye, how everything is upside down on the retina. Shit! The power to the speaker would be reversed, and in fact, it would give him a stereo effect. Why the fuck didn't I catch this? It was a simple fix, and I was over thinking it. I hate when that happens.

So, I tried it, and it worked. It was only seconds after that I had his bottom jaw back together, and he was talking like crazy. Pretty fucking weird knowing that he was the one who fixed himself, or Dean, or Dean's robot or, FUCK ME! I'm glad I had Brad input the fact that he is a program because it would be really fucked up if he was to think he was the real Dean.

Anyway, Brad has already retired to the guest room and I'm heading to bed as well. Tomorrow I will be taking him out for a dry run, and then we are going to fuck up this town.

Eat some snatch.

close: 1:22 a.m.

Sunday

Day 26, Sunday May 7th, 2000, 5:45 a.m.

Well, I've been up all fucking night and don't feel the slightest exhausted. I've done a lot of improvements since my last log. I realigned the ocular units and the 380-output giving the robot a wide-angle vision. The screen doesn't look as tightly focused as it used to be. I also tested the voice command shut off, and it worked just fine. After flipping his ass switch back on, I had the robot on for about three hours. We actually had a bullshit session about his final year at Tandam and what his future plans were.

I did a work over on his inputs that took me most of the fucking night. To make things easier and not to cause such a clusterfuck, I found a way to remove all memories about the experiment from DD inputs. He now knows Jack shit about the robot, how it was made, how it was designed and how it was completed. As far as what I did, he is Dean with the exception of knowing about this project. It was like setting a computer program to a prior date and time. Both Brad and Dean are going to get a hard on once they find out what I did. I'm such a fucking genius.

Well, shit, Brad wanted me to wake him up at six and we are going to call Dean and meet him somewhere for breakfast. That's where we will go over this week's agenda. I'm going to have fun with this shit because I get to be with the robot all week and play along.

Hey! I've got an idea! This will be the moose's dick!

Love that tit shit!

close: 5:55 a.m.

Day 26, Sunday May 7th, 2000, 6:34 a.m.

Good morning, Brad here. Curt really got me.

I woke up this morning with Dean shaking my shoulder wanting to get the day started. I told him that we were planning to call him and pick him up at Lynette's on the way to get breakfast and lay out our agenda. He asked me how soon I would be ready, and I told him about thirty minutes after I freshen myself up. That's

35

when my cell phone next to the bed rang and I answered it to Dean's voice on the other end.

I had been talking to the robot this whole time and didn't even know it. Curt came running into the room laughing and then the robot asked him what was so funny. I told Dean on the phone what had just happened and that we would be by to pick him up in about forty-five minutes. He counter suggested that he would ride into the Book Nook with Lynette and we could have coffee there. We all agreed.

I'll tell you this, if the robot fooled me, and I've been around it so long, I can't wait to get everyone at the college. It's time to clean myself up and get this day rolling. Curt is taking DD back downstairs and shutting him off. Ha, what a trickster.
close: 6:15 a.m.

Day 26, Sunday May 7th, 2000, 8:00 a.m.

Well, last night was a wonderful. After arriving back at Lynette's apartment, she fixed some hot tea with honey in it. Her sister was already asleep in her bedroom, so I didn't have to deal with her tonight. It didn't take long for me to fall asleep on the couch, and when I woke up this morning, Lynette was all cuddled up next to me. What a lovely way to wake up.

After getting off the phone with Brad, I took a shower and rode into the Book Nook with Lynette. She had to open this morning, and the fresh coffee and bagels really hit the spot. If only my eye didn't hurt so much, thanks Curt. About fifteen minutes later, Brad and Curt arrived. They also ordered breakfast and we all gathered around a four top table to belt out what our week will entail.

Brad put me in charge of the official log book entries during the tests since I'll be sitting at the 380 all week. Later tonight I've got to stock the refrigerator and set up a microwave so I don't have to go upstairs. The bathroom next to the pool room will be the only time I'll be out of sight from the 380, and I don't plan to place a bucket next to the unit like Curt suggested.

This week's schedule is as follows;

Monday
9:00am-12:00pm: 17th Century Literature with Professor Grubbs
2:00pm-4:00pm: Biomedical Engineering lab with Professor Bergin.
Tuesday
10:00am-12:00pm. I teach Intro to Mechanical Engineering.
Wednesday-no classes
Thursday
8:00am-10:00am: Engineering Statistics 3 with Professor
Allumbaugh
1:00am-3:00pm: Cinematography with Professor Burke.
Friday
10:00-? Open Laboratory work in the mechanic's room

In between times we plan to just walk around campus, go to
the local restaurants for lunch and pay visits to Professor's offices
just for fun. One of the professors is an old cranky relic and is
usually irritated that he has to deal with the students. I can't wait
to get him.

Holy cow! Is this good news! Lynette just stopped by the
table and asked what we were up to because we looked all serious
and stuff. Then she asked me if I was doing anything on Wednesday
because she had received two passes to the annual Governor's
luncheon. It included tours of Lincoln's Home and Burial Tomb, and
she wanted to know if I could go. Of course, I'll go! He He, Ha Ha.
That fills up the Wednesday spot and will also give us a great test
for DD in a public place.

As for today, Curt is going to take him out and around the
town for a couple of hours while Brad and I monitor from home.
Curt will take his Jeep and play it by ear. One thing that Brad
stressed to Curt was that he had to get it in his mind that it is Dean
he is with and not the robot. Looking at it in any other way could
confuse DD and cause a problem. Curt acknowledged that by the
time today is over with, all tests will be complete. I don't know
what he has in mind, but that comment sent a chill up the back of
my neck.

It's time to close this session and start this day.

close: 10:42 a.m.

Day 26, Sunday May 7th, 2000, 11:27 a.m.

Brad and I are now sitting at the 380 and Curt and DD just left in the Jeep. Curt's first stop is going to be his trailer by the lake. He said he needed to get a few things before going on the run. Brad says he is all goose pimply and ready for the ride of his life. I too, am excited and ready for fun.

close: 11:42 a.m.

Day 26, Sunday May 7th, 2000, 12:34 p.m.

Curt's stop at his trailer was a short one. His trailer is on the lake, which is great for a nice little get away to fish or even just to leave the stress of the city. Many times, I passed out on a lawn chair listening to the night sounds of the lake. Several times it was with Lynette, but ever since we bought the cabin at Shelbyville Lake, we don't go to Curt's any more.

When they walked up to the porch, Curt approached the security system on the right side of the front door. It looked like something from a science fiction movie, and he opened the small door on the unit and inputted his security code. I was always amazed at all the security he had installed around the place. There were at least fourteen cameras, six voice recorders and three alarm horns on the premises. He had, also, an automatic call to a security alert company which, in turn, notified the police. With all the equipment he had inside, I knew that nothing was going to be able to get in without being noticed.

Once the security box beeped an all-clear tone, they entered the trailer. DD performed really well and even commented on how messy the trailer was. That was something I always do every time I see it myself. Curt is always on the go and rarely cleans his house. He never eats at home, always out, and so he doesn't have dirty dishes or maggots crawling around the place. His refrigerator is normally either filled with beer or left-over pizza. He does stock the freezer with quick frozen microwavable items, but other than that, his cupboards are bare.

Of course, he had electronics all over the place. Since he does a lot of computer repair and design, he pretty much has set up his trailer as a warehouse. Everything has a category on the floor or table or even the kitchen counters. It is a double wide trailer, so he has a lot of room for a lot of parts. He actually turned his second bedroom into his office to manage his accounts. That is probably the only clean and organized place in the trailer. With all the security systems that he has designed around town, he probably has a really good nest egg.

First thing Curt did was check his machine in the office to see if he had any business in the last two days. Of course, since he was with us the last two days, he had at least seven messages. DD asked him how he was able to keep on top of all his clients with his lifestyle and once again Curt answered with a crude and yet funny remark. He said, in a roundabout way, that it depended on how high on the priority list was the situation that was going down, which lead us to his bedroom.

His bedroom is like his throne and trophy room. The front might be a business corporation, but in the back of the house, it's like a regular bordello, and even DD asked if anyone was passed out in the room before they entered. Curt had to think for a moment, then smiled and shook his head no. After another crude comment, they went in.

The bed was in its usual disarray but the room looked immaculate. Soft lights lit the room, a 51-inch flat screen was on the wall across from the bed and it included a collection of DVDs. Filling the wall was that wonderful sound system he picked up in Tennessee last year. DD asked if he reused the sheets after each encounter and Curt told him only if it was the same girl. DD asked what was the longest he went without changing them, and Curt replied three days.

Curt grabbed a couple of things out of his bedside table and then went back out toward the kitchen. He pulled a small box out of a storage cupboard and filled it up walking around the room and grabbing parts. After telling DD that he had everything that he needed, he armed his system and then they got back into the Jeep.

The next stop on the list was the Home improvement store because Curt said he needed one more thing before he was going to get the day started, and hopefully it would be there. They were soon talking up a storm and heading down MacArthur Boulevard.

Brad had left ten minutes ago to get some lunch and I have to go to the bathroom really bad. I'm going away from the 380 for the moment and be right back.

close: 1:38 p.m.

Day 26, Sunday May 7th, 2000, 2:37 p.m.

Wow, what an hour. I get out of the bathroom, approached the 380, and on the screen, I saw a pair of women's bare breasts. First, I immediately wondered what DD was doing, and then I noticed that he was looking in the rear-view mirror of Curt's Jeep and watching what was going on in the back seat. It seems our horny friend Curt found what he was looking for at the hard ware store. The girl that he met at the checkout lane two days ago is now giving him more than a phone number in the back seat. DD was being as casual as he could be, sneaking a peek when he could, like I would, and then excused himself from the Jeep. He told Curt he was going to walk around and Curt told him not too far because she had to be back at work in ten minutes.

At first this worried me, for without supervision, what if something would happen? How could we get him out of a jam if nobody is there to handle it? But on the other hand, this is a good field test to see how DD does alone. Damn, Curt, that's why I wanted you to take my phone. He hates telephones, and that is why he does all his business from that land line in his trailer. He will not carry a cell phone. He always makes the comment that phones make people stupid and lazy. "If you can't have a conversation with the person, you are with," he would say, "then what's the point on going anywhere?" Well, my friend, this situation is a good example of why it would be good to carry a cell phone.

40

So, DD walked around the front of the store looking at items they had on the sidewalk sale. He even had a conversation with a male employee about the craziness of how fast the season items change in a store. That's when the employee had told him they were starting to get things in for the holiday season already. DD then commented on how the world has changed so much that people, don't shop smart any more for what they need, but for only what they want. Priorities are really messed up with most people and then they wonder why most of them go into debt. Once again, that's actually what I would have said.

Then I saw on the screen the girl running past DD and in through the front doors, buttoning up her vest in the process. Obviously, Curt was done and DD returned to the Jeep. After asking him if he needed to go into the store to get his item, Curt replied that she was it.

Why didn't that surprise me? They then got into the Jeep, and Curt mentioned that he was hungry. DD said that he wasn't, but he would go ahead and go with him to the burger place. He also asked Curt, since they would be near the Book Nook, if they could stop by and see Lynette. Curt had no problem with it. I can't wait to get Lynette.

Speaking of food, Brad just got back, and he is heading downstairs. Whatever it is he picked up, it sure smells good. I'll fill him in on what just happened and then report after the next stop.
close: 2:44 p.m.

Day 26, Sunday May 7th, 2000, 3:50 p.m.
Wow, I'm glad I wasn't standing in the Burger Barn for this one. When Curt and DD arrived at the restaurant, there was a line of five people before them. A tall gentleman in a baseball jersey was the one in front of Curt. The first person in line must had been ordering for at least four people and wanted each order rung up separately, which was making the wait longer, and Curt more frustrated. I could see people looking at their watches and nervously fidgeting. If only I could see DD's face to capture his

expression, but I can hear him doing frustrated sighs, which is what I do.

Anyway, by the time the person was served, Curt yelled out toward the service counter to get someone to open another register, and the girl at the counter told him that there was nobody else available. Of course, he cursed and asked DD if believed this (insert curse word).

Then the guy in front of them stepped up to the counter, and when the girl asked him for his order, that's when he decided it was a good time to look at the menu. Curt flipped.

He started yelling at the guy about how he was more concerned about his watch than trying to decide his order. Everyone had been standing in line for at least ten minutes, and he didn't know what he wanted? It's was people like you that make poor employees like her look like their service is slow. Women trying to find that quarter in the bottom of the purse, men trying to get exact change, people wanting separate orders rung up and people like you! (Of course, ad SEVERAL curse words in this description).

The guy was so scared and flustered that he left and Curt walked up to the employee smiled and told her that he would have the double cheese bacon burger, Cajun fries and a large cup for here. She smiled back and asked DD what he would like, in which he responded that he wasn't hungry.
That was fun to watch from this side.
close: 4:23 p.m.

Day 26, Sunday May 7th, 2000, 4:57 p.m.
Am I really this boring? After they left the Burger Barn, they proceeded to drive to the Book Nook and DD chatted up a storm over the way the Burger Barn repainted its interior. Curt hardly spoke during the whole time, and I can see why. DD jabbered so much he couldn't get a word in. I guess this experiment is opening my eyes up to more things every day.

They will soon arrive at the Book Nook, and I still haven't eaten the Chinese food that Brad brought home. I love egg rolls! Anyway, I'm going to relinquish the throne over to Brad and eat.
close: 5:03 p.m.

Day 26, Sunday May 7th, 2000, 5:45 p.m.

Greetings, Brad here with an update. This day is really razzing my berries, and I hope it ends well. Curt and DD just left the Book Nook after talking to Lynette. Everything went well, besides the fact that the wireless internet for the Cafe went down while they were there. Lynette was running around trying to calm down the salty customers, and Curt looked at her system. He couldn't figure out what was wrong and could only surmise that there was interference in the air. Most people who sit in the cafe just come to either reads books for free, use the internet for free or possibly buy a drink. She does have a lot of loyal customers, but a few wet rags always visit.

It is good to see that DD is performing well and passing every test that Curt is putting him through. He tried offering food, drinks, and even asked if he needed to go to the restroom. DD turned down all of the offers.

Lynette didn't have much interaction with him because of the wireless fiasco, but from the short conversations they had, she didn't tell a difference. DD is really cookin'. At least he hasn't been shot down.

With Lynette so busy, DD asked Curt if he was ready to go, and they left. Curt said that they had one more stop before returning home.
close: 6:00 p.m.

Day 26, Sunday May 7th, 2000, 6:51 p.m.

That little snot! I wasn't expecting this! Curt took DD to Marvin's. When they drove into the parking lot, DD flat out refused to go in. Curt begged and begged him to reconsider, but DD wouldn't budge. Curt then asked him to wait outside, and again, DD refused. He said something to the fact he was not going to sit in the Jeep for hours at end waiting for Curt to return. That's when Curt smiled, leaned toward DD and said that the test was complete.

DD asked "What test?"

After laughing and saying, "Never mind", Curt motioned for them to go home.

That's when I noticed that DD had been driving all this time.

close: 7:00 p.m.

Day 26, Sunday May 7th, 2000, 7:37 p.m.

After a successful day, we are going out to celebrate at 'The Pizza Barn'. DD is already shut down for the night, and I'm taking the boys out, my treat. Tomorrow can't get here soon enough.

close: 7:04 p.m.

PART TWO

EXPERIMENT: A controlled procedure carried out to discover, test, or demonstrate something.

MONDAY

Just woke up and ready to get the party started!

close: 6:32 a.m.

"I don't believe this!" Brad resounded as he tossed his cell phone onto the kitchen island. "Of all the days for the Board of Directors to hold a meeting with me, makes me wonder how I made it through all these years with those putzes."

"What's going on," Dean asked as he started to butter a freshly toasted blueberry bagel.

"I have no idea; they just want me to be there at eight o'clock," Brad added as he walked over to the refrigerator, opened the door, and pulled out the orange juice container. "Has Curt done anything stupid recently?"

"Define stupid, Curt style." Dean said as he took a bite of the bagel.

"You're right," Brad sighed as he grabbed a large glass from the cupboard, and placed it on the table. He opened the orange juice and filled the glass. "Wait a minute," he said as he screwed the cap back on the container, put it back into the refrigerator and closed the door, "didn't he just attend an Honor Banquet last Friday night?"

"Oh yeah, I forgot about that," Dean said as he snickered.

Brad picked up the glass, took a couple of large swigs from it, and then set it back down on the counter "What's the snicker for, what did that lame brain do now?"

"Well," Dean said as he took another bite from his bagel, "he told me that a girl at the dinner came onto him and she, well, dared him to pull down her top."

"Pull down, WHAT? What was she wearing, a strapless dress?"

"I guess so," Dean mumbled through his chewing, "and he said she had a nice pair. Of course, I don't know the whole conversation, but I'm sure that Curt probably left a few parts out."

Brad took another gulp of juice, "No doubt and the Board of Directors are probably going to clue me in on those parts. What time is the American Gigolo supposed to get here?"

Dean looked at the clock on the kitchen wall "He should be arriving by seven. I've got 17th Century Literature at nine o'clock and Professor Grubbs does not like tardiness." Dean jabbed the rest of the bagel into his mouth. "I better get down stairs and start getting DD ready."

"Wait, bad idea," Brad said holding his hands up to stop him. "I think it would be a good idea that the robot doesn't see you anymore. With all your downloads into him, he might trip out seeing another him."

"Like traveling back in time and running into yourself," Dean contemplated the possibilities, "but freaking out because there is another you."

"Exactly," Brad added. "So, it would be best for you to stay upstairs until they have left."

The sound of the front door opening made them look up at each other and then turn their heads to see Curt walk into the kitchen.

"Good morning, turds, isn't it a lovely day?"

"What did you do at the Friday night Banquet," Brad snapped, "Full story?"

Curt looked confused at the question but then a large grin slowly took over his expression, "Oh yeah, the chick with the tits."

"What happened?" Dean pressed.

"Well, I was sitting there, minding my own business alone at a table, when this chick walks up to me and introduces herself. "Curt walked over toward the refrigerator and grabbed the bag of doughnuts on top of it.

"What was her name, "asked Brad.

"I have no idea," he said shrugging his shoulders and opening the bag. He reached in and pulled out a couple of mini chocolate doughnuts, and tossed the bag back on top. "But she had these huge tits, and the dress she wore was barely containing them."

Dean lifted his eyes into the air, "Did you even see what her face looked like?"

"Oh, yeah, she was fucking gorgeous, but anyway, she had told me that she had heard of my reputation and wanted to meet me. I asked if it was the reputation at the college, and she said no. One of her friends had told her that she went out with me a couple of times."

"What was her friend's name?" Brad asked again.

Curt turned his head toward him and shrugged his shoulder, "Beats the shit out of me. Anyway, I told her that she was good eye candy and couldn't wait to open the wrapper. Then she said what was stopping me now? "

"You've got to be kidding me," Brad said waving his arms around. "What kind of lady in this day and age says something like that? This didn't happen in the middle of the room, did it?"

"No, we weren't in the middle of the room; I was sitting at a corner table." Curt's eyes started to glisten, "And she had some beauties! The kind of tits that you could...."

"Ok, that does it for me," Brad added setting his now empty glass into the kitchen sink, "at least I'll know what I'm walking into." He started walking out of the kitchen.

Curt turned to Dean as Brad exited the kitchen and got a quizzical look on his face, "walking into what?"

"Board of Directors," Dean said grabbing a coffee cup off of the hanging cup tree; He then walked toward the coffee pot on the opposite side of the kitchen, "nine o'clock this morning."

"Oh, shit."

"Yeah, well you better get DD ready. Brad suggested that he shouldn't see me; it could cause a whole paradox thing, so I'll come down when you're gone. I've got Professor Grubbs at nine, so don't be late." Dean filled his cup and added sugar.

"Grubbs at nine, interesting," Curt stated as he walked toward the basement door, "Do you have your entire shit ready downstairs?"

"Oh, yeah, it's ready to go."

"Then let's get this fuck show going!" Curt turned toward the basement door, and Dean headed upstairs.

Day 27, Monday May 8th, 2000, 7:07 a.m.

Curt and DD just left, and I'm sitting at the 380 with a cup of coffee. I'm so excited that when I bit off one of my fingernails, it tore down to the cuticle. Man, that hurts. It's bleeding too. I better get some salve on it and a band aid, so I don't bleed all over the place. Here we go.
close: 7:09 a.m.

It was a warm sunny day, and the breeze flowing through the Jeep's open cab felt good. The top was down, and Curt had the radio turned all the way up, but you could barely hear the song because of the wind. Curt's Jeep also made a low rattling sound when he switched gears and at times, it sounded like the transmission was going to fall out. With all the things Curt could do, he hated working on cars. He always took his Jeep to a local family-

49

owned business. They always fixed the problem and at a decent price, as if money was a problem anyway.

They had just passed Stevenson drive and were turning onto the campus road. Between the noises of the wind, the radio and the rattling, they had to yell to get the other person to hear them.

"I really appreciate you driving me around this last two weeks; I just have to get that truck fixed," DD yelled.

"I don't know why you put up with their bullshit," Curt yelled above the howling wind. "They've been dicking you around ever since you bought that thing."

"It's all in the way they wrote that contract," DD proceeded, "the loophole is in between the first sixty days and the individual dealer's warranty. It has a gap of about three weeks. At least the part will be in this Thursday morning."

"I still say you need to shove the truck up their asses and go to another dealer. Those pussies have probably fucked over a lot of people the same way."

"True, true," DD said while nodding his head, "but someone needs to find a legal way to shut them down. Either way, I won't be able to get the transmission fixed until Monday, and then, I'll have to pay for half of it."

"That's bullshit, man," Curt yelled as they turned into the parking lot of Mckinley Hall. "They should cover the entire cost; the truck is only three months old. If the part comes in on Thursday, why can't they fix it then?"

"Because," DD answered, "The shop is booked up until Monday."

Curt swung the Jeep around and parked at a spot under a large tree. When he turned off the engine, the sound difference was a lot quieter. "You should just drive the thing until it fully breaks and then sue their ass."

50

"Then they would label it as owner neglect; I've already thought about that solution." DD opened the door and stepped out, "I've got to get to class."

"Wait," Curt said, exiting as well, "I'm coming with you."

"Huh?" DD got a really surprised look on his face, "You want to come to Professor Grubbs class? Are you nuts?"

"I've got no classes today, and it'll be like a refresher course." He added as he started walking on the sidewalk toward the Hall.

"Are you sure after the way you treated her? I mean, she was so furious..."

"I don't give a rat's ass; she can't kick me off campus property. I'm still a registered student." Curt said while holding his hand to his chest, "besides, I'm in good standing."

"Yeah, until you do another one of your stupid moves," DD continued his pace toward the hall, "How long has it been since you got on someone's nerves?"

"I'm on a good streak," Curt looked up into the sky for the answer, "Oh, it's been about, two days," he smirked as they reached the steps. Trotting up two steps at a time, they both reached the tenth step and the door. Curt opened the right door and gestured toward the inside. "After you, my Hine ass."

They both entered and the door closed behind them.

****

Brad always hated walking down the hall toward the Board of Director's office. All down the hallway were pictures of past members, and they all seemed to judge the viewer as you passed by. Some of the first founders looked like they would kill the first student that had a bad grade. Fifty pictures adorned the hall, and Brad had seen them more than enough. Only retired members were pictured on the wall, which meant that the people waiting in the closed doors ahead were all too eager to put their faces into the history of the University. Brad knew their faces all too well. Many times, he had been called to this place, several in protest to Curt, but this time was just bad timing. In fact, before he even opened the door, he could see in his mind who and where each person was sitting.

First there was the chairman, Jerry Mcward, who always sits at the chair facing toward the door. He's been Dean for about three years, and if it was up to him, he would have his face carved on the stone out front. Never looking for what's best for the college, but what was best for him.

Sitting to his left, should be Polly Geist, Administration Director, and the only thing louder than her dress was her mouth. She was always the undecided person whenever it came to any decisions. She would argue the fact until you turned blue and put off voting on things long enough for it to be either too late to activate, or it was just plan forgotten.

Sitting to Mcward's right would be Charles Herbert, the head of the Laboratory division. He was a good man, to a degree, if you needed something in the lab, but anywhere else, forget it. To him the lab was the entire reason the college existed, and all forms of funding should be provided to him first, others second. He could never truly understand that they all worked together to reach our goal.

Sitting to Geist's left would be Marshall Dunmire, Head of Finances. His checkbook probably has redder than a strawberry pie. He's been in the position for six years and at the end of every year, they always had to hire an outside accountant to straighten out the mess.

Sitting across from Dunmire would be the only friend Brad had in the room, Robert Foraker. He always watched Brad's back and kept him informed of the board's moves. It was Robert that helped him maintain control of the Mechanical Engineering department. Several times Brad was asked to run for the Board, but refused. He didn't like politics and never would. Nobody really cared about the individual, only how good they or their party would look in the end.

Politics, now that was an entirely different world. Most people saw it on a grand scale, like the President of the United States and Congress. All of them trying to make themselves look like they are looking out for the American people when in reality, they are not. Budget cuts where always found somewhere, but never in their own pockets. Funding was always cut off to people who truly needed it, but they could still have their paid vacations, jets, housing and even benefits untouched. Even when they passed laws, they did not have to abide by them. They somehow made themselves untouchable. If it was up to Brad, he would get rid of the Senate and the House and make one ruling building with equal number of parties and cut all their salaries in half. Of course, as he thought harder on the subject, he started to reflect back to his present circumstance. The same politics runs on a smaller level as well, and as he approached the doors, Brad stopped, took a deep breath and opened them.

Stepping inside, he saw that his predictions were correct except Robert wasn't in the room. Another gentleman, in his early forties, was sitting in his place.

"Good morning, Professor Crawford," stated Dean Mcward as he stood up to greet him, "please, come in." He turned toward a man at the table, "I would like to introduce you to Paul Dehart, I'm sure you know everyone else."

Brad reached over and shook the man's hand, "Pleasure", he smiled. The man returned the shake and only nodded in return.

"Please, sit down," Dean Mcward gestured toward the chair at the end, facing him. Brad sat down and scooted his chair up. "Mr. Foraker couldn't make it today; he is out of state on a business matter."

"So," Brad pressed on looking around the table at the faces looking at him, "What's burning on the fire this week?"

"Possibly the college's reputation," blurted out Polly Geist. "We have a situation that has to be addressed, a situation that should have been taken care of years ago."

"And that is?" Brad questioned.

All eyes turned to Mcward as he cleared his throat. "It seems that your wonder boy did some inappropriate behavior at the Friday night dinner banquet."

"Behavior that is so degrading and disrespectful, "added Dunmire, "that repercussions could hurt the finances of this institution."

"Not to mention enrollment for future students," Dehart voiced.

"And the possibility of donations being cut from the lab," Herbert finalized.

Brad sighed. It all played out as usual. Everyone was worried about themselves and their tiny little control they contained. By the end of this week, they all will be out of the spot light and his experiment will be in center stage. Once the word would get out about DD and the experiment, other Universities and Colleges would all be knocking at the door for information. Student enrollment would go up, funding would go up, and the overall standing of Tandem would be overwhelming.

"Ladies and gentlemen," Brad stated, "pulling down a woman's top will not destroy the financial state or the political balance of this institution. In fact, it might give us the media attention that we so much need. With that type of reputation, Mr.

Johnson could fit in quite well as a state senator or even the next president of the United States."

Outrage and muffled words ran around the table, and Brad couldn't understand anything anyone was saying, although he did manage to hold back a laugh. Mcward was waving his hands trying to calm everyone down when Dehart spoke up.

"Brad that was uncalled for," Mcward voiced.

"I apologize," Brad stated, "that was out of line."

"I want the man arrested and kicked out of this school, "said Dehart loudly.

"And your position in all of this?" Brad asked.

"I'm the father of the woman he raped."

Everyone got quiet. Only the hum of the air coming out of the floor vent could be heard. Apparently, nobody knew who he was, except Mcward.

"Rape is such a strong word," Brad stated. "Is your daughter pressing charges?"

"No, but I will," Dehart added as the scowl on his face got even deeper.

"Is she a minor?" Brad questioned on.

"No, she is twenty-four," he answered.

"Well, I do have a minor in Law, and if she doesn't press charges then no Judge will take the case." Brad summed up.

"Then I want him expelled!" the man yelled, slamming his fist into the table.

Silence once again took over the room.

"Obviously Brad," Dean Mcward calmly stated, "you know about this situation?"

"I was made aware of it this morning," he replied.

"Look, Brad," he said as he glanced around the room at the faces, "you have covered his problems far too long, and it's time to let go," Mcward added.

55

Brad looked upset. He was tired of this group, and the ignorance they had. "This University has been trying to get rid of this young man for almost two years now. Yes, I've come to his defense, many times, and with very good reasons. He is a genius!"

Several people shuffled in their seats clearly illustrating their disagreement.

Brad continued, "History has hundreds of geniuses that are not perfect, Ladies and Gentlemen," He glanced around the room, "And I've taught myself to look away from the faults and look at the strength of their talents."

"Name one genius," Dehart snapped.

"I'll name several. Michelangelo's domestic habits were so incredibly squalid that he practically lived like a Hermit; Mozart had a scatological humor and even Aristotle was accused of misogyny and being a sexist!" Brad lowered his eyes and scanned the room again, "and with the years I have at this institute, I can point out several things about members in this room that I also have taught myself to look away on."

Several voices filled the room until the Dean yelled just above the others.

"Enough!" Mcward said as he raised his hands in the air hoping that it would hush the crowd; but didn't work.

"Professor Crawford," Geist said while pointing at him, "This sexual behavior has no bearing on other people's conduct, not to mention people not even living during this time period! This day and age we must...."

"Please!" Mcward waved again, "Let's have order here! "

The room then returned to silence, but several facial expressions were still loud.

"Brad," Mcward said, releasing a tired sigh, "this time something needs to be done. I'm not going to authorize an expulsion, but I do feel that a suspension is in order."

Dehart didn't like the answer but remained quiet. Other board members shuffled their feet and Herbert scooted up his chair. Dunmire just looked like he was trying to get lost in his papers on the table, shuffling them around.

Brad took a deep breath. "Esteemed members," he said calmly, knowing what he had to do to derail this racing train and thought out his next sentence carefully. "I ask you to bear with me for a moment for there is something of extreme importance I must tell you, something that is going to not only put Tandem on the map, but bring in lots of money."

With that comment, all eyes and heads turned toward Brad. Even Marshal Dunmire stopped rattling through his papers and gave him full attention.

He had their full attention now. "I have been working on a very large project for several months now, and it is being tested as we speak."

"What kind of project?" Charles asked quickly.
Brad cocked his head toward the left, "I don't want to say anything until all tests are completed, but I need Mr. Johnson for this. He is a large part of its success and its future."

Many of the members looked confused, and then turned toward the Dean for an answer.

"What do you want?" Mcward said.

"I need two weeks," Brad said looking from eye to eye at the table, but not in the direction of Dehart's. "Two weeks for him to be untouchable. Then after that, you can do whatever you wish to him," Brad then turned toward Dehart, "Whatever you wish."

All the members stirred in their chairs but no response was given. Brad stared toward Mcward and waited.

"Two weeks then," the Dean submitted.
By the reaction around the table, many were not happy, but Brad knew that they would later challenge the Dean and his answer.

57

"Then, ladies and gentlemen," Brad said standing up and scooting his chair back, "I bid you farewell. I have a lot of work to do."

A couple at the table nodded their heads while others didn't even acknowledge his departure.

On the way down the hallway, Brad could have sworn that all the pictures of the past board members were smiling at him.

****

Professor Grubbs 17th Century Literature room still looked the same to Curt when they entered. The entrance was at the top row of seats facing toward the professor's desk and work area below. A large chalkboard on the wall flashed memories to Curt on how amazingly she could fit so much writing into the small space provided. At times many of the students had to walk down to the board just to read the small print. The desk in the middle of the room looked like a miniature library. Several books cluttered the top and a small book case was just to the right of it.

Several memories started to flow through Curt's mind of the wild things he did in this class. He had taken her class two years ago, and although he did learn things about many unknown writers, he found the time to work on other subjects in the class. Many times, he would bring in schematics of the robotics that he was working on and try to finish his work during her long-winded speeches. She tried several times to catch him not paying attention, but his complex mind could easily answer correctly anything that she threw at him.

The class was almost full when they entered, and the clock on the far wall indicated that it was about thirty seconds away from nine o'clock. Curt gestured to DD to sit toward the left in the top row just as two other students rushed in the door and further down the steps.

"Let's sit up here," Curt insisted as he sat in the first chair, "she will not see my ass if I'm this far back."

"I don't know," DD added, "You know how observant she is." He sat down next to Curt and opened up his notebook to the blank pages. He pulled his pen out of his folder and clicked it open. "I hope it's going to be an interesting topic today; I almost fell asleep last Monday."

"You, fall asleep? Horseshit! You're the most obedient person I know," Curt turned and pointed at DD's face, "You'd get a hard on just watching butter melting."

"Exactly," DD answered.

Just then the second hand passed the twelve on the clock and the door on the far right of the room opened. Professor Grubbs came walking in, carrying her brief case, and approached her desk. She was a short woman with long black hair that hung down her entire back. She had a spring in her step and her face looked like it glowed with excitement. She was always cheerful and loved to express her feelings, especially when it came to her passion about literature. Her high heels echoed throughout the room as she finished her journey to her desk and laid her brief case on top of it.

"Good morning," she said.

The class room returned the greeting.

She started walking around the front of her desk while glancing at the people attentive to her. "Today I have a special......Mr. Johnson, what are you doing in my class?"

Everyone in the class turned to look at the two sitting at the top row.

DD leaned over to Curt, "I told you that she would see you."

Curt cleared his throat and answered, "I'm observing."

"Observing what," she said as she placed her hands on her hips, "My patience?"

"Why no, not at all, "Curt said in a professional tone, "I merely wish to experience the extraordinary skills that you possess and see once again, firsthand, how knowledgeable you are in your field of study."

A few laughs could be heard around the room but quickly stifled when they noticed she was not smiling. Her eyes squinted, and she pointed her right index finger at him. "One curse word and out you go."

"Yes ma'am," Curt said with a nod.

"Ladies and gentlemen," she announced like a circus ring master while she leaned her backside up against the front of her desk, "You have all heard my Curtee stories from time to time. Some of them are so outlandish that even I have a hard time believing that they have happened." She then lifted up her right hand and waved it toward Curt, "Behold, the Creator, the Master and the originator of those stories. I give you Curt Johnson."

Everyone once again turned to look at the waving person at the top of the steps.

"I've always prided myself on being very aware of my surroundings," she continued, "and being very hard to catch off guard." She turned and grabbed a pen off her desk, "But, unfortunately, one day I stupidly challenged a class to try to get me. Mr. Johnson was in that class and took the challenge willingly." She looked up toward the corner of the room searching in her mind for past events. "Remember the story about the glued together notebook?" She pointed the pen toward Curt, and some people laughed. "Remember the story about the exploding ink pen?" Once again, she pointed at Curt. "How about the classic fake chalk sticks for my black board?" Several people laughed at that story, "All of these were Curtee stories by our guest." She shook her head from side to side, "Every one of them didn't really catch me off guard, but they did keep me on my toes for the entire semester."

She started to walk around to her chair behind the desk, "and as he continued that semester, his tricks became even more technically advanced. His greatest failure was when he designed a robot snake and put it in my top desk drawer." A couple of the women in the class got a disgusted look on their faces. "He didn't know that snakes didn't bother me, so I just picked it up and walked it up to him."

Curt was smiling the entire time and leaned over to DD, "that snake took me over a week to build. I thought for sure the oil on it would make her squirm."

DD nodded.

"Even the worms in my coffee cup didn't faze me." A couple of 'EEW's' could be heard in the room. "He may be one of the brightest students we have ever had at Tandem, but he failed in tactics 101."

The class started laughing, and Curt yelled something out that was unclear.

"What did you say?" Professor Grubbs asked.

"Spider," Curt said again.

The Professor's eyes widened to their fullest, and she took a deep breath. "Oh, I can't believe I completely forgot about that." She looked up at the ceiling and started to pale like she was going to faint. She started to shake her head side to side again and took another deep breath. "Class, another Curtee story for you today, and this one did get me."

She had the full attention of the class and their eyes were glued to her just waiting to hear the story. Several students closed their open books. She pulled out her chair and sat down in it. She rarely sits down in her chair, unless either there was a class study hour or she had to write something. She looked deeply into the eyes upon her.

"This one happened in the second half of the semester. I was sitting in my chair, here at the desk, when a spider slowly came down from the ceiling and landed on my paper work in front of me." She looked at her right arm and rubbed it with her left hand, "I'm getting goose bumps just thinking about it," she sighed. "I let out such a scream that I probably disturbed professor Alumbaugh's class next door. Curt had made a robotic spider that was about six inches in diameter. He was controlling it from his seat and once it landed, he proceeded to make it crawl toward me." She got lost in thought of the situation, "I hate spiders, and I loathe them." She continued with a shiver, "It only took me a second to regain my composure and when I did; my copy of Edger Allen Poe's complete collection ended its electronic life in a second."

The classroom rang out with a few laughs and Professor Grubbs got up out of the chair. "He did have me on pins and needles the rest of that day though." She walked back to stand in front of her desk, "but beyond that, he did make the semester quite challenging, to say the least and to that, I do take my hat off to you."

"With my pleasure," Curt answered with a salute.

"Now, moving on to other things, besides spiders, everyone knows my love for animals. Outside of Literature, I spend a lot of time helping the shelter in town and animal rights organizations. There is a strong problem in our society. I am very frustrated with the treatment of animals not only by careless individuals, but also by a government that hasn't put strict enough laws to help these defenseless creatures." Her expression changed from the shivers of the unexpected to anger. "Sure, we have laws in place for cruelty, but why do we put animals to death that naturally defend themselves?"

62

The class could see that she was really upset by this and watched her start to pace back and forth in front of her desk. "Animals are naturally instinctive and unique to nature. Humans are the ones who created the terms in which they are measured. I fail to understand why we have not required a training course on how to raise, treat and love an animal. They do it for new born babies, why not newborn puppies?" She sighed in anguish, "they are just as fragile as a child and as innocent."

She walked over to the chalk board and grabbed a piece of chalk off the ledge. "This topic is the center point of this week's assignment. Our assignment will be studying the writings of Rene' Descartes and John Locke, two writers who not only questioned the feelings of animals, but the treatment of them."

She started writing their names on the board.

****

Brad sat calmly at his desk in his office. He had already made a pot of coffee and was enjoying a little down time before he called Dean to find out an update. He lifted up his cup and took another sip. It was amazing how at times coffee could make you feel. When you took a drink, you could feel the warmth travelling down your throat and toward your stomach. The hazelnut aroma added to the sensation and calmed him even more.

Damn those stuffed shirts and their "holier than thou" attitudes. Their politically correctness frustrated him to no end, and they always had Curt in their target sights. Yes, Curt was annoying, rude, obnoxious and downright overbearing but he was one of the most gifted people he had known. Wait until next week when everything changes, and they see that control will be taken out of their hands. The seminar in Seattle is not only going to be informative, but many of the members in the audience have

63

financially backed him for years and would in a heartbeat support any future developments. Many of them are stock holders of Tandem and Brad was sure that a few heads would roll in the board of directors when he goes public with the robot.

He glanced at the stack of papers in front of him; all the notes he had been taking over the weekend for his presentation. He was glad that he had no classes today, so that he could start typing everything together. Tomorrow was a full day of classes for him, and he wanted to finish his report as soon as possible. He wanted Dean to look over the final draft before he stamped it with approval.

Suddenly, the phone ringing startled him out of his trance and he jerked, spilling a little coffee on the desk. He grabbed the phone receiver.

"Professor Crawford," he answered.

"Brad," said the familiar voice, "so how was your morning?"

Robert's voice was a good sound to the ears. In fact, it was many times that he chewed his ears off with stories, concerns, and just plain jibber jabber. "It would have been better if you were there, Bobby. Those vultures were after blood."

"I know," he responded with a laugh, "I would have called you to warn you but didn't get a chance."

Brad lifted an eyebrow, "You heard of the situation then?"

"Yes, pretty funny actually," he laughed again, "I wish I was there to see them; I mean the incident."

"No, you meant them." Brad said with a smile, "You were always a horny little kid when you were younger."

"Yes, I was, but now at our age any chance for a glance...."

"Where are you?" Brad interrupted as he started dabbing up spilled coffee with a couple of tissues from his desk drawer.

"I'm in Indianapolis recruiting students at the state college convention."

64

"Oh yes," Brad said throwing the now wet tissues into his garbage can, "I forgot that you were there." His thoughts started to dance around about how famous this college would become when the news gets out. "Well, if things go well with this project of mine, maybe this will be the last time you have to beg for students, Bobby. After this week is over, they will be swarming to this University."

"Oh, yeah, that reminds me," he paused as Brad could hear him take a drink of something, "when are you going to let me in on this little project of yours? I'm dying to know what it contains."

"Soon, my friend, very soon," Brad said as he took another drink of his coffee. "I can't let the cat out of the bag just yet; I have to do final tests. When they are complete, though, you'll be the first to know."

"Good, this waiting is driving me nuts." Bobby's voice sounded a little muffled as he obviously was chewing on something while he was talking. "I should be wrapping up things tomorrow and back into town on Tuesday. How about having a couple of drinks at Shenanigans when I get back?"

"I'll try to fit it in. Just give me a call when you're ready."

"You bet. Talk to ya later."

"Stay cool, my friend." Brad laid the receiver down and got up to refill his coffee. That's when he noticed that he almost finished a whole pot of coffee, and he was yearning for more. He turned to grab the coffee accessories and noticed that he had used his last filter.

"Swell," he mumbled to himself, "I'll guess I'll check in with Dean then go down to the cafeteria and get some more filters." He returned to his seat and picked up the phone.

****

It was now about 11:56 and Professor Grubbs was wrapping up her class. It was a very interesting topic and both DD and Curt were fully engulfed into the lecture. Curt had watched DD throughout the entire class and noted how accurate he was with Deans actions. He nibbled on the end of his pencil, like Dean did and even his handwriting was a perfect copy. Even though he was there to babysit DD, he found himself quite intrigued by the professor's topic.   The entire class revolved around the treatment and laws protecting animals, not only in this country, but other countries as well. She had gone over several court cases and writings that influenced animal activists and what programs developed because of their influence.

Curt was very impressed.

"Now to finish up the day," Professor Grubbs said as she walked over to an empty pickle jar on her desk, "I will be glad to take any donations for the local animal shelter. This is not a part of your grade, but please feel free to help in any way you can, every little bit helps." She then closed her briefcase which always signified that she was done for the day. "Have a good day, ladies and gentlemen."

All the students started getting up, putting their papers in order and leaving. Several went down to place money into the jar, and Curt and DD joined the line as well. They both stood back and waited for the other students to leave the desk area and when the Professor was the only one left, they approached her.

"Professor Grubbs," DD stated, "That was one of the best classes I've attended in a while. Your research and knowledge on this matter is very good."

"Thank you, Mr. Mitchell, it is a very touchy subject with me," she answered with a smile. "What was your assessment of its Mr. Johnson?"

"I'm very impressed," Curt replied, "I didn't know that so much cruelty happens like that in this country."

"It is sad," she added, "in fact, other countries have stiffer penalties than the United States when it comes to animal cruelty."

DD nodded his head, "Well, I'd like to throw in one hundred dollars to the shelter, but it seems that I forgot my wallet at home."

Curt got a Deja vu look on his face then got out his wallet and pulled out a wad of money. Professor Grubbs' eyes widened at the amount. "Good Lord, what did you do, rob a bank?"

"No," Curt said, "I don't trust banks. I usually carry what I need for my business."

"And what is..." she waved her hands, "I don't want to know."

"It's not illegal, if that's what you thinking," Curt added. Then he pulled out two hundred dollars and handed it to her. "Here is a hundred from each of us," then he turned toward DD, "you can pay me back later."

DD nodded his head.

The professor's eyes widened, "Thank you gentlemen, thank you very much. That kind of donation can help a lot of homeless animals."

"It's only money," DD stated, "and like you said, every little bit helps."

"Fuck'n eh," Curt responded.

The professor slowly turned her head to Curt, "Get out."

Day 27, Monday May 8th, 2000, 12:18 p.m.

Brad just called for an update, and I told him how everything was going. This is so cool and it's only the first day! I know I shouldn't get my hopes up so much because we have so much more to test, and there is bound to be some glitches but I'm excited! Brad had asked where they were at, and I told him they just arrived at the cafeteria to get something to eat. Brad said he would join them. That gives me a chance to cook up some pizza pockets and go to the bathroom.

close: 12:22 p.m.

When Brad walked in, he saw that Curt and DD were sitting on a round table in the middle of the room. He walked over toward the beverage area and ordered a large orange juice. He had enough coffee for the day and needed something to cool his throat. He loved the fresh taste of orange juice but could not stand pulp, so he always got the one with the least amount. After getting his glass, he went to the checkout lane and had the server get him a package of coffee filters from the back. All faculty members were allowed to purchase their supplies from the cafeteria, and even run a tab. Brad always paid for his up front because he knew others that would run up such a tab, they would forget what they got. When the monthly statement would come out, they would freak out on how much they owed. Not him, though, he had enough stress in his life not to add another stroke at the end of each month. Besides, it was easier to keep track of his finances this way. When they server returned, he was given a total and he paid, received his change, and walked to the boy's table.

"Mind if I join you two dead beats?"

"Have a seat, you old fart," Curt said signaling to the chair in front of him, "we just got here."

"I know you did," Brad replied as he set his glass on the table, pulled out a chair and sat down.

DD ruffled his brow and looked toward Brad, "How did you know we were here?" DD quizzically looked at him. "Do you have cameras following us?"

Brad took a sip of his orange juice, "No, I saw you two walking up the entrance." Then he glanced toward Curt and winked at him.

"Well, aren't you just the lucky shit, "Curt responded with a sneer toward Brad.

Brad took another sip of his juice, and Curt a gulp of his soda. Brad then looked at DD who was just sitting with his hands folded on the table and glancing around the room.

"Didn't you get anything to drink?" Brad asked DD, "By now you would usually have a full glass of chocolate milk gone."

"I'm just not thirsty right now," DD responded, "I don't have the craving for it, if you know what I mean." He then reached to the tooth pick holder and took a couple of picks.

Both Curt and Brad smiled at each other.

"So how did the meeting go this morning?" Curt added with a laugh, "Am I in trouble again?"

"What meeting?" DD asked.

"Brad was called to the Grand asshole table," Curt said as he laid his right hand upon his heart in a salute, "and he probably had a wonderful fucking time!"

"You're lucky, son." Brad said pointing to his face, "I was able to get you a two weeks furlough. They can't touch you for two weeks."

"Why two weeks," DD asked as he started to clean out dirt from under his fingernails with the tooth pick.

Brad looked at him, "because, two weeks would give me enough time to get Curt out of this situation."

"Situation, fuck, if you were in the same position, you would have done the same thing." Curt announced.

"I doubt it," Brad said.

DD looked back and forth at the two men in front of him with a confused look on his face. "Am I missing something?"

Just then, they all noticed two girls turning around from the cash register, with their food trays, and walking toward them. Both of them was wearing short skirts, white t-shirts and neither one of them were wearing a bra. Every detail of their breasts could be seen through their shirts. The nipples poked out and even the color of the skin tones could be seen. Their breasts bounced wildly as they came closer to the boy's table.

Curt watched them walk toward them, then around the table and sit at the table behind them.

"Yummy," he stated as he glanced from the girls back to the faces at his table. That's when he noticed the other two still staring at the ladies.

"HEY, "Curt said pointing at both of them, "Now you can't tell me that you were not staring at that?"

"I'm old, "Brad stated, "not dead."

"Looking is for free," DD added.

"Yes, looking is for free shithead," Curt declared, "but touching and licking is so much more fun! And tits have a language of their own."

"A language", Brad asked, "What do you mean by that?"

"I call it Titanomics. Pay close attention gentlemen, and I'll educate you," he said leaning forward to them, "I have uncovered another dialect."

Both DD and Brad leaned forward for his description, knowing that it was sure to be sexist and interesting at the same time.

"Titanomics is a language defined on how a tit wiggles, jiggles, and rotates. They give off a unique speech of their own. Some tits bounce in a circular motion, like a wheel turning on a car and other tits bounce just straight up and down." He took a gulp of his drink and continued. "Other tits jiggle side by side, but, and of course there are ones that do it all."

70

Brad was smiling about the details but also was nervous that someone might overhear them, "Talk a little softer."

Curt continued at the same volume, "Sizes play a part in the language as well. Small tits, medium tits and large tits contribute to the speech like an adverb. Small tits with an up and down bounce say, 'Look at me, I'm fresh and unique!' Large tits that bounce all over give the language of, 'I'm uncontrollably too much for you to handle, and I dare you to!"

"You thought about this all by yourself, did ya?" DD asked.

"Years of field work, gentlemen," Curt voiced proudly. "Now the language also has its own accents and nipples are what give the language its colorful flair."

Brad and DD couldn't help but be lost in this weird but unusual topic. They leaned in further as Curt continued.

"Nipples depending on their size and length give off unique additions. Short tiny nipples tease you with the thought of tongue action while long pointy ones you can actually pick your teeth with. With the added areolas, nipples can either stand out by themselves or serve as an appetizer to the larger area. How to talk back to this language is another subject in its own, which I could best describe as the tongue, fingers, and lip technique."

"You are one sick puppy," Brad said. "And this is probably what you work on during classes."

"A man has to research somehow, somewhere, and sometime," Curt added.

"A very fascinating perspective," DD pointed out.

"Indeed, it is," Curt said with a smile. "Now, pussy has a different speech."

"And with that," Brad said standing up, "I'm leaving. Later Gaters." He nodded his head toward the boys, picked up his now empty glass, and walked it to the dirty dish counter on the way out the door.

"You were saying," DD pushed.

"No time now," Curt said turning to look at the table behind them, "I've got to do more research." DD turned and saw that he was referring to the two girls behind them. Curt got up from the table and walked to the table with the two girls. DD sighed.

"Good afternoon, ladies," Curt said as he pulled up a chair.

Day 27, Monday May 8th, 2000, 1:38 p.m.

Just got done eating and now enjoying a cold beer. This is pretty neat attending my classes and having a brew at the same time. DD left the cafeteria leaving Curt with his new targets. He's on his way to my 2:00pm-4:00pm class with professor Bergin. Biomedical Engineering lab has always fascinated me and with new discoveries each day brings hope that many diseases could become a thing of the past. I hope that cancer will soon be one of those past problems. Ever since Brad's wife died of cancer, I have become more aware of the problem and its need to be cured.

I see that DD is approaching the lab building and heading to the room. Second act is about to begin, but this time, DD is alone. **close: 1:42 p.m.**

DD saw the large plaque above the entrance to Professor Bergin's room. It simply read: "TECHNOLOGY CURES". As he walked in through the doors, he couldn't help feeling like he just walked into a hospital ER room.

The room was very small, containing several chairs with arm desks, a large video screen in the middle front and several machines scattered throughout the room. The machines were all medical devices used to research, discover, and interpret the human anatomy. This happened to be one of the fields that DD was considering for a career, but he would have to also take medical classes and he tended to have a weak stomach when it came to seeing blood. He still could remember how sick he got when Curt showed him a video clip from "Hatchet attack".

72

He was the only one in the room, which was normal because he always liked showing up early to get himself relaxed and clear his mind of the previous hours. He moved to a desk in the middle of the room and put his satchel down on the floor in front of him. When he sat down, the door to the left front of the room opened and an older female came walking in. It was Professor Bergin, and she was walking with a pitcher of water over toward the coffee maker at the desk in the right corner of the room. As she poured in the water, DD couldn't help but smile about how many people drank coffee around this university. Brad drank it so much that he could still be drinking at about eleven o'clock pm and still have a good night's sleep. Curt always had a few cups in the morning and then switch to beer by night fall. DD would have one cup in the morning and that would be it. He would become edgy and shaky if he had more than two cups. Even decaffeinated would not help. Lynette, on the other hand, was liked Brad. She loved coffee. In fact, she always said it could be its own food group. Her favorite was flavored coffee, and since she had lots of access to different brands and brews at work, she made it a lifetime goal to try them all.

"Good afternoon, Mr. Mitchell," Professor Bergin said to snap him out of his trance.

"Good afternoon, ma'am." DD replied.

"In early as usual I see," she said as she flipped on the start button to the maker.

"Exactly," he responded, "just relaxing the mind and getting it fresh for the next topic."

"Well, our next topic is going to be hard," the professor said annoyingly. "I was planning to do today's class on brain scan technology and the ability to analyze the patterns, but it seems that the 380 unit has been misplaced."

DD got a quizzical look on his face, "What's a 380?"

"I'll explain it during class," she said getting her coffee cup out from under the cabinet, "At least I have the schematics and the manuals for the unit, I just don't have the unit to show everyone."

"Bummer," DD responded.

Just then, several more students started walking in to take their seats and the clock on the wall showed it was close to 2 o'clock. DD reached down and grabbed his notebook from his satchel and opened it up to the third tab. He grabbed his pen from the side, clicked it open and waited for the class to start.

Day 27, Monday May 8th, 2000, 2:02 p.m.

Holy smoke, this is funny. I can't wait to tell Brad about this.
close: 2:03 p.m.

It had been a while since Curt was in a dormitory, especially for this reason. It had also been a while since he had a threesome. Once again, his reputation preceded him. Both the girls in the cafeteria knew of him and wanted to meet him. Once they noticed him at the cafeteria, they went to the restroom, removed their bras and walked by him to get his attention. They did. Not only did they get him into their room, but he picked up some beer on the way there. Now all three of them lay naked in a puddle of mixed sweat on a sheet they had spread out on the floor. Curt had a cold beer in his hand and lying on is back, he had the bottle perched on his stomach. The two women were on each side of him, having beers as well, and exhausted from their adventure.

"Now that's how you kill two fucking hours, "Curt announced. The two women started to laugh.

"And ten pounds of fat," one of the girls stated.

"I have to pee," stated the other one as she got up and ran toward the bathroom. Curt watched her ass wiggle as she ran.

"So," said the other girl as she rolled over and put her arm around his chest, "you graduate this year, don't you?"

Curt sighed, "I don't talk shop when I'm playing, in fact, I just don't talk shop." He reached over and squeezed her right breast. "Let's talk about other things shall we, like, how fucking hard you can get me again and which one of you cums first."

"Sorry,' she said as she started to get up, "We both have class in an hour."

74

Curt got a discouraged look on his face, "What the fuck! That's bullshit. Skip it!"

"I can't, finals." she said putting on her panties and then her pants. The other girl exited the bathroom fully clothed and just as eager to leave.

Curt sat up and glanced over them, "Well then let's continue this shit later, when we have a lot more time, preferably a whole night."

The first girl finished snapping on her pants and started to slip on her shoes, "We can't, we live too far away." The other girl started to laugh.

"Live too far? What the fuck is that supposed to mean?"

They both grabbed their purses and headed to the door. The taller one turned toward him and smiled, "We don't go to this college." They both laughed and ran out the door slamming it behind them.

Curt sat on the floor, naked and dumb founded. "What the fuck was that shit about," he stated as he got up and grabbed his clothes off the bed. "Just two dick hungry women who wanted the best, I guess."

He put on his underwear and then started slipping into his jeans and that's when he noticed that his wallet was missing.

"BITCHES!"

****

Papers flew everywhere as the frantic woman that DD accidentally bumped into tried to catch her possessions as they dropped. She had been in a hurry, no doubt late for a class, and ran into DD as she ran around a parked car. He had been waiting for Curt to arrive at the Jeep, because his class ended thirty minutes ago, and started walking toward the bench in front of the car to sit down when the encounter occurred. DD started helping her with her things: several notebooks, pens and paper was scattered all over the ground and he was doing his best to get them all. All

75

during the time both of them were apologizing to each other and then they stopped and started laughing.

"I'm so sorry, "the woman stated, "I almost knocked you over."

"That's ok," DD added, "I was about to fall asleep waiting on a friend and you helped me wake up." He picked up the rest of her belongings and handed them to her. "At least there wasn't a wind, or we would have been chasing this all over the campus."

"Thank you," she smiled as she put her stuff together, "and again I'm sorry," then her eyes widened, "and I'm late!" She started her quick pace once again

"Take care," he waved at her, "and drive safely." He walked over to the bench and sat down.

He inhaled and let out a long sigh. Looking around the campus he noticed that it wasn't as crowded as it used to be when he was a freshman. He still remembered how busy it was and how the grass was always covered with students sitting in groups. Several times he himself sat under the trees getting lost in either one of his tech manuals or his notes from class. At times he would lose hours under a tree. It was easier for him to concentrate with only the sounds of birds, the wind, and distant talk surrounding him. He just could not relax in a stuffy closed up room or study.

Even when he helped his father with his business, he found himself out in the back yard most of the time when it came to reading tech manuals and schematics. He even built himself a table and chair under the old oak tree. He would always find himself drift away from the real world and practically be hypnotized into the studying, but he was always time aware and was never late for anything.

Thinking of late, DD glanced around again for Curt. Not seeing him, and looking at the large clock in the middle of the court yard, he noted that it was now five o'clock and Lynette would soon be getting off from work at six. He wanted to stop by the Book Nook before she got off and invite her to dinner at his house. He just recently saw a recipe for a Japanese dinner and wanted to serve her in style. He had everything in the kitchen he needed and was just waiting for a good night to do it. After all the work she did the last four days, she really needed to be waited on in style.

At times, he thought that she worked just too hard. She had three assistants, and all of them were quite capable of running the store. Lynette's problem was that she had to be involved with everything the store offered. It wasn't that she didn't trust them, but she felt more comfortable rolling up her sleeves and being a part of it all. Dawn was her first assistant, and always kept things in order. When it came to receiving, ordering, school functions, and even the Café, Lynette was involved. There had been several times that Dawn had to physically force Lynette to leave.

All together, they were a great team and had built a smooth-running store. The bottom-line profit proved it. The Book Nook had been achieving its goals for the last three years and not only did it achieve profit, but the bonuses for the manager staff was really good.

"Are you planning on sitting there all day or are you going to start masturbating?"

DD turned his head and saw Curt by his Jeep, "Where have you been, "he said angrily as he got off the bench and walked toward the Jeep.

"Well, I got fucked twice by two different ladies in two different ways. Damn bitches."

"What now", DD said as he opened the passenger side and got in.

"Do you remember those two braless bitches in the cafeteria today?" Curt hopped into the driver seat and started the car, "Well, they fucked my dick, and then fucked my wallet."

DD's face turned to disgust because this had happened to Curt before when they were in Vegas. "How much did they get?"

"Well, I think I had about fifteen hundred on me, fucking bitches."

"Fifteen!" screamed DD. "Why do you always insist on carrying that much money?"

"Because it's been too many times that I have someone call my ass to install one of my security systems and I have to get parts quick. I don't trust banks and hate checks and charge cards." Curt turned his head and backed out of the parking spot, then went forward toward the parking lot exit.

"You hate cell phones too, so why don't you just keep the money in your trailer then when you get a call on your home phone, get the money then."

"Because I'll get to the parts store and realize that I forgot the money. That's why I always carry it."

"YOU, "DD said in surprise, "You admit to a brain loss?"

Curt turned and glanced back at DD, "Even the best of us has brain farts, but you didn't hear that shit from me. And don't you go repeating it fuck head."

DD smiled then noticed that they were at the end of the lot. "Hey, can we swing by the Book Nook? I wanted to talk to Lynette for a second."

"Sure, I've had my dick hard already; you might as well have your turn."

The Jeep made a quick right turn and headed down Veterans Parkway.

Day 27, Monday May 8th, 2000, 5:10 p.m.

When is Curt ever going to learn? I remember when that happened when we were in Vegas two years ago. We went there for a Robotics battle competition, and we stayed at the Royal Cantina. This was about the fourth time we had gone to Vegas, and I truly enjoy the concerts and the shows. Curt, of course loves it for the gambling and the women. He loves to play blackjack and Craps, but I only venture on the slot machines. I play a little but enjoy the celebrity shows and the fine dining more. One of the best steaks I have ever had was in Vegas.

Anyway, he had picked up this lady at one of the crap tables when he had won it big and took her up to the room. He knew that she was an escort right off the bat and paid her one thousand dollars up front. After his show was over, she had emptied the rest of his winnings and left before he could get out of the bathroom.

78

He was furious and was determined to find her and knock it out of her. It took me several hours and drinks to talk him out of it. In that town you don't want to mess with who is in charge.

I see by the 380 that they are just now pulling into the parking lot of the Book Nook. I wonder what DD wants to talk to her about.

close: 5:33 p.m.

"Hello sweetie," Lynette said as she walked over toward the boy's table in the cafe, "are you feeling any better?"

"Yes, better seeing you," DD said winking at her.

"Did you guys' order anything to drink yet?" She said as she pulled out one of the empty chairs and sat down.

"I'm not thirsty," DD stated, "I don't know if Curt did or not."

"I was going to get up and get something for me," Curt commented with a disgusted look on his face, "but I don't have any cash on me."

Lynette got a quizzical look on her face, "No money, you?"

DD leaned over to her, "It's a long story."

"Bitches," Curt said under his breath.

Just then, one of the employees, a short haired girl with a red shirt walked over to the table, "Hey Lynette, the internet is down again."

"What? Again?" Lynette said in disgust. "That's the second time this week."

"You want me to look at it?" Curt asked in his sorrow.

"No," she answered, "it's probably just as simple as pushing the reset button. I'll be right back." She started to get up out of the chair when DD grabbed her arm.

"Hey, Lynette," DD said quickly, "are you still getting off at six?"

"Yes," she answered, "Dawn is over the flu and she came in at her regular time, why?"

"Good. I want you to come over to the house at eight for dinner. I've got a surprise I want to cook for you," his wink toward her made her smile.

79

"Sounds good to me," she said as she stood up and pushed in her chair, "I've got to get away from Kim for a while anyhow. She's driving me nuts."

"I still don't understand why you put up with her shit," Curt said. "She needs to get her fat ass out, get a fucking job, a place of her own and let you have a life. She's just a fat, bloodsucking leech!"

Lynette turned and walked away. "See you at the house, Dean" and started walking toward her back office. She had heard Curt's lectures about her sister too many times and wasn't in the mood to hear one now.

DD leaned over to Curt, "You really need to stop bothering her with your insight about her sister. She knows what she is and what she does. It's just hard for her to let go."

"I know, I know," Curt said shaking his head. "There is just only so far a dick can go up your ass."

DD responded quickly. "Until it clogs up the pipe."

Curt got a surprised look on his face, "Dean! That's fucking funny! There's hope for you yet!"

DD got a disgusted look on his face, "Can we go?"

"Yeah, let's go," Curt said getting out of his chair.

It wasn't long till both of them were in the Jeep and heading toward Dean's house.

Day 27, Monday May 8th, 2000, 5:51 p.m.

Ok, what was it that DD was planning to do tonight? I have got to find out soon because Lynette will be here in about two hours. I wish Curt would carry a phone, and I could call him and get him to find out what the plans are. Brad also just called and is on his way. I told him about DD's diner date, and he said that he would just help Curt pack away DD, and they would go out to eat somewhere leaving me to, what was the word, play whoopee? Well, when they get here, I'll have to get Curt to ask DD what he is up to. I hear a car pulling up, so I'm done.

close: 5:59 p.m.

Brad had been leaning up against the back of his SUV when Curt's Jeep pulled into Dean's driveway. He had finished the first draft of his presentation about an hour ago, and Dean called him to intercept the boys before they came into the house. He needed to know what DD was planning for Lynette. At the same time, they could all get together and compare notes about the first day of tests.

Curt and DD exited the Jeep at the same time and walked up to Brad.

"Good afternoon, Brad," DD gestured toward him with a wave, "What brings you here?"

"I need to talk to Curt about a few things, and I knew that he would be dropping you off after class." Brad then opened up the back door on the SUV and grabbed a green portfolio case off the seat and then shut the door. "So, what are you gentlemen planning on tonight?"

"I need to get my dick itched at Marvin's," Curt said as he rubbed the front of his pants, "After today's clusterfuck, I need some good old fashioned, local, snatch that I know."

Brad looked confused, and he glanced toward DD.

"I'll tell you later," DD stated.

"What about you, son," Brad continued to ask.

"I've wanted to cook a Japanese dinner for Lynette for quite a while now. Set the table up Japanese style, you know what I mean. After this weekend with all the overtime she worked, she could really use a good relaxing night."

"That is downright noble of you young man," Brad stated, "not many men around like you anymore, at least in this goofy decade."

Curt started to make puking noises and bent over the bush at the start of the front walk. "Fucking puke shit," he spat as he continued his fake gagging, "Your little goody two-shoes bullshit is what makes all the other bitches dig into their men's asses and scream at them. 'Why don't you ever do anything sweet like that?',

'Why can't you ever cook me a special dinner'," Curt said with a whiny voice.

"I think it's a very nice gesture from a kind gentleman," Brad added.

"A nice gesture would be to not slap her bare ass when she gets out of bed." Curt responded.

The three started to walk up the sidewalk and toward the front door. During the trip, DD started to slow down his pace as he fumbled around his pants pocket. He then started to get a really confused look on his face.

"What's wrong?" Brad stated seeing DD's face.

"I don't have my keys with me," he answered.

Both Brad and Curt gave each other an odd look.

"Don't worry, blue balls," Curt added in, "I've got my set." He pulled his keys out of his pocket and unlocked the door in front of him.

"It's a good thing that we made keys to our places for one another, I just don't trust hiding them somewhere on the porch." DD commented.

Curt turned toward him, "You do still remember the program code of my place? How they change with the date?"

"How can I forget," DD answered. "You drill me about it all the time."

Curt smirked, "well, with my place, I don't feel fucking comfortable either, leaving it on the porch."

When they opened the door the first thing everyone could smell was pepperoni pizza. In fact, the whole house smelled like a bakery.

"What is that smell?" DD said as he walked into the main room.

"Smells like someone shit their pants," Curt yelled out loud.

"Hardly the smell of that," Brad said as he laid the case onto the coffee table.

"Exactly," DD stated, "And why did you have to yell that so loud, we're all standing right next to each other."

Curt moved through toward the kitchen and up to the basement door. "It smells even stronger downstairs," he yelled again, this time louder.

DD came up behind him and gave him a look of annoyance, "Are you ok?"

"Of course," Curt answered, "just fucking ducky." Then he opened the door to the basement.

Brad was following close behind them as they walked down to the bottom.

"You're right, it is stronger down here," DD said as he sniffed the air.

Then a magic word later, DD was shut down.

Day 27, Monday May 8th, 2000, 6:17 p.m.

Test day one has come to an end, Brad here wrapping up today's events. After we shut down DD, we plugged him back into the 380 and sat him down into his chair for the night. Dean came walking out of the downstairs bathroom and we all started to compare notes when Curt told him about his dinner date with Lynette tonight. Immediately Dean rushed Curt to the super market to buy ingredients for his meal and left me to this log. From what I gathered, today went well, but we will not be able to sit down tonight to compare notes. Dean has his dinner with Lynette, Curt has his, well, plans, and I could use the rest. After overworking the noggin all weekend and with the meeting this morning, I need some down time myself. I have classes all day tomorrow, and Dean has only one class which is teaching Mechanical Engineering 101. It should be interesting. I also got to get Dean to proofread my presentation tomorrow as well. Once the boys get back, I'll suggest that we all enjoy a night off from this excitement and reconvene tomorrow morning.

close: 6:31 p.m.

It felt really good driving in a car with no radio on, no voices and just no sound at all. This last weekend was the most nerve-racking days Lynette had ever worked in a long time. With her assistant out with the flu last week and with summer just around the corner, sales were up at least 36% over last year. A lot of customer orders were placed and the local hospital had ordered several manuals for their upcoming classes, making that much more work for her to do. She was glad her assistant was back.

Lynette's head was going a hundred miles an hour even though she was driving in thirty miles an hour speed zone. She had been with the Book Nook for almost eight years come September and really enjoyed the job. She was an avid reader when she was younger and enjoyed all kinds of topics. She also grew very fond of coffee, which she drank every day, and could even drink a cup just before bedtime. Coffee relaxed her. Other people she knew would be wound up for hours after drinking a cup, but not her. The Book Nook was the perfect job for her to be the General Manger. The best of both worlds together; a book store and a built-in coffee bar. She had climbed through the corporate ladder quickly; first at the registers, then as a receiver, then assistant, then the GM. It was a dream job that came to very few people.

Most of her life she saw people, with families, struggling to make ends meet. They would have to work two jobs and pinch every penny they earned. No money for a night out, no special things for their kids and just cooped up in the house. Sometimes they created their own problems by getting pregnant without the whole marriage bit. Then the child would be pulled between the parents and really not have a good childhood. She often wondered why the government enforced training for driving a car, a boat or a motorcycle but never created a program to teach people to be a responsible parent. You can return a car, but you can't return a life. Soon, she thought, the government is going to be so in debt because of the assistance they provide, that they are going to have to start cutting people off. With the minimum wage and the ever-climbing cost of living, it's going to be hard to survive. They need to find a way to find people who are milking the system, like her sister Kim.

Kim, what was she going to do about her? She claims to have a medical handicap but Lynette knows that there is nothing wrong with her. She is just plain lazy. She wants to have everything handed to her on a silver platter and thinks the world owes her. Lynette had to work for everything she had, especially after their father's death. Their mother, rest her soul, died when she was very young. She is only two years older than Kim, and with her father's passing, was handed the responsibility of taking care of her. Her father always pampered Kim and was in full belief that she had an illness. Many doctors had been brought in to evaluate her and only concluded that she was depressed and placed her on antidepressants. So, in claiming medical handicap, she gets checks from the government which she spends on a new car, going out to movies and other entertainment. Kim doesn't even pay rent to stay at Lynette's apartment. Most of the time, Lynette comes home to an apartment that needs cleaned and laundry to be done. Both Dean and Curt had voiced their opinions; Curt a little more than needed, but in the end, she is the only family she has left.

She turned her car left onto MacArthur Boulevard which changed her thought patterns toward Dean. His house was only a mile down the road, and she started wondering what he had in store for her. After this weekend, microwaved hot dogs would be even accepted. Her love for him was exceptional. It's going to be three years this June that they would have been seeing each other. She still remembers when she first met him like it was just yesterday.

She was working as a receiver/stocker at the time and had noticed he was a frequent customer. They had talked several times and she knew that he had been going to Tandem for about two years. He also provided a shoulder for her to cry on when she was depressed. He knew that her father had just passed away from a heart attack and also that her boyfriend, Andy Sorenson was mistreating her.

She had just sat down with Dean on her break to have a cup of coffee in the cafe when her boyfriend walked in. At first his jealous rage took over and he demanded her to leave the table and she refused. Dean stood up and tried to talk sense into him, which was hard to do, and was shoved out of the way. That's when Curt, sitting nearby, jumped in. It ended with Andy being arrested, Lynette getting a two-year order of protection put against him, and about three thousand dollars' worth of damage to the cafe. Curt paid for all the repairs. Andy later moved out of state and she hadn't heard a word from him until last Thursday when she saw him in the Book Nook. He had surprised her at the service desk and told her he might be moving back. When he asked her how she had been doing, she told him 'Busy' and she went to her office until he left. The thought of him returning to town gave her a cold chill and another problem to add to here already heaping plate of complications.

The loss of concentration caught up with her, and she almost missed Dean's driveway. She had to stop quickly and turn left, almost hitting his mail box. When she stopped, she was parked a little close to the garage door. Her heart was beating faster on the adrenalin from the near miss, and she let out a sigh. She needed a few days off.

She turned off her car and sat looking at the house for a moment. It was now dark outside and it looked like no lights were on in the house. She knew that the truck was in the garage due to its transmission problem but still wondered if he was home.

She turned and grabbed her purse off the passenger seat, opened the door and stepped out. After locking the car door and shutting it, she placed her keys into her purse, shouldered it, and started walking toward the front door. When she approached the door, the door opened.

There stood Dean, dressed in what looked like a Japanese robe.

"Good evening, Ojou-Sama." Dean said with a slight nod of his head. "Please remove shoes," he added as he pointed toward a mat next to the inside of the door.

She smiled and laid down her purse and looked at her feet as she took off each of her walking shoes. When done, she looked back up and saw that he was holding another robe for her to put on. She cocked her head to the side in amusement and let him put the robe on her.

"Your teburu awaits." he announced as he walked her toward the kitchen in the back. She started to smile but her entire weekend still was embedded in her thoughts. Her tenseness still persisted as she followed him while tying the robe's front together. A faint glow from the kitchen was the only light on in the house.

When they stepped into the kitchen, her eyes started to adjust to the low light and she saw that he had moved the large coffee table; from the front room into the kitchen. Two large pillows were on the floor across from each other at the table and a candle decorated with flowers sat lit in the middle of the table, it was the only light in the house. The room smelled divine with the aroma of what was cooking on the stove.

Lynette smiled, "What are you..."

"Shhhh," Dean interrupted her as he put his right index finger toward his lips, "No talking. This is going to be a quiet get away from everything." He walked over to the under the counter music system and pushed the play button. Low Japanese harp music filled the room. He then gestured for her to sit down on the right-side pillow and she complied with another smile.

As she was getting comfortable, Dean walked over to the stove to prepare the first course. Lynette started to take into view the table in front of her; there was a vase of lilacs in the middle of the table and the candle next to them glistened on the blooms. He had tea cups, an oriental tea pot, soup spoons and a glass of thin cracker wafers upon the white floral patterned table cloth draped in a triangle shape over the table. An empty large plate was in front of both of their seating areas.

Dean walked over to the table, bent over and grabbed the tea pot. He proceeded to fill her cup, then his, replaced the tea pot and walked back to the stove.

She reached out and grabbed the cup, the warmth of the tea soothing her tired hands. As she lifted the cup, she could smell the scent of jasmine rising from its contents. She loved jasmine tea. As she sipped it, the warmth could be felt running down her throat and down into her stomach. It was sweetened just right, and she almost finished half the cup in one gulp.

Dean walked over again, carrying two soup bowls. He laid the first one in front of her, placing gently upon the large empty plate. He then placed the other one upon his and sat down across from her.

The smell of egg drop soup filled the air around her.

"This is..." she started to say.

"Shhhh." he repeated.

She smiled again and they both reached for their soup spoons and started to eat. Once again, the warmth of the liquid felt good going down. The taste of the chicken broth and the soft cooked vegetables sent her taste buds into delight. The soup was heavily filled with egg, which she loved and was a perfect balance between thick and thin.

Her eyes widened from the sensation and she started to open her mouth to say something, and then remembered his plea. She winked at his eyes across the table and then took another spoonful.

She was always fond of his cooking because she herself would burn water. Most of everything she ate was either bought from the cafe or microwaved at home. Of course, there was the eating out at restaurants, but nothing compared to what he was doing now. The quiet alone time away from everything was what she needed. No thinking about what to order, writing the next week's schedule, resetting the planograms for the upcoming sale, the....

"You're letting your mind drift," Dean said with a whisper, "stay in the moment."

Lynette laughed by lightly blowing air out her nostrils and then took the last drop of her soup. Dean stood up and grabbed both of their empty bowls and spoons and took them to the sink.

She then arched her back and stretched her arms above her head, crackling the tired joints and making her feel even more relaxed. She let out a long-winded sigh. That's when Dean walked over with the next course.

First, he placed down two small bowls of rice with chopsticks sticking straight up in them. He returned back toward the stove again and then brought a gravy boat filled with the smell of sweet and sour sauce. He lightly bowed toward her, picked up their empty plates and went back to the stove.

As she heard him scraping the next course onto the plates, she once again took in the condition around her. The room didn't look like something that was slapped together; this took some time. She even noticed the Japanese bamboo pictures that he had hung in several parts of the kitchen.

When he approached carrying their main course, she instantly knew what was being served by the aroma it carried, eggs. He placed the plates down on the table, sat down, grabbed the chopsticks from his rice bowl and started to eat.

She engulfed herself into the meal, which was egg foo young. She could see the chestnuts and bean sprouts in the mixture and then noticed the size of the shrimp that was cooked within. She loved shrimp, and together with the eggs, she was in heaven. She took a bite from the rice bowl and then grabbing the gravy boat, poured sweet & sour sauce all over   the ingredients. She then lifted up the boat and with a nod signaled toward Dean if he wanted any. He shook his head no and then pulled out from underneath the table a bottle of special hot sauce and placed it in front of him. She laughed and started to say something and he lifted his finger and wiggled it back and forth.

The first bite was an unlimited sensation of shrimp, egg, sprouts, spices and sauce which made her groan in pleasure. The flavor was outstanding. As she slowly savored that first bite, Dean reached over the table and picked up the teapot to fill her cup. She nodded and he replenished her.

What an event. All five of her senses were being fed. The music fed her ears, the flowers fed her eyes, the softness of the robe fed her skin, and the dinner completed her. All her troubles where gone. She closed her eyes and drifted away.

****

The dressing room looked like a clash of different worlds. In one corner was a neat and tidy make up table with a well-organized clothes cabinet, and in the adjacent corner was just the opposite; a piled-on mess of makeup, clothes, underwear and dancing props thrown about the table. You couldn't even see the chair. That piled up mess belonged to the main dancer, Valentine, who not only was the senior dancer, but was also the one in charge of the girls. She did the schedules, the ordering of outfits and equipment. If you were on her good side, you got things you wanted, but if you were on her bad side, forget it. Valentine was the only one who had her own dressing table; all of the other nine girls had to share the remaining four tables which meant that one table was shared by three. Above each of the tables, in small frames, were the names of each dancer assigned to that table.

Starting from the right of the door entrance and going clockwise was table one: Hot Tamale and Carmel. Table two belonged to Parmesan and Barbie. Table three was Valentines. Table four listed Heartache and Sweet Wine. The last table, which was to the left of the entrance, was for Jambalaya, Paradise and Dragonfly. All along the walls were pictures, posters and a Hodgepodge collection of knick knacks trying to bring a personal touch to the room. Together with the smell of perfume and smoke, this was a typical day at work.

A young Asian girl sat at the fifth table, putting on the remaining pieces of her outfit. She had been working there for almost a week and has made more money than she ever did at other dance clubs she had previously worked at. When she saw the ad for an Asian dancer, she applied immediately, even though she knew that she was going to have to move downstate to accept the job. When she was offered the position, she found residency in a nearby apartment building and dancing the next day. The move was quick; she had no family, and found the town to be very pleasant. The owner even went out of his way to help her find a place and to move in. The place was respectable and honest; not like some of the dives and terrible conditions she was accustomed to. This owner respected you and didn't want to get any extra favors from you. He paid well and the place was clean.

She snapped out of her daydreaming when she heard voices coming down the hall and toward the door. As she slipped on her second boot, the door opened up and a white woman with a Hawaiian girl stepped in laughing.

"I couldn't believe the look on his face," laughed the taller white girl.

"Oh, hello," the Hawaiian said as she noticed the Asian, "You must be the new dancer everyone is talking about" She held out her hand and the Asian took it, "I'm Maylee," she said shaking the girl's hand.

"And I'm Vera," replied the other girl.

"Hello," the girl replied, "I'm Krissy, aka Dragonfly." She released her shake and pointed toward the plaques on the wall, "You two are?"

The White girl pointed to herself, "I'm Heartache and this girl here is Paradise."

"Shake them coconuts!" she stated as she wiggled her large chest back and forth.

Heartache walked over toward her table as Paradise pulled up a chair next to Dragonfly. "Is this your first night here?"

"No, it's my second," she replied, "looking forward to this weekend. I hear they get really busy."

"Girl," Heartache said from across the room, "this place rocks on the weekend, not to mention the money you make."

"And there is plenty of money here," Paradise added. "So, I take it you're Asian?"

"Yes."

"Then the buffet plate is complete," Paradise added, "Marvin wanted to have a dancer for every ethnic group so that he could cover anybody's needs. You were the last one he needed."

"You can probably guess the other races by their names on the wall." Heartache said, "And we are a pretty tight group. We all get along really good and watch out for each other."

"What kind of info can you give me," Dragonfly questioned, "is there anyone I should watch out for?"

The two girls turned their heads to each other and in unison said, "Valentine."

The stereo effect that they put off made it emphasize the warning. "Is she really that bad? When I did the interview with her, she did come across as being a little overbearing but I just figured it was because she had been here so long." Dragonfly leaned forward toward the mirror and started to apply eye shadow.

"Overbearing is putting it mildly," Paradise added, "she prances around like she owns the place, but she doesn't."

"So, Marvin is the only owner?" Dragonfly asked.

"Mainly, he does have a silent partner," Heartache added.

"Oooo," Heartache exclaimed as she leaned backwards up against her table, "Speaking of partner did you see that the horse is out front?"

"Really," Paradise said, "I haven't seen him for weeks; I wonder what he's been up to."

Dragonfly looked puzzled for she was completely in the dark about what they were talking about. When Paradise saw her expression, she turned her chair toward the mirror, "The horse is Marvin's partner, and he contributes a lot to the business."

"He's intelligent, rich and pretty much in here every night." Heartache added, "And not to mention one hell of an ass kicker. He's like a private body guard for all of us."

"So," Dragonfly said as she finished both of her eyes, "why do you call him horse?"

Heartache started to smile, "Because he is hung like a horse and most of us like to ride him."

Paradise started to laugh, "I haven't, but I know several others that do."

Dragonfly got a sad look on her face, "Don't tell me that we have to do extras for..."

"No!" Heartache interrupted, "it's nothing like that at all. Please don't get that impression. He's like a big brother to us. He's very protective."

"He's also very hard to listen to," Paradise added, "he's cocky, raunchy and very rude at times."

"But that's how he is," Heartache continued, "Once you get past his attitude, he's really a great guy."

"But," Dragonfly added, "He's a gigolo?"

"Not at all," Heartache said, "he just loves to have a good time. He hates the idea of commitment and even settling down. You don't have to worry about this guy wanting to follow you home or even falling in love with you. He's what I call very safe."

Dragonfly stood up out of her chair and gave herself one more glance in the mirror, "Well I go on in five, any other advice about Valentine?"

"Don't sweat it, Honey," Paradise said, "If Marvin likes you, you don't have to worry about Valentine."

A large green bulb above the door flashed three times.

"Go get them girl," Heartache said as she stood up and walked over to Dragonfly. She put her left arm around her shoulders and leaned up to her face. "The horse would be the one sitting in the chair in front of center stage, his usual spot."

Dragonfly shook off her nervousness and went out the door.

Curt had just sat down in his chair by the dance floor when a large short fat man pulled up a chair and sat next to him. The man slapped his hand on to Curt's left shoulder, "What's up needle dick?"

"Marvin!" Curt yelled, "How's it going, fat ass?"

Marvin leaned closer to Curt, "Big things. Where in the hell have you been? I haven't seen you for days."

"Oh, I've been fucking off as usual," Curt said taking a drink of his beer. "Is everything going well here?"

"Real good, in fact, I've got news, shit head; I finally filled that Asian spot."

"No shit?" Curt said excitingly, "When does she dance?"

"In about five minutes," Marvin added "and she's hot. She came in from Atlanta and does this trick with chop sticks that'll freak you out."

"Bullshit, nothing freaks me out." Curt said.

"Well," Marvin said as he got up out of the chair, "nether or less, she was the last piece I had to fill to make this place complete, so try to not let her trip over your dick."

"Fat fucking chance," Curt answered. As Marvin walked away, the stage lights came on.

"Bring on the smorgasbord," Curt said with a smile.

****

The room was only lit by the crackling ambers of the wood that was burning in the fireplace. The only other sound in the room was the ticking of the clock on the far wall. The room was covered in shelves, even above the entrance door there were shelves running across the top. The ten-foot ceiling was lost further up in the darkness and the smell of leather encompassed the room. Only two recliner chairs and a coffee table were the only furniture visible. The chairs sat side by side, at an angle, and between them on the coffee table was a large chess set. The pieces where all scattered around the board indicating that a game was in progress. The pieces were gold and silver colored and were about six inches tall. A few pieces sat to the side of the playing board; obviously the ones lost in combat.

Brad came walking into his library carrying a cup of coffee and the day's paper. He sat down in the leather recliner on the left; its wrinkles and discoloration showed its age and its use. The creaking of its surface continued as Brad sat his cup on the table, the paper at his side and leaned back into it.

Brad sighed. Today was a very stressful day. He didn't expect the day to run so smoothly; in fact, all his worrying was for nothing. The robot performed so well that it even made him more nervous. Anticipation is always the stomach burner, and the first thing he had to do when he got home was to take some stomach medicine. He could never get used to that taste. With all the talent in the medical field, why couldn't someone make a chocolate or strawberry flavored medicine? Peppermint was always the adult flavor, and he hated peppermint. They have flavored medicine for children, why not adults? Do they think that adults actually lose their craving for taste?

Brad reached forward for his coffee cup and made the ancient chair creak again. As he sat back, he took a sip from its contents and he felt the hot liquid run down his tired throat and into his stomach. Closing his eyes, he tried to get himself to relax. His ears concentrated to the sound of the fire but were pulled away by the sound of the clock. He opened his eyes and saw that it was almost ten thirty, and he still needed to type up his speech for this Saturday. He forgot to check with Dean to see if he had the chance to proofread it. He was running out of time and with a full day of classes tomorrow, he didn't know when he was going to get it finished.

He glanced down at the chess board in front of him and wondered if Curt and he were ever going to finish this game. He thought about when they started it, perhaps weeks ago, and then tried to remember whose turn it was. Curt was always fond of chess because it was the only game that really challenged him. His only annoyance was that he could never beat Dean. Brad himself had only beat Dean once, which was about a couple of years ago. They rarely find the time anymore to do these types of things. It seems the older one gets, the less fun you have and the more work you have to do.

His tired eyes then looked toward the mantel above the fireplace and he saw his wife's picture. It's been almost five years since her death and he missed her so much. They had been married for forty-seven years when she died of a heart attack, and the cause was never found. Her health was very good and the last thing they expected was a heart attack. She was not overweight; she exercised regularly and ate very healthy foods. Many a times she tried to get him to eat healthy but he just couldn't give up that occasional pizza or bratwurst. She always called his meals 'Cardiac arrest on a bun' and told him that he was just only putting the coffin nails in quicker every time he took a bite. It just doesn't seem right that....

He shook his head to dislodge the thoughts and started looking around the room. Several items adorned the shelves between the books; each of them bringing back memories:

The little ship statue they won on a cruise in the Bahamas,

All wine corks above the door frame of each anniversary they had,

The mason jar of white sand and shells from a beach in Florida,

The framed tickets of their first movie that they went together,

It was truly amazing the power that an object had on the mind, even objects that were only trash to another person. One little object could bring in a multitude of memories and stories that could last for hours. His wife always held on to those little things and had boxes of them in the basement. He always saw it as clutter, but up until five years ago, he now understood the true meaning behind her collection. It was full of memories.

His mind was now in a full Olympic sprint and wouldn't slow down. He had to find a way to turn off the mind and join the rest of his body that was relaxed. He hated when he would get into situations like this. Either his mind would be tired with his body fidgety or his body exhausted and his mind racing one hundred miles an hour. He hated when he couldn't relax. His eyes were too tired to read the newspaper and his body was too tired to go to bed.

Maybe tomorrow will be more relaxed, maybe tomorrow will be a better day, maybe...

Brad fell asleep in his recliner.

Tuesday

Dean here and ready for day two. Curt called and said that he would be over at about nine thirty to drive DD to teach my mechanical engineering class from ten to noon. Curt then has classes all day, so I figured that we could have DD just walk around the campus for a while until Curt got out of class at two o'clock. I'm going to take a shower, get some breakfast, and call Brad again; he's not answering his phone.

Close 7:55a.m.

Brad bolted up in his recliner, a cold half-filled coffee cup spilled into his lap, and he heard his phone ringing in the other room again. He tossed the coffee cup onto the table and ran across the house to catch it before it rang again. His head was still fuzzy from the sudden jolt, but he managed to reach the phone on the kitchen counter before its fourth ring.

"Hello?" he said groggily.

"Brad, where are you?" a familiar voice said.

"Obviously home," he said shaking the cloudiness out of his head, "who is this?"

"It's Robert; your class is waiting for you."

Brad reached up with his right hand and rubbed the matter away from his eyes. When he adjusted his vision to the kitchen clock, he saw that it was a quarter after nine.

"Aw Duck water! Can you cover for me until I get there?"

"Yeah, no problem, but hurry, I've got a class at ten."

"I'm on my way."

****

DD walked into the classroom with his briefcase and a video he planned to show the students. All month he had them designing a blueprint of different pumps. They were split up into four groups; four students to a group, and today was the last day to finalize the project. The video showed the steps to take from blueprint to part design. The movie was about an hour long which gave him a chance to catch up on some of his lessons.

The class didn't start for another ten minutes and he wanted to get everything ready to go. The large screen TV needed to be pulled down and the video projector set up. Even though those things took minimal time, DD wanted to be ready; he always hated to be rushed.

At least Curt arrived at a decent time this morning to drive him to the campus. All the way there, though, he kept talking about the fun he had at Marvin's last night and about the new dancer. It kind of bothered him, in a way, how Curt looked and treated women. They were like a new sandwich that he needed to try. No concern about their feelings, their past or even their personality. He just saw them for one thing and one thing only, sex. It just goes to prove how the upbringing of a child is so important. They grew up in two completely different circumstances and homes. It does not take a village to raise a child, just two loving, caring parents who are there twenty-four seven.

After class, he was going to ask Curt to stop by the Book Nook again and find out why Lynette didn't stop by last night. He doesn't even remember cooking anything last night. He did remember seeing Brad at the house, though, but after that, he drew a blank.

Was he working too hard? Taking his last year too seriously like Curt says he is? Maybe he needed to relax and enjoy this last year. After his graduation and he finds out what job offers he could get, Lynette and he will get married.

The class door opening pulled him out of his daydream as he started watching students walk in.

"Good morning," he said.

A couple of the students returned the greeting.

Day 28, Tuesday May 8th, 2000, 10:10 a.m.

I'm kind of nervous about this part of the test for nobody, Curt or Brad, is there in case something goes wrong. At least one phone call would get Brad to the room in a matter of minutes. Of course, getting hold of Curt is a different story. Man, I wished he would carry a phone.

Close: 10:13 a.m.

Lynette wasn't bothered by how busy the store was; she was still thinking about last night. Dean really did the trick by helping her relax. The dinner, the music and the overall quietness of the night put her into a trance. After dinner, he lit a fire in the fireplace, and they snuggled up on the couch in front of it. He still insisted that they remained quiet for the night, no talking and no phones. A bottle of wine finished off the perfect evening and she was home into her bed by eleven thirty.

She was standing in the middle of the store at the Customer service desk and on her left, she could see that the cafe had every one of the tables filled, and more were standing in line. Her cafe manager, Carol, was in the center of the counter, taking orders and receiving the money. She was a good manager and had been running the cafe for the last eight months. In fact, she had doubled the sales over two years and had just hired a new assistant. Her assistant was working today as well and was keeping up with Carol's pace. She had previous experience at another coffee shop and was getting a real initiation today, for this was only her first day on the job.

She could see Dawn walking by the best seller's wall and talking to a group of kids. She did look a lot better than she did last week, when she had the flu, and it took Lynette a lot of begging to get her to stay home. She's a workaholic and just hates to miss work. She has been with her for almost five years and rarely calls off. She works about fifty hours in the store, goes home to a husband and two kids, and is a part of the PTO club at school. How she finds time to sleep was beyond Lynette's thoughts.

She started to think about Dean again and the feelings were so intense that she felt like she was wrapped up in an electric blanket turned on to the highest setting. She tilted her head back and let out a relaxing sigh.

99

"Hello, again," the male voice said snapping her out of her trance. She knew the voice and it instantly turned her warm feeling to cold chills up the back of her neck. She turned and saw Andy standing on the other side of the counter.

"Andy, are you here to buy anything?" she asked.

"Not really," he answered as he leaned both elbows onto the counter. "I just wanted to ask a question."

She gave him a grimaced look and waited. With his muscular arms still on the counter, she started to see that he really hadn't changed the last time she saw him. He was still very bulky, still just as tall; his hair was still brown but with a shorter cut. He still had the goatee and those eyes still gave the look of trouble. She still wonders why she stayed with him for so long.

"How about going out to dinner?"

She stopped breathing. The thought of doing anything with him was frightening. Memories started to flood her mind as she went through the days of their past...

They had met at the bowling alley, when she used to be on a league with friends, and he had bought her a beer one night. After a couple of dates, they decided to get onto a team of their own, and they were always the center of attention on Saturdays. He was an excellent bowler, and she was just as good. They had won first place on a doubles league and second in an elimination tournament. They enjoyed the same movies and found that they had a lot in common. They had dated for about five months until he tried, well forced...

"If not dinner, "he added as he signaled toward the cafe, "maybe a cup of coffee?"

"No, Andy, I do not wish to see you anymore. Now please leave before I call the police." She had looked toward the direction of the cafe, where he signaled, and she saw Dawn looking at her holding up her cell phone. Lynette shook her head at her.

"Your order of protection expired two months ago, I'm perfectly legal to be standing here," he said with a cocky voice.

"Your right, you are," she stated, "but if you think that the police wouldn't do anything when a GM of a store calls about a problem customer, you're mistaken"

"You wouldn't do that, would you?" His eyes trying to look hurt. "Even after all the fun times we've had?"

"Yes," she said, "I have a new life and a future, and you are not a part of any of it."

Andy leaned over the counter, "I will be," he said at a whisper, "I will not stop trying."

"Leave now," Lynette whispered back, "while you can still leave on your own."

He turned, winked at her, and started to walk away. "See you again, soon." He then turned and walked toward the exit.

Dawn slowly approached the counter while still watching him exit, "I was ready," she said as she held up her phone, "911 was already punched in, and all I had to do was hit dial."

"Thanks, Dawn. It looks like the week is going to get a lot more intense."

"Don't sweat it," she said smiling, "I'd love to kick his ass just once, besides, never mess with a chick with a set of these!" She held up her hands and Lynette saw her long sharp nails. "I'll gouge his eyes out."

Lynette started laughing, "Did I ever tell you how much I hate bowling?"

****

"Class, I'm sorry I'm late," Brad said bursting into the room. Robert sat at the desk in the corner of the room and stood up upon his arrival.

"That's ok, Professor Crawford, we had some interesting conversations while we waited." Robert said as he walked up to Brad and then whispered in his ear, "I've got to run, you owe me one. I'll collect when you tell me what the hell you've been doing."

"Soon, my pal, possibly tomorrow I can clue you in," Brad said as he patted him on the back. He watched Robert leave the room and then turned toward his students. "Now, class, I know that we were going to talk about hydraulics today, but I had a little smog in the noggin this morning. Due to certain circumstances this week, I'm kind of frazzled out. I didn't get a chance to get my things in order so I came up with another idea. I've got a wild idea for you to all chew on today. Taking in consideration of all available equipment, I want you to design a fully operational robot. I want your pros and cons to prove if it is feasibly possible. I'm not talking some pee wee size robot; I'm talking about a human size unit and fully independent on its own."

The students started to stir in their seats looking eager to address the question.

"Work together or independently and I'll give you two hours to get ready and thirty minutes to present your ideas. Knock yourself out!" Brad started walking toward his desk to sit down when a student called out to him.

"Professor Crawford?" a young man asked holding his hand up.

"Yes, Michael?"

"By meaning running independently, are you referring to a unit with no connecting wires?"

"Yes," Brad answered sitting down in his chair. "No connecting wires."

The class stirred again.

"I want all ideas to make it operate." Brad turned and looked at the clock, "You now have one hour and fifty-seven minutes."

The students started to pull out papers, pull into groups and chatter started to fill the room. Brad sat down at his desk and sighed. He thought that it would be fun to find out their points of view then throw the reality at them next week, when the entire campus finds out. He was really enjoying himself on this and was getting eager for the week to be over. It was too bad that they still had three more days to go. Somehow, he still had the jitters about something going wrong, but so far everything was peachy keen. Things were running too smooth for it to be safe. Somehow, something was going to go wrong and everything was going to blow. He got another idea and picked up the phone.

Day 28, Tuesday May 9th, 2000, 11:43 a.m.

Brad just called for an update. I told him how really freaky it was to watch DD teaching the class. He discussed the two units that were displayed in the video and then started looking over some of the student's blueprints. Being able to see the prints myself on the 380, he was handling the situation just the same way that I would have. I have probably said that line at least a hundred times in the log and will probably say it more.

Brad wanted me to make sure that I was proofreading his speech and I told him that I finished it during the video run. There were a couple of sentences that needed reworded and a few things that I suggested that should be added. Other than that, it covered everything really well, if you know what I mean.

He also told me that he made up invitations to several of the Professors at the college and wanted DD to hand them out. It was an invitation to his lecture hall on Monday night at eight o'clock. He was planning to 'Let them have it', he said, and DD, Curt and I were to attend as well. So, I'm going to type into the 380 a suggestion to DD to go see Brad at his office. He doesn't have to meet up with Curt until two o'clock, which will give him plenty of time to do the errand.

Well, DD is winding up the class, and we shall continue this day.

Close 11:54 a.m.

DD watched the last student leave the class room. He was really pleased with work he saw from the first half of students and was looking forward to next week when the other half would present their designs. Then, the week after that, he would present the students with their final grade. Some of the pump designs were very good and he knew that his father would have had a good time looking over them. Some designed hydraulic pumps, some designed water pumps and one even designed a pump to handle ice cream. Their presentations on their work were very well written, and each had great class involvement.

DD sat down at the desk and started to pack his things into his briefcase. He glanced over at the clock on the back wall and saw that it was ten after twelve. Curt wouldn't be out of his class for another couple of hours so he had some time to kill. He wasn't hungry; so, a trip to the cafeteria didn't interest him. There wasn't much to do in the lab either; he had just finished his semester project last week. Even reading a book didn't appeal to him.

Suddenly he got the urge to go see Brad in his office. Brad wouldn't have his next class until one o'clock, so at least he could kill some time there.

DD threw the rest of his belonging into the briefcase, snapped it shut, grabbed it by the handle and walked out of the room.

****

Curt sat in class completely lost from what the discussion was about. He kept thinking about the robot and how well it was operating. Its speech, its walk and even right down to his actions were perfectly copied. He really wanted to stay with it all week long to watch, but it would throw off the test and make the robot wonder why he was being followed. With the thoughts that it had, neither he nor Brad could change their habits or it wouldn't be a true straight forward test. Everything had to run as if it was an ordinary day or week for that matter...

Curt looks down at his right foot and saw that he was wiggling it with excitement. He never was this eager to get out of class and continue something. Even with his computer business, things would eventually get done but the robot was like a boiling pot of water and he wanted to be there to watch it boil. His mind was forever thinking about a million things at once but he found himself completely lost in the robot. He kept going over in his mind how the inside of its head looked, how the oculars were wired, how the 380 loaded into the unit, the additions he added to the 380, the...

"Mr. Johnson, did you hear me?"

Curt snapped out of his trance, "Huh? What?"

The professor looked rather confused as he looked at Curt, "Something else on your mind other than this class Mr. Johnson?"

"You have no fuckin Idea."

The professor shook his head, "I've never seen you this dazed and lost before," he said walking back to the map on the wall, "try to stay focused, shall we?"

Curt sat up straight in his chair, "Yes sir."

As the professor continued with his instruction, Curt wandered off again.

****

Brad was taking another drink of his coffee when someone knocked at the door. "Come in," Brad answered to the unknown face.

DD walked in with his briefcase, "Greetings, Professor, what's new in your neck of the woods?"

"Hey," Brad exclaimed, "What's shaken! Have a seat hipster, and we'll chew the fat,"

DD sat down in the chair in front of the desk and placed his briefcase on the floor to the right. "I heard through sources that you were late to class this morning, what's up"

Brad shuffled in his chair, "I overslept. I've been having a rough week."

"I think that you're just getting nervous about retiring. I mean, seriously, what are you going to do with all your time? You can't play chess and read books all day."

"Oh yeah," Brad smiled "Just watch me try."

"You only do three classes a week now, right? Hand off the rest of the year to someone, if you know what I mean. As for retirement, I think you should get yourself to a white sandy beach somewhere and just sleep to the sounds of the ocean." DD smiled at him, "That's what I call retirement."

"Oh hey, that reminds me," Brad said while opening his left-hand drawer, "Could you help me with something?"

"I've got time to kill; Curt doesn't get out of class until two." DD stated.

"Cool beans," Brad said as he pulled out a stack of yellow envelopes, "Could you deliver these envelopes for me?"

"What are they," DD asked as he grabbed the letters from Brad

"Invitations to a special get together I'm having this coming Monday night. It's going to be a kind of farewell, thanks for all the memories, good luck to me night. Could you do it for me?"

"Sure," he said standing up "I'll leave my briefcase here and get it later."

"If I'm not here, you have the key and if you don't mind, don't tell anyone what the night is about. I want it to be a surprise. You'll also notice that Curt, Lynette, and you don't have invitations, I'd rather invite you in person."

"I'll have to check with Lynette to see if she is off Monday, if not, I'm sure she'll have her assistant cover for her."

"Sounds good, see you later gator," Brad said waving at him.

"Later," DD said as he left and shut the door behind him.

Brad jumped up out of his chair, raised both hands in the air and took in a deep breath. He just couldn't contain his excitement anymore.

"Whoopee!"

Day 28, Tuesday May 8th, 2000, 12:43 p.m.

Ok, now it's time to mess with a lot of people's heads. This is going to make me laugh so hard that I better go to the bathroom before his first stop.
Close: 12:46 p.m.

Robert Foraker just sat down in his office when someone knocked on his door. Today was a nonstop day, and it seemed that he was never going to get time to himself. He sighed deeply before he spoke. "Come in."

Dean Mitchell came walking into the room. "Good afternoon, Professor, how is your day going?"

"Mr. Mitchell," Robert said as he held his hand out for a shake, "it's been, interesting. What can I do for you?"

Dean returned the shake and handed him an envelope, "Professor Crawford wanted me to hand out these invitations."

Robert looked at the envelope that had his full name neatly scripted on it, "What's it for?"

"I have no idea," Dean said, "he just wanted me to hand them out."

Robert looked at it hesitantly, "It's not going to blow up or ignite or something, is it?"

DD laughed, "No, I doubt it."

"Then, I guess, you can scratch me off your list."

"Thanks," Dean said as he grabbed the door knob, "I hope you have a good day."

"Thanks," Robert answered as the door was shut again. He sighed again and then looked quizzically at the envelope in his hand.

The walk across the campus didn't last long, and DD soon found himself back into Professor Grubb's class to deliver another invitation. When he entered, he saw that she was not in her main class area and thought that perhaps she was in her office room. He walked down the steps between the chairs and toward the door on the right and when he approached, he could see that the light was shining out from under the door and took a deep breath. He always enjoyed her teachings but yet felt uncomfortable around her. Maybe it was the fact that she was so well educated on literature that he couldn't help feeling inferior. He always enjoyed reading, which was another reason why he enjoyed Brad's company, and it put him at odds wondering how to strike up a conversation with her. He reached up to knock on the door.

"Who is it?" she questioned from within without the need for a knock.

"Dean Mitchell," DD answered.

"Please come in," she replied.

When he opened the door, he was overwhelmed with all the literature that filled the room. It was the first time that he had ever been in her office and his heart raced with the obstacles around him. Every wall was covered with books. Even the window that was on the back wall above her desk was half buried in books. The entire room smelled of heated leather and it seemed soothing.

"Wow," he exclaimed, "What a collection!"

"Oh yes," she said still sitting at her desk in the middle of the room. "And I'm very proud of this collection. Many are original works and sitting amongst them relaxes me." She started slowly glancing around the room. "Most people love their cup of Joe, but I tend to satisfy my senses with books. The smell, the sight and even the sound of the pages is like being wrapped up in a security blanket. Add a large glass of iced tea and I'd be lost for hours."

"Sounds all very relaxing; I know what you mean."

"So," she said sitting up from her slumped position, "what can I do for you?"

"Professor Crawford wanted me to drop off this invitation to you and before you ask, I have no idea what it is."

"Invitation?" she said quizzically as she reached out for the envelope. She opened up her middle drawer and pulled out a letter opener. She slowly opened the envelope with it and unfolded the paper. She quickly read it and glanced back up at DD. "Doesn't say much, does it?"

"No. I guess we will all find out Monday night."

"We?" she said as she tilted her head to the side.

"A few professors, the entire faculty board members, Curt Johnson and me."

"Any ideas?" she said raising her left eyebrow.

"Seriously, I have not a clue," DD said shrugging his shoulders.

"Then I guess I'll see you next Monday night."

"Before that, actually, you'll see me next Monday morning during class."

"Of course." she said smiling as she laid the paper on the desk and replaced the letter opener back into the middle drawer. "Thank you. You have a good week, and I'll see you Monday."

DD turned to leave, grabbing the door knob to her office as he exited, "I'll see you Monday, then. I hope I didn't take up too much of your time, you probably have a class coming up."

"Nope, not me, I'm off the rest of the day."

DD smiled and leaned forward, "then I let you get back to your dream land."

As he closed the door, she smiled and leaned back in her chair. She picked up the book on the desk in front of her and returned to her reading. With her other hand, she grabbed the large iced tea from a small table to her right, took a sip, and disappeared.

****

Several members of the board were sitting at their spots on the table when Jerry Mcward entered and sat down. They all just had their lunch break and were ready to resume their weekly board meeting. Same topics were brought up; finances, new construction, future projects and student enrollment. In fact, the rest of the afternoon was going to be Robert's report on his scouting convention.

"The chicken parmesan today was delicious!" Polly commented a she licked her lips, "I had two servings of it."

"I can't break myself away from the pizza, "Marshall added, "It's so good."

"One of these days, "Charles said, "you're going to turn into a pizza."

"That would be fun," Marshall said as Robert entered the room and sat down, "Think about it, though. There are unlimited things that you can put on a pizza. There is meat, veggies, dessert, even fruit. All the five food groups are deliciously supported on a pizza. What a better way to get everything at once!"

"Let me know when they come up with a rum pizza," Robert added, "then I'll be able to get drunk at the same time I get my daily essentials."

Everyone started laughing when a knock at the door stopped them.

Jerry quizzically looked at the door, "Come in."

In walked Dean Mitchell with what looked like a stack of envelops.

"Mr. Mitchell, good to see you, "Jerry smiled, "We are right in the middle of our weekly board meeting, what can we do for you?"

"Sorry for the interruption, lady and gentlemen, but I'm dropping off these invitations per Professor Crawford's request." Dean started thumbing through the letters.

"Invitation to what," Polly asked.

"It's an invitation to a get together in his room Monday night," Robert answered. "I already read mine and it doesn't have any information other than the time."

Dean started handing out the letters to the appropriate people, and when he was finished, he saw that he had only two left.

"Sorry I interrupted," Dean said as he walked toward the door, "have a good day."

"Thanks," said all of the members as they watched the door shut.

"I've always admired that young man," Polly said, "a fine example of an outstanding student. I still don't understand why he hangs out with Curt Johnson."

"Now let's not get started on that again," Jerry added. "Robert, I think it's time to see what you got for us in Indianapolis."

"You got it," Robert said as he opened up his folder.

****

After delivering the board member envelopes, DD walked out of the building and into a gentle breeze blowing outside. He took a deep breath and noticed how clear and refreshing the air was. He stopped and looked up into the blue sky above him and saw several birds flying. White puffy clouds slowly danced above the birds and he thought he saw a fish in one of their shapes. A rustle toward his left made him turn his head to observe two squirrels chasing each other around the limbs of a tree. Other trees on the campus added the sounds of chirping birds and windblown leaves which created serenity to the area.

The symphony of nature truly set him at peace. Only three more months of this campus and he would graduate. He had several offers already from many major corporations, but he couldn't make a decision yet on which road to take. He only knew that whatever road that he took would only be complete if Lynette would be with him.

He glanced down at the one remaining envelope in his hand; it was addressed to Professor Morgan.

"Seriously," DD yelled out loud. Why in the world would he invite Professor Morgan? That man is the most uptight, unfair and most hated Professor on the campus. DD still remembers that during his sophomore year, Professor Morgan yelled at him once for smiling too much. He was notorious for changing his requirements on assignments after most people were finished with them and then he would get mad stating that we didn't listen to him the first time. At one time, a class mate brought in a voice recorder to catch him but the Professor saw it and confiscated it. The man just gave off the impression that he hated kids and was annoyed every time he had to deal with them. If anyone saw him walking down the sidewalk on campus, most students would cross the street or walk out of their way to avoid him. By the time they became a junior, they had been fully alert to him. To the new students, good luck.

DD sighed and started walking toward Mckinley Hall, the main building that most of the students had to go to for the first two years. It is where he taught his class this morning and most of the other basic classes were held. It was one of the oldest buildings in the college and stood in the center of the campus. A large grass courtyard was in front of it, and a lot of the students usually sat around the area. Several benches lined the sidewalks and many trees provided ample shade.

DD looked down at his hand and noticed that he forgot his watch. Curt would be getting out of his class soon, and he hates to wait. Hopefully he would be on time. Knowing that the Jeep was parked on the other side of the campus, DD started picking up his pace and soon was at the entrance to Mckinley Hall.

As he stepped inside, he tried to refocus his thoughts about where Morgan's class was at. He knew it was on the fourth floor but couldn't remember if it was left or right. So, trying to bring up the memories, he started his flight up the stairs, passing several students going down, and soon found himself on the fourth floor. DD glanced left, then right, and then decided to take the right hallway and look at each door as he passed. When he got further down the hall, he saw a group of students walking toward him as they exited a door on the right. Their conversation became clearer as he approached.

"What a jerk," the female student said, "how in the hell did he become a professor?"

"Beats me," the other girl said, "I'm just glad to get out of his class."

DD stopped at the door they just exited, smiled and pointed toward the door, "Bingo."

Stepping inside he instantly felt pressure. The same feeling you get when you walk into a crowded elevator hoping that the people would move to give you room. The air felt thick like you could cut it with a knife, and it smelled stale. The smell instantly brought back memories of the class and the dread of entering three times a week. In fact, ...

"What do you want?" rasped the tired old voice.

"Sorry for the interruption, sir, but I was told to deliver this to you." DD walked up toward the elderly man sitting at his desk and handed him the envelope.

"What the hell is this, and who sent it," he rasped back as he rudely swiped the envelope out of DD's hand.

"It's from Professor Crawford, and for its contents, I don't know." DD thought that the comment would get him out of further conversation.

"I know you; I had you in one of my classes a couple of years ago. Mitchell, isn't it?"

"Yes sir, Dean Mitchell," DD replied.

"I remember you being a bright but very impatient young man. You could never focus yourself on the class. You always had your head in the electronics department. Hey, you're not still hanging around with that idiot Johnson student, are you?" Professor Morgan asked as he started opening the letter. "One of the biggest wastes of air on the planet, that boy is. Why was such a gifted mind put into such a disrespectful, rude, mean-spirited body?"

"I was thinking the same thing sir," DD said pointing the comment in a different direction.

"Thinking the same thing about what?" He ripped open the letter as he barked out his question.

"Never mind, and yes, I do still hang out with him," DD answered.

"Biggest waste of air." mumbled the professor as he stopped long enough to read the letter in the envelope. After reading its contents, the Professor glanced toward DD. "What could this be?"

DD shrugged his shoulder.

"Well, if I got the time, I'll go." He threw the letter toward the top of a filing cabinet on his right. "Always some damn meeting around here. If it isn't the students that want you, it's the faculty!"

"Yes, sir," DD said as he stated to leave, "have a good day, sir."

"And stay away from that Johnson kid," he yelled. Then he looked down at the planner on his desk and started to mumble. "Damn disrespectful, rude and mean. That's what he is."

DD shut the door and quickly exited the building.

Day 28, Tuesday May 8th, 2000, 2:20 p.m.

Oh, what a pot of gold we have. Wait until Monday night when all these people find out that they have been talking to a robot this whole time. In fact, even if Professor Morgan comes, I'd pay admission just to see his expression of being fooled.

Oh no, I just noticed the time, and DD is late getting to Curt. Curt hates it when people can't keep track of time.

close: 2:23 p.m.

Curt was getting very annoyed as he sat in his Jeep waiting for DD to arrive. He was ten minutes late, and he hoped that nothing happened to him. Curt did manage to get through the rest of his boring class and finish up his assignment. It only took him the last five minutes of the class to write the thesis for the project. He still can't understand why he has to finish these last two months for him to graduate. He only has four classes and all of them are generic courses. During his freshman year, he skipped them and went right to the required courses for his degree. Now all that remains is one English course, two science courses and a public speaking course. He found that the public speaking course was a little more challenging than the others. There, he had to watch his language and his opinions.

His Jeep was backed into the parking space and he had a pretty good view of the campus area. If DD was approaching, he would be able to see him several feet away. He started getting more upset about the wait; so, he leaned over and turned the radio on to listen to some heavy metal music. It always relaxed him. As the loud noise filled the speakers, he tilted his head back and closed his eyes. He felt the base vibrate the seats and the screaming singer drowned out any other sound around him. He was about ready to really get lost into the song when the music shut off. He opened his eyes and sat up to see DD leaning over the door and removing his hand off the radio button.

"Where the fuck have you been?" Curt barked at him as DD stood by the driver's door.

"Sorry I was late; I forgot to put my watch on this morning. What time is it?"

114

"Two thirty, dill hole, get in."

"Sorry." DD walked around the front of the Jeep and to the passenger side door. "I had to deliver invitations for Brad," he said as he opened the door and got in. "He's having some kind of get together Monday night. We're invited as well."

"Really," Curt said as he reached forward and turned the key to start the Jeep. "Who's all invited?"

"All the board members, Professor Grubbs and, get this," DD turned to look directly at him as he shut the door, "Professor Morgan."

"What? That asshole?" Curt looked at him squarely, "Why does Brad want that shithead to come?"

"I have no idea," DD added as he fastened his seat belt, "but delivering the letter was really uncomfortable, if you know what I mean."

"Yeah, what a shit fuck." Curt put the Jeep into gear and pulled forward out of the space with the speed as if he was entering the highway. Several people had to quicken their step just to get out of the way. He turned left and headed toward the exit to the parking lot. "That guy is just plain mean and a fucking ass to everyone. He's just a waste or air."

DD started to laugh.

"What's so funny, numb nuts?" Curt asked as he slowed the Jeep down at the end of the parking lot and then without stopping, accelerated it into a right turn.

"He said the same thing about you," DD answered as he held onto the door strap.

"Well fuck him, that piece of shit." His anger made him accelerate the Jeep even faster. "I should do something to that fat ass."

DD laughed again, "I wouldn't. You're in hot water with the board already. I'd just cool my jets until the end of the year."

"Yeah, but you're not me."

DD got a coy look on his face. "Seriously, when did you notice?"

Curt stopped quickly at the stop light at the end of the block, screeching his tires in the process. DD almost put his foot through the floor. Curt looked over toward DD and lifted an eyebrow, "well, anything you want to do?"

"Stop by the Book Nook, I've got to get some information about tomorrow."

"Why doesn't that surprise me?" Curt said shaking his head, "What info do you need now?"

"What to do for tomorrow's luncheon with the Governor. Things I need to know like when Lynette's going to pick me up, what should I wear, what things are we going to see, things like that."

Curt shook his head back and forth, "You two are so made for each other." He glanced up and saw the light had turned green and once again started his quickened pace of a race car driver down the road. "Going to things like that just doesn't seem exciting to me. There really isn't much action in it. I need some ball busting, spontaneous fuck me up action."

"Actually, that could happen soon," DD said in a low mumble.

"What's that supposed to fuckin mean?"

"Andy's back in town."

That comment got Curt's facial expression all knotted up into an angry mess. "That asshole better not show his face in my direction because I'll fuck him up. I know that you don't have the balls to do something, but I'm sick and tired of how he gets into Lynette's face."

"I knew there was a reason I kept you around," DD smiled.

Curt stopped the Jeep at the next red light and turned toward DD, "Bite me, Mitchell."

DD smiled then noticed that his right hand had an extra tight grip on the doors handle and it looked like he was bending the fabric. He always got so jittery when he rode with Curt because he drove like he was late for something that happened a week ago. He would zigzag his Jeep between moving cars, tailgate people and even cut people off to get where he was going. He was a good driver by all means, but most of the time it felt like you were in a roller-coaster without harnesses to keep you safe. Even the seat belt DD had around him didn't make him feel any calmer.

"So, what plans do you have tonight?" DD asked.

"I've got my Karate class at six tonight then I might stop at Marvin's for a drink."″

"Seriously, don't you ever get tired of that place?" DD looked in awe. "I mean, once you see them and know them like you do, what's the attraction?"

Curt looked at him squarely, "are you fucking kidding? Do you ever get tired of hot and spicy shit?"

"I'll never get tired of hot stuff," DD said as he looking at the stoplight. "It's green, Curt."

Curt gunned the car, "Precisely," he said back to DD. "You have a variety of sauces and objects that you eat all the time. I mean, once you eat them and know them like you do, what's the attraction?" Curt laughed throwing the line back in his face.

"Eating hot stuff and Marvin's are entirely two different subjects," DD added.

"Want to bet?" Curt's smile grew bigger as he turned the Jeep into the center lane. DD got a coy look on his face and decided to stop trying to point out the difference. As Curt turned onto Veterans Parkway, a car honked at him, and he flipped them off. DD's grip tightened even more as they sped their way toward the Book Nook.

Day 28, Tuesday May 9th, 2000, 2:37 p.m.

Wow, I'm on edge just watching Curt drive and I'm not even in the Jeep. I don't know how many times I've almost put my foot through the floor boards on the passenger side when he comes to a stop, but I sure hope that DD doesn't actually do it, if you know what I mean. Curt's a really pushy driver on the road, and he's even worse when he's riding his motorcycle. I tried to follow him a couple of times, but no matter how hard you try, a one-ton pickup is not going to be able to weave between cars and go down the center line.

117

I am glad that he is going to the Book Nook to talk to Lynette because there are a few details I need to get from her as well. This 380 is the neatest machine ever. It's like an Instagram.

Well, they are pulling, or should I saw, speeding into the parking lot of the Nook now, so I'll close for now.
Close: 2:49 p.m.

The Cafe area was crowded as usual, and Curt and DD started heading toward a table that an older couple was getting up from. The lady was adjusting her purse as the man was putting on his jacket when the two boys reached the table. As the elders started walking away, that's when Curt noticed the pile of books they left on the table.

"Hey, fuck face," he said picking up the stack and handing it to the man. "Do you have any idea how long it takes for the people working here to put this shit in order for you to find it?"

The man's expression was aghast and the woman looked like she had been slapped in the face.

Curt continued. "At your fucking age I would expect a little more courtesy and compassion, but hey, you're probably one of the people that bitch about the high prices, right? Scheduling more hours to clean up after someone's shit like this is what makes prices go up. They got to get the money somewhere, right?" Each time he said the word 'Right" it got louder emphasized. "So why not grease inconsiderate bastards like you who don't give a shit about the working-class crew who bust their ass trying to keep things in order, RIGHT?"

Curt turned to sit down and the confused people walked away without a word, but with the books.

DD sat down in the chair next to him, "Dude, you're not right, but I love your forwardness."

"Fuckin-a." Curt added.

The two boys looked around and didn't see any servers, in fact, they didn't even see Lynette. The cafe was always busy and produced a lot of business. When they first opened it, people had to walk up to the counter to place their order, and then when the

118

business took off, they decided to hire in table servers and expand the seating area. The room held twenty-five tables and two high counters. Originally it was just a book store that had many categories including a small children's area, but when the clothing store next door went out of business, the company expanded. Not only did they build a larger children's area, but they added the cafe and a stage for author signings and shows.

Suddenly, from out of nowhere, a waitress whom they never met walked up to the table. "Can I get you gentlemen anything?"

"Yeah," Curt stated, "A Venti caramel Frappuccino."

Then she turned toward DD, "And you sir?"

"I'm not thirsty, but if you could tell Lynette that Dean is here, I'd appreciate it."

She nodded her head, "sure, she's probably in her office. I'll page her, and I'll be right back with your drink, sir."

"Thanks," DD said as she walked away with the order. Curt leaned over and looked at her ass as she walked away. His face lit up with enjoyment.

"Nice ass," he said as he watched her walk toward the cafe counter.

DD shook his head, "don't you ever think about anything else?" He leaned over and started to wave his right hand in front of Curt's vision. "I mean, seriously, women do have more to offer other than being a, well..."

Curt took his gaze off of the girl and toward DD eyes, "Say it, Dean, you know you can."

DD's face frowned, "I won't," he stated shaking his head.

"Fuck machine, Dean," Curt said leaning over the table, "the description you're looking for is Fuck machine."

"I know what your point of view is," DD said disgustedly, "but I'm sorry I don't agree."

"Man, just give it up," Curt said throwing his hands up in the air, "it's a lost cause with me."

"I know it is. I would think that maybe some of me would rub off on you after all these years." DD sighed as he turned to see Lynette walking toward them with the new girl in tow.

119

"Hi, Honey," Lynette said as she leaned over and kissed Dean on the right cheek. The new girl set a large drink in front of Curt at the same time. "I want you two to meet our new Assistant manager for the cafe. This is Curt Johnson," she stated as she pointed at Curt, "and this is my fiancé Dean Mitchell. This is Shirley Mason."

DD froze. He didn't even blink. He looked like something on the far wall had him in a trance and wouldn't let him go. Every part of him had stopped. His chest didn't even raise or fall with breaths being taken. His mouth was slightly gapped open like he was in the middle of saying something but lost the thought.

"Dean," Lynette said staring at him with concern in her eyes, "are you ok?"

That's when Curt realized what had happened and sprang into action.

"Damn, Dean, you're a dumb ass," he yelled as he got up out of his chair and walked behind him. "How many times have I told you that when you tuck your shirt into your underwear you look like a fucking retard. Now your underwear is hanging out of the back of your pants."

Both girls got a strange look on their faces as they watched Curt start stuffing Dean's shirt down the back of his pants.

"Fucking retard," Curt voiced as he shoved the shirt farther down DD's pants. "We should drop your ass off at the mental institute one of these days for an evaluation." He continued stuffing the shirt farther down his pants and in the last-ditch effort, Curt slid his fingers in between DD butt cheeks and flipped the switch.

DD slowly turned his head toward Lynette, "I'm sorry, I didn't hear what you said."

"Are you ok?" Lynette asked.

DD got a quizzical look on his face, "yes, why?"

"You kind of zoned out on us for a second," she said.

"Sorry, what were you saying again?" DD asked.

Lynette started to repeat herself, "This is..."

"Yeah, yeah," Curt interrupted her as he walked back to his chair and sat down, "We heard who she is, but my question is does she suck dick?"

Shirley flushed red not in only embarrassment but in anger. That was one of the most vulgar things that she had ever been told. Her blank face turned to irritation and she looked at Lynette. "If you'll excuse me, "she said and walked away.

Lynette turned toward her in concern then quickly returned her stare toward Curt, "What the hell is wrong with you?"

Curt smiled and shrugged his shoulders.

Lynette turned toward DD and shook her head in disgust. DD shrugged his shoulders as well. "What did I miss?"

Lynette squinted her eyes and shook her head back and forth. The innocent look on his face made her think about last night and slow smile started to build across her face as she leaned toward his right ear. "Thanks for last night," she said in a whisper, "I really needed it." She kissed him on the cheek again and walked away toward the cafe.

DD, in his confusion, turned his head toward Curt. "What IS wrong with you, man?"

"We all have our reasons," he answered taking a sip of his drink.

"I don't even want to know," DD turned his head and looked at Lynette at the cafe counter, "but this is odd though. She just thanked me for last night, but she never came over. In fact, I don't even remember last night. I must have been really tired and fell asleep."

Curt's face got confused trying to figure out what he was talking about. Last night they had that dinner together and she...oh shit. The robot would have no clue what happened last night.

"Maybe she's drunk?"

DD got an annoyed look on his face, "yeah, right." He pushed out his chair and stood up. "I'll be right back; I'm going to talk to Lynette."

"I'll be right here," Curt said as he lifted up his drink. He then cautiously watched DD as he approached the counter and hoped there wouldn't be another incident.

When DD walked over toward Lynette, he saw that the new girl was behind the counter next to her. She was a short girl and had jet black hair. She did have the impression that she was very comfortable doing this job and probably had many years of experience. When he approached, both women looked in his direction.

"I'm sorry about my friend" he said looking at the girl, "he has, well, issues."

The girl shook her head, "well, I'm used to, issues. I was a waitress in a bar for about three years. I've heard a lot worse."

DD turned his attention toward Lynette, "do you have a couple of minutes to talk?"

"Sure, let's go to my office."

"Great," DD said, turning toward Shirley, "Nice to meet you."

"You too," she said as she headed back out onto the cafe floor.

DD followed Lynette toward the back right of the building. The office was down the back hall where the public restrooms were. The noise of the cafe soon was muffled by the silence of the rows and rows of books they walked through. Out here he could hear the music on the speakers better. She had the station set on old fifties rock and roll.

"Sometimes I wonder about Curt," she said as she proceeded toward the hall, "his mouth is going to get him into some serious trouble one day."

"I told him the same thing just yesterday."

They entered the hall and he could hear her high heels echoing off the hard wood floor. They passed both the men's, then the women's bathroom doors and up to the third door which contained a combination lock. She keyed in the numbers and after a click, she opened the door and they stepped inside.

A small hallway held two other doors and ended at the employees break room. The second door was her office. They stepped inside the room and sat in the two chairs within.

"What's on your mind, Mitchell," Lynette said leaning back in her chair.

"I have a suggestion. Are you off this weekend?"

"I'm off on Saturday and Sunday. Why?" She said wondering where his questioning was going.

"Can you get Friday off? I mean you did a lot of extra work this week for when Dawn was sick, if you know what I mean. I thought maybe we can get away and go to the cabin for a couple of days. It would be good to get out of the city and away from the noise, the phone, the TV," DD tipped his head toward the front, "and the friends."

"I'll ask Dawn," Lynette said as she smiled, "I don't think I'll have a problem with her covering. She does owe me one."

"Good. Then we could get an early morning head start and be curled up next to the fire by dusk." DD then leaned back in his chair, "Now about tomorrow; what should I wear, what time will you pick me up and do I need to bring anything?"

"It starts at nine o'clock at the Lincoln home. After the tour, we meet at the Governor's mansion at twelve for lunch then it reconvenes at two o'clock at Lincoln's tomb. I can pick you up about eight thirty."

"Sounds good, and what do I wear?"

"Obviously a suit and tie would be a good idea." she said stretching her arms in the air. DD heard her back pop a couple of times, and she let out a sigh of relief. "Why don't you wear that outfit you had on for the awards banquet. I'm planning to wear that green dress of mine."

"You mean the one with the black belt and silver heart buckle?"

"Yes," she answered, "that one."

"Oooo," DD said wide eyed, "Hubba, hubba."

"Get yourself in control, Mitchell," she said as she twisted her body side to side in the chair and a couple of more pops rang out. "Ahhh," she sighed, "a three-day cabin trip would suit me just fine."

Just then the speaker phone on her intercom buzzed, "Lynette, you there?"

"Yes, Dawn," she spoke out loud, "What's up?"

"Guess what," she said with an annoyed expression on her voice, "Internet is down again."

"WHAT," exclaimed Lynette, as she turned and looked at DD. "Can Curt look at the system for me? Obviously, something is wrong with it."

"Probably not," DD stated, "He's got his Karate class tonight, but I'll let him know that you need help."

"Well, the sooner the better," Dawn added. "The customers are getting really pissed."

"I'll find out when Curt can get in here to look things over," DD added.

"Sounds good to me," Dawn answered and then hung up.

"We have never had any problem with that system until this week. This makes the third time it has gone out," Lynette said. "Well, I better let you get back to work," DD said standing up, "Curt's probably ready to go." He turned and looked at the clock on the office wall, "He's got his class in two hours."

"I'll call you later if anything changes," Lynette said, "other than that; I'll see you at eight thirty."

"See you then," DD said as he turned to leave but Lynette grabbed his arm and pulled him toward her.

"Thanks once again for last night," she whispered in his ear, "I hope this weekend would be just as special." She tried to kiss him on the lips, but he quickly turned his head.

"I'm still not over this cold; it would be a good idea to still play it safe." He stood straight up, winked at her and left.

Lynette sat in puzzlement. He didn't seem to be ill but his lips did feel like they were very dry. The buzz of the intercom snapped her out of her trance.

"Lynette, are you there?" Dawn's voice rang out.

"Yeah, what's up?"

"A teacher from Iles School is here to put in a large institutional order."

"Cool, I'll be right up there, and Dawn, I need to talk to you before you leave."

"No problem."

Day 28, Tuesday May 9th, 2000, 4:10 p.m.

I guess we have a problem. Since it was me with her last night and not DD, he doesn't remember anything about it. I'll call Brad and talk to him what needs to be done. We also are planning to have a meeting tonight about our experiment so far. I don't know if Curt is going to be able to join us since he has his class tonight, but I could get his input before he leaves.

Curt fixed that problem really fast with the shut off to the unit, though. That was a close one. I really didn't expect us to run into anyone named Shirley. This is one reason I was glad Curt was with DD.

Well, at least I did get my answers that I needed for this weekend. I love this 380. Most of the conversation about the weekend I had typed in. I'm just glad that they didn't say Shirley again when he was at the counter. That would have been a real problem.

Well, going to give Brad a call to talk about what our agenda will be tonight.

Close: 4:22 p.m.

Within minutes after Dean set the ledger down, Curt and DD arrived. Dean ran upstairs as they approached the front door and waited until Curt gave him the ok to come down. It didn't take long for Curt to get DD downstairs and shut down, in fact, ever since Curt had blocked out everything about the operation, it was as if DD had a total memory loss when he went down stairs. Curt even had him sit in his chair on his own before the magic word was spoken. The last few times when they shut him off, they had to carry him to the chair. DD wasn't really all that heavy; about 120 pounds, but bending his legs was the hard part. It usually took two people to complete the process. Curt was happy knowing that he was crunched for time that DD cooperated with no hassles. Once DD was inoperative, Curt went upstairs and met Dean already sitting in the living room.

"So," Curt said "How's it feel to sit on your ass all day and do nothing?"

"Actually, I need to get a cushion for that chair," Dean stated, "my butt's really getting sore."

Curt started heading toward the door, "Well, I'd love to chat, but I'm in a hurry."

"Wait," Dean said getting off the sofa and walking toward him, "I need your input on the experiment so far. I just talked to Brad, and we are going to meet at the Steak Out restaurant to compare notes."

"I can't go, drip dick, I've got class, "Curt added with annoyance in his voice.

"I know that," Dean said as he opened the front door, "that's why you're going to tell me everything on the way over there. I need a ride. Then you can drop me off, Brad and I will concur and you can leave."

"You know what; I'm getting sick of this shit." Curt said following him out the door, "we need to go to that fucked up truck dealer and shove it up his ass, I tell ya"

"I know," Dean said pulling his keys out of his pocket as he shut the door, "but soon the parts will be in, and I can wash my hands of the whole situation." He inserted the keys into the bolt lock and turned it. "At least I don't have to pay for the labor."

Curt's pace quickened as they walked toward the Jeep, "I still say they are fucking you over big time. You dropped a lot of money at their door step." He opened the driver's door and hopped in to the seat. Dean joined him on the passenger side.

"I still have to go home, get my shit and switch to the bike," Curt stated turning on the car," I don't know if I'll have the time to drop you off!" Curt seemed a little agitated.

"The way you drive," Dean added, "You'll have plenty of time."

Curt gave him a cocky look, "It's your life, pal."

Curt turned and looked behind him and backed the car out of the drive. Once he put it into drive and sped down the road, their conversation turned immediately to the task at hand. During the entire drive, Dean didn't say a word, only a compliment on Curt's quick thinking at the Book Nook. Curt voiced his observations and added a few ideas to the plan. During the entire trip, though, Dean did observe that Curt had driven through two stop lights and a stop sign and by the time they pulled up to the restaurant, Dean's heart rate had to be doing double its speed. Curt pulled, or rather screeched right up to the front door and Dean quickly jumped out. Curt saluted a goodbye and sped off before Dean even had the chance to shut his door. The momentum of the Jeep, though, shut the door anyway, and Dean watched Curt speed off squealing around the corner. When he turned his head to look at the entrance, the four people standing outside gave him an annoyed look. Shaking it off, he proceeded to walk between them and grabbed the handle to the door, open it and walk in.

It had been a while since he had been at the Steak Out, in fact it was about six months ago when he took Lynette out for her birthday. He always loved the way the place was decorated. All the staff was dressed in outfits from the 1930's and old jazz music was always playing. The place was made to look like a back ally speakeasy; all with light tan wood, water pipes and crates used for the chairs. They even had whiskey barrels to hold the table tops.

They had men dressed up as gangsters carrying around machine guns and women dressed up selling cigars and cigarettes. Local actors were hired to even talk with a Brooklyn accent and to provide entertainment for the diners.

"Can I help you sir?" said a lady behind the counter interrupting Dean's concentration.

"Yes," he said as he leaned his right elbow on the counter, "I'm supposed to meet someone here, his name is Brad Crawford."

She looked down at the seating chart on the desk, "Yes, he is already here, he's at a table in the bar." She grabbed a menu and walked out from behind the counter. "Follow me please."

Dean let her pass and he followed her toward a booth on the left side of the bar. As he passed the bar, he once again got lost in its splendor. The back wall of the bar had many machine guns and pistols hanging all over it and in the center was a large head of a buck. It had many beer kegs sticking out of the wall along the back bar top and each one had a tap sticking out of it. The bar top itself was all wood and smooth as glass. What was unique about the bar though was it was riddled with bullet holes. Not only were there holes in the wall, but the mirror and even the buck head was shot up.

When they stopped, he saw Brad already sitting in the booth enjoying a tall beer and he slid into the seat across from him. He nodded a greeting in his direction and turned toward the lady.

"Thank you," he said with a smile.

"Your server will be right with you."

Both the men said their thanks, and she walked off. Brad and Dean glanced up at each other, and they both started to grin. The thought of how successful the week was going filled both of their heads and gave them a warm tingling feeling.

"Well," Brad said grinning, "How's things on your end?"

"My end is getting very sore sitting in that chair all day," Dean added as he wiggled back and forth on the booth's cushion, "but other than that, just fine."

"Did you get any info from Curt?" Brad said just before taking another sip from his beer.

"Yes, some great points. In fact, a few we missed."

Brad licked the foam off of his lips, "such as?"

"Good evening gentlemen," an accented waiter interrupted as he approached the table, "Are you eating tonight or just going to wet the whistles?"

"Oh, we're eating," stated Dean as he lifted up the menu. "We just need a couple of minutes."

"Fine," said the man dressed in suspender supported slacks and a white long sleeved dress shirt, "Can I get ya anything to swallow?" he asked.

"A large light beer, whatever you have on tap," Dean said without hesitation.

"Then I'll be right back with the house specialty, the bullet. Is that a short barrel or long?" he questioned as he leaned over the table.

"Long barrel," Dean said rather fast, "and with plenty of lead."

The waiter got a smile on his face "it'll be loaded and ready for you to shoot." He stood back upright and turned, "I'll be right back." He turned and he walked toward the bar.

"Must be a lot of fun working in a joint like this," Brad commented as he took another swig of his beer.

"I don't know," Dean said with questioning eyes, "I'd go crazy just trying to keep up the act."

Brad smiled and set his half empty glass down, "Ok, son, clue me in."

"First," Dean said as he cleared his throat, "we need to make sure that we dress him accordingly. I've been forgetting to put my watch on him. Also, I've never put my wallet in his pocket. What if he wants to buy something and he has no money?"

Brad's face lit up in illumination, "I'm surprised we missed that. Totally forgot about the jewelry. That really touches home."

"Not to mention if Lynette asks DD where my gold ring is that she bought me. I'm surprised that she hasn't noticed that yet." Then Dean's eyes widened, "Or what if police ask for ID?"

Brad raised an eyebrow, "That could be very crazy."

"Seriously," Dean added. "Well, I'm starving, outside of the dinner with Lynette, I've eaten nothing but microwave food all week." Dean lifted up his menu and started looking at its contents. Brad followed suit.

The Steak Out was obviously the best place to get a steak. They had all the cuts; sirloin, rib eye, New York strip, prime rib, filet and the T-bone. They even had one called the Godfather which was a two-pound porterhouse steak. Their twice baked potato was so big that it could pass as a meal in itself. Most of the meals came with honey glazed dinner rolls, salad and choice of vegetable. You could never leave hungry from a place like this.

After a couple of minutes with their noses in the menu, the waiter returned with Dean's beer. Dean leaned back to allow him to set the glass down in front of him.

"Well, gents, what'll be?" He asked as he lifted up an order pad and pen.

Brad nodded toward Dean to go first.

"I'll have the twelve-ounce New York strip, medium rare, with the twice baked potato and put everything on it." Dean's thoughts were salivating, "and I'll take a side order of butter beans."

"House or mixed salad with that?"

"Oh, the house, of course, with blue cheese dressing," Dean answered.

The waiter finished writing down Dean's order and turned toward Brad, "And for you sir?"

Brad grunted out a low growl, "I'll have the sixteen-ounce T-bone, medium my good man." he said as he tried to attempt to do a Brooklyn accent. "Top it all off with butter mashed spuds and green beans, and be quick about it. I've got people to ice and cement shoes to cast."

Dean started to smile; he always loved it when Brad loosened up.

The waiter leaned over toward Brad, "Not anybody I know, is it?"

"Cut the gas, punk," Brad blurted out, "do you want everyone in the joint to see us with are pants down?"

The waiter stood upright and glanced behind himself to the right and then the left. "You're right, Joe, I need to watch my P's and Q's."

Brad leaned back in the booth, "that's better, bloke."

"Say, Mack," the waiter said in a lower voice, "are you going to have the House or mixed salad?"

"House with thousand island dressing," Brad concluded.

"That's the ticket, Mack." He finished writing the order down and tucked the booklet under his arm. "I'll be right back with a couple more barrels right after I put in your order."

"Great," Brad continued with the accent, "now beat it, boy, ya bother me."

The waiter smiled and walked away.

Dean started to clap slowly, "Impressive, seriously impressive. But I wouldn't quit your day job."

"I'm retiring," he said as he lifted his glass, "remember?" Then he downed the rest of the beer.

"You should retire that accent. Sounded like someone in the fifties trying to imitate a British prime minister." Brad was laughing out loud during Dean's grilling, "and isn't 'Bloke' an English slang term?"

"How should I know; do I look British to you?" Brad continued to laugh.

"Only from the back of your head," Dean answered, "that bowl haircut always stands out."

The waiter quickly returned to the table with two full glasses. "Enjoy these ten cent beers, gents; I don't know how long we can hold out from the cops."

"My men will take care of things if there is any funny business," Dean responded in what sounded like a garbled mess. The waiter just looked at him very suspicious, nodded his head and walked away.

Brad shook his head back and forth, "now that was in Nowheresville. What was that supposed to be?"

Dean just smiled and shrugged his shoulders.

Brad once again changed to a gangster's accent, "just leave all the talking to me."

They both laughed and then Dean finished his first glass. Brad started his second.

"Ok," Brad said as he licked the foam from his lips, "what other things happened with DD?"

Dean shook his head, "we had a close one at the Book Nook today. Lynette has a new assistant named Shirley."

Brad's expression came to one of alarm, "don't tell me that..."

"Yep, he shut down." Dean took a drink of his beer. "Add Curt's quick thinking and he was back on line in no time."

"How'd he, do it?" Brad still had the troubled look on his face.

"He played off that my pants were tucked into my underwear and it was sticking out. He tucked it back in himself and flipped the switch in the process."

Brad's face turned to disgust then to relief, "I bet that looked odd."

"I was embarrassed just knowing what he was doing, and I wasn't even there, technically." Dean's thoughts went to the next problem, "we do have a problem, though."

Brad's mind started to race. He knew that somewhere a problem would develop and they would have to scramble to fix it. "What's the snafu?"

"DD has no knowledge of the dinner I did for Lynette last night. He told Curt that he thinks that she never showed up."

Brad's eyes widened with surprise, "of course. Since he didn't make the scene, he was blinded by the fact that it never happened."

"I know what you mean," Dean added. "What can we do?"

Brad leaned over and looked deep into Dean's eyes, "You know there is only one way to correct this."

"Another download," Dean stated hesitantly.

"Yep, and we've got to do it tonight; we don't want him flying blind tomorrow."

Just then the waiter walked up with their salads. "Blue cheese for you sir," as he set the bowl in front of Dean, "and thousand island for you." He sat the second bowl in front of Brad.

"The meals will be up shortly," the waiter added and then walked off again.

Brad continued from his last train of thought, "Also, you cannot see Lynette until this test is over. I'd hate to chase around the bush every time you do something that he is not aware of."

132

"Understandably," Dean said as he picked up a fork and started stabbing at the salad. "I'm going to have to type in a joke in the 380 to cover his forgetfulness."

"Good idea," Brad agreed as he shoved salad into his mouth.

"That 380 console is wonderful," Dean said with a mouthful of salad, "not only did it give me a chance to ask Lynette about tomorrow; it also let me tell Curt that Andy was back in town."

Brad stopped chewing, "Andy? Lynette's ex?"

"Yes. I thought it might be a good idea to let Curt know in case they were to bump into him. She told me last night after dinner. I guess DD will get that in his download tonight." He took another bite of his salad.

"Well, that will correct the loose ends, but I tell ya, when he came into my office to get those envelopes, I felt like I was in Fat city."

"What?" Dean asked.

"Never mind, it was just fascinating watching him operate."

Just then the waiter walked up with the two steak dinners, "New York strip for you sir," as he laid it in front of Dean, "and the T-bone for you." He then laid the other plate in front of Brad. Behind him was another server with their beers.

"Gentlemen," she said as she sat down the drinks, "enjoy your meals."

When she walked off, both men looked at their steaks and their eyes widened.

"Now this is a steak," Brad exclaimed.

"Indeed," Dean added.

****

Curt pulled up to the building on his motorcycle and saw that he was four minutes late. He hated tardiness and always penalized anyone who arrived at training late. He propped his cycle up on its stand, took off his helmet and walked toward the front door. He could hear that it was very quiet inside and when he opened the door, everyone seated in the workout room along the wall, jumped to their feet and yelled, "Sensei."

Curt bowed, "Brothers, take stance against the wall," he said as he took off his jacket and threw it with his helmet into a chair in the corner.

The students shuffled around into a pre designed line where the tallest was the first and the shortest was the last. They were ten students in all, dressed in white outfits and supporting several different colored belts; 3 black, 1 red, 2 purple, 2 green and 2 oranges.

Curt walked out to the middle of the room and faced toward them. His reflection on the wall mirror behind them showed how tired he looked. He really didn't get a chance to freshen up, so a shower after class would be very soothing to end the day.

"I apologize for the tardiness and stand to be corrected," Curt said to his group. "What should be my punishment?"

They all got confused looks on their faces and eyed each other back and forth waiting for someone to pass on punishment. A taller boy in his twenties, with the red belt, stepped forward and stamped to a stance.

"Sensei" he yelled, "since you are the master, I suggest to triple the punishment that you enforce to us."

Curt nodded, "So three hundred pushups on my knuckles?"

"Yes, Sensei," he yelled back.

"But on only one hand," yelled another student from the back.

Curt stomped toward the line of boys. "Who yelled that out without presenting themselves?"

One of the boys in a green belt stepped forward and made a stance. "I did, Sensei"

Curt got up into his face, "Do you think it was fucking proper for you to blurt out when Brother Jason had the spot?"

"No, Sensei," the boy yelled back.

"Then I suggest one hundred jabs into the bag, Brother Steve, each hand. And I want to hear them."

"Yes, Sensei," the boy yelled as he bowed. He then walked over to the far back of the room where all of the training equipment was kept. He immediately took a stance against a hanging bag and started hard jabs with his right fist. With each hit on the bag, he yelled a 'Kia.'

Curt turned back to his standing student, "So accepted, Brother Jason. Three hundred pushups," he turned to look at Brother Steve at the bag, "on one hand." He got a cocky smile on his face and turned his head to the left, "Brother Rodger."

One of the black belts stepped forward," Yes, Sensei," he yelled.

"Get the others into position to practice fist strikes. I want to hear them. I will join you when I'm done with punishment. And after that, I want to teach the class the proper way to roll when you're knocked down, no matter how fast you're going. Tuck and roll will always regain your balance." The boy bowed to him in acceptance. Curt returned the bow and walked to the far side of the room mat and got down into a push up position. With his right hand on the mat, with curled knuckles, he started his count. Each push up was finished with him yelling the number.

Brother Rodger turned to the other, "Brothers, break out and prepare to practice fist thrusts."

The class fanned out across the mat and soon everyone in the building was yelling.

Day 28, Tuesday May 9th, 2000, 10:23 p.m.

Brad here with a few lines. After we left the Steak Out, we quickly returned to Dean's house and plugged him back into the 380. It shouldn't take too long to do the upload. It already has all his brain patterns and will only upload things that have not been recorded, mainly the dinner they had last night. Also, with Curt's input about omitting any information about the project, we should have no problem about what we talked about tonight. I still feel queasy like something is going to happen. This ride feels like it's on overdrive and just waiting to blow a tire. I'll stay here until he wakes up and then probably head home. Come to think of it, I

don't have any classes tomorrow so I just might stay here and give Dean the company. Tomorrow is going to be a big day, with the tour and Governor's luncheon; I might just park here and enjoy the show.
Close: 10:39 p.m.

Wednesday

Since it had been so late when finishing up the previous night, Curt opted to just stay overnight at Dean's house. They quickly ate breakfast and headed out toward the dealership. Dean was driving the truck, which other people could hear grinding every time it changed gears, and Curt was following him in his Jeep. Curt's craving to drive fast
was halted because Dean always drove the speed limit. Not to mention that if the truck did break down, he would need to assist. The dealership was only four miles down the road and it didn't take long for them to enter the parking lot. Dean pulled the truck up to one of the front spots in front of the two big glass doors, and Curt parked in a spot next to a van.

Day 29, Wednesday May 10th, 2000, 7:36 a.m.
Brad here, starting this day off with a nice hot cup of joe and a blueberry bagel. Dean and I have already dressed DD and have placed him on the front living room couch. The only thing left is to wait for Lynette to pull into the drive. We haven't turned him on yet, but when we hear her car pull in, Dean will motivate downstairs, and I'll turn on DD.

This time we made sure that his wallet was in his pocket with money, and his watch was on his wrist. He's dressed in a nice dark blue suit and has on black leather shoes. I didn't realize how hard it is to try to put shoes on someone else. It proved harder than putting on the suit. After we got him upstairs, Dean made the coffee and bagels which we are now enjoying.

I did stable that horse of mine into the garage last night so that Lynette wouldn't know I was here. It would also look odd to DD if he was to see my clunker sitting in the drive way.

Today should be a real test of time if he fools an entire dining room of people, or it could be the biggest disasters if something goes wrong. Once again, that feeling in my gizzard is rising to the top. Without anyone chaperoning him; Curt or me,
137

there would be no way of explaining if he were to be exposed. I can only hope that everything works well.

Close: 7:57 a.m.

"Are you sure it's ok that I come along? I don't want to get you in any trouble."

Lynette shook her head back and forth, "No, Kim, it's fine. You can come with us to the House and the tomb because they are free, but you will not be able to eat at the luncheon. I suggest that you eat at one of the fast-food places nearby."

Lynette was driving her compact car in anticipation to Dean's reaction when he finds out that Kim was coming along with them. She was so tired of her whining and crying about how she never takes her sister to things anymore and feels left out of her sister's life. She has been known to go into a depressed state to where Lynette would end up taking care of her even more. That was the last thing Lynette wanted to do.

And she has heard it all. Everyone she knows gives her advice what to do with her. Some suggest kicking her out, others suggest forcing her to pay for half of the rent and most people just can't stand being around her.

She does have the nasty habit of becoming ill when something really needs to be done or a project was planned. It was just last December when they all were going to help Family Charities with bagging Christmas baskets for the needy. That morning, Kim developed one of her anxieties and had to stay home. After eight and a half hours at the center, they came home to find out she had gone to a movie and dinner. Dean was mad.

"How long do I have for lunch?" Kim asked.

"Well, we meet at the Governor's mansion at noon and then reconvene at the Tomb at two," she said as she turned into Dean's driveway, "there are several restaurants by the mansion."

"I could try that Italian place downtown; they say it's really good."

Lynette pulled the car to a stop, put it into park and turned off the motor. "I thought you already ate there."

"You're thinking of 'Mario's', this place is called the 'Mama's Kitchen'."

"Oh," Lynette grunted as she opened her door and got out. "Why don't you stay here; I'll only be a couple of minutes."

"Ok," she answered.

Lynette started walking up the long sidewalk toward the front door. Her dark green dress was lightly swaying in the breeze. As she stepped up on to the first step to the porch, she nearly stumbled when her shoe came into contact with loose rock. She stopped, grabbed onto the porch rail and regained her footing. She then looked down and noticed that there were several real deep scratches in the step. It looked like someone had taken a hammer to it or something very heavy had been dragged across it. She lifted her right leg and readjusted her high heel and then continued walking. Just before she grabbed the door knob, DD opened it from the other side.

"Ready?" he said as he stepped out.

She looked at him in the suit that he had on. It was the one that he wore during their anniversary date last year. It was a dark blue suit with red trim and bow tie. He looked sharp. "Well, well, well, handsome," she said as she put her arms around his waist, "where have you been all my life?"

DD got a slow smile on his face, "always in your back pocket."

She pulled him closer for a tighter hug, "you'll never forget that, will you."

"Not, ever," he stated, as he stepped back and looked at her. The green dress she wore held her thin figure nicely. The collar in it was a low cut and her cleavage was very visible. She was wearing a gold belt that connected on her right side and the ends just hung down past her waist. She, of course, was wearing high heels. She always wore high heels. She didn't want anyone to notice how short she was, and she felt that the height gave her a different presence around people. Only a few people have ever seen her at her true height. With her shoes on, she was the same height as him, and it made her even more comfortable.

DD looked into her eyes, and they glistened. Her beauty was indescribable. He felt very lucky knowing that they had found each other and his life ahead would be complete. He started to get that warm feeling again that always glowed in his chest when he would think about her. The same sensation you get when you drink hot tea, and you can feel its temperature going down your throat into your stomach. That great feeling you get when you're wrapped up into an electric blanket on a cold winter's night. That wonder feeling you have when you're hugging the one you love, and your bodies' together start to...

A honking car horn broke his concentration, and he quizzically looked around Lynette and toward her car.

"Hurry up," Kim yelled out her window, "we're going to be late."

DD's eyes turned back toward Lynette's only this time with different warmth. "Why is she with you?" His eyes burned with anger.

Lynette let out a long sigh, "I know what you're going to say, but she started getting on my nerves, crying, and asking me why I didn't do anything with her anymore."

"We only have two tickets," DD said lifting up two fingers on his right hand, "how is she going to go?"

Lynette took his hand in hers, "the Lincoln Home and tomb are free, and she's going to go somewhere else to eat."

"Really, on whose money?" he said really annoyed.

Lynette returned the annoyed look but said nothing.

DD shook his head like he was trying to erase the situation. "Ok, let's go. I might as well try to play nice."

Lynette leaned forward and kissed his left cheek, "Thanks sweetheart."

They started to walk toward the car when he noticed that Kim was sitting in the front seat. He walked around the passenger side of the car and approached her open window. "Are you getting in the back?" DD questioned.

"I can't ride in the back," Kim whined. "It hurts me. The front seat is more soothing to my bad back."

140

DD sighed and walked further toward the back door and opened it. He climbed into the back, shut the door and then buckled the seat belt. Lynette, at the same time, climbed back into the driver's side, shut her door and started the engine. As she reached back to pull the seat belt forward, she turned and winked at DD and whispered a 'Thanks'.

DD could only nod.

Day 29, Wednesday May 10th, 2000, 8:10 a.m.

Are you kidding me? Seriously? Why in the world did she have to bring her along?

Close: 8:11 a.m.

Curt awoke in his trailer wondering if he should get up and get ready for class. It was going to start in about an hour and a half, and he really didn't want to go. He laid on his bed, the fan on his night table on full blast blowing upon his nude body. He could never sleep at all unless there was a fan on him. He had no problem having a sheet covering him, but anything other than that he would sweat all night. He found it a lot more comfortable and a better night's rest with that fan. He has had to buy three new fans in the last two years because since they ran all night, they would burn up quickly. Even the hum of the fan seemed soothing to his ears.

He turned his head and looked at the clock again and saw that ten minutes had passed since the last time he had looked at it. He sat up in bed and then swung his feet around to the right side of the bed and dangled them off the edge.

Boy was he sore. Last night's class really gave him a work out and he stiffened up when he got home. He did pick up a couple of burgers at the drive up from the Burger Barn on the way home, but ended up only eating one of the burgers before he decided to call it a night.

He belched and immediately tasted onion in his breath. He took his tongue and rolled it around his teeth in his mouth and felt how filmy they were. Perhaps a long shower would get his inspiration going.

He leaned forward and groaned his way to a standing position next to the bed. His knees popped a couple of times and he raised his hands toward his face to attempt to wipe away the grogginess. He let out a loud fart. Bad smell; must be the onions again.

He walked down the hall and into the bathroom. Flipping on the light next to the vanity mirror, he looked deep into his bloodshot eyes.

"I think you need the day off," he said to the face in the mirror.

He walked over to the shower, opened the door, and turned on the water. The one true place that he enjoyed was the shower. It was like a sanctuary away from everything. In the shower he felt like he did his best thinking, and at the same time it would wash away all his troubles. He never took fast showers, never, and today he was looking forward to a long soak. Just when the water was at his favorite temperature, he stepped in and closed the door.

The water doused on top of his head and he felt the soothing heat run down his aching body. The water was so hot that it singed his back and made him unwind. At times he would have the water so hot that when he got out, his skin would be a light shade of red.

The phone rang.

"Fuck, you," he yelled out, "I'm not getting out."

It rang again.

"Piss off," he yelled out.

It rang again then clicked to the answering machine.

He drowned himself away into the water face first. He could hear the answering message of his voice playing out but totally cut away from whomever it was leaving the message. He, of course, would check it later, but nothing was going to make him jump. That's why he hated cell phones. They always became top priory and people would drop everything to answer them. It was rude and disrespectful to the people they were with. It was as if they said,

"Hey, this ringing phone is more important to me than anything you are about to tell me, so fuck off." There was one time when he saw a younger couple on a date, at the Golden Egg, and they were both talking to other people on their phones telling the others how their date was going. Stupid, stupid, stupid.

His mind had drifted so much that his time lasted longer than usual, and he noticed that the hot water was losing its heat. He must have emptied the water heater. It was time to get out.

He reached over and turned off the knobs and stood for a while letting the water drip off his body. The steam in the enclosed shower soothed him even more. When he opened the door, a slight gust of cool air hit him, and he grabbed the towel off of the rack and dried himself off. Once he was dry, he walked toward the front of the trailer and up to the answering machine. It was blinking with a message. He pushed the play button.

"Good morning, Mr. Johnson, this is Professor Blair. An unexpected personal problem has occurred, and I will not be able attend class today. We will extend our assignment on the theory project for one more week. Enjoy the morning, and I'll see you next week."

Curt sat down on his couch and stretched his arms above his head

"YESSSS," he yelled out loud. Now all he had was the afternoon class which was English History. Maybe he could just pass that up too.

Jumping up off the couch, he got an idea as he walked toward the phone.

Day 29, Wednesday May 10th, 2000, 8:42 a.m.

Brad here with a couple of lines. Curt just called and told us his class had been cancelled. I hope everything is ok with Professor Sheldon I know that his family has been through some rough times recently. Curt found out that both Dean and I are parking it here at his house all day so he decided to come over and join us. Instead of a boy's night out, it'll be a boy's day in. He said that he had to finish up getting ready and he would be right over.

It didn't take long for Lynette to find a parking spot, and for them to find the Park Ranger holding the sign saying "Governors Party" at the entrance to the Visitor's Center. They were asked for their invitation tickets and were handed the free passes to the Lincoln home tour.   While they stood waiting for the rest of the people to arrive, DD, Lynette and Kim all leaned against the brick wall along the entrance.

"I've never been to this place," voiced Kim, "has either one of you?"

"Twice," DD answered. "It's very interesting, to a point, if you know what I mean."

Lynette smiled at him and turned her head toward her sister, "I've been here only once, but that was a long time ago. I barely remember it."

"I did a study on Abraham Lincoln when I was in high school," Kim said with a smug look on her face, "Did you know this was the only house he had ever owned?"

"Really?" Lynette said, "I thought he had other houses in Salem and Decatur."

"Only rented houses and property, "Kim answered, "In Salem he lived at the store he ran."

Just then the Park Ranger interrupted her history lesson, "All guests for the Governor's tour please follow me." He walked them toward the front door of the visitor center and opened the door for them. As people headed in, he greeted them one at a time as they entered. When DD passed, he nodded a greeting.

"Good morning to you," DD said as he walked through the door frame.

"Good morning to you too, sir," he replied kindly.

Four other people behind them brought up the last of the party and the Ranger followed them in.

Everyone was gathered into a large room that had a movie screen on the front wall. It looked like the group was about only twenty people and they all were dressed like they were going to the grand Ball, except Kim. She was wearing dirty worn-out jeans and a yellow blouse that looked like part of her breakfast came with her on it. The Park Ranger moved up to the front of the room and gestured to the guests,

"Please move in and take a seat in the theater. We have a small presentation called, 'Abraham Lincoln- A journey to Greatness' that you will enjoy."

People started taking their seats and DD, Lynette, and Kim slid into the third row toward the middle. The Ranger continued;

"I'd like to introduce myself, my name is Park Ranger Paul Webster, and I'm the officiating Ranger of the entire area. And what that means, ladies and gentlemen, is that you can't find a higher-ranking officer in the area. Any problems you have will need to be directed toward the Governor himself, that is if he's taking any phone calls."

Several people laughed, and Kim, sitting on Lynette's left, leaned over toward her, "Wow, we're getting the royal treatment."

DD, on Lynette's right, leaned toward Kim, "He's joking, Kim, remember who this group is?"

"Oh yeah" Kim said as she leaned back.

The ranger continued, "A little history on the house, if I may. Lincoln bought the house in 1844 at the price of One thousand and two hundred dollars. At the time, it was only a one-story house and they later added a second story in 1856. This house was the only home that Lincoln ever owned."

"Told you," Kim blurted out. The row in front of her not only heard her, but the Ranger showed a reaction on his face too.

"Shhhh," Lynette whispered.

He continued on. "The family lived in it for seventeen years up to the point when they moved to the White House. They had four boys; Robert; born in 1843, Eddie, born in 1846, Willie, born in 1850 and Tad born in 1858. Eddie only lived for four years and died in 1850. Willie died in the white house in 1862 and Tad died in 1871. Only Robert lived to full adult hood and passed away in 1926. He inherited the Lincoln home in 1887 and donated it to the State of Illinois upon the request that it would always be free to the public. Of course, he never knew about the future parking."

People laughed again and Kim leaned over again, "They could at least put a cushion on these benches. This is really going to hurt my back," she groaned. DD got a disgusted look on his face but bit his tongue on what he wanted to reply with. Lynette hushed her again.

"Several things in the house are authentic, but many things are replicas. I will be conducting your tour and will point these things out as we observe each room. As for now, sit back, relax and enjoy the movie." He walked off from the front and headed up toward the back on the right-hand side.

"How can you enjoy the show on such uncomfortable seats," Kim blurted out, "If they would..."

"Oh, shut up," Lynette voiced in, "We'll be up and walking in no time. Just enjoy this." She turned her head toward DD and gave him a reassuring smirk and he smiled back.

The Lights dimmed down and the projector started to roll. The first picture shown was a portrait of Lincoln himself sitting in a chair. The picture had a crack running through it signifying that it was a real old photograph. Then the soundtrack started to play.

Suddenly, loud screeching sounds omitted from the speakers and half the people in the room jumped. Others covered their ears. Kim held her palms to both her ears and yelled out in anguish. Lynette and DD's faces both cringed in pain.

The movie stopped.

"I'm sorry, ladies and gentlemen," Park Ranger Webster said from the back, "I don't know what caused that. We will look into this problem and have it going again in a couple of minutes."

Kim squirmed on the bench. "My butt is starting to hurt," she whined.

"If it's that bad," Lynette added, "then go stand in the back."

Kim turned her head back and forth, looking behind them and then got up. "I'll be over there," she said pointing toward the entrance door. Lynette nodded. Kim slowly made her way past them and past three other people at the end. She never bothered excusing herself when she rudely shoved her way through. Within a couple of minutes, she had found a place to lean up against the wall.

DD leaned over toward Lynette, "We've been here for only ten minutes and I'm about ready to kill her. Can't she be pleasant about anything?"

Lynette sighed, "You know the answer to that."

DD sighed back, "Unfortunately, I do."

"Sorry for the inconvenience, ladies and gentlemen," Ranger Webster said from the back, "Things look good, so we'll start this again. The hamster in the projector motor needed some water."

A few more laughs and the picture flickered again of the image of Abraham Lincoln. His proud stance in the chair gave him a strong image, even though the picture was taken at the height of the Civil war. He looked toward his left in one of the most famous pictures ever taken of him. His beard fully grown and...

The music soundtrack screeched again only this time with a lot of static noise. People once again jumped and covered their ears. The movie was quickly shut down. People sat in confusion looking around to see if they could somehow see the problem. Several heads turned left then right, only to see three Rangers in the back working in the small projection room. Ranger Webster came walking out and toward the front of the room again.

"I'm sorry, ladies and gentlemen, but we cannot figure out what is causing the disturbance. I know that this group is on a time crunch so we will proceed to the Lincoln home for the tour."

Several people grunted in dissatisfaction and started to get up.

"Please accompany me this direction and we will walk toward the home." He moved to a door on the other side of the room and opened it to the outside. Several people were gathering their belonging as Lynette and DD stood waiting for Kim to catch up to them from the back.

"Well, that's a bummer," DD said as he looked at Lynette. "I was looking forward to that."

"Me too," Lynette added when her sister caught up to them.

147

"This sucks," Kim said a little louder than needed. "I hope the rest of it isn't this bad."

"It's a nineteenth century house, what could possibly go wrong?" DD asked as he walked toward the exit. When they stepped outside, they saw that the Ranger was standing on a wooden walkway that led the distance down through the Historic Park.

"You mean we have to walk?" Kim complained. "I'm going to be sore in the morning."

DD whispered through his teeth, "You're going to be sore if...." His opinion was silenced when Lynette put her right palm over his mouth.

"Once again, I apologize about the inconvenience," Ranger Webster added, "We are now standing on the main street that leads toward the Lincoln Home. Several other families occupied the street. Back in their time, though, each home didn't have a street number; they had the family's name on a plaque mounted on the front door."

He started walking down the walk way and toward their destination.

"The Lincoln Home," he said as he pointed to the home on the right, "was registered as a National Historic Landmark in 1960 and belongs to the National Park Service. It is the only National Service property in the state of Illinois. That is why you only see Park Rangers on the premises, not police. You don't have to worry, though, we don't write tickets."

People laughed and continued to walk with the Ranger right up to the front entrance of the home. Ranger Webster walked up the front steps and turned around facing the crowd below. He pointed at the plaque on the front door. "Here is the home identification for the house. This is a reproduction of the original plaque with 'A. Lincoln' engraved upon it. When we step inside, I kindly ask you to gather and wait in the front entrance way until all people are in. Then I will proceed with the tour."

He opened the front door, and the crowd started to move in.

Day 29, Wednesday May 10th, 2000, 10:12 a.m.

Oh wonderful! Curt just got here and he brought some lunch for us. I can't remember the last time I had fried chicken. He brought all the trimmings too; mashed potatoes, gravy and corn on the cob. Brad ran upstairs to get plates and silverware, but I plan to eat it right out of the box. I mean, seriously, isn't that why they call it finger food? Brad's the only person I know who eats fried chicken with a fork. It's really weird too when we are at the Pizza pub and he eats pizza with a fork as well. Any way, we caught Curt up on what was going on, and he, too, is scarfing down his from out of the box. I will admit, though, eating the mashed potatoes without the utensils would be a little hard.

Well, they just finished the downstairs tour and are heading upstairs. Hopefully the day will get better than the movie.

Close: 10:25 a.m.

"As we go upstairs, you will see that Abe and Mary had their own separate bedrooms." Ranger Webster continued with the tour, "It was customary in their time to do this. It also gave Mary time to sleep since Abe worked late nights at his lap desk. And no, we're not talking a computer."

People laughed.

"One thing you can say about this guy," DD whispered toward the two girls, "he does have some good wit about him."

Lynette smiled and nodded her head. "He does know how to work the crowd, doesn't he?"

"It's all very corny if you ask me," Kim added.

"I didn't ask you," DD snapped back. Kim turned her grumpy face into a pouting one. Lynette gave DD the look of 'Stop it'.

"First room on the left," Ranger Webster said with a motion of his arm, "Is Mr. Lincoln's room. The bed is not the original bed, but a replica of a bed during that time period. It was big enough to hold his six-foot four-inch body."

People, one at a time walked up to the railing and peered inside the room. When it got to their turn, Kim butted her way up

149

into the front a leaned over the rail. DD and Lynette had to lean in sideways to get a glance.

"Not really much room was there," Kim said.

"At least Abe and Mary had their own rooms," DD said, "The boys had to share theirs."

The rest of the group followed the Ranger down the hall toward the next room on the left. "Next is Mary's room," he said, "A nice and cozy room with a small bed, a hope chest and a makeup table." DD, Lynette and Kim caught up to the group as the Ranger continued, "She had the most elegant colors in the house, next to the front parlor, and she always was neat and tidy."

Kim started getting antsy as she kept rising up and down on her toes, "I want to see."

DD turned toward her with disgust in his eyes, "will you calm down, you'll get a chance."

Several of the people walked away from the railing and then Kim saw her chance and trotted up to the railing. The Ranger, next to her, gave her an annoyed look, but he continued. "The wallpaper is not the original nor is the Hope chest. A lot of the furniture in the house, as well, is not the original. They tried to match as close as they could with photographs and furniture of the time."

Kim moved away and DD and Lynette got to walk up together, alone, to see into the room.

"Mostly reproduced, huh?" Lynette questioned.

DD turned his head to her and raised an eyebrow, "You own your great grandfather's hammer. Since he has had it, it has had three handles replaced and two new heads put on it. Is it still your Great grandfather's hammer?"

Lynette chuckled.

"I don't get it, "Kim said behind their shoulders, eavesdropping.

"And you never will," DD said as he turned from the railing and walked toward the rest of the group at the end of the hall.

"This small room to the left is the servant's quarters," the Ranger continued. "It was just big enough for the bed, dresser, and chair."

DD, Kim, and Lynette peered into the room after the others walked on. Because the way that Kim was acting, DD and Lynette had slowed their pace down so that they were not as close to the group. Without saying a word to each other, they reached this result. So many times, they had to deal with Kim's impatience and had to derail many problems that occurred. One time they went to the St Louis Zoo, and she was in such a rush to get a cotton candy that she knocked an ice cream cone out of a little girl's hand and onto the concrete below. Lynette had bought the girl another, adding a double scoop to the mix and she was happily on her way. Kim, on the other hand, never apologized.

When they caught up with the group around the corner, The Ranger had just finished explaining the contents of the boy's room. Several of the other people had already looked in the room and moved on when they approached. Kim, once again, rushed to the front to look in. The Ranger was still standing next to the railing.

"Where's the bathroom?" Kim asked.

The Ranger got a coy smile on his face. "The main outhouse is out in the backyard but do you see that white ceramic bowl under the wash basin table," he said pointing at the object, "that's called a chamber pot."

"Ewww," Kim resounded. "You mean they had to go in that and let it sit all night?"

"Yes. And that was one of the chores the maid had to do in the morning. She was also responsible for making the fires, cleaning the lamps and carrying the water," the Ranger repeated what he had earlier said at the Maid's room.

"You mean she had to clean up everyone's shit?" Kim yelled. Many of the people in the party turned their head and looked.

Lynette walked up to Kim and grabbed her arm, "Shhhh, watch your language." DD stayed toward the back. He didn't want to get involved.

"But that's gross," she continued. "I hope she got paid for it."

"She got paid a dollar fifty a week," the Ranger answered.

"What? She only got that much for cleaning up people's shit? That's disgusting and unfair."

Everyone in the party was looking toward them now, and looking very annoyed. Lynette grabbed her arm tighter.

"If you don't stop now, I won't take you to the Tomb, do you hear me?" Lynette said in a low whisper. Her eyes were glaring with anger.

Kim nodded her head. "Ok, but still..."

"Shhhh," Lynette added.

"The next room," the Ranger pushed on trying to draw attention away from the incident, "is where Robert slept when he was at the house. When he left for the service, it was turned into a guest room." The crowd followed him down the hall, and DD didn't move. He signaled toward Lynette to go on ahead, with a wave of his hand. She nodded and slowly kept Kim at arm's length. DD leaned over the rail of the boy's room to get a better look.

They both shared one large bed. The wash basin table, and the chamber pot, was on the left side of the room. They had a dresser in front of the bed, along the wall, and several wooden alphabet blocks were stacked on the floor. This kind of reminded him about how Lynette and Kim had grown up.

They shared a room together as well. She had told him several times how she had to deal with Kim's impatience and her spoiled brat tendencies. He understood a lot about why she acted the way she did. Kim was very close to their mother, who had died in a car accident when they were very young. Lynette, at the time, was thirteen, and Kim was only ten. Their mother had pampered Kim a lot. They spent a lot of time cooking in the kitchen and knitting which to this day Kim still does. Lynette was more of a tom boy and attached to her father. She loved Football, fishing and, of course, reading books. After their mother's death, Kim wasn't the center of the attention anymore and over the years had become dependent on others. She is very intelligent but chooses to take a path of laziness and annoyance. She has convinced her doctor that she is in severe depression, and he has her on heavy medication, which in turn grants her government assistance. She's not handicapped, but at times people tend to think of her that way. A lazy spoiled brat is the real definition. If only people would understand what life's misfortunes can do to a child, then maybe the world would get a better understanding on how to live together.

A hand placed on his shoulder and lightly shaking it snapped him out of his trance.

"Hey," Lynette said, "Are you ok?"

DD unclouded his mind, "yes, I'm fine. I just dazed off there for a moment."

"Well, they are ready to head downstairs," she noted. "We are supposed to get on a charter bus and be driven to the Governor's Mansion for the Luncheon."

"Are they going to allow Kim on the bus since she doesn't have an invitation?" DD said as they both started walking toward the stairs.

"Yes, I already cleared it. When we get there, Kim will walk to Mama's Kitchen and eat lunch. Then we are to board back onto the bus to take us to the Tomb." Lynette grabbed the hand rail as they proceeded down the steps. "After that they will return us to the Home where we can return to our car and leave.'

"Seams easy enough, but you know something will happen."

They both reached the bottom of the steps, where the rest of the group was exiting the house. Kim was standing at the bottom of the stairs looking at them as they approached.

"What took you so long? I want to get a good seat on the bus," Kim announced.

"Be lucky you have a seat at all, "Lynette added, "I had to pay for your transportation."

"Let's go," Kim said trotting out the door.

Day 29, Wednesday May 10th, 2000, 11:22 a.m.

Someone really needs to slap the shit out of that bitch, Holy fuck, what an annoyance. Brad has taken over the 380 while Dean takes a long shower. I don't know why they won't let my ass watch the 380, well…, yes, I do. Because I'll probably have DD SLAP THE SHIT OUT OF THAT BITCH! At least she won't be there at the luncheon to piss and moan. Henceforth why God gave women two pairs of lips; one is for pissing, and one is for moaning. I mean, Dean has explained to me why she acts that way, but give me a fucking break. Even I at times know how to behave myself let alone support myself. What a fucking brat.
Close: 11:27 a.m.

The last of the group got off the bus, and it pulled away from the front gate of the mansion. Most of the group started walking toward the entrance, and others noted that they still had enough time to get in a quick cigarette. DD, Lynette, and Kim stood on the sidewalk going over the plans.

"Now listen up," Lynette said, "the bus will be here to pick us up at two o'clock sharp. Don't be late. That'll give you plenty of time to get something to eat, relax, and get back. Make sure to give yourself plenty of time for the walk."

"I understand," Kim answered. "Do you have any money I can borrow?"

Borrow. DD started laughing in his mind. Why does she always insist on using the word 'borrow' when she knows that she will never pay her sister back? Lynette opened up her purse and gave her sister forty dollars.

"Here, this should be enough." Lynette turned and started walking toward the mansion, "remember, two o'clock."

"I'll be here," Kim said as she wadded the bills into her pocket and started walking away.

DD turned and started walking along Lynette's side and then took note of the people still smoking along the front walk. They all had smiles on their faces, probably due to the fact that Kim wasn't joining them for the luncheon. His eyes then turned to Lynette again, with her dress lightly blowing in the wind. God, she was

154

gorgeous. He was very lucky to have such a woman in his life, someone that not only was so attractive but very intelligent as well. She had such a great personality and her added wit and humor just made her all the more exciting.

When they reached the doors, an attendant held the door open for them and as they walked in, he nodded a greeting to them.

Soothing jazz music filled the air as they approached the Maître de at the front entrance hall. Several people were talking in the room which gave a low rumble to the sound of the music. When they approached the attendant, he held out his hands.

"Invitations, please."

Lynette opened her purse and pulled out the two tickets and handed them to him. He looked at them and then turned to a waiter behind him. "Please escort them to table twenty-nine."

The attendant bowed and looked toward them. He extended his arm out for Lynette to grab onto, "Please follow me." Lynette wrapped her arm around the young slender man and turned her head around to look at DD behind them. She stuck her tongue out at DD, and he laughed. They walked into the middle of the room where they were seated with five other people. The attendant pulled out the chair for Lynette to sit down, and after she did, DD took the seat to the left of her. All the faces at the table were new, so they didn't have to deal with any questions about Kim. They too were elegantly dressed and talking amongst themselves. One older man nodded a greeting toward DD.

"Good day," said the man toward them, "It's nice to see a younger crowd among our midst, and an attractive one at that!"

"Thank you," DD said.

"Ah, honey," Lynette said, "I think he was talking about me."

"Oh, of course he was." DD added.

The man got a serious look on his face and then started to laugh. He raised his glass in a salute, "and to you sir, for a quick wit."

"Thank you." DD said. Looking down in front of him he saw the place setting. Three forks, two knifes two spoons and a small menu lying upon an elegant gold rimmed plate. To the right was his napkin folded into the shape of a swan. He grabbed the napkin, unfolded it, and then placed it into his lap. Lynette did the same.

"Better start looking at our menus," the older man said. "They'll be by any moment to take our order."

Lynette picked up her menu and started glancing through the list. A seven-course meal was on the agenda.

APPITIZERS
Melons & peas with Prosciutto

SOUP
Chunky Gazpacho

SALAD
Northwest Wild Greens

PALATE CLEANSER
Lemon Sorbet with fresh mint

COURSE 1
Roasted Filet of Beef

COURSE 2
Roasted Pigeon with Pickled Red Cabbage
Or
Glazed Salmon with Bok Choy & Shiitake

DESERT
Vanilla Pannacotta with Blueberry Sauce
Or
Poached Pears in Mulled Wine

Her mouth started to water as she tried to decide what she wanted for the last two choices. "Which one are you going to pick," Lynette asked as she turned toward DD.

DD suddenly got a nauseated look on his face. "I'm not hungry," he stated. "I've had an upset stomach all day."

Lynette put her menu down and put her hands on his shoulder, "Oh, honey, I'm sorry that you're not feeling good. Perhaps a drink of water might help."

"I'm afraid not," he continued, "it's one of those when if you take a bite or drink of anything, it's probably going to come right back up."

Lynette's eyes were deeply concerned, "Have you been this way all day?"

"Ever since we got to the Home; I tried not to ruin everyone's day." he answered.

"Well, just relax, and if you need to go to the bathroom quickly, I'll understand." She kissed him on the cheek and picked her menu back up to make her decision.

"At least I have the day with you, that's enough to cure anything," DD smiled.

Lynette smiled back and mouthed 'I Love You' to him.

DD returned the words.

Day 29, Wednesday May 10th, 2000, 12:17 p.m.

Well, darn it, this isn't fair. I could be enjoying a seven-course meal, and a delicious looking one at that, but no, I have to sit here on this chair all day playing experiment. And it's not fair either when the other two are laughing at me because of it. Brad told me that he would be glad to take me out to a seven-course meal anytime. I told him that it just wouldn't be the same. That's when Curt said that Brad could always borrow the green dress of Lynette's. They both started laughing at me again. I really hate those guys.

Close: 12:19 p.m.

DD had plenty of time to look around the room while the others were eating. He couldn't understand why his stomach all of a sudden got upset; he just knew that he didn't have an appetite for what was offered. The food looked really good, though. As he watched Lynette savor her every dish, he took account of what was around.

Sharing the table with them was a lawyer and his wife, and a Senator with her husband. DD didn't catch if she was a Republican or a Democrat; he only knew that he never enjoyed the whole political scene. There were just way too many politicians for this state. Nobody could ever agree on anything which meant that the regular citizens either worked harder or waited longer. Most of the time, one house was controlled by one party and the other by the other one. In true reality, it meant that whatever one wanted passed, the other one would deny. The only thing that got done was that the state deficit grew bigger and bigger. They keep spending and spending but tax the people more and more to take up their loss. DD always saw that when they raised taxes to help cover costs, they would come up with a new spending which put them deeper in the hole. Then they would start all over again. Taxes up, spending up, taxes up, spending up; everyone was out of control. If he was to try that system for the bills in his house, he would have no electricity, phone, water, TV or even food. He probably wouldn't even have the house anymore. Why can't anyone in the State Capitol balance their check book?

Most of Politicians got salaries that alone would take care of six families each year. And, of course, they always received their annual raise. They loved to prance around like they were all mighty and untouchable. Behind every one of them is probably some scheming criminal waiting to get caught. The main table itself, up on stage, had quite a few of those stuffed suits sitting and drinking their mixed drinks. They were all laughing and carrying on without a worry in the world except making their next tee time at the Country club. DD did notice that the Governor was nowhere to be seen. He was probably at the golf course now.

The bussers cleaned up the last of the dirty plates and had removed all that was left on the table besides what drink people were still working on. One of the larger men, on the front stage, stood up and walked over to the podium in the middle of the stage table. He started hitting his drink with a spoon to get everyone's attention in the room. Of course, everyone else in the room started to join in on the annoying noise as well. Once everyone's voices were silent, he set the glass down and reached up and turned on the microphone.

"Ladies and Gentlemen, thank you...."

A loud screeching resounded all over the room and several people held their ears. The man turned off the microphone, silencing the noise, and looked toward the left at a couple of attendants at a speaker box. They fumbled around with the cords and then nodded back toward the man with reassurance that the problem had been fixed.

He turned it on again, "Sorry about that, we..."

This time it was so loud that it sounded like a glass cracked somewhere. The man waved his hands toward the attendants and signaled them to leave it off.

"Sorry, once again," the man said without the use of the microphone, "My voice carry's so I don't need the microphone."

A couple of the men at the front table laughed, and someone yelled something that made more people join in on the laugh.

The man pointed his finger toward one of them, "The electrician must be on your payroll, Sam."

More laughter rang out.

Lynette turned toward DD, "I can't believe this has happened to us twice in one day."

DD smiled, "It's got to be all those sparks you're putting out from your good looks."

She winked at him and put her hand on his hand lying on the table. Then they both turned their attention back to the speaker.

"I've got bad news for everyone. As you all have noticed, the Governor couldn't make it today, so he had me take over the luncheon." The man reached over and took another sip of his drink and sat it down again. "I promised him that this wouldn't be a political debate, topic or even a fundraiser. We are here to celebrate a good year. Of course, it gets better and better depending on how many drinks you have had."

DD laughed out loud with the others. "Now that was a good line," he said to Lynette.

"Over the last year, we have seen a lot of firsts in Illinois. We have seen the first female Lieutenant Governor ever appointed."

Several people clapped, and many women cheered.

"We have seen," the speaker continued, "the first African-American secretary of State."

More people cheered, added with a couple of whistles.

"And we have a Governor who was the first US Governor to visit Cuba in the last 40 years. I guess the main office finally ran out of cigars."

Laughter around the room burst again and the speaker took another drink of his beverage. "Our population has dropped down to about twelve million, four hundred and thirteen thousand; which made us lose a seat in Congress, and the districts were reorganized from twenty to nineteen. That's one way to cut state spending, I guess."

A couple of grunts and groans moved throughout the crowd.

"But several good things have happened and are on the horizon. One of the biggest moves was for our Governor to declare a moratorium on executions in the State."

Cheers filled the room and several people started to give a standing ovation. The roar of the clapping slowly died down, and the people once again took their seats.

"But the biggest project coming up is an idea that is almost one hundred years behind in the making and should have been done a lot sooner. A project that will bring in so much tourism to the state of Illinois that people would be proud to be a citizen of this state." He lifted a fist to his mouth and let out a little cough,

"We are building a large fence around Chicago and changing its name to Joy Land Amusement Park."

That joke got several jeers from the crowd and both Lynette and DD moaned in unison. Chicago was always known as being Illinois, everything else was just 'Down State.' If Chicago wanted it, no matter what it was, there was a 95% chance of it being passed. Most of the politicians were from Chicago, and since the town had almost three million people, it overpowered the rest of the state. Springfield only had about one hundred and fifty-two thousand people, but ever since it became the State Capital, Chicago has been on the defensive.

"I know, I know, bad joke." The speaker started to laugh, "Just trying to see if you were paying attention." He took another drink and set down the glass. "This project, in reality, is one that is very dear to my heart. One of the greatest Americans in history and we only celebrate his legacy in statues, monuments, a home and a tomb. Soon we will be showing the world many things about his life, his dedication to not only his family but to his country as well. Next year we plan to break ground on the Abraham Lincoln Library and Museum."

This got everyone standing and clapping. Lynette and DD also stood up and joined in the celebration. It was a huge move for Illinois and, yes, it was years behind in the making. Several other past Presidents had museums, but somehow Lincoln was left out of the mix. Springfield tourism would skyrocket.

The clapping continued which felt like two minutes long to DD and then people started to sit back down into their chairs.

"One more thing before we go," the speaker added. "I'm very happy to be a part of this year's elected officials. With the Governor, the house, the senate and all the district representatives; Illinois will be a state that will be moving forward. Progress and business growth will be the main focus to bring Illinois into a land of competition. A place people would be proud to live in, a place that everyone will be comfortable with their elected officials to do what's best for them. A place where Government doesn't control the people, but the people control the government. We will be a state that not only gives equal justice and prosperity to the upper, middle and lower classes, but listens to them to make their lives a better place. We will be that blanket that comfortably tucks your family in at night, giving them a feeling of fulfillment and joy." The speaker lifted up his glass in a toast, "This state will prosper!"

Once everyone stood up again, cheering and clapping. The entire room roared with applause as the speaker walked away from the podium and shook hands down the line at the front table. When the clapping started to die down, people started to gather their things and leave the room.

Lynette looked down at her watch, "Perfect," she said to DD. "It's five till two which gives us just enough time to catch the bus out front."

DD put his arm around Lynette and they both slowly moved through the crowd toward the exit. Several of the suited people were just lingering around to hobnob with each other and catch up on the times. It didn't take long for them to make it past them and through the opened door of the entrance.

"That was different," Lynette said as they walked down the steps and onto the front walk. "I was really expecting a political lecture."

DD shook his head, "I wasn't. Most of the officials just got elected into office, so they really didn't have to preach to the choir. This was like a 'High Society' frat party."

Lynette laughed. "Good call," she commented as she looked up and saw the tour bus parked at the end of the walk with its doors opened. As they approached, both of them looked up and down the sidewalk and scanned around the bus.

Kim was nowhere in sight.

Day 29, Wednesday May 10th, 2000, 2:12 p.m.
Why does this not surprise me? I knew that something was going to happen today and this was it. The bus waited till ten after, and then left without them, Curt got so frustrated, he went upstairs and turned on the TV to get his mind off of it. Brad just shook his

head in disgust and then followed Curt upstairs as well. So, here I sit, watching DD wiggling his feet as they sit on the brick wall along the front walk waiting for her non caring sister. At least I got a good long shower and feel refreshed. Now if I can only wash out the thoughts in my mind about Kim.

Close: 12:17 p.m.

Kim slowly walked down the sidewalk, still eating what was left of the ice cream cone that she had bought. When they saw her, DD and Lynette hopped off of the knee-high wall they were sitting on and stood waiting for her. Lynette had her hands on her hips, her frustrated annoyed cat look, and DD knew that this wasn't going to be good.

"Do you have any idea what 'BE ON TIME' means?" Lynette blurted out.

Kim took another bite of her cone, "sorry," she said as apologetically as she could, "I found a real neat video game and I lost track of time."

"You also lost our tour of the tomb," Lynette yelled back. "The bus left without us."

Kim got a real sarcastic look on her face, "well the tomb is free right? We can still go, can't we?"

"And just on how do you expect us to get there?" Lynette said as her voice rose louder and louder. DD knew better not to say anything; in fact, he started picking little leaves off of one of the plants to look like he wasn't paying attention.

"Your car, of course," Kim stated in a smart mouthed tone.

"And where do you see my car?" Lynette lifted her right hand and waved it toward the street.

Kim got a look of revelation on her face, "you mean..."

"Start walking, sister." Lynette's tone was at its peak. She took her right thumb and pointed it toward the street in front of them, "Get moving, it can't be more than maybe twenty blocks!"

Kim let a big sigh out and starting walking in that direction, dragging her feet. She started walking across the street to the sidewalk on the left-hand side, and DD and Lynette started walking

163

with her but about ten feet behind her. As Kim reached the sidewalk, she threw what was left of her ice cream cone at the side of the building, and it ended with a crunching splatter.

"Don't get upset," Lynette voiced, "It was your own actions that caused this. This is a perfect example why I don't take you anywhere."

Kim didn't respond; just kept shuffling down the sidewalk.

"Could be worse," DD said, "it could be raining."

First Lynette gave him a 'don't push it' look, then shrugged it off, smiled, and took his right hand into her left. "You're right; it is a lovely day for a walk."

"Yes, it is," DD answered. "And there is no rain in the forecast for today or for the rest of the week. The cabin is going to be great."

Her hand tightened on his, "I'm really looking forward to it. After tomorrow I'll really need the getaway. I'm pulling an open to close so that Dawn doesn't overwork herself the whole weekend. I gave her Thursday completely off."

DD smiled, "which means plenty of time for us to be away from it all."

They both looked up and saw Kim still shuffling her feet ahead of them, but about a half a block away. They both started to quicken their pace and soon found themselves caught up to her. They only completed three blocks and there were many more to go.

Day 29, Wednesday May 10th, 2000, 3:12 p.m.

Well, one thing is for sure, DD is getting plenty of exercise. He's really biting his tongue too because I know what I'd be yelling at Kim right now. After all the things that I had seen that girl do, I know it's better to keep my mouth shut because Lynette wouldn't appreciate it if I didn't.

I can hear that Curt and Brad have the TV on upstairs and from what I can tell it's another Science fiction movie. Soon they'll get into one of their debates again and over exaggerate the topic. I'm glad I'm down here.

Close: 3:22 p.m.

As the Captain walked down the gangway of his ship, he saw that his Engineer was at the relay beacon by the perimeter of the landing zone. He always got edgy when they had to investigate a distress call, especially when it was this far from the system. Only this time it really wasn't a distress call. A repeating message called not for help, but for a response. This post was a deep space exploration site but nobody had heard anything from them in years.

When the message was received, they were ordered to check it out. The entire trip took only six weeks, but he could see that the crew was still restless.

The captain approached his Engineer, "So how soon till we get the perimeter secure?"

The bulky Engineer, in a knelt down position, turned his head toward the captain. The sweat was dripping off his face so much that he had to wipe it off with his long sleeve. "I don't know, Captain," he said with a raspy voice, "All the disturbances around the area are messing with the radio frequencies. It seems that something is transmitting on such a powerful Amplitude Modulation that it's disrupting the regular current of our equipment." The man stood up and brushed the ground from his knees, "We can't get a clear signal to........"

"HOLY SHIT FUCK," Curt yelled as he jumped up from the coach. The sudden outburst made Brad jerk in a startle, and he screamed.

"Why did you do that?" Brad yelled as he tried to catch his breath, "are you trying to give me a heart attack?"

"Don't you see?" Curt continued at his voice level as he pointed to the movie they were watching on the TV, "the frequencies!"

Brad looked confused, "What, you mean how they said about setting a perimeter?"

"No, not the movie," Curt yelled again. "The internet at the Book Nook, the movie at the Lincoln set, the microphone at the luncheon,"

"What are you babbling about?"

"It's fucking DD!"

Then Brad finally caught on to what he was trying to tell him, "The kilowatts that he's transmitting!"

"Fuck, yeah," Curt said as he pointed toward the stereo remote on the table next to Brad, "Quick, change the system to the radio."

Brad reached over and picked up the remote to the stereo console. He looked for the button that said TUNER and pushed it. Suddenly a loud screeching filled the living room, and Brad quickly shut off the unit.

"It's Fucking DD that's disrupting everything!" Curt started waving his arms in the air. "That solves everything!"

"Quite obvious, Dude," Brad answered. "Now we know what to expect."

They heard footsteps running up the steps, and soon Dean was in the living room with them. "What in the world was that noise?"

"It's DD man," Curt answered. "His frequency is so powerful that he's been the one causing all the transmission malfunctions; including the wireless at the Book Nook. No wonder I couldn't find anything wrong with it."

Dean's face turned to surprise, "Wow that explains a lot. The movie at the Home..."

"The microphone at the luncheon," Curt voiced in. "Shit, he's probably messing with a lot of things. I wonder if it's fucking with cell phone transmission."

"Different frequency," Brad said jumping in, "Not to mention that is a satellite transmission, not a radio."
Dean looked around the room for his phone, and then realized that DD had it. "I wonder what the perimeter of his disturbance is."

Brad scratched his head, "the only way to figure that out is to do a perimeter test with a radio. This is definitely something I'm going to have to add to my speech for this weekend."

"Maybe we can test him later," Curt added.

"Speaking of him," Dean said, "He should be home really soon. Lynette's calling it a day and is bringing him home."

The urgency hit them all as Brad stood up, "Ok. Curt, you need to hide your beast outside. Dean you get downstairs and type in something about not letting the ladies into the house. Me, I'll get things cleaned up here until they arrive. Gentlemen, let's motivate!"

****

DD could see that Lynette was furious as she was driving him home. She made Kim sit in the back seat and told her not to say a word the entire trip. She had her teeth clenched which DD rarely saw indicating that she had reached her boiling point.

During the walk, Kim started complaining that her feet hurt, and she wanted to sit down a lot. They had passed several stores, and each one enticed Kim to want to look inside at what they had. Lynette refused and kept walking. After the fourth store, Kim started to whine about how she never gets to do things that she's wants to do. That's when Lynette blew.

DD had never seen her this angry. She had backed Kim up against a wall and got into her face, yelling and screaming. Almost everything that people had been saying about Kim came out of Lynette's mouth at that time. She didn't hold back anything; in fact, Lynette let out a few curse words that DD had never heard her utter. Not only did he feel shocked about the outburst, but he felt relieved that she was getting it off her chest. Not a word was spoken the rest of the walk to the car.

Now, here they were, about six blocks away from his house, and still the air was thick. He had that uncomfortable feeling you get that goes up the back of your neck and to your ears. Even he was scared to say anything. He tried to even get a glance from Lynette so that he could wink at her, but she was in complete trance just watching the road.

As they pulled into the empty drive, Lynette put the car into park, and she turned toward DD, "I'll call you later."

167

"Ok," DD said as he got out of the car. He walked around the front of it to the driver's side window as she retracted it down. He leaned in toward her, knowing that she was in no mood for a kiss and whispered to her. "Try to remember to breathe."

Lynette, with a strong effort, smiled at him. "I'll call you."

And with those last words, she put the car in reverse and backed out of the driveway.

DD started walking toward the house as he pulled his keys out of his front right pocket. When he reached the front door, he tried inserting the key to find out that the door was already unlocked. He got a quizzical look on his face, turned the knob, and then slowly walked in.

When he entered the living room, he saw Curt and Brad standing in it.

"What are you guys doing here?" he questioned.

"Shirley," Brad said.

Then there was darkness.

"Why did you say that up here," Curt exclaimed, "now we have to carry his ass downstairs."

"Sorry, got carried away for the moment," Brad answered. "It's so cool. You can always turn him back on again."

"No thanks, fuck that shit," Curt exclaimed, "I've already stuck my hand down there once already, and I'm not doing it again. It's just weird."

"You're the one who put it there," Dean said as he walked in from the kitchen. "So, what's the plan for tonight?"

Brad sat back down in the recliner he had used all afternoon, "I'm calling Professor Foraker and meeting him for dinner somewhere. If it's alright with you boys, I'm going to tell him about the project."

"Fine with me," Curt said, "He's not going to tell anyone, will he?"

"No, he won't let the cat out of the bag," Brad reassured, "I've known him for a long time and we have covered each other's hinny's many times."

"I have no problem either, but seriously," Dean said as he sat down on the couch. "I've got a question for you two." Both Curt and Brad gave him attention glares, "Do you think we could let DD sit out tomorrow? I mean, the test runs these last three days have been pretty good. I've got to run the truck to the dealer tomorrow morning, and then I want to get packed for the weekend."

"The weekend," Brad said, "What's going on this weekend?"

"You remember, Brad," Curt said sitting down on the couch next to Dean, "He's planning to go to the cabin with Lynette and just watch each other grow old."

"Oh," Brad exclaimed. "I'm sure they will find other things to do."

"Checkers and cards maybe, but I doubt there will be any fucking or boob squeezing."

Brad got an annoyed look on his face, "What they do is their business, young man, and I think you should watch your mouth when it comes to Lynette." The sudden outburst had the boys with surprised looks on their faces. "You're just too raunchy when it comes to them and for Pete's sake, you're his best friend!"

"Who's Pete?" Curt asked.

"Never mind," Brad said. "I think you just need to ease up, that's all. She is a special lady and it's very rare to find anyone like that. You have to cherish every moment that you can."

Dean started raising his hands, "Its ok, Brad, I'm used to it."

"You shouldn't have to be," Brad added, "It's just not right."

All three of them got really quiet and the only thing that could be heard was the ticking of the clock above the fireplace. Curt swallowed hard and looked at Dean for a response. Dean only shrugged his shoulders in confusion. After a couple of minutes, Dean stood up.

"Well, since we are giving DD the rest of the week off, I need to get something to eat." He turned and looked at Curt. "Want to join me?"

"You pick the place," Curt answered. "I'll eat anything right now. That chicken for lunch really didn't fill my ass up."

"Burger Barn," Dean answered.

"Perfect," Curt said standing up. "A big fat juicy piece of meat is always welcomed."

"Then let's call this day's experiment over and split," Brad said as he stood up and walked toward the door.

"Hey, Brad, "Curt said stopping Brad's momentum toward the door, "If it really bothers you, I'll try to be a little more careful around Lynette."

"You should be more careful around him too," Brad said pointing toward Dean. "He's pretty much the only friend you got."

Curt nodded as Brad left the house.

Dean shrugged again, "I'm going to write one more entry in the journal, and then we can go."

Day 29, Wednesday May 10th, 2000, 4:42 p.m.

Well, this week's experiment is over and DD has passed extremely well. Not only did he fool all of the professors but several random people as well. I think we are ready to show him off. Brad will go to the Seattle conference this weekend; Lynette and I will relax at the cabin. I'll tell her, and Curt, well, will probably spend the whole weekend at Marvin's. He'll probably sleep on top of one of the tables, or one of the girls, or maybe both.

As for the rest of tonight, DD has deserved a long rest in his chair downstairs and we will probably not turn him back on until Monday when we all meet at the university to show him off. I can't wait to see the look on many of the faces attending. Curt and I are going out to eat at the Burger Barn, and Brad is going to join his friend to tell him about DD. Although I sat in a room by myself for three days, this experiment did go by fast.

As for tomorrow, I'll drive the truck to the dealer and get it fixed. Curt will probably have to follow me so I can get a ride back. Then after that, I'll have to pack for this weekend. I am looking forward to spending the time with Lynette and to also tell her what she has been with all week.

I do wonder why Brad got so upset with Curt. He's always talked that way and Lynette and I have learned let it go in one ear

170

and out the other. Something must be bothering him, but I can't understand what it could be. Everything is going so well this week, and with his trip this weekend, he should be really relaxed. Oh, my word, this weekend, it just dawned on me. This Sunday would be the fifth anniversary of his wife's death. No wonder he is so strung up. I'll have to remind Curt.

Speaking of Curt, he's yelled at me three times to hurry up and I am hungry. So, without any other problems, the next log in this book should be Brad with his report about the Convention.

Until next time.

Close: 4:52 p.m.

It took only three rings for Robert to answer the phone, and he sounded extremely tired. "Hello?"

"Good afternoon, Slick," Brad said, "what are your plans for tonight?"

Recognizing Brad's voice, Robert's voice perked up. "Well, I've got a lot of stuff I've got to finish before I go home."

"You're still at the office?"

"Yes, and I don't know what time I'll get home."

"Can it wait until tomorrow?"

"Not a chance. The board wants my final report about this week's recruiting on the desk tomorrow morning." Robert sighed. "Why do you ask?"

"I was hoping to take you out to dinner and spill the beans."

"Really, Cool! I'd love to, but..."

"How about lunch tomorrow then, after you hand your report to the goon squad."

"Great," Robert replied, "I'll call you when I'm ready. Are you coming in tomorrow?"

"No, I'm taking the rest of the week off. I've got an outing I've got to do this weekend and I'll fill you in on that too."

"Then tomorrow it'll be."

"I'll be waiting," Brad finished as he hung up the phone next to his recliner. Then tilting his head toward the library wall, not particularly staring at anything, he started going through his mind

171

on what he needed to take with him to Seattle. His clothes were already packed, and the only thing he needed was his toiletries. His briefcase did need to be given a double looksee to make sure that everything about the experiment was in it; his report, the schematics, the diary. Oops, the diary was still at Dean's. He got a frustrated look on his face realizing that he was going to have to go get it. He just got done taking off his clothes and was relaxing in his library's recliner, only dressed in his boxer shorts. He had just poured himself a glass of wine, too. Now, he was going to have to slip something on and rush over to retrieve it.

He slowly stood up, grabbed his glass on the end table and took another swig of the wine. The cool chill of Riesling felt good going down. He carried the glass up the two steps leading out of the library and down the hall toward the kitchen. When he reached the refrigerator, he opened the door and placed the glass inside.

"I'll be right back, my friend," he said as he walked toward his bedroom.

****

Sitting on the table was a masterpiece. Two quarter pound patties, medium rare, lay nestled between two toasted slices of onion bread. The sandwich also contained lettuce, tomatoes, onions, spicy habanero sauce, Swiss cheese, jalapenos and bacon; lots of bacon. The French fries were so dense that you couldn't see any of the plate holding the special.

Across the table was the other work of art. Two half pound patties, medium, was wedged between two slices of toasted rye. Its other compliments included mushrooms, sauerkraut, Thousand Island dressing, Havarti cheese, pickles and grilled onions, lots of grilled onions. Once again, you could not see the bottom of the plate for this setting had a lot of onion rings.

Dean looked up from his bacon special and looked at Curt's plate. They had to use a long pick to hold the sandwich together and even that didn't help it from tilting toward the right.

"How in the world are you going to get that in your mouth?"

Curt smiled and grabbed the sandwich with both hands and lifted it off of the plate. "I'm just going to cram it in. Who gives a shit how much falls off onto the plate?"

Dean started to pick up his own, which also needed two hands to hold. "The real trick is to set it down after a couple of bites and then picking it up again."

Curt coyly smiled back, "Who said I was going to put it down?"

Dean nodded toward his plate, "but how are you going to enjoy the rings?"

Curt bobbed his head down toward the plate and picked up a couple of rings with his teeth. He started laughing as he started to eat them.

Dean started laughing and took a bite of his sandwich. The mix of bacon, jalapenos and meat hit him all at once, and he sighed in satisfaction. Once he swallowed his first bite, he looked up at Curt. "I know what's wrong with Brad."

Curt, after swallowing his mouth full of onion rings, squinted his eyes. "Oh yeah," he exclaimed, "What the fuck was his problem?" He then took the first bite of his sandwich.

"This Saturday is the fifth anniversary of his wife's death."

Curt's chewing slowed down, and he got a real concerned look on his face. He groaned a response because he couldn't open his mouth to say anything. Dean took another bite of his sandwich, and for the moment, the table was free from talk. When Curt swallowed, he cleared his throat. "I know the man loved his wife dearly, but if he lets it bother him this way, he's going to have a stroke one of these days." Curt took another bite and started chewing.

"Seriously?" Dean said in surprise, "Brad's the calmest individual I know. In fact, he should let his feeling's flow once in a while because keeping it bottled up could give him a stroke." Dean held onto his sandwich with his left hand and picked up his beer with his right and took a drink.

Curt swallowed again, "Either way, the shit's not right. I'm glad he's going to Seattle this weekend; he needs to get away from this fucked up place."

Dean nodded in agreement. "Oh, by the way, what are your plans for tomorrow?"

Curt swallowed again, "I'm skipping the rest of the week. I don't really have anything required of me for the rest of the year. Those bullshit extra courses can just blow me."

"Good," Dean answered. His mind started to drift toward the weekend coming up again and his time with Lynette. "Could you do me a favor?" Curt waved his hands for the question. "Follow me to the car dealer so I can drop off the truck to get repaired? I'll need a ride home."

"No problem. What time did you want to drop it?"

"About eight o'clock. That way I can start packing and getting ready for Friday. And if things go right, the transmission will be in tomorrow morning, and the truck will be done by Friday."

"What if it's not? I take it Lynette would be driving to the cabin?" Curt asked taking another bite.

"Yes, if things don't go right. Either way we are getting away from it all and neither one of us are taking our phones. I'm going to be totally non reachable." Dean took another bite of his sandwich. "We both will."

"Does she work tomorrow?"

After swallowing, Dean answered, "Yes, she plans to open and then get off at four." He took a couple of French fries and put them in his mouth. The Cajun seasoning on them sizzled his taste buds. "What are you going to do the rest of the week?"

Curt bobbed for another onion ring. "I'm going to the Amateur night at Marvin's tomorrow night and from there, who gives a rat's ass." Just then, half of Curt's sandwich fell out from between the bread and splatted all over his onion rings.

"I didn't know that you ordered a salad!" Dean laughed, "Do you need a fork and a bib?"

"No, shithead, but I do need a straw for my beer. I'm not setting this fucker down."

Day 29, Wednesday May 10th, 2000, 9:22 p.m.

Hello, Brad here. Well, it didn't take me long to get the diary, in fact I had to use my keys because the boys were still out probably feeding their faces. I double checked everything with DD, and he is shut down. The 380 is purring like a kitten and everything else seems to be keen.

I'm back at home now, and on my second glass of wine. I plan to hit the sack in the next few minutes. Tomorrow I'll meet Robert for lunch and let him know about our little secret. By the sound of the way the boys were talking, I wouldn't doubt that they too will take off from the rest of the week. Well, they deserved it.

It's now down to the wire and the horses are ready to take the rails. I can't wait for this weekend. My flight leaves at 7:30 a.m. Friday morning, and I'm the Eager Beaver.

Goodnight.

Close: 9:35 p.m.

Lynette hung her keys on the hook just inside the apartment door and she walked toward the kitchen table. Kim slowly, walked in from behind her, shutting the door and scuffling her feet across the wood floor. Lynette set her purse upon the kitchen counter and grabbed one of the table chairs and pulled it out.

"Sit down, please," she said gesturing to her sister to sit at the chair across from her. Kim slowly walked over and pulled out the chair and sat down.

Lynette sat down and pulled the chair up toward the table. "I want you to listen to me really well, and don't interrupt me, understand?"

Kim nodded her head.

"I love Dean very much, and soon we will be married and living together, WITHOUT YOU."

The words hit Kim hard, and she flinched.

"You need to get a life of your own. You need to stop feeding off of me and get a job. I'm no longer going to pamper you.

I have a future, and it's with Dean. You will still be my sister, but not my roommate, understand?"

Kim nodded again.

"I don't want to hear you whining about anything anymore. You need to start getting yourself together and building YOUR future." Lynette sighed and leaned back in the chair, "I'm giving you to the end of June to be out of this apartment."

Kim's eyes widened, "But how…"

"Kim," Lynette said raising her voice, "you will do it. If you can't, then I'll help you move to the nearest homeless shelter."

Tears started to run down Kim's cheeks.

"I cannot go on living this way," Lynette emphasized. "I want my life to be spent with Dean. You and I are far beyond the time of being young children. You MUST find a job and start YOUR OWN life. Do I make myself clear?"

"Yes," Kim said through her tears.

"I'll bring the newspaper home every day from work so that you can look at the Want Ads, I'll even help you find a job and a place. I'll even go as far as putting the deposit down for you, but YOU MUST be out by the end of June."

Kim nodded her head.

"Now, I'm going to take a shower and get to bed. I've got to open the store tomorrow morning and pack when I get home." Lynette stood up and slid the chair back under the table. "I'll bring the first paper home with me tomorrow, until then, just get some sleep and start thinking about what you want to do." She walked over toward her sister and then kissed her on the forehead. "Goodnight," Lynette said as she walked toward her bedroom and shut the door behind her.

Kim sat at the table for the next two hours.

Thursday

Hello, Brad here. Woke up this morning first with the smell of coffee from the automatic and boy did it taste good going down. After a couple of sips, the phone rang and it was Dean telling me that they were going to take his truck over to the dealer when it opened. I asked if he needed any help, but he said that Curt was taking the rest of the week off as well and things were taken care of. Those two gents did a lot of work on this project, however; Curt not as much since we brought him in late, but they really used the elbow grease to make it a success.

After the first cup of coffee was gone, Robert called me and said that he had handed his report in. He said that he was so excited about meeting with me that he stayed up last night until it was done. We plan to meet at Sabastian's Italian Restaurant at noon. Sebastian's is a great place with private booths. I don't want anyone else to hear what I'm going to tell him.

Now all that is left is to fill up another cup of coffee and finish packing for tomorrow morning.

Later, Gater.

Close: 7:55 p.m.

They both exited their cars and without a word between them, they entered the building.

Inside were several cars on the show room floor; two trucks, a minivan, two family cars and one convertible sports car. Facing the front doors was a large counter that had a man sitting on a chair behind it. Above him was a large banner that said, "Let us put you in the ride of your life." Both boys saw it at the same time, and Curt laughed.

"Got that shit right, ride of your life, more like fuck of your life."

Dean put his hand on Curt's shoulder, "Just let me handle this, will you?"

177

Curt nodded and pointed to the sports car over toward the right, "I'll just piss the time away over there."

"Thanks," Dean said as he approached the counter. The man behind it was fully engulfed into the morning newspaper and didn't see him walk up. Dean had to clear his throat to get his attention.

"Oh sorry," said the fat man as he quickly tried to fold the paper up and move it out of his way, "can I help you?"

"Yes, my name is Dean Mitchell and I'm here to drop my truck off to get the new transmission installed."

"Dean Mitchell? Let me call the maintenance bay and find out what door you need to take it to." The man picked up the phone and pushed a button.

On the other side of the room, Curt was deeply looking over the sports car. It was bright yellow, was a manual and by the look of the speedometer could top 160. As he had his head deep into the front seat, another man approached.

"Nice set a wheel's, isn't she?" he asked as he put his arm over the top of the hood.

"Sure, if you like the color piss yellow, do you give test drives?"

The salesman got an alarmed look on his face, "not this car, but we have several others in the lot to test drive."

"No, I'd rather test drive this car," Curt said as he mimicked the salesman by putting his arm up on the opposite side of the top. "I see the keys are already in the ignition, so let's take it for a spin, Sparky!"

"You just don't take a hundred-thousand-dollar car for a 'Spin', young man." The man sounded irritated.

Curt was about to let go with all kinds of stuff but yelling from the front desk caught his attention. It was Dean yelling. As he walked closer, he could hear the words clearer;

"What do you mean it's not here yet?" Dean yelled again. "I was told that it was going to be here this morning?"

The fat man was now standing up and holding both hands in the air. "Calm down sir, there was a problem with the delivery truck, and it will not arrive until later this evening. Sorry to upset you."

That's when Curt came around the corner, "Upset?" Curt yelled as he leaned over the counter into the man's face, "You don't know what upset is dickhead. Why don't you fuck shits get your heads out of your asses and learn how to be customer fucking focused!"

Dean just backed up and let the pit bull loose.

"Ride of your life?" Curt said pointing at the sign, "More like 'Bend the fuck over so we can all dick you in the ass and watch you bleed,' ride." His ranting has drawn the attention of many other employees, and they were all walking over to see the commotion. One of them dressed in a three pieced suit approached them directly.

"Sir," he said calmly, "please calm down, other customers are in the building. If you could please come to my office..."

"Who gives a fuck about the other customers," Curt threw out, "You don't give a shit about them anyway!"

"Sir, if you do not stop," the manager said, "I'll be forced to call the police."

Oh no, Dean thought, there it was, the one word that always set Curt over the edge. Police.

Curt started pointing his finger in the guy's face, "Go ahead, fucker, call the police. Then when the media arrives because of the outburst, I'll inform them of everything that this shit in the hole does to people. Not only will I tell them about the fucked-up way you do business, but I'll also tell them about how you claim you have security cameras watching their cars. I know for a fact that you don't have shit. The cameras are empty shells and you don't even have a system for them to run to."

The manager got a real worried look on his face, and Dean started to step forward toward Curt. He figured that it was time to leave but was also happy that he got all of this off of his chest; even though it was through Curt. It also amazed him how Curt knew about the security system. It didn't really surprise him because Curt's business depended on it, but it was a good touch.

"Sir," Dean said interrupting, "sorry for my friend's outburst, but it's my truck that needs serviced. I was hoping to get it fixed by tomorrow."

"It's your truck?" The manager asked as he pointed at Dean, "So why is..."

"Just let it go, "Dean said. "When should I drop the truck off tomorrow?"

"You can leave it here tonight if..."

Both Curt and Dean shook their heads no. "I think it would be safer at my home for now," Dean said.

"Tomorrow morning would be fine," the manager said with a sigh. The incident left him exhausted and huge perspiration stains under his armpits.

"Let's go," Dean said to Curt as he grabbed his arm.

Curt turned and then looked back at the manager, "Better get some deodorant that works, shit for brains." The manager looked down at his shirt and when he looked back up; both boys had already exited.

****

Brad and Robert had already been at the restaurant for about thirty minutes when the waiter walked up with their meals. Each of the men had already drunk one beer and enjoyed the bread sticks that the place offered. At first, Robert was very jumpy about hearing the news that Brad had to offer, but Brad said he wasn't going to say anything until they finished eating.

The entrées looked delicious as usual. Brad had ordered the spinach lasagna and Robert had the House spaghetti special. The spaghetti had four large sausage meatballs on it and lots of parmesan cheese. Brad's lasagna was at least four inches high and had lots of cheese running out from between the layers. Each dish was served on an oval plate that curved up to hold all the sauce on it. One true thing about Sebastian's was that none of their entrées were dry; everything was just drenched in sauce.

The two men each lifted their forks and hesitated.

"I never really know where to start," Brad said. "Do I start a little bit on the side or do I just cut that beast in half?"

"Same here," Robert added, "Do I go for the meatball or the noodles drenched in sauce?"

Both men just dove into their plates without another word. They let out sighs of acknowledging the taste was fabulous. Even when the waiter returned to ask them how everything was, both men had their mouths full and couldn't answer. Robert just pointed his finger at the two closely empty beers and then held up two fingers. The waiter nodded and left them to their enjoyment and went toward the bar to get another round.

Brad swallowed, "It has been a while since I've been here, and I forgot how good this place is."

"Well, with the whole family running the place, and being from Italy, what else do you expect?" Robert said as he watched Brad take another bite. He didn't bother to take one for himself because he froze into a stare at Brad across the table.

Brad looked up and saw his status, "What?"

"I'm not waiting anymore...tell me now or you're going to get spaghetti all over you!"

Brad put down his fork, grabbed his napkin and wiped his mouth. "I don't know if I should. I wouldn't want you to blow a noodle out of your nose."

The comment got Robert thinking about a time that happened years ago. "You mean like that time you had me laugh so hard that I shot milk out of my nose?"

Brad started laughing, "Yeah, like that. In fact, I almost paid for that because I was sitting across the table from you at the time. I dodged it pretty good that day."

"Well, you're not going to be so lucky today," Robert said as picked up one of the meat balls, "If you don't start now, you're going to wear this."

Brad leaned back and smiled, "Ok, but first put down the weapon and relax."

Robert complied. Brad reached over and took another sip of his beer and leaned forward. "Do you remember on Tuesday when

Dean Mitchell came to your office and delivered my invitation to you?"

Robert ruffled his brow and took a sip of his beer. "Yeah."

Just then the waiter returned with two fresh drafts and set them down on the table. "Is everything still ok, gentlemen?"

Both men turned and nodded.

"Enjoy the rest of your meal then and I'll return when you're finished." The waiter turned and left them alone again.

Robert turned his head back to Brad and waved his hand, "So what about Mitchell?"

"That wasn't Mitchell," Brad smiled, "it was a robot."

Robert's face froze. Then his left eyebrow raised, and he slowly got a smile on his face, "You're funny, Brad. Next, you're going to tell me that the entire board is zombies, right?"

"No, I'm serious Robert. I started the project about six months ago with Mitchell, and we have been test running it all this week. That's why I'm going to that conference in Seattle this weekend to present the experiment."

Robert still had the look on his face that he was been fooled. "You're pulling my leg, old man. How could that be Mitchell when I saw him walk into the office with no wires?"

Brad lifted up his briefcase from the floor and opened it on his booth seat next to him. He pulled out his report and the diary and laid them on the table. "It's all right here. The speech I'm planning to present, and the diary that we kept during the whole process. Feel free to look it over." Brad took another bite of his lasagna as Robert opened the diary book.

Time passed and Robert got totally lost in the diary and wasn't even eating. Brad kept shoveling it in. By the time Brad's lasagna was almost gone, Robert had a pretty good look at the report. He shut the book and looked back up toward Brad with a wide-eyed look that only a kid in a candy store could give.

"When can I see it?"

"Monday night, "Brad said wiping his mouth again. "That's what the invitations were for."

Robert looked dazed, "Who's all is coming?"

"I invited the entire school board, a few of the professors, Dean Mitchell, of course, and Curt Johnson."

"Johnson? Was he involved in it too?" Robert questioned as he continued into his meal.

"He was toward the last end of it, in fact, he was like the chaperone for the week."

"You know," Robert said as he wiped his mouth and took a sip of his beer, "you always said that someday you were going to tell me how and why you're so attached to that kid. I know he's a genius and a major problem, but what in heaven's name made you become so close?"

Brad sighed and took a long sip of his beer, "I know that I should have told you years ago and maybe you too would understand. It's a long story."

"I'm done for the day, and from what you said, so are you." Robert leaned across the table, "I'm all ears."

Brad smiled, "After we finish eating, we'll move to the bar."

"Agreed," Robert answered.

****

The entire day at the Book Nook had been exhausting. The local schools had what they called an 'Inservice' day and the kids had the day off. The kid's area was trashed, the magazine area was in shambles, and everyone needed help finding what they were looking for. The Café had its usual long line, but the employees at that spot had no trouble keeping up with the demands. The Head Cashiers were in full focus at the registers, and the sales floor employees looked like they had roller skates on. With all of this going on, Lynette felt rather relaxed knowing that she would have the next three days off.

She was at the customer service desk when she saw Dean walk in. He had a spring in his step and was heading straight toward her. The look on his face looked happy but, in a way, frustrated as well. She leaned over the counter as he approached, and she started to glow with anticipation to hear his voice again.

183

"Good morning, Sunshine," he said as he stopped at the counter, "and how's your day going?"

"You tell me," She answered as she waved her right hand for him to follow it and see the crowd to the right.

"Busy. Huh?"

"That's an understatement," she smiled. She started looking around behind him in curiosity, "Where's Curt?"

"I think he's heading home right now, why?"

"Didn't he drive you here?"

"No, I've got the truck. I was heading home from the dealer and swung by here on the way home."

"So, it's fixed then," She asked while hoping for the best. Then she saw his happy face turn to sourness. She tilted her head and gave him a concerned look. "What happened?"

"No, it's not fixed," he said angrily. "The part didn't come in. It will not be in till tomorrow, which means the truck will not be done till at the least Monday. I was mad at first, but when Curt stepped in, I felt a lot better."

Lynette got one of those, 'I know what you're talking about' looks. "Did he punch anyone?"

"No, but I bet anything that the manager had to change his pants, if you know what I mean."

Lynette laughed, "So why are you risking damaging the truck more by swinging over this way?"

"Just verifying a few things," he said, "like, you're still getting off at four, right?"

"Yes, everything is taken care of, and Dawn has it all under control."

"And, are you packed and ready to go?"

"All I have left is my toiletries."

Dean took a big sigh and let it out through the large grin on his face, "Then let's go after you get off."

Lynette's face first crinkled under the thought of jumping at it so fast but after thinking about it, started to smile back. "And your reasoning on this, Mitchell?"

"First of all," he said as he leaned both elbows on the counter, "we won't have to get up so early tomorrow to leave; second, we could sleep in tomorrow morning and third; I want to be with you so badly."

Lynette stared into his deep blue eyes and her face started to glow. "I get off at four, get to my house by four thirty, put my things into the car and can be at your place by five thirty."

"Sounds like a plan," Dean said standing back up straight, "I'll hold you to five thirty."

"I'll be there," she said in a whisper, "just don't forget the body oil."

Dean's smile almost cracked his face. He winked at her and turned and left.

Lynette's mind was at ease. This weekend was going to be one of the best weekends ever.

****

Curt just pulled up to his trailer, parked the Jeep right in front of the porch, and jogged up the steps to the security console on the wall. After entering his code, the door clicked, and he pushed it open. As soon as he stepped in, his mind was in motion. First, he ran over to check the answering machine in the office and saw that the light was blinking. He had messages. He pushed the play button and continued to roam the house for what he needed. He had wired speakers throughout the house attached to the answering machine so that he could hear it anywhere he moved.

BEEP: "Hello, Curt, this is Stacey. We met two weeks ago at the Grocery store. I wonder if you'd like to do something tonight. Please call me. I know you got the number, Bye!"

"Fat chance," Curt talked to the air around him as he entered the kitchen, "The only thing that needs to go near your fucking mouth is a thick piece of duct tape."

BEEP: "Hello, my name is John Whitrock; I'm the owner of Carson City Salvage yard, and I've been told that you're the person to talk to about a security system. I would like to get together with you sometime and discuss a system that will cover approximately fifteen acres."

"Oh, fuck me," Curt yelled as he starts rummaging through a pile on the kitchen table looking for a pen or pencil.

"I will also need an update on my computer system for the business. I need a system that can categorize and inventory everything on the lot. My number is 555-1138. If I'm not there please leave a message. I'm looking forward to meet you."

Curt pulls a pen out of the pile and flips over a piece of paper on the table. "555-1138, John Whitrock, got it." After writing down the message, he took the piece of paper and put it halfway into one of the overhead cabinet doors in the kitchen. The paper stuck out of the bottom of the door; a system he used to identify priority tasks.

BEEP: "Hey good looking, it's Jambalaya. I'm looking forward to seeing you tonight. I've got good news; Dragonfly is going to join us at the table. I hope you'll be here because we missed you last week. See you soon!"

Curt got a smile on his face as he opened the refrigerator and pulled out a cold beer, "oh, I'll be there, sweet ass, don't want to miss another one." He twisted open the bottle and then threw the cap somewhere near the garbage can in the corner. The triple clinking told him he missed the can but continued to walk into the living room.

BEEP: "Hello, big brother, its Heartache, looking forward to seeing you tonight. It sounds like most of the girls are going to be here. Even Barbie says she's going to sit in. Missed you last week, don't be late."

Curt leaned over toward a large round marble clock that he had on the wall, "I won't be, little lady." He grabbed the left side of the clock and swung it open to the right like a cabinet door. Behind it, on the wall was a safe. He started turning the dial.

BEEP: "Don't ditch out on us again, Hon, you better be there tonight."

The accent told Curt right away that it was Sweet Wine. He shook his head back and forth thinking about how much of an impact he had on that place. Sure, he had fucked a few of them, but next to Dean, Lynette, and Brad, the dancers were really the only other people he cared about. He knew all about their lives and problems. He had seen several come and go, but tonight is their night out, so to speak. They were like the sisters he never had. He shook his head again, thinking how sick it would be to fuck your own sister.

The click on the wall told him that the safe opened. He grabbed the handle, lifted it up, and opened the door. Several shelves were within it and he reached into the top shelf and pulled out a stack of bills. "I guess about a thousand should do it for tonight. That should take care of the ladies' thirst." He counted through what he needed and put what was left of the stack back into the safe. He shut the door, pulled the handle down, spun the knob, and closed the clock back into place.

BEEP: "Hey, Baby, It's Carmel. You better be there tonight, bitch, I'm looking at having a good time. Don't let me down."

Curt walked over and flopped down on the couch with his beer. He pulled out his wallet from his back right pocket and put the money inside it. After a couple of swigs from the bottle, he realized that there were no more messages. That's when he started glancing around at the room he was in and took note of its condition.

"What a fucking mess. I need to hire me some bitch to do all my cleaning." He started glancing around the room and saw the picture of Dean and Lynette standing in front of Dean's truck, which was on the end table. That was the day that he bought it. The morning fiasco returned to his mind again, "Fucking assholes," he yelled as he downed the rest of the bottle. He was getting ready to throw the bottle toward the garbage can when a large box in the corner caught his eye.

"Yeah," he said with a smile, "Fucking yeah!"

****

The cold draft, in the frosted mug, felt good in his hands as Brad sat at the bar waiting for Robert to come back from the bathroom. The old bar top had shown its age, and the chair was as comfortable as the first time he ever sat in the place years ago. The entire bar's countertop used to be at a bar in Chicago, a place called, "Little Chicago," in the northern area. It had seen its time throughout history first as a pub, then changed to a drug store during the prohibition and then back to a bar after. When the place had a fire in the 1950's, the only thing that remained was the countertop. It sat unused for several years until it was auctioned off and moved to Springfield and was made a permanent fixture here ever since. It was made of marble, and still had its luster. It had to be at least thirty feet long and he was told that the brass foot rail on the front was original as well. The thought of how much it weighed crossed Brad's mind and added the wonder of how they transported it.

"Sorry, that took so long, "Robert said as he sat in the bar stool to Brad's left, "Sometime garlic hits me fast. What were you thinking about, you looked lost?"

Brad rapped his fist on the bar top, "This old thing. It's amazing how good it looks after what it's been through."

Robert took a sip from his beer, "Hopefully I'll look this solid when I get that old." He leaned in close toward Brad, so that no one else could hear him, "I can't wait to see this DD. You're going to drive me nuts making me wait until Monday night."

Brad sniffed in a short laugh, "If it makes you feel any better, I'll let you come in a couple hours before everyone else to get your paws on it."

Robert lifted up his glass in a salute, "why thank you sir, you are a gentleman and a scholar. Now tell me about Curt."

Brad nodded his head and took another sip of his beer. "I met Curt about seven years ago at the State Tournament for science that was being held at McKinley Hall. Dean Mitchell was there as well whom I met the prior year at the same tournament. Dean won that year, by the way, and tickled my fancy ever since."

"As I started a quick walk through the area, in which I do before I initially start the grinding of the wheel, I noticed a table over by the wall that looked like someone had piled a bunch of garbage on it. Disregarding it as just that, I proceeded to the end of the room and met with the other Judges in the back kitchen. You know the spot; it's the room where we usually hold the annual Honors banquet."

Robert nodded his head acknowledging the place.

"About halfway through the day, I reached that garbage pile and saw that it was one of the entries. There standing at the table was this kid, about 19 or 20 at the time, blue eyed and blond with a calm attitude with himself. I asked his name and he told me Curt Johnson and then asked him what it was. He told me that it was a generator."

"Now at first, I had to hold back a chuckle because this thing looked like it was dragged down the strip. It consisted of dented up cans of all sizes, copper wire, tin foil, coat hangers and I think I even saw a muffler in it. I tell you, it looked like he had just raided the local bone yard for scrap. It had several light bulbs all over, which was the only thing that didn't look broken, and a bar that ran around the top made of what looked to me of a shower curtain rod."

"I asked him to turn it on and the only thing he said was that I had to wait for it. Now my thoughts were on complete and utter disgust on how this kid even made it in here."

Brad stopped long enough to take another drink of his beer. He saw that he had Robert's full attention and continued.

"Now this whole show started about five in the evening so by the time I got to him it was about seven thirty, and it started to get dark outside. Also, to add to the darkness, we had a storm front coming in, and we were under a Thunderstorm Watch until about midnight."

"I was about to the end of the room when the storm hit. That watch had quickly been upgraded to a warning, and we were in the dead center of it. You could hear the wind and the rain hitting the side of the building, and it was loud. All of the Judges

189

gathered together to discuss whether we should postpone the event and get the kids to safety. That's when the power blew out."

"At first it was pretty dark in the room and then the emergency lights kicked on. Then with further observation, we noticed that it wasn't the emergency lights. Curt's 'generator' was in full swing and lighting up the entire other half of the building. Several of the other contestants rushed to see the contraption, and soon the judges followed. When I got there, he saw us approaching and smiled. His first words were, 'I told you to wait'. He explained to the judges how it worked, and why he requested a wall table. The night before, he had climbed up on the roof of McKinley Hall and put up a lightning rod. He had it wired down the side and in through the window that was right next to the table. I followed his description and did see the wire running up the wall and out."

"Needless to say, he won that year. His ingenuity was beyond anything that I encountered, and I was quite impressed." The bartender walked up to the two gentlemen and noticed that both their drinks where almost gone, "Another round, Gentlemen?"

"Please," Robert said, "and put this on my tab."

The bartender nodded and placed two fresh napkins in front of each of them. "Be right back," he said as he walked away.

Brad downed what remained in his glass and continued. "Now after this day was all said and done, I was dreading going outside. I had parked at the end of the lot, like I always do and outside was a solid downpour. Me being the 'I believe it when I see it guy', didn't bring an umbrella. I was going to get soaked."

The bartender walked over with two fresh drafts and set them down on the napkins and walked away again. Robert finished the older drink and scooted the fresh one to the front.

"I open the door to a powerful rain that I couldn't even see past half of the lot. I stood under the awning trying to get the guts enough to dash across the lot and that's when I noticed this small tent toward the right of the yard. Well, it wasn't really a tent, but a tarp that had been thrown over an object. It had a bicycle perched up against it and I saw this boy tying up the bike and crawling under the tarp. It was Curt Johnson. I made my way over to the tarp and lifted it up to find his machine sitting on a small flatbed carrier and him tucked under the trailer. I asked him if he was ok and if he needed a ride home in which he proceeded to answer, "What home?"

"We ended up putting his machine in the wagon and going to the Golden Egg to get something to eat. He insisted on buying his own meal, because in his words, he didn't want to owe anybody favors. He seemed like a very nice young man."

"Nice?" Robert said with a surprised look on his face. "He says things that would make a Sailor blush."

"I know," Brad said taking the first drink from his fresh draft. "His cockiness wasn't into full bloom at that time, but his ingredients for the pudding were."

"So, what are the ingredients?"

Brad took a larger gulp of his beer. "Curt Dwayne Johnson was born April 14th, 1975. And if you tell him I told you his middle name, I'll Jap slap you. There are only about four people that know it."

Robert nodded.

Brad let out another sigh, "His Mother died when he was about two years old which left him in the custody of his alcoholic father. His father frequently beat him. His favorite spot to slap him was the left side of his head which rendered his left eye partially blind. And once again very few people know that he is blind in that eye, so keep it to yourself. His father had an addiction to prostitutes whom he frequently brought to the house. Curt was given his own prostitute for his twelfth birthday, a present that his father told him that he would never forget. Due to the home being so uneasy, Curt had found other things outside the house to do. He secretly got a job at an electronics store, which his father didn't know about, and he quickly learned the trade."

"Other kids ignored him due to the fact of how he was so closed up. He ended graduating High school although he had missed so many classes. He once missed two weeks because his father had beaten him so severely that he couldn't even get out of bed. He became more and more dependent on himself and viewed

191

the entire world was against him. That's when he started taking control of his own life."

"First, he studied electronics at the library as much as he could. He became the best electronics repair guy at the shop and was saving up his money to open his own store. He became good friends with the son of the owner, who was about seven years older than Curt, and he trained Curt in Karate. "

"Then one night, in a major drunken state, his father realized that the old hands beating wasn't enough, so he picked up a crow bar. Curt's rage finally kicked in, and he had beaten his father so badly that he was taken to Memorial Hospital and stayed on Life support until he died three weeks later."

The story really had Robert in shock. His chin had dropped down and he was completely astounded at what he was hearing.

"Once again, nobody knows about this, so keep it under your hat."

"No problem." Robert answered, "What did the police do?"

"First, they were going to try to arrest him for attempted man slaughter but when the owner of the Electronics store stepped forward with information about his father and photographs to back them up, the charges were dropped."

"Why didn't the store owner turn his father in?"

"Curt wouldn't allow it."

"You would think that the school would or should have done something," Robert said in an agitated voice.

"His school really didn't care, which is sad. Schools need to be more aware of problems like that and have extra authority to get involved."

"I agree," Robert said.

"So, back to the story," Brad continued wetting his whistle with another sip, "That night in the rain was followed by him staying overnight at my house. Shirley took a shine to the boy right away, and weeks went by and his visits became more frequent and he loved doing chores and errands for her. It wasn't long after that that I gave him a tour of the college, and I could see the spark in his eye."

192

"How in the world did he get accepted there?"

"I had to pull a lot of strings; I even threatened to resign if they didn't accept him." Brad lifted his drink as if to toast, "it's a really great feeling when you know how much power you have to get things done."

Robert lifted his glass and tapped it into Brad's. "You got that straight, buddy."

They both took swigs.

"Now I can fully understand why he acts that way," Robert added. "It makes me look at him in a different point of view. Who was the store owner, by the way?"

Brad got a sad look on his face, "Do you remember Drestens?"

"Yes," Robert answered and then his face got a surprised look. "That was the place downtown that burned to the ground and took the lives of about four people, right?"

"Correct," Brad sighed. "The owner, his two sons and a firefighter all died in that disaster. That day, Curt lost the only people he truly trusted."

The bartender walked up again, "you two went through that serving quick. Care for another round?"

"One more," Brad said. "And put it on my tab."

The bartender nodded and walked off and Brad turned toward Robert. "After this drink, I've got to leave to finish packing for tomorrow."

"Then, this'll be the last one for the road," Robert said.

****

Dean looked at the duffle bags and suit cases that he had piled on the living room floor and slowly started to grin. Anticipation about this weekend was driving him crazy, and he still had three more hours before Lynette arrived to pick him up. He started to walk to the kitchen when the doorbell rang. He turned and approached the door and saw Curt's face through the glass, so he grabbed the knob and opened the door.

"Why didn't you open it?" Dean said then realized that Curt couldn't. He was carrying a large cardboard box.

"Because my arms are full, dick weed, open the screen door."

Dean reached the screen door and opened it and stood back so that Curt and his box could get by him. "What's in the box, boy?"

Curt walked it to the living room coffee table and laid it down upon it. "Revenge, redemption and satisfaction."

Dean walked over to peer into the box that Curt had started to open.

"It's all the fireworks I had left over from last year's Fourth. I figure we could head over to the dealership late tonight and put some sparkle up their ass, not to mention some fucking burn marks on all the cars." Curt pulled a large lighter out of his pocket and flipped the top up. A large flame emitted from its wick after his thumb flicked the switch.

"Ah, sounds fun, but..."

"But what" Curt interrupted, "Are your balls sucked up so far up your crotch that you're going to turn this offer down? It would be fucking great!"

"Oh, I don't doubt it will be, it's just that Lynette and I changed plans, and we are leaving to the cabin in about three hours."

"Well, fuck me," Curt yelled as he turned off the lighter and set it on the mantle above the fire place. "I was looking forward to this."

"Sorry, but you will probably have your hands full with something else tonight, anyway. Isn't it amateur night at Marvin's?"

"Oh, I'm already aware of that, I just thought I could bring along the winner with me tonight. I've never fucked anyone in a dealer's lot before."

"I'm sure you'll have plenty of opportunities in the future," Dean said as glanced into the box again, "and I'm sure you'll find a better use for these."

194

Curt nodded his head. "True, on both accounts."

"Well, if you can do me the favor of checking on things while I'm gone, I'd appreciate it."

"I always do," Curt answered. "I'm going to head out and get a bite to eat before I head to Marvin's to get a bite to eat."

"Later, man, take it easy," Dean said laughing as he watched Curt head out the door.

Day 30, Thursday May 11th, 2000, 4:22 p.m.

Hello, Brad here. Robert took the information about the robot like a kid in a candy store. He's dying to meet it and can't wait for Monday night. He was a bit surprised about the other story I told him, which I will not put its topic into this diary. It did give him a better understanding of why things are.

I plan to shut this down and get myself something to eat and then hit the hay. Everything is ready to go for tomorrow's flight and the only thing left to do is to tuck this journal into the brief case. Next time I write in this, I'll be in Seattle.

Good night.

Close: 4:27 p.m.

When Lynette entered her apartment, she was greeted by an overly excited sister. She first looked like she was going to wet her pants, but Lynette realized that she had something important to tell her.

"What are you all jumpy about?" Lynette said as she set her purse on the kitchen table.

"I might have a job!" Kim yelled in excitement.

Lynette's facial expression glowed, "That's great, Kim, where at?"

"You know that ice cream parlor around the corner; I have an interview Saturday afternoon."

Lynette grabbed her sister's neck, pulled her forward and kissed her forehead, "I'm so proud of you!"

Kim walked over and sat down on the couch, "I might have to buy my own uniforms, though."

"Don't you worry about that, I'll take care of it when you get the job, my way of celebrating your victory."

Kim smiled back, "So, let's go celebrate out to eat somewhere."

"Now?" Lynette questioned her, "You don't even have the job yet, slow down. Besides, Dean and I are leaving for the cabin right now. I've just got to get a couple of more things and I'm ready to go."

Kim started to panic. "But, what do I do for an interview? What should I wear? What if…"

"You'll be fine, Kim. If you need to, I've got a book in my room called 'Get that Job'. You're welcome to use it."

Kim looked toward the hallway leading toward the bedrooms, "Okay."

Lynette went to her purse and pulled out her wallet. She pulled a few bills out of it then walked the money over to her sister. "Here's about sixty dollars in case you need it." She said handing the money to Kim. After Kim took it from her hands, Lynette continued. "Use it sparingly. There is plenty of food in the fridge, but if the interview goes well, get yourself something good for dinner to celebrate."

"That sounds good," Kim answered, "and after the interview, I'll call you with the results."

"Honey," Lynette said, "you know that neither Dean nor I take our phones with us to the cabin. It's a complete dead zone in the area and besides, we want to get away from it all."

Kim nodded her head in acceptance.

"I'll hear the good news when I return on Sunday," she said smiling at Kim.

"And good news it will be," Kim added.

Lynette smiled again and walked to her bedroom to complete her packing.

****

196

Curt had picked up two cheeseburgers through a fast-food drive through and already had them gone as he pulled into the parking lot of Marvin's. He wanted to bring the motorcycle but didn't want to drive all the way back to the trailer across town and return. Besides, it was supposed to rain tonight, and he didn't want to chance it. He knew that the motorcycle was in his side shed, locked up, and the alarm was on. He had no idea if he would return home tonight or possibly, hopefully end up somewhere else. He parked the Jeep behind the building, a spot that was reserved for him, locked it up and entered through the back entrance.

The music was already pounding the walls when he entered and he waved to the staff as he passed through the kitchen. When he walked up to the service door and peered out, he could see that the table he sat at on Thursdays was full, except one empty seat for him. He opened the door and walked toward it.

Getting closer he could see the women around the table, seven in all. From left to right he saw; Paradise, Jambalaya, Heartache, Carmel, Barbie, Dragonfly and Sweet Wine. The empty seat was between Jambalaya and Heartache. He knew all of their real names but for safety purposes, he refrained from using them while they were at the establishment. Tonight, was the dancers' night off, like every Thursday, and they all gathered to enjoy each other's company without having to impress anyone. They did have another day off during the week but not all at the same time like tonight. They also enjoyed seeing other talent in the area and possibly get ideas for their own act. Marvin, himself, ran the Talent night, so he didn't need any of the ladies. This night was what they called their ladies night out.

As Curt approached, they all recognized him, smiled, and waved him over. Jambalaya stood up and grabbed the empty chair next to her.

"Here's your seat, sweetie, I've already told them to bring your drink when you arrive,"

"Ladies," Curt said as he sat down, "I'm really looking forward to this evening. It's been a long-stressed week."

"Well, forget your week," said Carmel, "and kick off your shoes and relax."

"Oh, I plan to," Curt said. Then he saw Dragonfly looking at him, and he nodded a hello at her. She smiled back.

"I'm ready to see what's so great about ladies' night out," Dragonfly stated.

"Oh, Honey," Paradise said, "Every Thursday is a different tale, you'll see."

The waiter walked up and placed a drink in front of Curt. Curt then looked side to side around the table, "Ok, Ladies, order the fuck up!"

The waiter was bombarded with drink requests.

****

Dean heard the rumble of a car in the drive and quickly jumped up from the couch. He ran over toward the front window and pulled open the corner of the curtain just enough so that he could peak outside. He watched as Lynette opened her door, stepped out and then leaned in to fumble with something in the front seat. He loved watching her. She was so prim and proper that she looked elegant. She then shut the door and started walking toward the front entry way. Her walk was slow and dainty like she had been trained to balance books on her head as she moved. Her body was very erect and her stride flawless. Even in jeans she looked gorgeous. Dean's attention to her made him warm up inside about how much he really loved her. His life was now relaxed and fulfilled because of this lady and he looked forward to every day to come. The wedding would make it complete.

He pulled away from the window and jumped in front of the door as she opened it.

"Hello, gorgeous!" he yelled as he wrapped his arms around her.

She hugged him back, "You were watching me out the window again, weren't you?"

He leaned back but still held onto her shoulders, "Of course I was. I love watching you walk, it's like its own art form."

She smiled, "before we leave, I have to use the bathroom. The trunks unlocked and you can load up your stuff while I pee."

"I'm on it," Dean said as he turned and grabbed the duffle bag and case off of the floor. Lynette walked down the hall and into the bathroom. Dean pushed open the screen door with the case and stepped out onto the porch. He started whistling as he walked to the rear of the car and set the stuff on the ground behind it. He pushed the button on the trunk and the lid flipped open showing stuff that she had already put inside. There were her bags, a cooler and a rolled-up blanket. He started moving around the contents to fit his stuff in when he noticed that the blanket was a little heavy. He unrolled it to find two bottles of wine.
'Well, well, well what do we have here?" he said softly out to himself, "a bottle of champagne and a bottle of rose'. Looks like it's going to be a good weekend."

He heard her walking out through the screen door and quickly wrapped the bottles back up and slid them to the side. He didn't want to ruin her surprise.

"What are you doing back there," she questioned as she walked up to him.

"Just scooting things around to make them fit better," he answered.

"Well, you can always through that duffle bag in the back seat. There is enough room next to the cooler." Dean walked with the duffle to the back car door and opened it and saw it was the wrong side. The cooler was taking up the seat space. He shut the door and walked around to the other side, opened that door, and then tossed in the bag.

"Ok, I've got one more thing to get, and I'll be ready," Dean said as he walked toward the house.

"I'll be waiting, "she said as she shut the trunk and walked to the driver's side door.

Dean stepped in and did one more walk through the house. The kitchen appliances where all shut off, the back door was locked and most importantly, the basement door shut.   He hurried back out the front door, locking the door knob, then the dead bolt. He turned and saw that Lynette was already in the passenger seat waiting for him. She didn't like to drive long drives and he did, besides, she would always fall asleep.

He returned to the car, opened the driver's side, and seated himself inside. After fastening his seatbelt and shutting the door, he let out a long sigh.

"Ok, where's your phone?" he asked.

"Setting on my kitchen cabinet," she answered. "And where's yours?"

"On the island in my kitchen," he responded.

"Then," she said with a smile, "we are ready to go."

Dean put the car in reverse and backed out of the driveway.

****

Everyone at the table grimaced when the girl dancing on stage slipped off the pole and hit her head on the floor. Marvin immediately rushed out and helped her to her feet. Jambalaya even went up on stage to help her. The girl was nodding her head that she was ok and everyone clapped for her as she left the stage with Jambalaya's arm around her. Marvin walked up to the end of the stage with his microphone in his hand

"That is one tough little lady, but she seems fine. Just a little shaken, that's all." He started fumbling through a list he held in his hand and continued. "Once again, welcome to Amateur night, at Marvin's. I'm Marvin and tonight's winner can walk out with one hundred dollars. Then that winner will compete in our Quarterly Dance Off for the chance to win five hundred dollars." Whistles around the room showed favor to the announcement.

"Next up we have a lady who claims to be a mix of Fire and Ice. Ladies and Gentlemen, I give you, Misty."

Several whistles and claps drowned out the talk and the music that followed drowned out the claps. It was a country western song, and the tall brunette came out dressed in a cowboy outfit. She started waving her right arm around in the air and hunched down like she was riding a bull. She turned and reached down and pulled off her rip away jeans. Whistles commenced.

Curt wasn't paying too much attention to the dancer because he was in a deep conversation with Dragonfly. Throughout the night, as usual, people at their table would move around to different seats to talk to each other. Being so close to the stage, the only way to hear what the other was saying was to talk directly in the others ear. Dragonfly and Curt's conversation was in full gear.

"So, you did dancing for five years and with no boyfriend," Curt yelled in her ear, "That's a fucking record around here. With all the horny bastards in this town, they can't wait to show you off to their friend's face and brag about how far they can stick their dick down your throat."

Dragonfly laughed at the comment, "but they'd never tell their friends about how much I kicked their ass when they touched me wrong."

Curt started to laugh, "I like you girl, you got a big set off balls."

They both smiled and reached for their drinks and slugged them down to the bottom.

"Who needs another one?" Curt yelled out as he held up his empty glass. About four of the women at the table held up their hands and so did Jambalaya when she returned and sat at the table. It only took moments for the waiter to notice the empty glass in the air, and he was at the table to replenish.

The country song finished and the now naked lady bowed and walked off the stage. Marvin returned to the front of the stage.

"Just a reminder, draft beers are one dollar and imports are two. Don't forget to tip the waiters tonight; they are trying to keep up the pace." Marvin started to look at his sheet again. "For tonight's contest, the judges are our very own dancers sitting over here at table one." Marvin gestured toward their table. "We've already seen five dancers and we are about half way through tonight's performances. We have twelve contestants and it looks like some great competition."

"Get your fat ass off the stage and bring on the tits." Someone yelled from across the room. A lot of laughter ran around the room, but Marvin paid no attention to the outburst. Curt turned his head in the direction of the noise, just to get a sight of the unreasonable guest, but couldn't see through the smoke.

"In due time, wise ass," Marvin said which brought on more laughter. "When our sixth girl dances, there will be a thirty-minute break, and we will return to the action." He looked down at his notes again, "our next lady is root'n for attention, ladies and gentlemen I present, Rodeo."

Another country music song came on and a short girl with a lasso came twirling it onto stage.

Curt leaned over to Paradise on his right, "What the fuck is with all this county music shit? Bring on some rock and roll!"

Paradise nodded her head in agreement.

Dragonfly tapped Curt on his left shoulder and he leaned over to hear her. "What's with all this fucking county shit? I want some hard ass rock," Dragonfly said angrily.

Curt got a big grin on his face. This new girl was a good time looking for some fun. She was gutsy and somewhat crude as well. "Fucking eh," he replied back. This Dragonfly caught his eye when he saw her dance on Monday night. She could wiggle her ass pretty good too. He turned his head toward the stage in time to see the little dancer pull her top off and see her long nipples.

"Holy shit," Curt yelled, "those are some long ass nipples! Someone can get their eye poked out with one of them fuckers." His trance on her breasts was pretty intense when Marvin walked up behind him and tapped him on the shoulder.

"Hey, numb nuts," Marvin said with his low deep voice.

"Yeah," Curt answered without taking his eyes off the dancer, "What do you want, fat ass."

Marvin knelt down to Curt's level at the table. "Did you see who it was that yelled that out?"

"No, I couldn't see for all the smoke, why bother, his dicks just taking over the thinking."

"Well, I saw, and your comment couldn't be more right."
Marvin let out a sigh. "It's Andy."

Curt's head turned away from the dancer and he looked at
Marvin's face. "Do you need me to…?"

"No, not yet," Marvin said standing up, "but I'd thought I'd
give you a heads up about it."

"One wrong move and he's fucking toast." Curt said, his eyes
narrowing in anger.

Marvin patted Curt's shoulder and headed back to the stage.

Dragonfly leaned over toward Curt, "What was that all
about?"

"There's this guy in here that caused a lot of trouble in the
past. Not only with some friends of mine but he fucked up this
place twice. He gets so drunk that he'll start trying to either kick
someone's ass or gets too grabby with the dancers. I wasn't here
for either of the altercations but they did manage to get his ass out
the door."

"How much damage did the shit head do," Dragonfly asked.

"The first time he picked up a bar stool and threw it at the
mirror behind the bar. Shit scattered everywhere, several people
were cut and then three people jumped him. The fight was taken
out into the parking lot where he got in his car and left." Curt took
a drink of his beer, "the second one happened when he pushed
himself onto Barbie, and he fucking tore her dress off. The bastard
tried to get close, and she kneed him in the nuts. Once again, he
was pushed out into the parking lot and told to leave, but this was
after he had fucked up several people."

"Someone needs to fuck him up, it sounds like to me,"
Dragonfly said. "How long ago did this happen?"

"About two years ago. He's been out of town for a while.
He just returned last week. He's a big ass hole and thinks his size
intimidates people."

"Aren't you a little wary of messing with this guy?"

Curt got a real dumbfounded look on his face, "Fuck, no.
The big ones are a lot more fun to beat the shit out of because
there is more area to hit"

203

Just then the music stopped and the naked girl wrapped in her lasso bowed and left the stage.

"Any of these dancers looking good to anybody," Heartache yelled.

"Fuck no," Curt yelled back. "Get rid of this country shit."

Marvin walked back out on stage, "Now for our last girl of the first half, I bring you Storm." Marvin moved off and a heavy metal song started to fill the airway. Everyone at Curt's table screamed and started wiggling in their chairs with their arms in the air. It was a really loud song that started with the main guitar screeching out the notes.

"Hell yeah, this is more like it!" Curt yelled. The girls all yelled and moved their bodies to the tune. The tall blond came out wearing black leather and carrying a whip.

"Yeah, baby," Curt yelled, "Spank my ass!"

All the girls at the table started laughing.

Day 30, Thursday May 11th, 2000, 10:38 p.m.

Oops, I forgot one more thing before I hit the sack. There were a couple of extra parts that we had for DD that I'm going to take with me. There is a pair of ocular units, a hand that we had to replace and several left-over wires I plan to show as well. I had packed them into a separate suit case and will take that along with me as well. I hope security at the airport lets me on with this, if not, I'll have to settle with only the drawings.

Good night, again.

Close: 10:42 p.m.

The entry road to the cabin was at least a half a mile long and they had seen two deer run across their path on the way in. Other than the lights from the car, the moon was the only thing lighting the night. The grinding of the gravel under the tires brought on memories of past trips and the times they had together. It was funny how certain sounds and smells could bring the mind to other times. Even songs could flood you with the memory of a place or even an event. The song, 'We'll live on forever' always reminded

Dean about the first time he saw Lynette. It was playing on the Book Nook's speaker system, and he just sat down to order a coffee. Smells had the same effect as well. The smell of baked bread always reminded him of his mother. She loved to bake things; pies, cakes, and many types of bread. What triggers the mind is amazing.

As they pulled up to the cabin the lights from Lynette's car shined on the front door and a rabbit ran out of a bush and scurried away. Dean put the car in park but left the engine running.

"It's amazing how that old rundown cabin looks so inviting," Lynette said.

Dean sighed, "I'm looking forward to this weekend, in fact, I think this is going to be the best time we have ever had to date." Dean opened his door and stepped out, "I'll keep the car lights on until I flip on the power." Lynette nodded her head and stayed inside the car as Dean walked up to the front porch to a panel on the right side of the door. He opened up the panel and looked at the keyed alarm pad installed inside; courtesy of Curt. After he punched in the seven-digit code, the outside perimeter lights came on, and he walked back to the car.

"All ready to go. You can go in and get things turned on why I bring the rest of the stuff in."

"Not on your life, Mitchell." Lynette said with a dead stare, "I'm not walking in there alone again and running into another raccoon." Lynette crossed her arms. "You go in first."

Dean smiled, "Oh yeah, I forgot about that. I'll be right back. Then, you can get the stuff out."

Dean started walking toward the door as Lynette got out of the passenger seat and opened the back door. She pulled out Dean's duffle bag and started walking with it towards the porch.

When Dean opened the front door a really bad odor hit his nose. It smelled like something had died in the room. He turned and flipped on the light switch and the large chandelier over the family room lit. Nothing looked bad in the front room so he proceeded toward the kitchen. As he got closer to it, the smell got worse. It only took him a minute to find the dead squirrel that lay in the sink. Above it was the broken kitchen window that it must have used and he could see dried blood all over the broken glass. He told himself that he was going to have to go out back to the shed and get something to cover the window and get rid of the carcass.

"Good Lord," Lynette yelled from the front. "What is that smell?"

"Don't come into the kitchen unless you want the answer to that," Dean yelled back.

"Is it another raccoon?"

"No, but by the looks of it, it had to have happened less than a day or two ago. I'll go out back to the storage shed and get some things to clean it up."

"Ok, I'll start opening the windows to air things out," she said as she laid the duffle bag on the couch. "Do we still have those fans in the closet?"

"I think so," Dean said. "I'll be right back."

Lynette heard him flip the switch for the back area lights and step out through the back door. "Pew," she yelled.

****

The music stopped and the lights came up as Storm left the stage, completely naked. Marvin walked out again, with the microphone in his hand and addressed the audience. "That concludes the first half of amateur night. We will return in thirty minutes with the second half. Get your glasses filled up and hit the bathroom because something tells me that it's only going to get better."

"Good idea," Curt said as he stood up, "I need to piss a river, ladies. I'll be right back."

"You're not the only one," Barbie said as she got up, "I've been holding it through the last two dancers."

Sweet Wine, Carmel and Heartache all got up as well to join the others to the bathroom. The table seemed rather empty with only Jambalaya, Dragonfly, and Paradise holding the spot.

"You know, I really like Curt," Dragonfly said, "I really don't see why he's gotten such a bad rap."

"Well, it's his attitude," Paradise said. "It rubs people the wrong way, and they can't handle it. I love how he so straight forward about everything. He doesn't hold anything back."

"He tells it like it is," Jambalaya added. "You really don't have to worry about mind games with him. What you see is what you get."

Dragonfly picked up her drink, "So, is he dating anyone?"

Both Jambalaya and Paradise looked at each other and start laughing.

"What's so funny," Dragonfly asks.

"He'll never settle down with someone," Jambalaya stated, "He's, how shall I say this, not the committing type."

"Why?" Dragonfly really liked Curt and wanted to get to know him better. She found him unique but troubled as well. His overbearing rudeness was a cover-up, she thought. Somewhere deep inside was a person asking for help, for companionship.

"I can't really tell you," Jambalaya said, "you see, he's had a hard past and doesn't really open up to anyone about it. I think I'm the only one that he has opened up to in the group. I've known him longer than any of the girls here."

"I've known him just a little less than her," Paradise speaks up, "but he tends to try not to get so personal with people."

Just then someone grabbed Curt's chair and pulled it out from the table. "Hello tramps, what's new?"

It was Andy's.

"Ah, that's seat is taken," Dragonfly said as Andy sat down.

"It is now," Andy said as he leaned forward and looked toward his right at Paradise and Jambalaya. "I've done seen you two naked several times, but you," he stated as he turned to Dragonfly, "I haven't seen at all."

"You better leave, Andy, before shit hits the fan," Jambalaya said as her face showed anger.

"Oh, I'll leave, but first I'm going to have some oriental food." Andy reached out and grabbed Dragonfly's left breast and then leaned his large body on top of her, pinning her against the chair. Jambalaya got up and jumped on top of his back, but with a quick thrust from his right arm, Andy swung Jambalaya off onto the floor. He then leaned closer toward Dragonfly's face and tried to lick her cheek. His grip on her breast was strong; it was bringing tears to her eyes, but she found the strength to shove him off. He was just about to force himself on her again when she took a right fist to his mouth. His grip released her, and he sat back up in the chair. With a disgruntled look on his face, he reached up to his mouth, and pulled out a broken piece of tooth. He looked down at the bloody tooth in his hand and his angry eyes fixed onto her face once again.

"You bitch," he yelled as he pulled back his right arm to punch her.

The punch never swung because someone from behind him grabbed his arm in a firm grip and Andy could not move it. He stood up out of the chair and spun around to come face to face with Curt. Before anyone could even move, Andy punched Curt in the stomach with his left hand and it sent Curt into the table behind him.

Everything was quiet. Curt's head slowly lifted from staring at the floor to looking directly at Andy's eyes, a trickle of blood flowed from his mouth as a large grin started to grow on his face.

"Now," Jambalaya said from behind Andy. "You've done fucked up, asshole."

Curt round house kicked Andy on the side of his face with his right foot and sent him flying into the table to the right. People scrambled out of the way as Curt was on him again with fists flying. Then suddenly, two other men ran up behind Curt and tried to jump him, which only succeeded in making Curt's smile even wider. His first kick went to the blond man's midsection, then another kick to his face. The blond man fell to the floor. The other man swung at Curt and missed due to Curt's quick dodge and was hit in the back of the head with a right chop. That was followed by another kick to the man's right knee which in turn bent the other way. The man screamed in agony as his right leg folded the opposite direction and he collapsed to the floor.

Andy stood back up again and with all his strength went full speed toward Curt. Curt, once again dodged the attack and kicked him in the face as he passed by and he followed up with another round house to the back of Andy's head. Andy went down on top of the man with the broken leg and he screamed even louder.

As quick as it started, it ended. Three men lay in their own puddles of blood. Andy was dripping from his nose and mouth; the blond man was spitting up blood, and the other with the broken leg had the still held it in agony.

During the fight, all the other girls returned from the bathroom to the table and witnessed most of the brawl. Barbie was the last one to arrive. "Marvin called the cops," she said as she approached. "We need to get Curt out of here."

"Why?" Dragonfly said as she walked up toward the crowd. "He was defending himself."

Jambalaya took over the situation, "Curt has a past with the cops and it won't go down too good with them. I'll take him out of here."

"I'll come with you, "Dragonfly added.

"No, sweetie," Jambalaya added, "you can't. You got to stay and tell the cops your involvement in this. Andy did attack you. Make sure you press charges because if you don't, I know that Marvin will."

Dragonfly nodded in agreement. "Okay, call me later and let me know how he is."

"Oh, he's just fine," Paradise said, "Probably upset that he couldn't continue the fight."

All the girls started helping the waiters pick up the tipped table and chairs, and Jambalaya walked toward Curt.

Curt was standing above the three writhing on the floor waiting for any of them to get back up. Soft caressing hands came across his shoulders, and he turned to see Jambalaya behind him. "Come on, baby, Marvin had to call the cops. I'll take you out of here."

209

"But, shit, I was just starting to warm up! Can't I play a little longer?"

Jambalaya started to laugh, "No, little boy, it's time to go to bed now,"

Curt's eyes opened wide with her remark, "Bed? But I'm not fucking tired."

"Who said anything about sleeping," Jambalaya said.

Curt held out his elbow for her to wrap her arm around, "Then you best tuck my ass in then."

She slipped her arm around his and smiled, "I'll do more than tuck that ass in," she added.

"Let's fucking blow this joint then."

They both hurried out the door and were just pulling off in Curt's Jeep when the cops pulled up.

****

The fireplace was the only thing that illuminated the cabin. The crackling of the wood sent memories drifting to other times, to other days of happiness. The warmth of the fire created its own comforting blanket on this cool evening and sparkles of tiny embers danced up its chute. The smell of the burning oak tickled the nose with an aroma that relaxed the mind and the body.

There it was again, the mixture of the senses bringing so much into perspective and flooding the mind with unforgettable times. Dean was laying on the floor, cozily tucked into a sleeping bag made for two and took in the surroundings like a dream from heaven. His nude body under the bag felt soothed and relaxed. He truly enjoyed these get away times. Behind his head, upon the floor, was an ice bucket holding a perfectly chilled bottle of wine. The cork had already been opened, and the light aroma drifted around the area.

Lynette walked in from the kitchen, dressed in a white bath robe, and was carrying two empty wine glasses. She bent over and set the glasses next to him in which he immediately took on the task of grabbing the bottle and filling them.

"Is it nice and toasty warm under there," Lynette asked.

"It's ready any time you are," Dean replied.

Lynette slowly pulled off her robe and exposed her nude body. The light from the fire danced around her glistening skin as she draped the robe on a nearby chair. Dean could see the curvature of her breasts and how the light teased them. She was a beautiful woman and her hour glass figure stirred him inside. They had snuggled many times before, in the nude, but he still respected her wishes to remain a virgin until their wedding night. As Curt said, touching and licking was so much more fun but looking was still free.

With that thought, he slowly took in the lady in front of him. Her hair flowed over the top of her shoulders and ended just touching the top of her breasts. Her breasts were not large but like the size of a lemons, and the nipples were hard and erect. Her tenderness continued down her sides and to a belly button that looked like it was perfectly tucked in. From the waist down she was memorizing. Her legs looked smooth as silk and were tall and elegant.

Lynette saw his eyes looking over her and smiled, "Taking it all in, Mitchell?"

"Oh, yeah," he said, "it's been a while since I've seen you like this. In fact, Curt still thinks I haven't even seen your body yet."

"Well what Curt don't know," she said as she got down and crawled under the sleeping bag, "won't hurt him."

Dean reached over and handed her a filled wine glass. "Here's to the most beautiful woman I have ever known."

"And to the best man I could ever have," she added. They tapped their glasses together and then took a drink.

Their bodies snuggled close to each other and Dean propped his elbow up and rested his head on the open hand. "I've got something to tell you, something that will really shock you."

She sat up and the sleeping bag fell off her shoulder exposing one of her breasts, "I'm not going to be mad, am I?"

"Maybe, yes, we will see," he said with a smirk on his face, "You see, I haven't left the house all week."

Lynette got a confused look on her face, "What do you mean you haven't left the house all week? You have been at the Nook at least three times that I know of."

"Yes, but It, a, it wasn't me," he said with a smirk on his face.

Lynette cocked her head sideways in confusion.

Dean took a sip of his wine. "About six months ago, Brad came to me with the idea to build a robot. Not some of the ones you see in movies that are all stiff, or a bunch of arms or even on wheels, but a life looking robot. He had already designed the schematics for it and after going through them I believed that we could do it."

Lynette still looked confused but didn't lay back down either, "So you're telling me..."

Dean held up his hand to stop her, "let me finish and then you be the judge."

She laid back down and propped her head upon her bent elbow like Dean was.

"He came up with a way that we could make a mold of someone's body and make it work. He wanted me to be the guinea pig so then after several days in plaster, I had a double. Then we had the long and tedious task of trying to build the rest of it. To make a long story short, we finished last week and have been testing it all week. I didn't even go to classes. DD did."

"DD?" Lynette questioned as she took another drink.

"It stands for Dean's Duplicate. It was a way that we could talk about the robot and nobody else would know who we were talking about. It also made it easy if anyone was overhearing us." He took another drink, and so did she. "So, what you saw all week was DD in action."

"Even the dinner you or he cooked me?"

"Dean started shaking his head, "Oh no, that was me. You see, the robot can't eat."

Lynette cocked her head to the side again, "You're pulling my leg, Mitchell."

"Honestly, I'm not," he stated as he grabbed the bottle to fill both glasses again. "Let me explain how it works,"

And he continued the rest of the night.

****

Turning into Dean's driveway was a Jeep that looked like it had no direction at all. When it stopped, it was slightly crooked as it parked on top of one of the front yard bushes. As soon as the engine cut off, you could hear two adults laughing.

"Oops, shit, I think I fucking killed a bush," Curt said in his drunken state.

"Maybe it had it coming to it, "Jambalaya added with a laugh and a few slurred words. She held up the empty whiskey bottle that they had both been drinking and tossed it over into the grass, "Now what, we finished the second bottle." She leaned over to Curt and grabbed his shirt and pulled it, "I NEED MORE!"

Curt gave her a coy smile, "There is more in the house."

She looked up and tried to focus on the building in front of them, "whose house is this?"

Curt opened his driver side door and stumbled out, "A very good friend of mine, I'm house sitting for him."

Jambalaya stumbled out of her side and staggered toward the door. "Then let's go in and get it."

They held onto each other as they attempted to walk a straight line up onto the porch and to the door. Curt pulled out his keys, dropped them twice, and then finally succeeded on unlocking the house. When they stepped in, they were immediately hit with a hot house.

"Dean, you dumb ass, at least you could have left the air on," Curt said as he stumbled toward the thermostat on the entry wall. He flipped open the panel and turned on the air.

"So, his name's Dean, huh," Jambalaya stated, "What kind of guy is he?"

Curt started walking toward the kitchen and stopped in the door way, turned, and propped himself up against the entrance frame. "He's pretty much a goodie two shoes who has his fucking life all in order, a fucking hot looking lady that could probably melt my dick and doesn't really have a care in the world.... what was I doing?"

"Getting another drink," Jambalaya said as she glanced around the room. "It's fucking hot in here, I'm getting comfortable." That's when she reached down and pulled her top up over her head but didn't succeed in completely getting it off. Her bare breast bounced around as she tried to pull the turtleneck sweater off of her head. Curt was watching her in amusement. He couldn't wait to crawl all over that body again. She almost lost her balance twice in the struggle, but then finally succeeded on completing her task. She wadded up the now free top and threw it into the recliner. She then started to work on pulling off her jeans. She unbuckled the top and started to wiggle her way out of the tight-fitting pants. Curt could see that she had a pair of light blue underwear on and that they were laced. Wine me, dine me, sixty-nine me, he thought.

"I'll get another bottle and be right back," he said as he headed into the kitchen. Trying to keep his balance, he made it to the liquor cabinet on the right side and opened the door. He saw four bottles, grabbed two, and started walking back toward the front room. Twice he had to lean on the counter to recollect his balance and then he proceeded on. When he walked around the corner, he saw Jambalaya; she had passed out on the couch and was only successful on getting her jeans down to her ankles.

"Hey," he shouted as he knelt down and crawled over to her, "I've got something for you." He laid the two bottles on the coffee table and proceeded to crawl the rest of the way to her body. He could see the sweat glistening on her chocolate-colored breasts, and he was ready to devour them when he suddenly heard her snoring. It completely turned him off. He slumped down on the floor and propped his back up against the couch, "Aw, shit," he sighed, "I'll fuck her in the morning."

He crawled back toward the coffee table and grabbed one of the bottles. While he uncorked it, he looked at one of the many pictures that covered the mantle above the fireplace. One of them was a picture of Dean, Lynette and that troublesome truck sitting in front of the cabin. Instantly the situation at the truck dealer came to his mind.

"Dean," he said as he raised the bottle in the air, "Here's to the luckiest son of a bitch I know."

He lifted the bottle to his lips and took a large swallow. Within seconds, he spit it out all over the room.

"What the fuck is this shit?" He yelled as he lifted the bottle to read its label. It was a nonalcoholic beverage. It was a sparkling wine.

"Dean, you pussy," he yelled out loud again. "Now I've got to deal with pissy girly drinks? What the fuck!" He took the bottle and tossed it into the open fireplace. Glass shattered all over the inside.

"You seriously need to grow a manly set of balls, dude.   If there was a way that I could give you a part of my brass balls, I would, In fact...."

Suddenly, an idea hit Curt like a tornado hits a trailer park. He put his right hand up to his mouth and held it there for a moment. A grin started to grow across his face.

It didn't take him long to get things hooked up, in fact he had the hardest time just trying to get down the steps. After stripping down to just his underwear, he attached the transfer clips in all the right spots and was ready to flip the switch on the 380 when he noticed that his chair was too far away. He went to the cleaning closet around the corner and got a corn broom and took it back to the chair with him. It would be the perfect length. Once he got himself settled into the chair, he stretched the broom out, handle first, and proceeded to tap the switch. It took three tries but he managed to throw the power.

Everything went black.

PART THREE

TAINTED: A trace of something bad, offensive or harmful that causes an infection making the object to spoil or become corrupt.

Friday

Several birds outside created a musical wonderland as the sun lit up the room. There were high notes, low notes, and several in between, bringing a calming effect to the ears. The warmth of the sleeping bag felt like peace itself had surrounded her and engulfed her. She couldn't hear any crackling from the fireplace which meant it was either in low embers or completely out. She had her head buried in the bag and slowly opened a small portion just enough to feel the cool air gently touch her face. That's when the scent of food hit her nose, waking up more of her senses. She could smell coffee, eggs, and some type of meat within the air and the aroma started to awaken her more as she turned to sit up right.

She still was in a daze not only because of the good night's sleep but because of the story that Dean had told her last night, a fully functional robot that looks just like him. He told her about the 'No' list and also about why he never kissed her all week. After thinking about it, he was right. He never kissed her except at the dinner that he cooked her on Monday. She couldn't wait to meet or see this wonder that they had built. Actually, she thought, she had already met it. It still amazed her that she couldn't spot a difference.

Lynette stretched her arms above her head and heard her back and shoulder pop. The feeling soothed her, and she sighed in the moment. The sleeping bag slid past her shoulders and fell down to her lap, exposing both of her breasts. The cool air chilled them, and she quickly pulled the bag back up over her chest, trying to recollect the heat from within. She glanced over on the other wall and saw the clock. It was eleven thirty, and she shuddered. It had been a long time since she had slept this late. She felt refreshed and invigorated than she had been for weeks, and she was pleased with herself for doing it. She then heard utensil noises coming from the kitchen and turned her head toward the opening just as Dean came walking into the room with a bed tray in his hand. He was only wearing his underwear.

"Good morning, sunshine," he said as he knelt down with the tray and set it beside her. "Have a good sleep?"

She smiled and nodded her head several times, "Beautiful, I feel so relaxed."

"Good," Dean said, standing back up, "That's what we are here for." He smiles, turned, and walked back into the kitchen. Lynette looked down and started to take in what was laid in front of her.

The bed tray had a cup of coffee, utensils, a small bowl of strawberries, and a plate with an egg mixture on it. The added vase with one red rose touched off a perfect morning. The steam of the egg dish started to pillow around her head as she took in its aroma. It was a mixture of scrambled eggs, cheese, onions, mushrooms, and meat and she turned her body counterclockwise to face the tray. As she picked up her fork, the sleeping bag fell past her shoulders again and down to her lap. Her breasts were exposed again, but this time she didn't fight the cold.

Dean came walking in with another try and sat down on the floor in front of her. His tray had the same ingredients, minus the rose. As he adjusted himself on the floor, she took the fork and stabbed it into the mixture. When she lifted the fork, the cheese seemed to stretch on forever, and she had to grab it and wrap it around the fork until it broke.

"Got enough cheese on this?" she asked before she shoved the mixture into her mouth.

"There is never enough cheese," he replied as he popped a strawberry into his mouth.

Lynette started chewing and the flavor was heavenly. The eggs were fluffy, the vegetables were perfectly crisp and the meat was very well seasoned. She swallowed her first bite and groaned a yummy sound. She quickly picked up another bite.

"What kind of meat is this, it's delicious," she said as she shoved the loaded fork into her mouth.

"Squirrel," Dean said.

She stopped chewing and got a disgusted look on her face.

"Just kidding," Dean said quickly. "Its Italian sausage and I added some spices to it as it was sautéing."

She swallowed the bite and picked up a strawberry, "very funny, Mitchell, very funny." She held the fruit out toward him.

He leaned forward and took the strawberry from her hand with his teeth. He smiled as he chewed it and swallowed it.

"Any plans for today?" she asked as she took another stab at the mixture.

"I'm going fishing and catch some dinner for a good feast tonight." Dean took a drink of his coffee and then took another bite of his eggs. "I plan to pan sear it."

Lynette's eyes widened, "It's been a long time since I had your pan seared fish. It's so yummy!"

"I figured that you could take down one of the chairs and read a book like you always do. It always relaxes you."

She held up her fork and waved it at him. "I even brought a book just for this occasion. It's a book that I've wanted to read for a while. It's called 'The Sacrifice' and its sounds really good."

"What kind of book is it?"

"It's a science fiction, of course, and I was told it's got a lot of humor in it and action as well." She took a drink of her coffee and felt the warmth of it run down her throat. "Dawn has already read it and she says it has a couple of really hot scenes in it too."

"Seriously, maybe you can practice them on me." Dean said while he took another drink.

"Do you think I need a book to instruct me on that?"

Dean smiled. "Not on your life, you give me all that I could ever hope for and more." He leaned across the table and they kissed. As he leaned back, she popped another strawberry into his mouth and they smiled at each other.

****

Brad tried to walk down the concourse but the three bags he was carrying kept putting him off balance. The flight was really comfortable, and he slept most of the way, but it was hard to sleep when it was so bright above the clouds, and most everyone one was talking around him.   Even when the stewardess came by with the drink cart, she woke him and asked him if he wanted anything. That's when he decided to arise and join the rest of the passengers. He knew that he would probably get sleep tonight, after the get together, and then stay up late tomorrow night after the announcement.

He finally reached the end of the entrance and staggered into the gate seating area where he tossed two of his bags into an empty chair. He started to reorganize his carry-ons when someone behind him grabbed one of the bags.

"Let me get this for you, you old fart," said the man picking up one of Brad's bags.

Brad turned and saw the familiar face, "John, so good to see you." The two men laughed and shook hands.

John continued laughing as he returned the firm handshake, "It's been too long, my friend. Care to share a ride to the hotel?"

"Love to," Brad answered, "just got to get the rest of my bags. Did you just get in?"

John picked up one of Brad's bags and put it over his shoulder, "thirty minutes ago at the gate across the carpet. I saw that the gate board had a flight arriving from Springfield so I took a shot at thinking you were on board. So, I just parked myself at the little bar over there and waited. And here you are."

"And here I am," Brad added.

"So, buy you a drink?" John said as he pointed his thumb at the bar next to the gate.

"Not now, but later at the hotel, you can buy me all you want. I have some delicate equipment that I need to pick up at the baggage area." Brad reached down and picked up his other two bags.

"What are you carrying, liquid nitrogen?"

Brad laughed, "that would be rather fun, wouldn't it? No, it's nothing like that, but it is some pretty nifty stuff. I'll let everyone know tomorrow. Until then, let's motivate and get settled in."

"Sounds good to me," John said as the two headed toward the escalator for the baggage area.

****

Suddenly it felt like someone had thrown a bucket of cold water at his face, and Curt jolted up right in his chair. His body tingled all over, and his hands were shaking. He was disoriented and couldn't get his bearings on where he was at; even his eyes were out of focus. His entire body was covered in sweat and the coldness in the air made him shiver.

He must have really got drunk last night, he thought, and slowly put his hands up to his face and wiped back his hair.

"Oh, fuck me," he said out loud still trying to get his bearings. Looking around, his eyes started to clear and he saw that he was in Dean's basement, and he was sitting in the transfer chair. Suddenly he remembered what he did and turned to look at DD in the other chair.

The chair was empty.

"OH, FUCK ME," he yelled. Quickly he pulled off the connections and ran upstairs, looking for the robot. When he opened the door at the top of the stairs, he noticed how quiet the place was. He ran around the corner and saw that the front room was empty.

"Fuck me; fuck me, where the fuck is he?" He yelled out loud as he ran toward the door to look outside. That's when he saw the note on the door. It was written on a sheet of yellow paper, and it was addressed to him;

Curt,
I tried to wake you up this morning, but you were really passed out. I guess we were both pretty wasted. I don't remember you even leaving the room. Anyway, since you wouldn't wake up, I called Paradise, and she came and picked me up. I had to get home and get ready for tonight. Thanks for the great time, even though I don't remember any of it. By the way, did we fuck?

See you later, Jambalaya.

Curt threw the paper down on the floor and opened up the door. He stepped out onto the porch, still only dressed in just his underwear and saw that his Jeep was in the yard parked on top of three bushes.

"Where the fuck is he?" He questioned again as stepped further out on the porch. Then it suddenly dawned on him, the 380.

He ran back inside, and his adrenalin had him taking two steps at a time down the basement steps. When he reached the 380, he glanced closely at the screen and was shocked at what he saw. DD was driving the truck.

"Well, I can't shut him off; I'm going to have to hunt him down." Soon he had his clothes on, and he was driving his Jeep away from the house.

****

"Everything came through approved," the man at the desk said to the young couple sitting across from him. "I just need your signatures at the red X on the bottom of each page, and then you can drive away with the SUV today."

The young man smiled at his wife and grabbed the pen from the salesman. "This is it, Honey. No more riding the bus."

"Makes me happy," she answered.

The salesman leaned back and looked around the room as the couple signed the papers. It was a busy day. Every salesman had people waiting. His desk was the first one sitting in the lobby and three other desks were in line behind his. They were toward the back wall of the lobby because the front area had the show vehicles taking the space. Toward the right front was the large counter that welcomed people in and a small seating area with coffee and donuts which kept the waiting customers comfortable. A television, hanging in the corner, was playing the four o'clock news. He took in everything that was going on inside the building which is why he didn't expect the truck on the outside.

Dean's truck crashed through the main entrance doors at full speed and ran into the service counter. The man sitting at the counter was instantly smashed to the back wall, and his body disappeared under the truck. Blood sprayed everywhere. People in the waiting area scrambled and screamed, but two of them didn't get clear enough from the debris as it flew through the air. Their eyes were pierced with flying glass, and their backs were splinted with shards of mixed glass and wood. The computer from the service desk was flung into the air, and the screen hit a little girl in the back of the head knocking her down to the ground.

The truck continued plowing through the building. The two new car owners didn't get a chance to move as the front grill of the truck hit them so hard that their skulls smashed into pieces upon the front hood. The salesman, at the first desk, was crushed into the other three desks behind him which also contained many people. Blood splattered all over the walls, the floor and spots dotted the ceiling. When the truck finally came to a stop, it was upon the piled-up mess of wood, computers and bodies. The engine still was running as the driver's door opened up, and DD stepped out of the vehicle.

He glanced around and looked at the carnage in front of him. Screams and sounds of electrical sparks filled the air, but he was searching for someone. Four steps later, he found his salesman pinned on the floor between what was left of the last two desks. The man lay bleeding from the mouth and he was gasping for air. The desk in front of him, like a spear, had cut his mid-section in half, and his intestines were spread around the floor. DD leaned down toward him and dangled the truck keys at him.

"I've changed my mind," he said tossing the keys into the man's face, "I don't want the fucking truck no more."

He stood up and stepped over the piles of debris and walked up to the sports car. He opened the door, sat inside, and started the engine with the keys that hung in the ignition. The car roared to life and DD put it into gear. He firmly planted his foot on the gas pedal and exited out through the front windows of the dealership. Once on the road, he shifted to a higher gear and sped off.

****

His line pulled tight, and Dean jerked hard at the pole. When he felt the weight, he knew that he had snagged the fish and started to reel it in. The fish started to pull toward the right, and Dean stood up off of the rock he was sitting on to get a better leverage. He pulled back the pole, then reeled and then repeated the process until he had the fish close to the shore.

"I've got a doosie," he shouted.

Lynette looked up from the book she was reading and watched him through her sunglasses. She was comfortably sitting in a reclining chair and on her left side was a small table with a glass of wine on it. She watched him struggle as he reeled and then pointed the tip of the pole down toward the water line. When he pulled the pole up, he lifted his catch out of the water and she saw that the fish was no bigger than her wine glass. She started to laugh.

Dean turned his head back toward her with a serious expression on his face and grabbed the fish with his left hand. "Well, it felt a lot bigger in the water."

She laughed again, "Maybe you better try again, you old sea dog." She laughed again and returned to her book.

"How's the book?" he asked as he pulled the hook out of the small fish and tossed it back into the water.

"It's really good," she said as she reached over and grabbed her drink. "The ship character is really funny and it has a lot of action." She took a sip of her wine and sat the glass back down. "The main character reminds me of you."

"Really," he said as he re baited his hook and then casted his line back out into the water, "is his name Dean?"

"No, it's Jason."

"Jason, huh," Dean continued. "Is he handsome and smart too?"

"Shhh," she said lifting her finger toward her mouth, "Get back to your fishing, I'm at a good part."

Dean sat back down on his rock and slowly tightened up his line. He always loved fishing on the bottom. He couldn't stand using bobbers to fish. Most of the time, he would only catch small bluegill when he fished with a bobber. His experience always found that the catfish were easier to catch on the bottom. Bass was good as well, but he hated the task of always casting out and reeling in to attract them. It was always calm and peaceful just to bottom fish, and he always had two poles in the water. The calmness of the breeze in the air, the ripple of the water, and the sounds of nearby birds always relaxed him. Fishing was the perfect getaway.

Lynette, on the other hand, would truly get lost in a book. She would get so involved in the story that she wouldn't hear the breeze, or the water, or the birds. She would tune out any noise that tried to surround her. When she would zone out in this world, at times, you had to say things two or three times just to get her attention. She loved the way that books would take her away from the real world. She would get so in-depth into her books that she would experience every emotion possible. She would laugh out loud, she would cry, she would even sigh in ecstasy during really steamy parts. She literally would lose herself in a book. This, to her, was the perfect get a way.

Suddenly, one of his lines yanked hard, and Dean grabbed it to set the hook. He stood up and started to reel it in when his other pole pulled jerked toward the left. He stomped his left foot on the reel and yelled.

"Hey, help me here!"

No answer.

"Lynette," he yelled, "help me."

Lynette lifted her eyes up from the book again, and with an irritation in her voice answered,

"What?"

Dean's eyes got wide, and he gestured with a nod of his head toward the pole that was yanking hard under his left foot. "I could use some assistance here."

She laid her book down and jumped up to help him. "I knew that fishing with two poles at a time would get you into a situation like this." She stepped toward him and reached down and grabbed the pole under his foot. "If I smell like fish after this, you'll be sorry."

"Who cares what you smell like," he added, "do you want to eat tonight?"

She pulled the pole hard and started to reel it in.

****

Curt was driving furiously and weaving around cars just trying to figure out where DD was driving. He wasn't programmed to eat so that ruled out any restaurants. He didn't like women's exploitation, so that ruled out Marvin's. He had no classes today, only lab work; so that ruled out the college. The only places he could be were; Lynette's, the Book Nook, or Brad's house. He was on the way toward the Book Nook when from behind him, a police car, with its lights and siren on, came roaring up behind him. He looked down at his speedometer and saw that he was going fifteen miles over the speed limit.

"Shit," he yelled as he pulled over to the curb. He put the Jeep into park and was ready to get out his wallet when the police car continued its momentum and passed him. Curt's expression changed and he pulled the Jeep back out into traffic.

He turned down Dirksen Parkway and saw the entire road was covered with flashing red and blue lights. Several ambulances, police cars, and fire engines littered the road.

"What the fuck happened here?" he said as he slowed the Jeep down to a crawl with the traffic. A police man was directing traffic through the stop light and everything was really chaotic. When he passed through the intersection, Curt finally saw the glimpse of the carnage. Many people were running around the dealership where Dean purchased his truck at. Paramedics and policemen covered the area, and several gurneys were scattered

226

throughout the parking lot. It looked like a tornado had hit the building. Glass was everywhere. Then he saw it.

Dean's truck was sitting in the center of the building.

"Oh shit, fuck me!" he yelled. He couldn't understand what was going on, but if it was DD causing this entire disaster, he better find him quick. Concentrating on the building, he didn't notice that the cars in front of him had proceeded ahead and the car behind him honked. Curt regained his attention to the road and sped off into the direction of Dean's house. He had to shut that unit off no matter what.

****

Lieutenant Ann Parker thought that she had seen it all, but this tragedy had her speechless. First officers on the scene had already blocked off not only the parking lot, but the roads that surrounded the dealership. They had already run the plates on the truck that caused all the damage, and an APB had been put out on the sports car. She had already gotten a report from the sergeant on the scene, and she went over the gathered facts in her mind.

First, she was standing in the middle of a blood bath. Pieces of bodies were strewn all over the place, and two of the bodies were so badly smashed that the faces were unrecognizable. Blood was splattered everywhere; the walls, the furniture, and even the ceiling was dotted. One of the bodies had been wrapped around the back tire of the truck, and emergency personnel were still trying to pry it out. Several ambulances had arrived to search the debris for life. The deaths included two managers, two employees, and five customers. One of them was a six-year-old girl.

Second, the video that they uncovered in the main office proved to be totally useless. The entire system was a fake and no recordings were available to view. They did have the owner of the truck's information, and she had sent a couple of units to the address. There were no other businesses around the area that could provide a possible camera angle to the lot, so that evidence would not be available.

Third, the dispatch had provided a description of the convertible that was taken off the lot and all available units were searching the area. It was a bright yellow convertible sports car, with no license plate other than the dealer's logo plate. The tire marks had indicated that the driver had headed south bound on Dirksen Parkway.

"Lieutenant Parker," a male officer said breaking her concentration as he approached, "Here's that list you wanted of the employees scheduled for today."

"Thanks, Officer Start," she replied as she took the note from his hand, "did we also find a list of family members to notify in case of emergency as well? I don't want them to find out from the news first. I want this quickly taken care of."

"Yes, ma'am, Officer Tucker is getting that information together and will notify people. He'll start calling when you give us the order."

"Have the family report to me directly," she added. "And have them wait for me in that first repair garage at the end of the lot. I think its garage number three. Under no circumstances are they to set foot in this building, do I make myself clear?"

"Yes, ma'am," said the officer as he headed back toward the back office.

Whoever did this, she thought, has no concern for life. She turned and looked toward her left were one of the blood-soaked sheets covered up the body of the child. This maniac has no concern, not even for the age. She looked at another report that she was holding in her hand, the identification of the truck owner, a 'Dean Mitchell' who lived in the Jerome area.

"We need to get this man before he causes more deaths," she said under her breath.

****

"Everything is ready for you sir," the Hotel attendant said as he held up a card key, "You're in room 531 and the bell hop will be glad to help you upstairs with your luggage,"

228

Brad took the card key from him and put it into his front vest pocket. "Thank you, young man."

Suddenly a hard pat on his back startled Brad to look behind him. "What's up, you old fart?" The man said with a smile.

"Smitty," Brad said turning to shake the man's hand, "I didn't think you were going to be able to make it."

"Last minute change in plans," he said returning the hard shake. "Ruby got the flu, and she didn't feel well enough to attend her family reunion," said Smitty as he started to fake a sad face, "it really broke me up knowing that I'd have to miss it too."

Brad laughed. "Yeah, I bet my bottom dollar that you burned rubber all the way to the airport."

"Two sets, my man," he answered laughing. "Are you going to be at the mixer tonight?"

"As soon as I check into my room and freshen up. It's at six, right?"

"In the King's Room," he said pointing down the hall toward the right, "First drinks on me."

"I plan to get a lot of drinks after every one hears what I have to tell."

"And that is?"

"Not until tomorrow, my friend."

Just then the bellhop walked up to the two gentlemen pulling a luggage cart with suitcases on it. "Mr. Crawford?"

Smitty pointed at Brad. "That's me, son," Brad acknowledged."

"Are you ready to head to your room, sir?"

Brad waved his hand forward. "I'm right behind you."

"See you at six," Smitty waved as he walked off.

"I'll be there," Brad stated as he followed the bellhop to the elevators.

****

DD pulled into the main parking lot of the college and slowly drove around in font of McKinley Hall. The sound of the engine purred so smoothly that it was barely noticeable that the car was turned on. The brightness of the yellow paint reflected the sun so hard that people had to squint as they looked at it passing by. Even with the top down, the car still couldn't cool off enough inside from the heat of the day. Many heads turned to look at the car, including two girls who were walking down the side walk.

DD thought they looked familiar.

He pulled the car up toward the curb just as they were walking by, and they both stopped to look the car.

"Nice set of wheels," one of them said as she pulled her sun shades down and peered over the top of them. "Looks like it would cost as much as it shines."

DD put the car into park and turned toward the women. "Nothing really special, I'm just borrowing it for a while."

Both the girls stepped off the sidewalk and walked up to the car. They were wearing tank top shirts and he could clearly see that neither was wearing a bra. When they reached the car, they leaned on the passenger's side door and one of them glanced down at the dashboard.

"Wow, most of the interior is leather," she said as she leaned over to look farther down into the car. DD could see right down her shirt.

"Borrowing it, huh?" the other girl questioned as she looked at the back seat. "Are you on a business trip or out for a joy ride?"

DD smiled. "Just cruising around, would you like to tag along?"

Both of the girls smiled. "Love too," one of them said as she opened the side door."

"Why don't you both sit in the back seat," DD gestured with his thumb. "You'll get more wind in your hair back there. This sun is pretty wicked today."

Both the girls climbed into the back seat, and once the door shut, DD put it into drive and drove away.

****

Curt pulled around the corner in hopes to getting back to Dean's house to throw the switch on the 380. As he pulled onto Dean's Street, he didn't expect to see all the cop cars blocking the road.

"Fuck, me" he said as he slowed down and turned into the first driveway he reached. He put his Jeep into park and looked down toward the house. With all the attention, he realized that he would never be able to get to the house unnoticed.

He threw the Jeep into reverse and turned back around toward the direction he came.

****

The aroma of fresh fish frying filled every room of the cabin. The scent tickled the nose with many spices and even gave a taste to the air. Lynette loved Dean's cooking and savored every time he experimented with dishes. He rarely followed recipes because he enjoyed the adventure of coming up with his own creations. Several times he had pointed out that there were so many cooks, chefs and books about cooking that it would be an endless subject. One person could cook a different meal every day and never be able to eat every dish created. As many styles there were in cooking, how and why would you take the time and effort to do so many recipes? 'Just wing it' he'd always say. If you're good, nobody would know. And she knew that Dean was a great cook and enjoyed doing it. If he wasn't so good in his mechanical engineering field, he would have opened his own restaurant.

Lynette had been in the shower for almost twenty minutes trying to get the fish smell off of her skin. Thanks to her help in catching tonight's entre, she got fish all over her shirt, pants, and shoes. She even gave up on reading her book until later because she didn't want fish on the pages. Now thanks to her strawberry shampoo and body wash, she smelled and felt better.

She turned off the shower and stepped out onto the fuzzy mat. Her toes soaked down into the softness of the rug and she scrunched her toes. She grabbed a towel off the linen shelf, and started drying her hair, then her chest, her back, her lower torso, then her legs. She felt refreshed. She grabbed a house robe off the back door hook and put it on. After tying the robe's belt, she wrapped the towel around her head and stepped out into the bedroom.

The spicy air was strong and smelled delightful. As she walked out of the bedroom, she saw that he had set up a small table in the living room in front of the fire place. It had two settings and a bottle of wine chilling in an ice bucket. She proceeded to walk into the kitchen. On the island prep table, she saw that he had a large bowl of mixed greens and a fruit bowl of mixed berries. He had his back toward her as her was frying the fish at the stove; she walked up behind him and put her arms around his waist.

"Smells delicious," she said as she looked at the large two-pound filet that he was frying. "That's the one I pulled in, right?"

He turned his head and looked at her, "Yes, don't you remember? The bait on the other line ate the fish I had."

She started to laugh, "Oh, yeah, I forgot."

"Why don't you slip into something comfortable, and I'll get the rest ready."

"Ok," she said, lightly kissing him on the right cheek. She walked toward the front room and turned back toward him. "I've never felt this relaxed in a long time."

He winked at her.

****

Lieutenant Parker was sitting at her desk when her phone rang. As tense and stressed as she was, she grabbed the phone so fast that she dropped the receiver on the floor. She yanked it back into her hands by its cord and managed to get the receiver to her ear.

"Lieutenant Parker."

"Ma'am, this is Officer Tucker with a report."

"Go ahead, officer."

"Several police have searched the grounds of Mister Mitchell's house and we have found it to be vacant." The officer sounded very tired and upset. "Looking through all windows and doors we see no activity and even the lights rigged on a timer has come on, showing more vacant house. What are you next orders?"

Parker sighed, "I want every available unit on the streets to find that sports car. Let's leave one unit at the residence, but tucked out of sight. If he returns or any activity arises, call dispatch immediately."

"I'll park myself at the house and direct others to the search."

"Thanks, Officer Tucker, keep me posted." She hung up the phone and grabbed her cup of coffee on her desk and took a quick swig.

It was cold.

****

Curt walked into the Book Nook in a fast pace and up to the Customer Service desk where he saw Dawn standing. She got a disturbed look on her face because he normally doesn't come in alone. His urgency was noticed when he interrupted a customer standing at the front of the counter.

"Excuse me, I have an emergency," he said as he butted in front of the man. "Dawn, have you seen DD, fuck, I mean Dean?"

"Why should I? Lynette and Dean are at the lake. They won't be back until Sunday." Her voice suddenly went up an octave, "Why, did something happen?"

"Yes, no, Fuck, I can't say. Did you see Dean?"

Dawn shook her head no.

Curt pulled out a card out of his pocket and handed it to her. "This is my phone number, call me if you see him, ok?"

She took the card from his hand, and in her confusion, nodded her acceptance.

Curt turned toward the man he pushed out of the way, "sorry for interrupting you."   He turned and left the building as fast as he had entered it.

****

"So, Brad, what's this I hear about you having a Grand announcement tomorrow?"

Brad turned to see another familiar face in the crowd. "Well, Eric, you're just going to have to wait like the others."

Another man walked up to Eric's side and put his arm around him, "I think we should just find a way to get into his room and find his work."

"Either that," Eric replied, "or get him so drunk that he'd just hand us the keys."

"Now, gentlemen," Brad said as he put his drink down on the table next to him, "you all are going to have to cool your jets until tomorrow. Besides, you both know that I can drink either one of you under the table any day."

Eric turned to the other man. "He's got a point, Randy."

"So, this announcement," Randy said, "it's not retirement. We already know about that."

"Maybe he evented a time machine," Eric added.

"If that were the case, and it's not," Brad said, "I would have messed everyone up in this place by now." Brad reached for his glass and took another drink. "Do you actually think that the DeHart brothers would be in here? Do you think that Combs would be the council president? Do you think I'd be buying my drinks when I should own this place?"

Eric looked toward Randy and smiled, "No, that's not it. Maybe he's found the missing link!"

Brad smiled, "The only missing link is in your heads, now drop the subject. You're not going to get anything out of me."

"Then what can we do," Randy said with a slight slur.

Brad drank down the rest of his drink, and then held the glass out to them, "Fill up my glass with scotch and let's mingle."

Eric grabbed the empty glass from Brad's hand and held it up in the air. "Gentlemen," he said turning toward the left, "this way to the bar." All three of them walked together across the crowded room.

****

The sun had set an hour ago and the wind through the car's open top felt good. DD had driven the two girls all around the lake and also bought them some beer at a drive-up liquor store. During the ride, he found out information about each girl; including their names, their favorite movie, their ages, and how long they had been at the college. Of course, he didn't believe them for a moment.

Bitches.

He recognized them right of the bat and it was time to get even. For several miles he had been taking them deeper and deeper into the back roads, and they hadn't shown any sign of awareness. Through the rear-view mirror, he could see that the coolness of the air was making both of their nipples hard and they were giving shape to their already tight tank tops.

"So," he said loudly, trying to talk over the wind, "I'd have to say that you both have the nicest looking pair of tits, I've ever seen."

The sudden change of casual talk toward such a topic threw both girls off, but they soon picked up on the idea.

"I'm glad you noticed," one of them said. "What would you give to see them?"

DD answered quickly, "probably all the money I have, including what I have in the bank."

"Really," said the other girl, "and how much would that be?"

"I'm not giving out figures, but I like this car so much I might buy at least three or four of them. Shit, I might buy one for every day of the week. Different colors, of course."

Both girls turned their heads toward each other and smiled. They had found themselves another sucker. This area was just too

235

easy to rob gullible idiots like him. They always scoped out the colleges, because that's the best place to find the money. They even went as far as to find out which rooms were vacant and sneak in. They generally did about three to four jobs at one location, and then moved on, but this place had a lot of money and idiots. At times they would research an area to find specific people who would give a big payoff, or at times, they would be lucky, like now.

"Come on, Ladies, pull those tops off and let those titties fly!"

Both girls grabbed their tank tops and pulled them off. They threw them on the floor in front of them and held their hands up in the air. They screamed loudly in excitement as the wind blew across their bare breasts.

"Yes!" DD yelled loudly as he looked behind himself, "those are some beautiful tits!"

"Want to play with them," one of them asked.

"Not until you answer one question."

Both girls put down their arms and gave him their full attention. "And what question is that?

"Have you ever heard of the name Curt Johnson?"

Things got really quiet in the back seat.

"I know who you are, and what you did," DD said as he leaned over the back seat. "You gave him a ride of a lifetime, now it's time for me to return the favor."

DD threw the car down a gear and sped the engine up to a faster speed. He was already going fifty miles an hour but in the next few seconds was up to eighty. He reached down with his left hand and pulled the latch to the driver's door and the door became ajar.

"Now, bitches, this is how you get fucked," and DD jumped out the open door. He barrel rolled on the ground and when he regained his balance, he stood up and watched.

Both girls screamed and tried to scramble over the front seat to the steering wheel. Their breasts bounced wildly around as the car quickly ran off the road and was hitting all kind of bumps. It flew down the ditch, launched itself into the air, and it crashed head on into the first tree in the woods.

Wearing no seat belts, both girls were thrown from the back seat. One girl sailed up through the air and hit face first into the tree the car hit. Her head smashed into the bark so hard it splattered. Pieces of brain littered the leaves and blood colored the bottom of the tree trunk. Her lifeless body bounced back into a pile of mangled bone and flesh onto the roof of the smoking car, and then rolled off to the left side.

The other girl went further. She had missed the first tree but hit the second at a horizontal angle. The snap of her back could be heard several feet away and her body split open like a busted can of biscuit dough. Her body fell down toward the bottom of the tree and all of her internal organs lay scattered along the ground.

The car caught on fire as DD brushed the dirt from his pants.

"You have to learn how to tuck and roll, bitches," he said as he started to walk away from the accident. Looking around the area he took note of his position. If his calculations were correct, he didn't have that far to walk to get to his next stop. In fact, it should only take an hour.

"Damn," he said looking at the starry sky, "I'm fucking brilliant."

Saturday

Curt was out of ideas; he only knew that he was hungry and he had a hard time trying to think on an empty stomach. He decided to fill himself on breakfast and soon found himself at the Golden Egg, sitting at the high counter. Looking over the menu, the waitress walked up to him and had to speak twice to get his attention.

"Sir, can I get you something to drink?"

Curt looked up at her, "sorry, black coffee, no cream." She walked off to fulfill his request. He glanced at the menu and saw the assortment off omelets that they offered. The 'Everything Omelet' was always his favorite. Besides, it looked so pretty when you threw up after a long night of drinking. The waitress walked back over with a cup of coffee and a creamer cup. Curt took immediate note of it.

"What the fuck, I said…" he looked up at the startled waitress in front of him. "Sorry. I'll take the Everything Omelet with hash browns and a side of sausage." She started walking away when he spoke again, "Wait. Make that bacon, not sausage." She scribbled the change on her ticket and clipped it on the order wheel.

Curt grabbed the coffee cup with both hands and took a long sip from it. As he tilted his head back, he saw the clock on the far wall. It was four thirty in the morning. He couldn't remember the last time he slept. This fiasco is going to be a nightmare. Suddenly he overheard a couple of people talking at a table behind him, and he eavesdropped on the conversation.

"How many did you say was killed?"

"Seven and they say another two are in critical condition."

"What was that maniac's problem?"

"So far the investigating team has a name, a Dean Mitchell, and the truck he drove into the building had some issues with the dealership, and they think it was a revenge strike."

"Do they have any leads?"

"None, it's like this guy has left town."

Curt lost his concentration when the waitress brought over his order. "Anything else," she asked.

"A refill please."

She walked away to get the coffee pot.

"What the fuck am I going to do?" Curt said under his breath.

****

"What a feast," Brad said to his friend, Eric, as they both held their empty plates at the start of the breakfast buffet line.

"You're telling me," Eric added, "I haven't seen a line like this since I was in Vegas two years ago."

The line moved forward a little bit, and it shifted just enough for the two gentlemen to reach the first part of the table. Several fruit trays were laid out before them, and Eric quickly grabbed the tong from the first platter. It contained an assortment of strawberries, blueberries, raspberries, and black berries. Eric grabbed a couple of large strawberries and placed it on his plate. Then he handed the tong to Brad who grabbed raspberries and black berries.

The line shifted again.

Next were two platters; one with several types of cut melons, and the other held whole fruits. Eric grabbed a banana off of the second platter and Brad took notice of it. "You better save some room on that plate," he said as he pointed on down the line, "That's one heck of a spread."

Eric looked down the line and saw what was coming. The next set was a bread assortment, then several pastries and then last in the cold entrees was condiments. Steaming away in the next area was a large table that housed sausage, bacon, ham, pancakes, scrambled eggs, French toast, and waffles.

"Maybe I should have grabbed two plates," Eric laughed. Just then, Randy split the line between the two gentlemen and made himself present.

"Good morning, gentlemen," he said, "How's the brain's functioning this morning?"

"Great," Brad said. "My room was very comfortable. The freshness of the air and the coziness of that blanket made me sleep like a newborn. I bet you slept quite well after all the drinks you had last night."

Randy cleared his throat, "Fell asleep in my clothes, actually."

"Have you eaten yet?" Eric asked.

"Nope, I'm just getting in here."

"Good," Eric added, "Then there'll be food left for us."

"Oh, Hardy Har Har," Randy said as he backed up. "I'm going to get in line, save me a seat, will you?"

"No problem," Brad answered.

Randy walked away and toward the now long line that weaved out of the room and into the hall.

"One thing is correct about what you said," Eric said, "my room was rather comfortable as well. In fact, this whole hotel is impressive. The front desk was very professional and polite; the get together was well organized, and the welcome packet in the room was not generic."

"They really outdid themselves this year," Brad added. "Kind of like they knew this was my last year. Maybe they did this all for me?"

Eric got a coy look on his face and laughed. "Oh yeah, It's all for you. As a matter of fact, after dinner tonight, they plan to have a girl jump out of a cake for you."

Brad snorted a laugh, "Blond or brunette?"

"Both," Eric said.

Brad shook his head, chuckling and took another step forward. They had reached the sausage.

"Now," Brad stated, "I'll need the extra plate."

****

Lieutenant Parker was startled when the phone on her desk rang. She had fallen asleep in her chair and knew that this was the best spot she could be reached. The last time that she saw her wall clock, it was two thirty-two in the morning. It was now seven forty-five. She started to try to regain her bearings when the phone rang again.

"Lieutenant Parker," she managed to get out through her dry throat.

"Lieutenant, this is Officer Knox. We have found the stolen sports car."

The news woke her up like a bucket of ice water. "Good work and the driver?"

"Not in the vicinity," he relayed, "but there is more bad news."

She sat upright in her chair and braced herself for the report, "Go on."

"Two women are dead here at the scene. By the look of it, the car ran off the road in a high speed and crashed into the tree line. Identification has been confirmed of the two women, but..."

"But what, Officer?"

"It's going to take some time to, a, pick them up."

Suddenly, Parker got a nauseating feeling in her gut. If it was anything like the dealership, they would need several personnel.

"What's your location," she asked as she stood up out of her chair.

"Far south side of the lake," he said, "out on Meadowbrook Road about three miles from the Lakefront intersection."

"I'll be there in about a half an hour."

"Yes, Ma'am," he said as he hung up.

Parker hung up the phone and then walked toward her office door. When she flung the door open, she saw that two secretaries were at their desks working on reports.

"Casey," she called to one of them.

"Yes, Lieutenant," the blond responded.

"Get me homicide," she said shaking her head to wake up, "and a large thermos of coffee with lots of sugar in it. It's going to be another long day."

"Yes, ma'am," she answered as she picked up the phone.

****

Lynette felt so comfortable that she never wanted to move. The night before, after they had eaten their dinner, Dean and she played gin rummy for about three hours. They laughed and snuggled the whole evening. By the time they had settled down together in the sleeping bag, it was almost three in the morning. She hadn't had an evening like that for a long time, in fact; she was never able to sleep as late as she did this morning. It felt really good not to be rushed.

Then, a sudden rotten smell hit the air around her. It was strong, not persistent. She said up from the floor and turned to see Dean, propped up on his elbow, with a large grin on his face.

"Did you just fart?" She asked as she held her nose with her right hand.

"Of course," he replied, "you know what fish does to me."

"Pew, it smells worse than that dead squirrel," she said as she jumped up out of the bag. Dean watched her nude body run to the bathroom. "I wonder if there is such a thing as wearable butt freshener."

Dean chuckled, "you have done some bad ones in your time don't deny it."

"Never," she said from the bathroom. Dean could hear her opening and closing several cabinet doors. "Women don't fart."

"Seriously? If that's the truth, then every woman on the planet would be so bloated you could pop them with a pin, and don't tell me women don't fart. There have been times when you have peeled wallpaper off of the walls."

Her giggling from the other room warmed his heart. Her laugh always made him smile, and he felt good knowing that she

242

was happy. He heard her open another cabinet door and close it. "What are you looking for," he asked.

"This," she said as she came around the corner fully armed with an aerosol can. She started spraying it around the room and toward his direction. Cinnamon apple started to take over the scent in the room, but she continued spraying. "Stand up so I can spray your butt."

Dean stood to his knees and grabbed her body with both arms. He twisted her around so that she fell down on her back, and he rolled on top of her. Her arms fell out to the side and the aerosol can rolled out of her right hand and across the floor.

"Maybe you can just shove the whole can up there, and the next time I do fart, it would spray."

She started laughing and put her left hand up behind his head. She started running her fingers through his hair, and she looked deep into his blue eyes. "I love you so much," she said, "this weekend has been so needed. I really appreciate the things that you do for me."

"That's because I love you more than anything in this world." He leaned down and gently kissed her on the lips. Her arms started caressing his back, and she moaned in excitement. She parted her lips and he stuck his tongue into her mouth, swirling it around her teeth and gums. Her mind raced about how he kissed and how it aroused her. She remembered that one time he told her to try to guess what he was writing with his tongue, and he spelled out, 'I love you' in her mouth. He had a real unique way of kissing.

She felt her insides starting to boil and her love for him burn in desire. He was propped over her on his elbows and he had her head in his hands. He rubbed her hair gently and caressed the tip of her ear. She felt complete, she felt relaxed, and she felt it was time.

She reached up with her left hand, grabbed his right hand, and pulled it down to her left breast. She pressed his hand against it. Dean stopped kissing her and leaned back, in somewhat of a surprise.

No words were spoken from his lips, but he did raise an eyebrow. She smiled and nodded back at him. The connection between their eyes said it all. She wanted him, and he wanted her. She knew that this was the man she wanted to be with forever and wanted to open up to him, completely, now.

Their bodies started to melt together as one.

****

Curt pulled up in front of his trailer and turned off the Jeep. Fatigue was starting to set in as he laid his head upon the steering wheel. He had been driving around ever since he left the breakfast house and still no sign of DD. He was running out of places to check and was getting tired of using the Jeep to get around. He figured that he would swing out to the house, pick up some extra cash, and then take the motorcycle. The wind in his face while riding it would keep him awake and he would be able to move around faster. Not to mention how much gas he was burning up in the Jeep; the motorcycle got better mileage. Shaking his head, he opened the driver's door and stepped slowly out of the car, His legs felt like lead every time he stepped closer to the front door and up the steps. When he reached the door, he leaned his hand up against the side of the trailer, to balance himself, and with his free hand, entered the security code to the entrance.

The door clicked open.

He turned the knob and stepped inside to find it hot inside. Although it wasn't that hot outside, sometimes the trailer could quickly become a toaster oven when he wasn't around to rectify it. The first thing he did was to walk over to the thermostat on the wall and flip the switch toward the cool side.

When was the last time he was in here, he thought, was it Thursday or Friday? His head was so groggy that he looked at the couch and almost threw himself upon it to go to sleep, but no, he couldn't. That thing was out there somewhere, and he had to find it. He knew that he was going to be on the search for a while, so he made a turn toward the wall safe to get some more money.

It went like clockwork, as usual. The marble clock swung out of the way easily and in no time, he had the combination entered. He lifted the handle and pulled open the door.

The safe was empty.

"What the Fuck," Curt yelled out. "Where's my fucking money?"

He ran toward the kitchen and opened a corner kitchen cabinet. There, sitting inside, was the security system for the entire house. He punched in a few codes to see if there was a breach and then saw on the activity screen that the entry code was correctly entered at five twenty-five this morning.

"How the fuck," he stated until he noticed something else on the log that cut his sentence short.

The security code to the garage was used as well.

Curt, now fully awake and pumping with adrenaline, ran back out the front door and toward the garage on the right of the trailer. He punched in the code and the garage door hummed to life and slowly opened.

The motorcycle was gone.

****

The noise in the lunch room consisted of clinking glasses, silverware scrapping on plates, laughter, and a lot of voices that drowned each other out. The meal was almost to an end, and most of the group had moved onto idle chit chat. Another buffet was served, only this time it consisted of cold cuts, soup and salads; a quick and inexpensive way of serving the almost two hundred people in the room. The real expense would be the dinner tonight. Many were looking forward to steak, chicken, or fish. Of course, after that meal would be the biggest bar party this side of Texas.

The Scientist's Association of America, or SAA for short, always held an annual get together toward the end of the college year. Professors and scientists would get together to share ideas, update projects, announce future projects, and, of course, celebrate. It was an exclusive club that had member fees, and the

245

cabinet members would evaluate potential future members by inspecting their contribution to the field and position they held in society. It was the best of the best in the field of science. One thing that did stand out was that there were no women in the SAA. It was a 'Men's only' organization and it gave several of the members a chance to relax, unwind, and let themselves go. There was another organization for the women, The Women's Science Association, or WSA, that held their annual convention at the beginning of the year. Theirs would be relaxed as well, but in an entirely different experience.

The tone of silverware being lightly tapped onto a glass came from the front podium of the room and others soon joined in on the activity. It didn't take long for the talking to stop and the sound of pinging glass to become the main noise. Within the sound, the breaking of a glass was heard, and someone cursed.

"Gentlemen, gentlemen," the speaker standing up said into the microphone. "I thought that at least all of us in this room would know what the impulse pressure from a metal object to a glass cylinder would cause upon increasing the compression thrusts."

Several people laughed and someone in the audience yelled. "What else do you expect, he's an Engineer."

The roar of the room took a couple of minutes to die down.

The speaker continued. "First of all, gentlemen, let me welcome you to the twenty third annual SAA Celebration, I'd like to start by introducing this year's board members." He glanced from left to right and took in the four members sitting at the table with him. "To my far right is Robert Basil; professor of Science at Western Cal University."

Robert stood up and was greeted with applause. When he sat down, the introductions continued.

"Next to him is Tom Start; Professor of Mechanical Engineering from Southern High-Tech Institute." He stood, bowed, and the applause continued.

"To my far left is JD Pitcher; a computer design analysis from Whitewater University. The clapping continued but was drowned out by six voices yelling the University chant.

"White, White, Water, Water, ugh ugh ugh!" JD held up his right hand in a fist and pumped it with each 'ugh' that was yelled. People started laughing again as he sat back down.

The speaker chuckled as he continued, "and then to my immediate left is Doug Glick; Top biomechanical engineer at Stromming University."

The room applause finally died down. The speaker continued on. "I, of course, am Jim Howard; a Physicist at Pepperdine Tech." Claps started again, and he waved it off. "Let's get right to business, shall we Gentlemen. It seems that one of our esteemed members is retiring this year." Claps started to build up again, and the speaker waved them off. "He has been with us the entire time we have been an association. He called me a few months ago asking, no, begging me to let him talk to all of you. He says he has the granddaddy of them all."

The laughing started to rise again, and several heads were nodding around the room.

"This man said he busted a gut this year to create the ultimate device. It's hard to believe that a Mechanical Engineer busted a gut, but I decided to bring him up and let us judge for ourselves." Jim reached down and picked up his coffee cup and took a sip from it. "Before he comes up, I know that a lot of you in this room are just as excited as I am to find out what this so-called device is, let me just say that I'm just as in the dark as all of you. So, without further ado, I give you the Professor from Tandem University, Brad Crawford."

Brad stood up from his chair at the table and the applause was astounding. As he walked his way up toward the podium, people started standing up to give him an ovation. Several people patted him on the back as he went by. When he reached the stage, he shook each Board member's hand, and then turned to see the entire room on their feet.

"Thank you, thank you," Brad said. "Please sit down before you all fall down." Laughing accompanied the scooting chairs as everyone took his advice. When the noise dropped down low, Brad started.

"My fellow members and friends, this project was started about seven months ago, and I'm plumb tuckered out." He took a deep breath in and let it out slowly. "To get straight to the point, I've built a robot. Not any ordinary robot. I have developed a way to transfer brain wave patterns from an individual and into the data processor of the robots Nero net brain. Everything that the subject feels, knows, does, and says, the robot performs."

Several shuffled feet and groans from the audience gave the appearance of disbelief.

"I'm as serious as fleas on a hound dog, gentlemen. But to make things even more realistic, the subject I transferred the brain waves from also was put through a casting mold, and the robot looks exactly like him. Just last week we did an experiment with the robot in the students place and nobody, I mean NOBODY noticed the difference."

"But Brad," someone from the audience yelled, "how did the power continue throughout the University? Did it have a battery cell?"

"Not at all," Brad said shaking his head, "We used a high frequency radio output that tied into the brain wave machine, and it boosted the refractive index. By the time it was sending, the MUF optimal frequency was eighty nine percent."

Several whistles went through the crowd.

"Yes, it was strong and during our test we found out that it was knocking out a lot of other transmissions."

"In theory," said another voice in the crowd, "a radio frequency that strong wouldn't reflect off the ionized layers of the atmosphere. It would essentially transmit into space."

"Correct," Brad answered back, "But I found a way to bend the transmit wave so that it would return back to the machine and act as the atmosphere itself."

Once again grumbles came from the crowd.

"I've got everything in this journal," he said as he held up the tan leather book, "and would love to share everything with you. I know it sounds fuzzy, but I brought samples of the parts we made. I had a Dickens of a time trying to get them through the airport."

"Did you bring the robot?" someone yelled within the room.

"No, I wanted to share the information with all of you before I took it public."

Several hands in the audience went up and Jim Howard moved back toward the microphone. "I know a lot of you have questions for Brad, but this meeting needs to move on to other things. I'm sure Brad would love to get with you all afterward and discuss this in detail. I do suggest that we all buy him a drink tonight to help him celebrate not only this breakthrough, but indeed his retirement. I cannot think of a greater loss to this organization when you leave us."

"Thank you," Brad said as he shook the hand of Jim Howard as he left the stage, "I look forward to the questions as well as the drinks."

Once again, a standing ovation was given.

****

Once again, Lieutenant Parker was a loss for words. The Officer's comment on the phone was right; it was going to take a while to clean up the area. The crime scene was unexplainable. She had seen several car accidents in her career but never this intense. The entire area looked like a war zone, but it was astonishing how only one car did this much damage.

First, the report came in because someone driving down the road, which, by the way, was a low traffic area, saw the smoke billowing from the trees. When the fire department arrived, the car was completely engulfed in flames. Due to a wet summer, the fire was contained quickly, but once the fire was out, they found the bodies.

The first girl closest to the car was unrecognizable. From the splatter of her blood and pieces of her brain, the Homicide Detectives was able to piece together her demise. According to them, her body was thrown from the car and hit the tree face first. The bark from the tree had literally peeled off her skin, and still was dripping with blood and skin when the Lieutenant arrived. The impact had broken her neck, and according to the coroner, she died on impact.   Her body then rebounded back to the car; explaining the large indentation on the hood, and bounced off to the left side of the car. She landed about ten feet away. She was lying on her back and had no shirt on. Her face was gone. One of her eyes was dangling out of the socket and her nose was smashed up into her skull. Several ants were crawling all over her skin and the task of cleaning them off without tampering the evidence was hard. Cans of compressed air was the easiest way to do it.

The second girl was about forty feet away from the accident laying on her back as well. She too had no shirt on. According to Homicide, her body was thrown from the car and impacted the tree sideways. Her back was broken and the impact had ripped open her abdomen, spilling her internal organs all over the ground. Her body was bent in half, at the waist, and the expression on her face still held a look of surprise. Her hands and fingers were incased in mud and the front of her chest was muddy as well. The coroner pointed out the marks on the ground behind her; several groves indicating her clawing and her blood smeared into the ground. He concluded that she had fallen on her belly, tried to drag herself out of the area, and then rolled over onto what was left of her back. A trail of intestines supported his theory. Several of her ribs had broken and were protruding out through her skin. Both lungs were punctured, so no oxygen was staying in her lungs. She died moments later. Ants, once again, were covering the body.

Later, during the autopsies, they will be able to determine if the girls were sexually assaulted before the crash. The detectives never found their shirts, which led them to believe that they perished in the fire. They did find several empty beer bottles spread around the scene.

After placing together, the scene, Homicide concluded that both girls were riding in the back seat, with their shirts off, when the car veered off into the woods. The blond was sitting on the back right side of and the other was on the left. Neither of them was wearing a seat belt. All the evidence was clear on the crash and how they ended up in the end, but it still didn't explain why they were topless, and their pants were fully intact. No tire marks were present on the road; thus, indicating that the car did not lose control. This accident was deliberate. No other tracks or evidence could give a clue to who was driving, but Lieutenant Parker knew.

She shook her head and then looked at Officer Knox standing next to her.

"We've got to catch this Bastard, Kenny, before the death toll goes up again."

****

Curt took the steps two at a time up to Lynette's apartment building. This would be the last place to check; places that DD would see a need to go to. The building itself was well secure; in fact, he was hoping that someday he could land the account for the system. It had twelve buildings, and each building housed four apartments. It would be another stack of income to his pocket.

Income reminded him again about the incident at his house. After seeing that the motorcycle was gone, he went back inside and brought up the security camera video. When he saw that it was DD who had entered, it made sense. Dean knew his codes and how to shut off the alarms.

Curt's mind drifted back to the present and opened the first glass door and entered the foyer. It contained the box to press for intercom entrance into the building. Then the person from their room would press their security release for the next glass door. He looked down and saw Apt# 4 and pressed the button. After a couple of seconds, there was a response.

"Hello." It was Kim.

"Kim, this is Curt. Have you seen Dean?"

"No," she answered. "They went to the lake. I didn't think that they were supposed to be back until tomorrow. Why, did something go wrong?"

Fuck, Curt thought, if she only knew. "No, I just needed to see him about something."

"Curt, guess what," she said with a bubbly baby voice.

Shit, not now, Curt thought. She always had to have you guess whatever it was that she wanted to tell you about. And he hated it when she would talk baby talk. She would do that every once in a while, because she thought it was cute and funny. It was actually annoying and irritating, and he really didn't have the time for it. "What, Kim."

"I got a job at the ice cream parlor down the street."

"You got a job? Well fuck me, that's cool. Does Lynette know?"

"Not yet," the intercom responded, "I'm going to tell her tomorrow. Then we'll go out to celebrate."

"No doubt on her money," Curt quickly said, "at least she could rely on you to feed your own fat ass from now on."

The speaker got silent.

Curt got a funny feeling up the back of his neck like a cold chill. He felt a little annoyed at himself for spitting out such a comment. "I'm sorry about that comment, Kim. Good luck to you. I'll talk to you later; I have to go."

He turned, exited the building and took the three steps that led to the side walk. His forward pace slowed, and he sat down on the bottom step.

"Now what the fuck do I do?" he said looking into the night sky hoping to find an answer. He had tried every spot that DD would assume would be a place to go. He surely wouldn't go to a restaurant because his programming forbids it. He tried Dean's house, his house, Lynette's apartment, the Book Nook and even thought of going to the college, but he changed his mind.

The whole town was looking for Dean, now, and if he were to walk into the middle of it, he would be in some major trouble. There was only one thing to do, Curt thought as he stood back up and walked toward his Jeep. He pulled his keys from his pocket, opened the driver's door, got in, and started the Jeep. He was going to drive to the Cabin and warn him.

He put the car in reverse, backed out of the parking spot, and soon found himself on the highway.

****

DD walked into Marvin's with a big smile on his face. It always felt good coming into a place that you knew, around people that you knew, and with the expectations that you always got. The music was roaring loud and from the front entrance, he could see that Sweet Wine was dancing on stage. She was fully clothed; which meant that she had just started her dance, and he made it just in time to watch her. He continued walking toward his regular chair, and then the feeling of embarrassment overwhelmed him. He couldn't understand why it came; only knew that it was sudden, and he tried to shake it off. He even felt a cold chill up the back of his neck. What would Lynette think if she knew that he was in here? The discomfort took over and became so irritating that he walked over to a bar stool and sat down. Why was he here in the first place? How did he get here?

"Good evening," the lady bartender said to him from the other side of the bar, "what can I get for you?"

DD tuned his head slightly to hide his blushing face, "Nothing, thank you. I'm not thirsty."

"Are you sure? We have one-dollar drafts and a whiskey special that lasts until midnight."

DD turned his face directly toward her, "Listen, bitch, if I was thirsty, I would tell you. So, get the fuck out of my face."

The lady's eyes widened and she threw up her hands. "Sorry, mister," she said as she walked away.

DD turned his back toward the stage and saw that Sweet Wine had just pulled off her top. Damn, she had some big nipples. He loved chewing on them from time to time and maybe tonight could be another time. He stood up from the stool and started walking toward his regular table again when he saw Dragonfly sitting at a booth on the left, alone. He changed his direction and headed toward her. She was a cute little shit and maybe, some time, he would have her too. He arrived at the booth and put his hands upon the table

"Hello, cutie, what's new?"

Dragonfly turned her attention from sweet wine and looked at the person next to her. She got a quizzical look on her face and tilted her head to the right. "Do I know you?"

"Right, funny," DD said, "how about sliding over, and I'll buy you a drink."

She started shaking her head, "No thanks, I don't take drinks from strangers."

"What the fuck?" DD looked in utter confusion. "What do you mean, strangers?"

"I mean, I don't know you," she replied.

DD got a confused look on his face and started to try to slide into the other side of the booth when Marvin walked up from behind him.

"Excuse me sir," he said as polite as he could grabbing DD's elbow, "I'm told that you were rude to one of the bartenders, I'm going to have to ask you to leave."

"What the fuck? Marvin? It's me; have you all gone fucking nuts around here?"

"Now I AM telling you to leave. I don't need any belligerent drunks in the building."

Dragonfly slid further into the booth, and Marvin slid around to the other side of DD.

"But Marvin, it's me!" DD's mind was in total confusion.

"Ok," Marvin said as gently as he could, "you are you but you need to...."

Three people at the front door caught Marvin's attention, and he had to cut it short.

"I'm sorry," he said to DD as he turned to lean toward Dragonfly. "Call the police, we're going to have trouble," he whispered to her. Then he walked away leaving DD standing next to her table.

Marvin quickened his pace toward the newcomers at the front entrance as his stomach started to churn. His ulcers had been back for about two weeks and tonight was going to be a rough ride. The closer he got to them, the more details he could see; the bandages, the cuts, and the bruises.

Andy and the two accompanying him didn't get five feet in the door before Marvin cut them off.

"Gentlemen, you are banned from this establishment. You can take your business elsewhere."

Andy didn't even glance at Marvin, "I don't give a rat's ass about your place, I just want that blond fuck head."

"If you are referring to Curt, he's not here."

"Bullshit, I saw his motorcycle out front. If you don't send him this way," Andy said as he turned to look at Marvin, "you're the first on the death list."

Marvin started to open his mouth when he got interrupted.

"Don't' worry about this pile of shit," DD said coming up from behind, "I'll take care of it."

****

Lynette was sitting in a lawn chair on the back porch of the cabin with only a dark green robe on. The intimate morning that they had with each other was still swirling around in her mind. She never imagined that it would feel that good. He took her gently and caressed her throughout the entire encounter, and she felt complete. She knew that it wasn't the first time for Dean; he had been with two other women before her, but he didn't overwhelm her with confidence. He showed a new freshness just like it was the first for him as well. They had lain in each other's arms for hours after they had finished, and she didn't even look at the clock. For once, she didn't feel rushed or needed to know the time. She always had an agenda, had to be precise with everything, right down to the last minute, but today, she didn't care. Neither one of them bothered to get dressed, in fact they took a shower together; washing each other, and when they got out, they threw on their robes and had been that way ever since. She felt completely relaxed like someone who just went through an hour-long message. She tilted her head back and looked at the clear blue sky above her. A couple of birds flew over, and the light breeze was slowly rustling the branches of the trees.

255

The sudden smell of steaks on a grill made her turn her head toward the left and look at Dean. He just opened the cover on the grill to turn the steaks, his yellow robe beaming brightly in the sunshine. The aroma tickled her nose and teased her stomach creating a sensation of pleasure. If only she could be here forever and never return to the....

No, she wasn't going to think about it. This was their time and the world can just wait.

"Should we eat out here," Dean said interrupting her thoughts, "or inside?"

She looked back up at the clouds and took in a deep breath, and slowly let it out. "Out here would be nice."

"I'll get a couple of tables," Dean said as he shut the hood on the grill and walked toward the back door. Before he could grab the handle to the screen door, Lynette grabbed his arm and pulled him toward her.

"I love you, very much," she said.

He leaned forward and kissed her on the lips. After a few seconds, they released and he straightened back up. "I love you as well, he said with a smile. "Be right back," and he entered the cabin.

She started to lose herself into the calmness of the area again. They were the only cabin within two miles and had the private lake area to themselves. Dean's parents had bought the cabin as a getaway spot from everything, and it truly worked its charm. She was saddened that she would never meet them, and from everything Dean had told her about them, they were very unique people.

Banging behind her made her turn around to see Dean trying to walk out with both of the TV tables under one arm and attempting to open the door at the same time. "I can get the door," she said as she started to get up.

"No, no, you just stay put, I've got this." Dean used his right foot to push open the door and then he swung the tables out and around from the frame. He walked up to her chair and folded open one of the tables and placed it next to her. He then opened the second one and placed it to the empty chair to her left. "The steaks are almost done; I just have to get the plates and the rest of the meal. You stay put. I've never, NEVER seen you this comfortable before. Enjoy this time."

She looked up at him and smiled, "I enjoyed this morning very much, and look forward to your warmth once again. Let's never leave."

"Seriously?" I'm game if you are."

"No, I have to...." She started waving her hands, "No, I'm not going to think about it." She tilted her head back and looked at him standing next to the screen door, "Help me once again to forget the outside world. Love me like you did before."

"First, let's eat," he said as he opened the door and stepped inside. "Then we'll have dessert," he said through the screen.

"Corny, Mitchell, really corny," she said as she lay her head back down and looked at the sky again. This was the true definition of paradise.

****

"Well, look who's here," Andy said with a smirk on his face, "It's the college fuck. What you doing in here? Did you have to see what a real tit looks like?" His friends started laughing. "It's almost midnight, isn't it past your bedtime?"

DD lunged toward Andy, and in the process knocked Marvin toward the ground. He tried to break his fall, but his arm hit the ground awkwardly and he heard the bone snap. DD's hands shoved into Andy's chest so hard that the man quickly staggered backwards and hit the wall next to a dart board machine. Andy slid down to the floor and remained seated. The man on the right side took a swing at DD; which he dodged with no problem. When the attacker noticed he had missed, he pulled his fist back again but was met with DD's right foot as a round house kick connected with the right side of his face. His jaw shattered instantly and sent teeth and blood splattering toward the left. The man fell down toward the ground in agony.

The other man pulled out a knife and jabbed it into the right side of DD. They both froze. DD looked down at the knife, stunned, wondering why he didn't feel it. The other guy, just as stunned, wondered why the man had no reaction. That split hesitation was all that DD needed. With one thrust of the palm of his right hand, he jammed into the man's nose and sent fragments into his brain. The crushing of his skull was loud and the man fell to the ground lifeless, dropping the knife onto the floor.

Marvin, still sitting on the ground, could not believe what he was seeing. The attacker was small, in fact he didn't look like a fighter at all, but he just took out three large men within seconds. His attention was diverted when Jambalaya kneeled up against his back side and put her hand on his shoulder.

"You alright, Boss?"

"I think my arm's broken," Marvin said as her looked back at her. "Get everyone into the back."

"Already did, and the cops are on the way."

They then both looked back at the unknown guest as he slowly walked up to Andy and squatted down in front of him.

"So," DD said as he watched the blood slowly drip from Andy's mouth, "how you feeling now, hot shit?"

Andy's breaths were slow and wheezing very loud. The shove that DD applied had broken three ribs and punctured one of his lungs. Andy's anger was still raging, but he was also in a state of shock about how the college boy had caught him so off-guard. He could feel the blood in his mouth and the pain in his chest but had more determination to get up and beat the shit out of the little geek. He started to try to get up, but DD waved a finger at him.

"No, no, no, my little fuck head, you're not going anywhere." DD put his hand on Andy's chest and applied pressure. Andy grimaced in pain. "Let's talk."

Andy's eyes started to look scared.

"I've never liked you," DD continued, "because of all the shit you have done to my life and hers. The way you treated her at the bowling alley, the way you made me miss the Motocross race, the way you hassled her at work, the way you broke all of my security equipment at the electronics show, and let us not forget what you tried to do to Lynette. She didn't want me to do anything to you, and because of my honor for her, I promised I wouldn't, but now, it's time to pay."

Andy was utterly confused. The man in front of him seemed totally different, it seemed like he had gone mad.

"When you tried to force yourself upon her, she fought you, and you didn't like that. So, in the struggle, you had boxed her in the ear." DD shook his head from side to side, "do you know that she couldn't hear for a week? Her doctor had to give her drops and antibiotics that knocked her out, and she couldn't function. We had told everyone that she had fell off a stool and hit the side of her head because she didn't want to put you behind bars. We were told to let it go."

'We', Andy thought in even more confusion.

"Needless to say, it's time to pay the price. I figured you could feel what she went through, but twice as bad." DD cupped both of his hands and held them up in the air. "Let's box both of your ears and see how you like it."

Andy tried to take in a deep breath to prepare for the pain, but he couldn't. DD pulled back his arms and then slammed his cupped hands into both of Andy's ears. The force from DD was so intense that Andy's head smashed inward, exploding the top of his head off and splattering the wall with blood and brains. Andy let out a yell and then quickly silenced as his body slumped over toward the right.

At first, DD was shocked at what he just did. He misjudged his own strength and his face was showing a display of disbelief. Then, slowly, he started to get a cocky grin on his face as he looked at the outcome. "Fuck me, "DD said out loud, "looks like I just popped a zit!" He stood back up and shook off all the blood on his hands down to the floor. When he saw Marvin and Jambalaya still sitting on the floor, his thoughts turned toward one of concern. "Marvin, are you alright?" He voiced as he walked toward them.

"Get away from us," Jambalaya said, "you need to leave."

Just as she said that, the front door opened and a police officer stepped in. His reaction to the carnage in front of him hit him quickly, and he held up his hand, "Everyone freezes, nobody moves."

"The cops, Marvin," DD said as he looked back at the man still on the floor, "You called the cops on me, after everything that we have been through?"
Marvin looked at him in confusion. "Mister," he said, "I don't know who you are."

DD looked puzzled, "Oh you're fucking with me. Jambalaya, you know me. Remember Thursday night?"

Jambalaya shook her head no.

Officer Knox stepped forward, "Until I get some answers, sir, you need to put your hands behind your back."

DD twirled and kicked the officer in the right knee, and he fell to the ground. He then grabbed the officer by both sides of the head and then thrust his left knee into his face. The crunching noise that followed made Jambalaya and Marvin wince. DD let go of the officer and the lifeless body fell toward the floor.

"Thanks a lot, Marvin," DD said heading toward the door, "I guess this shows real friendship."

Moments later they heard a motorcycle start and fade away.

****

"This thing you created, sounds great but what purpose would it serve?" Eric asked his question between his bites of lasagna. The dinner tonight was a buffet of Italian food. Several choices included spaghetti, Italian sausage, calzones, stuffed pasta and Lasagna. The question he asked was across the table where Brad was eating a plate full of spaghetti and meatballs.

"A lot of things could be developed," Brad answered before he took a drink of his wine. "What if we were to load several doctor's input into one unit. Even though I don't approve war, it would be a good thing to have on the battle field if needed. If they were killed, it would be no loss of life."

The others around the table nodded their heads in agreement. The table consisted of six people, Brad, Eric, Randy, and three other people Brad was not acquainted with. This dinner was the last before they got together for one more evening of drinks and celebrations, and then the convention would be over tomorrow morning.

"Other things could come into play," said one of the other men at the table. "Bomb demolition, Police officers, fire fighters: any dangerous job that puts human life in jeopardy. Think of all the jobs lost."

"But think of all the jobs gained," Randy said as he enjoyed his Fettuccini Alfredo. "Factories to build them, maintenance people..."

"Not to mention the people needed for the download," Eric added. "They could be paid for their brain patterns"

"Many possibilities," Brad added.

"I'm sure there are more people here that will be asking you a lot of questions at the mixer tonight, Brad."

"Sorry, gentlemen, but I will not be at the mixer. I have to catch a flight at five thirty in the morning."

"Why leave so early?" The question was on everyone's mind, but Randy was the one who voiced it.

"I have a lot of things to do when I get home. I've got to ready the robot for presentation to the college, get all the schematics together and more people to contact."

"At least have a couple of drinks with us before you leave, old man," Eric said, "before you don't talk to us anymore because you're too famous to associate."

"Yeah, right," Brad laughed, "like that will ever happen. You deadbeats are the only people who understand me. Ok, a couple of drinks, then I have to hit the sack."

"I'll buy the first round," Randy said.

****

261

Lieutenant Parker was driving her car down 5th street when she heard the code 10-33 go across her radio. They reported a 415 in progress at Marvin's and requested backup. The officer reporting mentioned that the disturbance was caused by the fugitive that they were looking for and witnesses described him perfectly. He also said that three men were dead, and an officer was down. Instantly, Parker picked up her receiver.

"Dispatch, do you copy?" she said into the microphone.

"Dispatch ground, go ahead."

"Dispatch, this is Lieutenant Ann Parker, patch me through to the officer at the scene, on the double."

"Yes ma'am, connecting," the female voice said. "You're patched through."

A couple of clicks later and a male voice answered. "Officer Fuhrman."

"Officer, this is Lieutenant Parker, I'm on route and should be there in about ten minutes. What's the status?"

"Three men are dead and an officer is down on the scene."

"Who is the officer?"

"It's Officer Knox, Ma'am."

Parker went cold inside and shook her head to try to regain her attention on the road. Tears started to build in her eyes and she had to shake her head to refocus on the road. Her foot pressed harder on the acceleration pedal and she opened up the mic again. "I'll be there in five, hold the area and don't let anyone leave or come in except me. Do you understand?"

"Yes Ma'am."

****

Kim was getting ready to take her first bite into a pizza she had just baked when the buzzer for the front gate went off. She sighed in frustration, got up from the kitchen table, and walked over to the intercom by the front door. She pushed the speaker button with her pizza sauce-soaked finger.

"Yes, who is it?"

"Kim, its Dean. Can I come up?"

Her face got confused. "I thought you were at the lake. Is Lynette with you?"

"No, that's why I have to come up. There's been some sort of a mix-up."

"Ok," Kim said as she pushed the release button and opened the front door.

Sunday

Curt was speeding and he knew it. He didn't care if he was going to get pulled over or not; he just needed to get to the cabin. About a half an hour into the trip, he turned on his police scanner and found out about Marvin's. They didn't list the names of the dead; with the exception of the police officer, but he was very worried about everyone he knew. They did say "Four dead men", so he was relieved that it wasn't one of the girls. Still, they could be wounded, and he wouldn't know.

He never thought of looking for DD at Marvin's. Dean never went in the place and didn't like idea of women stripping anyhow. Maybe Curt thought his own download made DD curious. The entire situation was his fault, and he knew it. If he wouldn't have done the download in the first place, things would be normal, and eleven people would still be alive. He had to get to Dean before the police did.

****

She still remembers the night that he gave her the engagement ring. It had been a long day for both of them and neither of them felt like cooking, so they went out to the "Stakeout" restaurant. He always liked his steak well done and thick, so she knew that it would be a long wait. They were up at the self-serve salad bar, and he was picking through the cherry tomatoes, with a tong, and he got a really disgusted look on his face. "What is this gross thing doing in the fruit salad?" he had said as he lifted the object, with the tongs, and showed it to her. It was the engagement ring. He had planned this for weeks and told the owner that he would buy the whole bowl of salad if he needed to. As she inspected it, he knelt down and asked for her hand in marriage, and she accepted. She had later that week picked out a male engagement ring for him because she thought it would be nice that they would match. After all, they were a matching pair, why split them up?

264

Now, she looked deeply at his ring once again; splattered with blood and hair. The ring that meant so much to her and the man it was attached to. Officer Kenny Knox.

Lieutenant Parker tried to hold onto her professionalism and at the same time control her anger. Officer Fuhrman, at the scene, said that Knox died moments after he logged off from her call. He didn't say anything because most of his jaw was shattered. The rest of the scene she hadn't even started looking through yet; her mind couldn't focus.

"Lieutenant Parker?"

Silence.

"Lieutenant Parker?"

She shook her head clear, "yes, Fuhrman," she whispered through her anger.

"Coroner is here," he answered, "Shall I send him over?"

She could only nod her head.

****

Brad sat relaxed in his first-class seat and had already finished his glass of orange juice. He always flew in the coach section, but this trip was special. He had booked the flight months ago with the anticipation that the robot would be finished by then. Things worked out just fine, and he didn't even feel rushed during the whole project.

All his colleagues were very impressed with his report and wanted to see the robot as soon as possible. He was going to have to find a special transportation to get DD to the next seminar; which was to be in Tampa, Florida, next November. By then, he hoped that DD would be a national sensation.

The flight was only going to take four hours and twenty minutes and should arrive in Springfield about nine o'clock in the morning. He always hated going backwards in the time zones because it made the day so much longer. He decided that he would just put on the head phones, free of course, and snooze away to the sounds of the big bands. Within moments, he was snoring.

****

"What's going on?" Kim asked as she opened the door to the apartment.

"Beats me," DD said as he entered and walked toward the kitchen, "I haven't seen Lynette since Wednesday."

"Wednesday," Kim said in confusion, "But you both left together on Thursday morning."

DD looked at her confused as well, as he sat down on one of the kitchen chairs. "What the fuck are you talking about?"

Startled by the curse word, Kim sat at the chair across from him. "When she left Thursday morning, she was on the way to your house to pick you up to go to the cabin."

DD said in a low and frustrated voice, "but I haven't seen her since Wednesday!" His eyes flared with rage as he glared toward her. "What are you trying to hide from me, Kim?"

"I'm not hiding anything from you!" Kim yelled back, "You two packed and left for the cabin on Thursday morning!"

DD stood up quickly and knocked the chair over in the move. "Who's she with, Kim, because she's obviously not with me."

"Nobody," Kim said as she quickly stood up scared by his actions. "She was supposed to be with you."

"Where's your phone, I'm calling her."

Kim started backing up, "...b-b-but her phone is right there," she said pointing to the unit on the kitchen counter. "You guys never take your phones to the cabin."

DD stepped forward to her, "you lying little bitch, who's she with and where are they?"

"I don't know," Kim answered as she backed into the living room and toward the hallway, "I don't know!" She yelled as she turned and ran toward her room. When she stepped inside, she slammed the door, and then locked the knob.

DD slowly walked down the hall, up to her door, and pressed his face close to it. "I'm so sick and tired of you, you little piece of shit. You're just like a fucking leach, and you suck up everything that Lynette has worked so hard to get."

"Go away, or I'll..."

"Or you'll what, bitch?"

"I'll call the police."

Something snapped in DD. The mentioning of the police infuriated him. He took a couple of steps back and then kicked open her door. The wood from the frame splintered across the room and the top of the door broke off of the hinge. Kim, startled, stepped back in surprise.

"Call the police!" DD yelled as he stepped forward, "you little bitch." And with an open right hand, he slapped Kim across the face. She fell down on the floor hard and started crying.

"Oh, my god," DD said in a softer voice, "I'm sorry, Kim, I'm sorry." A cold chill went over him as he knelt down, grabbed her arm, and helped her stand. "I'm so sorry," he said again. When she got back on her feet, he saw that she had a busted lip and blood was running down her cheek.

Kim's eyes were very wide in horror. She never in her wildest dreams would ever think that Dean was capable of doing such a thing. She was crying in deep breaths and trying to understand what just happened. He was gently holding onto her arm and lifted up his other hand to lightly touch her lip.

"I'm sorry," he said again.

Through her gasps, she spoke. "My cheek really hurts, could you help me?"

DD eyes changed to rage again. "Help you? It's always, me, me, me, with you, isn't it? You always half to have the center of the fucking attention, don't you?"

Kim's eyes widened in fear again, "Don't hit me again," she said.

"Oh, shut the fuck up," DD yelled and back handed her across the face so hard, her jaw broke. She fell back into the night stand next to her bed, knocking off the lamp and several knick knack items down toward the floor. DD approached her continuing his rage.

267

"You always have to have it you fucking way with no consideration to Lynette's feelings," he said as he reached down and picked her up by her shirt collar. Kim was bleeding all over her shirt and she could not speak. Only whimpers and cries came from her mouth.

DD started shaking her. "We had sacrificed so much because of your selfish attitude and I'm fucking tired of it. We missed parties, dinners, social events," he said as he emphasized each word by shaking her shoulders, "camping, concerts and even the shit you pulled at the luncheon this week. We missed the book fair, the motor cross race, the Karate competition, and even the campus homecoming. I've had enough of you fucking up our life!"

DD hit her again, this time with such force that she flew upon the bed, face down, and unconscious.

"I'm tired of your shit, Kim," he yelled pointing toward her, "and from now on, stay away from us!"

He walked out of the room and headed back toward the kitchen.

****

When Curt pulled up to the front of the cabin, daylight had just peeked out from the horizon. The trip only took him forty minutes, and he was lucky that no cops were on the road. With the Jeep still running, he took a deep sigh and looked around.

There was no breeze and the entire area looked like a picture that was made for a calendar. The trees were not moving, white puffy clouds pillowed the sky in the morning redness of the rising sun, and the air smelled crisp and clean. Birds were flying around and even a couple of geese flew over his head. The calmness of the area still did not clear his mind of all the chaotic events that led up to this moment and he still could not come up with a clear plan to end it. This cabin may be a spot to get away from it all, but unfortunately, the 'All' didn't want to be left behind. Curt tried to regain a clear mind but couldn't, and in the midst of this serenity, he heard a loud disturbing sound; a sound that was louder than his Jeep's engine, and he cocked his head to identify it. When he turned the ignition key off, the sound became more prominent.

Loud classical music was blaring from the cabin.

Of course, there were no neighbors for at least five miles, and the noise would never be able to disturb them, but the thought of Dean blaring music this loud was unheard of, especially if Lynette was with him. She would always tell him to turn down the music because someday he would be deaf. She didn't really like to go to the movie theater anymore because it was just too loud. From his seated position, Curt could even see that the glass plane was even rattling to the loudness of the music. He knew the song; it was familiar, but he couldn't put a name on the composer.

He took a deep breath again, opened his door and stepped out. He started walking toward the porch trying to work up an idea of how he was going to tell them, and he was so engulfed in his thoughts that he left the door open. His footsteps were crunching the dry pine needles that were strewn all over the yard but he could not hear them; the music was that loud. Stepping up on the porch, the creaking boards and the hollow sounds of his boots still were unheard, and he reached for the door knob. It was unlocked. He opened the door and stepped in.

What he saw threw off his thoughts so much that he stood there in awe with his mouth gaped open. Never in his wildest days would he ever expect this. He knew the stereo was on the left, next to the fireplace; he knew the furniture arrangement perfectly; he knew the pictures, the rug, the curtains, and even the color of the walls, but he never knew that he would see this.

Dean and Lynette were totally nude on the couch. Dean was sitting down, with his head tilted back looking at the ceiling, and she was facing him while riding on top of him. Lynette kept raising herself up and down upon Dean's cock and shaking her head back and forth. They were having sex, MY GOD, they were having sex! He could see the curves of her naked back and wanted to get a glimpse of her breasts but an overwhelming sense of embarrassment swarmed over him. He turned his head quickly away from them and walked over toward the stereo. When he reached it, he pushed the power button?

Everything in the room went silent, with the exception of their panting. Lynette turned her body at the same time Dean tilted up his head to see what happened to the music and that's when everyone bolted to alertness. Lynette screamed. She grabbed a quilt next to them and pulled it around her body.

"What in the world are you doing?" Dean's voice sounded between embarrassment and frustration.

"Sorry," Curt said, "I had to come, we have a problem."

Lynette stood up and wrapped herself completely with the quilt, "I'll say we have a problem."

"I'm truly sorry for interrupting," Curt said again. Then he looked directly at Dean,   "Does she know?"

"Know what," Dean responded.

"About the fucking robot?"

Lynette stood with her arms folded around her front, "Yes, I do. It's really neat that..."

"It's gone, and I can't find it," Curt said interrupting, "It's even killed a few people."

"What," Dean said in shock as he stood up off the couch completely exposing himself to Curt. "How did this happen?"

Curt bowed his head in disgust, "I happened."

Dean cocked his head to the side and sat back down. "What did you do," he asked as Lynette sat back down on the couch next to him.

"On Thursday night I was pretty drunk and, well, got pretty upset on how you never stand up for yourself." Lynette leaned over against Dean's shoulder as Curt continued, "I was thinking that if there was a way that I could give you a set of balls to not be such a wuss that maybe..."

"Don't tell me you downloaded yourself into the robot," Dean said.

Curt nodded his head, slowly.

Dean tilted his head back and shook it back and forth, "Dude you planted a Trojan!"

"I did not; I only downloaded some of me." He responded back.

Lynette got a confused look on her face and looked toward Dean, "What's a Trojan?"

Before Dean had a chance to answer, Curt responded. "A Trojan is a program that appears to perform a valid function but contains, hidden in its code, instructions that cause damages, sometimes severe, to the systems on which it runs." Curt got wide eyed and turned to look at Dean, "Oh, shit, I created a Trojan."

Dean started nodding his head, "Precisely."

"But you said it killed people," Lynette added, "why would it do this when neither one of you would?"

Both of them went into thought process. Dean spoke first.

"Maybe because the mixture of me, you, and the alcohol was a contributing factor, how much did you have to drink?"

"Too much," Curt said, "way too much, but that's not the problem. So far, he has killed at least seven people." Both Lynette's and Deans shocked look on their faces didn't fade as Curt continued, "And the big problem is, every cop and person in town thinks it's you."

Once again silence hit the room, and this time Lynette spoke first.

"Dean, what are you going to do?" She put her hand on his right shoulder, "We could call the police and explain."

Dean glanced at Curt, "No one has a phone to do that."

Curt shrugged his shoulders.

"Well, someone has to explain this," she said.

"Brad," Dean yelled while snapping his finger, "he arrives at the airport at about nine o'clock."

"We could meet him there and get him to contact the police," Curt voiced. "I'd feel better if he was in on this."

"Me too," Dean said. "It's about six o'clock now, if we hurry, we could be there when he arrives. I'd hate to have him walk into this mess blind folded." He turned and looked at Lynette, "if you don't mind, I'll throw on some clothes and ride there with Curt. You get things packed up here and head to your apartment. I'll call you when we contact Brad."

"I'll be waiting in the Jeep," Curt said as he exited the cabin.

When the door slammed shut, Dean stood up and started heading toward the bedroom, "Well, guess I have no time for a shower. I'll just put on some clothes and go. Will you be okay doing this yourself?"

"I've done it before," she answered. "I'll just get the things that are needed and leave the rest here. You'll probably arrive at the airport before I get home, so don't be surprised if I don't answer the phone for a while."

"I understand," Dean said as he kissed her left cheek. "I better get going."

He started to head toward the bedroom when Lynette spoke up, "there is one thing that did throw me off,"

"What was that?"

"Correct me if I'm wrong, but did Curt apologize?"

"Yeah," Dean said with a confused look, "twice."

****

Officer Parker had been sitting in her car for over an hour contemplating her next move. Going back to her office was pointless and unwanted; she wanted to be as far away from all the activity that surrounded the tragedies. If she needed to be reached, her police radio was on, but still, she didn't want anyone to call. She didn't want to hear about another death; she didn't want to hear about another crime scene; all she wanted to hear was the report of finally locating this maniac and she would be the first one to get to him.

She hoped he would put up a fight, and then she could put him down.

Justice in this town sucked. Police officers, inspectors and anyone tied to the streets put their life on the line every day to have an attorney tap dance in front of a judge and get the lowest punishment available to the guilty. Many sympathizers would try to emphasize that the criminal has rights as well and therefore should be dealt with fairly. Sure, fairly. Explain that to all the families who now can only visit their loved ones standing in front of them with six feet of dirt on top of them.

The only justice this murderer should get is dirt on top of him.

And of course, once judgment was passed, the criminal would get so many years in a government run 'Resort' where they would get access to movies, work out rooms, books, food, and cable TV. They would get all the comforts that over half of the working middle class couldn't afford. They got it all through the taxpayers; the same ones who couldn't afford those luxuries. Very ironic, wasn't it? You work so hard to have a decent life, can only afford what you can, and your taxes pay for criminals to 'live comfortably' while they were incarcerated. And, of course, if they were good, they would get out early for good behavior. Then it would start all over again.

Isolated rooms with no windows, no luxuries, and they could only eat canned food and drink water. That would be true justice.

Then, once they were out, only a hand full of them would change their life around. The others went right back to where they left off. Burglaries, drug dealings, assaults, and killings would continue for them until they were caught again, and put right back into jail. Most criminals had a better life inside than they did outside. There were just too many people who didn't care about society and the respect to their neighbor. That's what has happened to this town; this world. People have lost the ability for common courtesy and other people's lives. You hear about death all the time, and it becomes common place, regular information, just another story to talk about around the water cooler.

Until that death is part of your life, and then it changes the whole perspective.

Kenny, Kenny, Kenny, she repeated in her mind, she could only hope this was all a dream. They were going to be married right after the Holiday season, on January fourteenth, in a private ceremony with a few close friends. They had been through a lot to come to that point. They had met in a local bar several years ago; both of them fighting off demons of their life. He had a bitter divorce and custody fight, and she had an addiction. They both vowed to help each other with their problems and together they successfully defeated them. The strength they had for each other built into a very loving relationship and for once she was happy with her life: content.

But now, everything had come crashing down.

She had to watch as the coroner declared that he was deceased. She had to watch as they put his body into a bag and seal it. She had to watch as they carted him away on the gurney and into the ambulance.   She had to watch it all. Other officers at the scene knew about their relationship and left her pretty much alone. She had told one of the senior officers to take charge of the situation and contact her if anything changed, if they find him.

So now she sat, in her car, watching an empty parking lot across the street and pondered her future. The radio chattered with other calls; improper lane usage, fender bender on Walnut, and a leaf burning in the city. She let out a long breath and turned to look at what sat next to her on the right.

The demon in the bottle she fought so hard to get rid of, the demon that Kenny had helped her defeat two years ago, the demon she so needed right now.

With another sigh, she grabbed the bottle she had just purchased at the nearby convenient store, twisted open the cap, and downed half of the contents.

****

Curt and Dean were sitting at gate two waiting for Brad's flight to arrive. It was delayed twenty minutes, and it gave the boys the chance to get something to eat at the Airport Restaurant. The restaurant was right across from the gate and everything on the menu was triple the cost of anywhere else. The quality wasn't that good either.

So, after filling their stomachs, they both got a drink to go and moved themselves to the waiting area. They had talked in the ride from the cabin on how they were going to tell Brad, and Dean came to the conclusion it should be him. Curt was far too stressed to deal with it, besides; Dean noticed he was acting different. Not the usual Curt difference, but, different.

"So," Curt said, leaning over to Dean, "one thing is for sure."

"What's that?" Dean questioned.

"Lynette sure has a nice pair of tits," he said with a smile. "And I don't mean that in a raunchy kind of way, if you know what I mean."

Dean creased his forehead brow then decided to shake it off. "I will let her know the next time I see her."

"Seriously," Curt continued, "I didn't expect that at all. I didn't think you would hear me knocking over the music. I'm surprised she let you play it that loud."

Dean started nodding his head. "Well," he added as he took a sip of his coffee, "she said it really enhanced the moment, and it made her feel..." Dean froze while still holding his coffee cup close to his chin, "why am I telling you this?"

Curt shrugged his shoulders, "Bragging rights? Hey, she opened herself up to you, ONLY YOU! I have had so many women; I can't count them. Most of them all sluts in their own way, but you got the cream of the crop. You got a decent, gorgeous, and very intelligent woman who only has had you." Curt lifted up his coffee cup and raised it like a toast toward Dean, "for someone to release herself like that is a very rare and special moment. I envy you very much, my friend. I'll never find someone like that."

Dean started to smile, "Thanks."

"Attention, attention ladies and gentlemen," the airport speakers announced, "now arriving at gate two is flight 1321 from Seattle. Once again arriving at gate two is flight 1321 from Seattle."

Dean and Curt stood up and worked their way up to the exit where they would catch Brad on the way out. They first had to wait for handicapped individuals and then families with small children to disembark. After that, it only took a couple of minutes for Brad to walk down the gangway and into the area. Immediately the boys rushed him.

"Brad, we need to talk," Dean said as they reached him.

"Well, howdy, buckaroos," Brad said as he juggled the carry on that he had on his right shoulder, "what brings you here to welcome me home?"

Dean grabbed his shoulder and pulled him away from the crowd toward an empty area near the corner windows. Curt closely followed.

"Don't tell me that you two gents need to...."

"DD is loose and has killed at least eleven people." Dean said cutting him off.

Brad's first expression was one of shock then he started to smile, "Funny, gentlemen, very funny. Next, you're going to tell me that he has sprouted wings and flew to Florida."

"No, Brad," Curt said cutting in, "this is serious shit. I've been running all over town trying to find him. He's not acting his usual self."

"What do you mean, 'His usual self'?" Brad questioned.

Dean sighed, "Curt downloaded some of himself into DD on Thursday night. He was drunk. The mixture between the alcohol, Curt's transfer and mine really messed up the unit. Curt had to drive out to the cabin to get me."

Brad got a really angry look on his face and turned toward Curt. "Why do you always insist on fucking things up?"

Both the boys froze in shock. They had never heard Brad utter a curse word, let alone that one.

"Brad said 'Fuck'," Curt said.

"I heard," Dean replied.

"Knock it off, both of you," Brad said as he sat down in one of the chairs. He started thinking out different options to try. "Has anyone tried to shut off the 380?"

"I tried to get to the house," Curt said, "but the cops have the street blocked off."

Brad lifted up his right hand and rubbed his palm all over his face. He then slowly pulled it down over the top of his eyes and stopped on his chin. He let out a long and loud sigh. "Has anyone called the police?"

"We thought it would be best to get you with us to help corroborate the story," Dean said, "Coming from us two it might be farfetched, but from you, they would take it more seriously."

"Then I suggest, gentlemen that the first thing we need to do is shut him down." Brad stood back up and lifted his bag over his shoulder again. "I've got to get my luggage from the baggage claim first, and then we can be on our way." He stopped and then noticed that both boys had a blank stare on their faces and were looking at something behind him. Brad turned to see the TV mounted on the wall. The speaker wasn't turned on but the closed caption was clear to read.

"Local authorities are searching the area for an individual responsible for thirteen deaths, including a police officer. If you see this man, please notify local authorities immediately and give all information that you can. Do not attempt to approach this person for he is very dangerous. Local law enforcement has issued a request to stay in your homes until the threat is offer."

A picture of Dean flashed on the screen.

Brad turned and grabbed Dean by the arm, "Here are my keys to the wagon," he said pulling them out of his pocket and handing them to Curt. "I'll meet you there after I get my luggage. We have got to get him out of here."

****

Lynette pulled up to her apartment complex and parked her car. Her entire trip felt like it lasted twice as long. She had listened to the radio on the way in and couldn't believe what she had heard. Thirteen dead, including a police officer was mentioned. The radio said there was an all-points bulletin out for Dean, he was dangerous and they said, under no circumstances, try to approach him. Life had changed in the blink of an eye and she was a part of it.

This robot they had created sounded like a vision of extraordinary talent and would have brought them a glorious future, especially Brad. His idea would have done a lot for the safety and development of many companies, including even the medical field.

But now, it had become a catastrophe.

She pulled herself together and exited her car and headed up the steps to the entrance door. After sliding her security card key in the slot on the wall, she opened the door and walked up toward her apartment. Each step she took made her go deeper into thought. She was tuned out to the noises around her: the baby crying in the first apartment, the loud television in the second one, even the humming of the air conditioner didn't detour her attention. Her mind was swarming about the possibilities of the near future. What if Dean were caught? What if they could never stop the robot? What if she… her thoughts were interrupted by the realization that she had reached her apartment door. When she reached for the knob and found it unlocked, she opened the door and stepped inside.

The kitchen light to her left was the only light on. When she made a few steps into the kitchen, she noticed an overturned chair at the kitchen table. She sat her purse down onto the table and bent over to pick up the chair when a voice behind her startled her.

"It's about time you got home," DD said from the couch.

Lynette sat the chair up and then walked toward him, "How long have you been here? I thought you guys were going to the airport?"

DD stood up, "Now why would I go to the airport? Am I going somewhere?" He tilted his head to the right, "and where were you?"

"Well, I left the cabin about thirty minutes after the two of you left. I just barely had enough time to get things together. Then I drove straight here. Where else would I be?" Lynette asked in confusion as she sat down on the couch.

"Where else indeed," DD said sitting back down next to her. "I've been wondering that myself for the last few hours."

She looked at him in utter confusion, "What are you talking about? Have you blacked out or something?"

DD started looking her over. He noticed that her hair was matted up, which concluded that she didn't take a shower this morning. He also noticed that she hardly had any make up on. She always had made up on. She never had to do heavy makeup because her face had a natural beauty about it, but she would always wear lipstick. Her lips were untouched.   Then, after further observation, he noticed that she was wearing a flimsy blouse and her breasts were lightly visible through the fabric. She was not wearing her bra.

"I see that you're letting your tits breath today," he said with a raised eyebrow, "I don't think I've ever seen you go bra-less."

"Well, I didn't have the time," she noted. "I just threw this on, grabbed the other stuff and hurried here."

DD started to get an angry look on his face, "let's stop playing, shall we? Who were you with?"

Lynette got a shocked look on her face, "you're kidding, right? I was with you! How could I be with anyone else when we spent the whole weekend…" she started shaking her head, "Dean, this is not the right time for this."

"NOW IS NEVER THE TIME!" DD yelled as he lunged at her. "Let's see what those bitches taste like. I'm sick and tired of just looking at them. Looking is for free, but touching and licking would be so much more fun!" DD grabbed her and shoved her down on the couch. In one quick move, he had torn open her blouse and exposed her breasts. "I've waited long enough, and you tease me like this!"

She started struggling and tried to sit back up but his strength was too much for her. "What are you doing? After last night and this morning, wasn't that enough for now?"

This time DD got the confused look, "are you out of you mind, we've never done it! Now start pulling off those jeans before I rip them off." He stood back up on the side of the couch, "I'm going to give you the fuck of a lifetime. I'm going to cum in you so hard it's going to run out of your ears!"

Lynette froze. She had never seen Dean act this way and she was in total shock at his behavior. Why would he do this to her? Why would he force himself this way? And the vulgar cursing, she had never heard him curse like this. Maybe he…. then it dawned on her. Her body started to quiver in fear and her mind raced with the terror that she was in. This wasn't Dean. It was the robot.

A cold shiver went down her back. She couldn't fight it; she knew that she wouldn't be strong enough. She slowly started to unbuckle her belt to let it know that she wasn't going to object. She wasn't going to get it angry. She was going to keep as calm as she could and do everything that it would ask. She didn't want to be added to the death list.

As she started to try to wiggle out of her pants, she started to cry. DD's look on his face changed from angry to sympathetic.

"I'm sorry," he said sitting back on the couch next to her, "I didn't mean to come off that way."

"It's alright," she said through her gasps of air while she tried to hold herself together, "you've been through a lot."

"Yes, yes I have." He started to get that crazy look in his eyes once again. "And a good fuck would relax me intensely!" He straddled above her with his knees on both of her sides and started to unbuckle his pants when his facial expression changed once again to awkwardness. He wanted to continue but something crossed his mind like a cold bucket of ice water. He shuddered and felt not just uncomfortable, but incomplete. Something didn't feel right about this and he couldn't understand how to do what he intended to do. Once he would get his pants off, he would…what? How did he…which way would… maybe if…. how do you?

DD stood up from the couch in complete disarray. Lynette noticed his state and calmly spoke. "Dean," she stuttered, "what's wrong?"

DD turned his head toward her, "I don't know. I feel, like I can't, like this situation…"

Lynette closed her eyes in horror. This is it, she thought. The robot's going to flip out and kill her. It looked like he was malfunctioning and any minute now, he would lose it.

"Lynette," DD said, "I'm sorry. I don't know what's wrong with me." He turned and headed toward the door. "I'm going home." He opened the door and stepped out. "I'm sorry," he said again as he shut the door.

Lynette exhaled a breath of relief. She sat up and put her hands to her face. She let loose the cry that she had held in. Her eyes had let go so many tears that she had trouble seeing when she tried to buckle her pants back up. She had also noticed that three buttons still remained intact on her blouse, and she buttoned up what she could.

He was going home, he said.

She quickly jumped up and ran to her phone in the kitchen. When she flipped it open, she pushed speed dial number one, Dean's number, and it quickly started ringing. There was no an answer. Closing up her phone, she grabbed her purse and quickly headed toward the door. She had to get to Dean's house to warn him. She had to tell him that he was coming.   When she locked her apartment door behind her, she was unaware that her sister was lying dead, in a large puddle of blood in her bedroom.

****

Officer Tucker was still sitting in his police car, out of view from the Mitchell residence. His wife, Debbie, had just brought him a large club sandwich and a thermos full of coffee. He had taken his first bite into the sandwich when he saw a motorcycle pull up to the residence and a person with a helmet on walk up the main entrance and enter the house.

****

"Lieutenant Parker," said a voice through the radio.

Parker reached over, groggily and grabbed the mic. "Parker here," she answered.

"Lieutenant, this is dispatch. Officer Tucker has reported that there has been an arrival at the house. An individual with a motorcycle helmet has entered the home. He did not see the face and cannot verify if it was the suspect."

"Dispatch, notify him that I'm on the way, send in any available units, arrive silent. No sirens. I don't want him to know that we are surrounding the house." she said as she hung up the mic and started the car.

"Dispatch, copy."

****

With Curt driving, Brad in the passenger seat, and Dean lying down in the back seat floor; they were moments away from reaching Dean's house. Dean tried to stay out of sight of anything or anyone they passed. He wished he had a chance to clear the floor of the articles that Brad had lying around, but decided that he could bear the mess for the moment. The empty orange juice containers were not a problem, nor were the old newspapers, but the tire jack and crow bar dug into his side. Every time the car hit a bump, it reminded him of them. Soon, they would be done with this problem and then they could start the process of explaining it.

****

Officer Tucker started his car to move it when he noticed a station wagon pull into the drive way and three men get out. One of the men, wearing a blue shirt, fit the description of the person at large. He slowly pulled his squad car out from the hiding spot, across the street behind a garage, and moved it in front of the house.

Parker pulled her car right up next to Officer Tucker's car and got out. As she approached, other police cars started arriving in the area. She walked up to Tucker's car as he rolled down his window.

"Officer Tucker," she said in a raspy voice, "I want you to take charge of the other units. I want the street blocked off and a line of cars parallel to the house. All officers behind their units and ready to shoot, if need be."

"Yes, ma'am," he answered as he got out of his vehicle.

They all got into position and waited.

The house was dark inside, even though it was daylight outside. All the curtains were drawn and Brad, Curt, and Dean all stood in the living room trying to figure out their next move.

"I didn't think we were going to get in here so easily," Curt said. "The place was crawling with police last time I drove by here."

"It really doesn't mean that it's all clear though," Brad whispered, "they surely have the place staked out."

"Well, let's get this thing over with," Dean said as he headed toward the kitchen. "Once we shut the 380 off, he'll be done."

"He's here, alright," Curt said as he pointed at his motorcycle helmet on the couch, "we can't let his ass get out of here again. Once he's off, we have a lot of shit to clear."

"When he's off, I'll call the police from here," Brad added.

Just as the three reached the doorway to the kitchen, DD stepped out in front of them.

At first, DD looked confused.

"What the fuck?" He voiced as he looked back and forth between Dean and Curt. At first, he thought he was dreaming because how else could you be staring at yourself without the use of a mirror. These two were perfectly identical to him. The hair, the faces, even the build of their bodies looked the same. He saw himself on the left, and then he saw himself on the right. Was he having double vision? Was he having hallucinations? Then he noticed Brad standing there and he raised his eyebrows quizzically.

"What the fuck is this, Brad? Am I dreaming? Who are these two? Did you...why they...how could I be two different individuals when...this is fucking nuts! What the shit!"

"Yes," Brad said quickly and calmly, "you are dreaming. We need you to sit down on the couch, and I'll go to the kitchen and make some coffee." He was hoping that DD would buy the story and then he could easily go down to the 380 and shut it off.

DD cocked his head to the left, "but I'm not thirsty."

"Well, sit down anyway," Brad continued, "And I'll go make myself some and we can talk."

"Seriously, I don't want to sit down," DD replied.

"FUCK THIS SHIT!" Curt yelled as he quickly put DD into a head lock. "Quick, someone flip that Ass switch!"

Brad reached around DD's back side and tried to put his hand down his pants. It was hard to even try because of all the struggling, but he had to do it.

"What the hell are you faggot's doing?" DD yelled in surprise, "Bastards, get your fucking hands off me, you dickheads!" And in one swift move, DD flung Curt off of him and onto the floor. Curt landed hard but was back up on his feet again. Dean had to step back because Curt had almost landed on him. Brad continued struggling with DD alone, but was not successful. In another quick move, DD swung around and elbowed Brad in his right temple. Brad fell unconscious to the floor.

"Quick, "Curt yelled at Dean, "get something so that we take this asshole down, SOMETHING HARD!"

"There's a crow bar in Brad's car," said Dean as he rushed toward the front door, "I'll go get it. Hold him!"

Curt turned and looked at DD and took a deep breath, "alright, mother fucker. Let's dance."

****

Lynette knew that she was speeding, but she had to get to Dean and warn him. She only had a couple of more miles to reach the house. Hopefully, it wouldn't be too late. She pulled up to the police car that blocked the street and got out of her car. She walked up to the officer that was standing next to it.

"Ma'am," the officer said, "you can't enter here. You're going to have to go around."

"Sir," she said holding her hands up, "I know what's going on. My fiancé, Dean Mitchell is not the person you want. His professor and he had created a robot look alike, and it has gone bad. Please believe me, sir"

The officer looked her like she had told a joke and he didn't get the punch line. "Lady, I think you need to leave before…"

"No, please, I'm telling the truth. Please tell whoever is in charge that a robot has been doing the killing. I was at a camping area the whole weekend with Dean and can prove it." She started to cry again and pleaded with him once more. "Please tell them. He's a senior at Tandem Institute of Technology, and they spent at least six months building this robot. Please, we don't have time."

The officer saw the seriousness in her face and grabbed his radio. Within minutes of his report, another officer arrived.

"Ma'am, I'm Officer Tucker. I know from my point of view, this sounds farfetched, but…"

"Please, take me to the house and the person in charge. What harm could I do?" Lynette started begging again, "Dean is in danger."

The officer let out a sigh, "Okay come with me."

They started walking down the block toward Dean's house, which was about four doors down, and Lynette could see the line of police cars across the road. All of their lights were off and they looked like a predator waiting on its prey to step into the clear.

"You say this is a robot doing all the killing?" The officer asked as he walked along her side.

"Yes, a robot that his Professor, Brad Crawford came up with," she replied.

"Brad Crawford?" The Officer questioned in surprise, "My father and he used to be in the same lodge together, before his death. Brad's a very talented and intelligent man."

"Then you know that what I say couldn't be unreal!' Lynette said as they approached the first car in line, "I'm telling the truth."

The Officer stopped and looked at her, "Ma'am, I'm not doubting you at all."

When they reached the second car, the one directly in front of the house, the Officer walked her up to a female. "Lieutenant Parker, this is the woman that told us about the robot."

Lieutenant Parker turned and her face showed disbelief. "I find that story a little hard to take, miss…?"

"My name is Lynette Ashbury; I'm Dean Mitchell's fiancé."

"Well, Miss Ashbury; I really don't have the time for this. We have the house surrounded and as far as we know there are four people inside."

"Yes," Lynette said, "four. There would be Brad, Curt, Dean and the Robot. Please do something before someone else gets hurt. Please get inside before it's too late." Lynette started crying again.

"Lynette," Parker said very calmly, "right now I'm holding ground until we reach someone inside. Do you know his number? We don't have a listing for a land line."

"Yes," Lynette said pulling her phone out from her back pocket, "It's speed dial number one."

Just as Parker took the phone from her, someone came running out of the house and toward the station wagon. The individual caught everyone off guard and that person was in the back seat before anyone could react.

Dean was in hysterics as he ran from the house and toward the car. He knew where that tire iron was at so he pulled open the door and jumped down into the mess on the floor. After scooting several newspapers out of the way, he found it, and lunged for its handle when he heard someone outside.

"Freeze," said one of the officers with a bullhorn. "Step away from the vehicle and put your hands up."

Dean stepped out of the car quickly, still holding the iron, and held up his hands.

"He's got a weapon," someone yelled.

It was time to put this thing to an end. This was the machine that killed so many people; the machine who had the entire town in danger; the one that killed men, women, and children; the one who took down Kenny.

Lieutenant Parker was the first one to draw her weapon and fire. Several other shots fired out, following hers, and the target staggered. First, Dean was hit in the leg, then in the right arm, then several times in the chest. He had dropped the tire iron after the first shot, then Lynette screamed and started running toward him.

That's when Lieutenant Parker noticed the blood splattering on the car. This wasn't the robot; this was a real person. "Cease fire, dammit, cease fire now," she yelled loud enough for the others to hear her. The gunfire stopped.

Dean fell to the ground just as Lynette got to his side. Several bullet holes lined the station wagon along with Dean's blood. She fell to her knees and cradled his head in her lap. He coughed up blood and his blank eyes looked up at her.

"Ouch," he said through his blood.

****

Just as gun shots were heard outside, Curt lunged toward DD. He grabbed around his waist and tried to bring him down. If he could get past him and to the basement, he could shut this thing down, but it looked like it was going to be easier to say than to do.

DD flung him off once again, like a person would fling off an unwanted coat, but Curt kept control of the move. He spun back and round housed kicked DD right in the face. The contact was rather hard and Curt felt the stinging in his foot, but still continued his attack. DD shook his head and started moving toward Curt. Curt tried another kick, but DD dodged it and followed up with a kick of his own. He connected to Curt's chest, and he went flying into the couch, knocking the helmet off in the process. Curt rolled off the couch, back up onto his feet and started throwing punches at the robot's mid-section. Hopefully, he thought, he would bust up something inside, and the robot wouldn't be able to function properly. He had thrown several punches until DD blocked one and then sent several back at Curt. One busted his lip, another cracked two of his ribs, and a third broke his right forearm. Curt attacked again; his adrenaline hyped up, and kicked the robot twice. One connected to its jaw, breaking its left connection, and one hit him in the right side. DD's jaw hung awkwardly to the right, and he reached up and touched it with his hand.

"Wa thh fck, yoo s hoo", was the only thing that came out.

Curt stood back up in front of him again, ready to strike, and he was bleeding in several places.

"Come on, shit head, BRING IT ON!"

DD sent a quick kick that sent Curt into the fireplace mantel, knocking his forehead into the brick and sending him down to the floor. Several items fell off the shelf as he hit it; Dean's phone, the picture of them with the truck and other items. The picture shattered on the floor and glass stabbed into Curt's face as he fell into it. The phone hit him in the head and Curt laid there motionless. He had his eyes closed waiting for the next hit. He started to try to think on how he was going to take DD down, if he could at all. Since he was loaded into the unit as well,   DD would know all his moves as well as his abilities. He was fighting himself when it came to his Martial Arts training. How does one beat yourself? When he regained his bearings, and opened his eyes, he saw his lighter laying on the rug in front of him. Then he remembered something. The fireworks he brought were in the box sitting on the coffee table. He quickly snatched up the lighter and stood up in front of DD. To DD's right, on the floor, Curt saw Brad still unconscious, and calculated his next move. He flipped open the metal top and flicked the wick igniting a tall bluish yellow flame.

DD stopped, confused at what he was trying to do.

Curt, through his puffed eyes, and bleeding face, smiled at him. "Happy fourth, you mother fucker," and he tossed the lighter into the open box on the coffee table.

At first, DD had no knowledge of what was in the box, until he heard the hissing of fuses. Several firecrackers went off first, but the box only just begun. When a roman candle ignited, DD ducked behind the couch, and Curt made his move. He grabbed Brad's unconscious body, with his right hand, and started dragging him toward the front door. The pain shot up his left forearm from the break, but he had to push on. Just before he got to the door, one of the Aerial units went off. The place was engulfed in light. Paper particles from the blast covered Brad and him, but Curt managed to open the door and get them out before everything went full force.

DD stood up and tried to see. The exploding box had engulfed the room and had started several fires. Powder burns started to lace DD's body and he tried to find a way out. Suddenly, the main bulk of the box went off and a barrage of light over took everything.

Lynette held Dean's head in her lap and she could tell that his breathing was slowing down. She kept trying to talk to him, but he couldn't answer. More blood flowed from his mouth, and his eyes were fixed on hers. Suddenly large explosions from the house made her look up toward the front door and she saw Curt dragging Brad out of the house. Several blasts and rockets shot out the open door as they escaped, and she ducked her head down to cover Dean's face.

Curt, still bearing the pain in his arm, dragged Brad up toward the side of the station wagon, where he saw Lynette sitting on the ground, and carefully placed Brad next to her. He put his hand on her shoulder and she lifted her head back up to look at him. Blood was smeared all over her face as she looked at him with tears falling down her check. That's when he noticed Dean lying in her lap. Dean's eyes were glazed over, and his face was covered in blood. His mouth was slightly gapped open with a line of blood running down his lips. Curt reached over and laid his fingers on Dean's neck to feel for a pulse. There was none. Curt's face turned white as he realized his friend's fate.

Lynette saw his expression and looked back at Dean. She too, saw that he was not breathing anymore. She started crying harder as more and more fireworks went off in the house. She pulled his body up to hers and held him tight. She couldn't believe what was going on, she wished it was all a dream, and everything was back to normal. She squeezed his body so hard that she forced the remaining air out of his lungs, and she heard the last breath. Her crying turned into a full out bawl and Curt, himself started crying as well. Lynette lifted her head in the air and saw the Lieutenant walking toward them, holding her hands in front of her face to cover her eyes from the fireworks still going off.

"You killed him!" Lynette yelled at the Lieutenant, "'YOU MURDERED HIM! I HATE YOU ALL!" She pulled his body back toward her and that's when the front window of the house exploded. Glass and fireworks shot out across the lawn and everyone ducked to protect themselves. Curt wrapped his arms around Lynette and pulled her toward the ground.

That's when DD saw his chance.

He leaped out of the opening that was once the window, and ran toward the motorcycle. Nobody noticed him because they were still taking cover from the bombardment that engulfed not only the house, but the front yard as well. He climbed onto the motorcycle, started it, and headed away from the house by cutting in between the house next to them. When everyone was able to look up, all they saw was the tail lights. Many officers jumped into their police cars and started a pursuit. The fireworks inside started to subside, but the fire they created was in full force. Flames were already leaping out of the second story and the sound of breaking glass filled the air. The roar of the fire was intense and the heat coming from it was scorching.

Lieutenant Parker knelt down toward Lynette and Curt, "'we need to step away from this before it engulfs us. I'll have a unit call an ambulance and the Fire Department."

"No fire department," Curt yelled as he stood up and looked at the house. "Let the fucker burn."

Other officers arrived around them and they picked up Brad and carried him away to a safer area. Lynette started to fight off the helpers as they tried to pick up Dean, but she soon gave in to their assistance. Curt just stood in the same spot and watched the house.

Flames started to shoot out of the rooftop as the siding started to melt. Creaking and snapping wood could be heard as the left side of the house fell in. Soon it would be nothing but burnt ashes.

Down deep in the basement, the 380 continued. The electricity in the house already had been blown, but the 380's back up battery still kept it going. When the side of its casing started to bend in from the heat, it started to throw sparks. That's when the house fell down upon it.

DD started to get dizzy. Maybe that fight caused more damage than he thought. His eyes kept getting fuzzy, and he blinked several times to clear them. He felt tired and just wanted to get some rest. His body started to get tingly all over and his back started to shoot out pain. Then he noticed that he could no longer move his fingers, and his feet felt limp.

The motorcycle started weaving back and forth then made an abrupt right turn toward the ditch. DD was thrown off the motorcycle and landed in a tall patch of grass. The motorcycle flipped three times before it ended in a smoking pile of crushed and twisted metal.

EPILOGUE

The hospital room was very comforting. The soothing light tan walls kept the mind calm and relaxed. Sunshine through the window showed little specks of particles floating in the air and could hear birds chirping outside. Other than the walls, everything was white. The floor tile, the end table, the bed, the sheets and even the trash can were white. The only noise that could be heard was the television that hung on the wall, continuing its five o'clock report;

"…. then when everything was over with, Lieutenant Ann Parker, person in charge of the man hunt, briefed us in on the story. The man that they were searching for was not a man, but a robot built at Tandem University. Its advanced state had run into problems and it went out of control. The death toll has been upgraded to fourteen deaths and one person still remains in serious condition at Memorial Hospital. We have not been told the name of the individual, but since this tragedy ended two days ago, pieces are still sketchy. We were told that this robot was being tested all last week throughout the city, which means that anyone in town could have possibly had interaction with it and not know it. The Attorney general said that the investigation still continues and that no charges have been filed."

"They are continuing with tracing where the robot had been through the past week, in hopes that no more dead bodies will be found. As of now, the robot was shut down and has been dismantled.

"What started out as an advanced project that was a major breakthrough in science, has now turned into the largest disaster that this area has seen in years. We tried to contact the Board of Directors at Tandem, but no phone calls were returned. Reporting from the police headquarters in Springfield, I'm Marcia Edwards."

The TV was turned off via remote leaving the only sound in the room the beeps from an electrocardiograph machine.

Sitting in the two chairs in the room were Curt and Lynette. Curt was all bandaged up. He had received several third-degree burns, three cracked ribs, damage to the ligaments in his left ankle, and three busted fingers. His right arm was in a cast and a sling due to a broken radius bone. He was also on a lot of pain medicine. His room was three doors down, but he wanted to be with Lynette during the visitation hours. They were both wearing hospital garments and slippers.

Lynette hadn't spoken a word all day and he could see that she still had the look on her face of disbelief. He, himself was trying to understand what happened. Their entire lives were on hold right now; he could care less about his business, and she didn't even want to step foot into the Nook. They both just wanted to hide away from all the media, the people and the town. They both decided that once he would be released from the Hospital, they would go to the cabin and stay. They didn't care how long, possibly forever. The town didn't feel comfortable anymore. He didn't even care to return to the college, for he was tired of playing their games and having to deal with those high-strung people on the board.

This entire incident was supposed to put Tandem on the map, but its conclusion might damage the University's future.

Two hours after the house burned to the ground, authorities found Curt's motorcycle and DD about thirty feet from it. No movement came from the robot so they tossed it into the back of a van and delivered it to the police station. To this day it still lies locked up in one of the cells. It's been heard that several people from the University visited the robot. Even in the end, it was still being treated like it was real.

Just after the paramedics treated Curt and Lynette at the scene, she requested for an officer to go check on her sister at the apartment. When she received the news about Kim, Lynette had a nervous breakdown. The doctors had to sedate her and keep her overnight at the hospital for further observations. The next day, she had to go to the morgue and identify the body. Kim was barely recognizable. Her face was all bloated up and her jaw was dislocated. A shock of horror was still shown on her face. The coroner said that she might have been alive for hours before she passed.

They had to sedate Lynette again. Her room was on the floor above Curt's.

Dean was pronounced dead at the scene. He had taken three bullets; the one to his chest was the fatal hit. In all the shooting, it was never found out who delivered the shot, but Lynette was planning to bring up charges against Lieutenant Parker. She drew and fired first. After the incident, all officers who discharged their guns were screened and tested. Lieutenant Parker had been drinking and had an alcohol level above the legal drinking limit. She was relieved of her duty without pay until further investigations were concluded.

A large gasp got both of their attention and they stood up and walked toward the bed in the room. Lynette, on his left side, put her arm around Curt's waist to help him support his ankle. He, in turn, wrapped his left arm around her shoulder. When they reached the bedside, he unbraced her and grabbed the bed rail with his left hand for support. They both looked down in the hopes to see someone's eyes open. They did not.

All bundled up in the sheets, was Brad. He had several IVs attached to his arm and many recording wires connected to his chest. The machine above his head continuously sent out random beeps, showing that his heart rate was still normal. He had been unconscious ever since the blow that DD delivered to his right temple, and brain scans showed that there had been some damage. Only time would tell if he would either recover or be able to move again. The intense pressure that he had received caused a brain aneurism which in turn could render him incapable of even speaking. The doctors performed surgery that next day and after two days, there still was no change in his condition.

They did find out, through a friend of Brad's, that Lynette had been given the power of attorney over Brad's estate. In a document that he had in his home; in the case if anything like this were to happen, it said that he felt like she was a daughter to him. He had no other family and, of course, no offspring. She was also granted the power to decide whether or not to end his pain. A power she didn't want to have.

Dean's will, in a safe deposit box at his bank, was opened yesterday. He too had left everything to Lynette. She gained control of his accounts that he inherited from his parents, the cabin at the lake, and all of his possessions. There wasn't must left of his house, but the inheritance could easily build another. Everything he had was now hers.

Curt couldn't get it out of his mind that all of this was his fault. If he would have never downloaded himself into the unit, things would be fine. He still recalled something that Dean said last week; 'one of these days, your actions are going to get you in a lot of trouble.' A tear ran down his check as he thought of his friend.

Looking down at Brad, he saw no movement, with the exception of his chest lifting and falling from the aid of the machine.

Lynette sighed. Her lips opened and she spoke very softly, "He looks so peaceful."

"Yes, he does," Curt added. "Any second now I'm expecting him to sit up and say one of his weird words."

"He's probably thinking about cruising down the road right now." Lynette said as she let go of Curt's waist and reached over and lightly brushed a hair off of Brad's forehead. "I often wonder how the mind works when you're in this type of condition."

Curt leaned over and got close to Brad's face.

"They say that you can hear everything when you are in this condition, you know what I mean. It makes me seriously wonder what he's thinking right now...."

AUTHOR PAGE

Richard Crane Is the author of three books. He is a veteran of the United States Navy and spends most of his time watching movies, drawing, or supporting his favorite sports team. He's a diehard Science-fiction fan and also enjoys a good horror movie. He's a collector of many movie items and enjoys long walks with his dog. He currently lives with his family in Central Illinois.

Other books by Richard Crane;

"The Sacrifice"

"The Resurrection" (Sequel to The Sacrifice)

"The Angel"